THE LAST CHRISTIAN

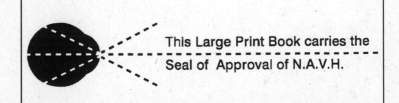

This Large Print Book carries the
Seal of Approval of N.A.V.H.

THE LAST CHRISTIAN

DAVID GREGORY

THORNDIKE PRESS
A part of Gale, Cengage Learning

GALE
CENGAGE Learning

Detroit • New York • San Francisco • New Haven, Conn • Waterville, Maine • London

GALE
CENGAGE Learning™

LIBRARY OF CONGRESS CATALOGING-IN-PUBLICATION DATA

Gregory, David, 1959–
  The last Christian / by David Gregory.
    p. cm. — (Thorndike Press large print Christian fiction.)
  ISBN-13: 978-1-4104-3104-2 (hardcover)
  ISBN-10: 1-4104-3104-5 (hardcover)
  1. Artificial intelligence—Fiction. 2. Large type books. I. Title.
  PS3607.R4884L37 2010b
  813'.6—dc22   2010027331

Published in 2010 by arrangement with WaterBrook Press, an imprint of Crown Publishing Group, a division of Random House, Inc.

Printed in Mexico
1 2 3 4 5 6 7 14 13 12 11 10

To my dad

ACKNOWLEDGMENTS

My heartfelt thanks go to Bob and Jan Mugele for schooling me on missionary life and to Bob for his assistance with the Inisi language; to Lisa Stewart, Rex Campbell, Todd Herder, Doug Reed, Rod Pauls, and Glade Diviney for their invaluable comments on the manuscript; to Drs. Robert Cockrell and Dana Penner for their insight on medical procedures and terminology; and to Dr. Gary Ferngren for helping me understand the professorial life. I am indebted to my editors, Shannon Marchese, Steve Parolini (noveldoctor.com) and Carol Bartley for forming a team that made this a much stronger book than my solo effort would have produced. Thanks finally to my wife, Ava, for your continual support and encouragement and advice to keep cutting.

My thanks to David Hazard for the painstaking work required to make the writings of the early Christian disciples accessible to today's reader in *You Give Me New Life: A 40-Day Journey in the Company of the Early Disciples,* from which I borrowed several quotations. Hazard's entire Rekindling the Inner Fire series is a spiritual gold mine.

Writing *The Last Christian* required extensive research in the fields of artificial intelligence, future trends, and jungle and missionary life. The two books upon which I relied most were a riveting personal life story, *Child of the Jungle: The True Story of a Girl Caught Between Two Worlds* by Sabine Kuegler, and a fascinating look into the possible future of artificial intelligence, *The Singularity Is Near: When Humans Transcend Biology* by Ray Kurzweil. I am indebted to these authors for helping shape my thoughts in their respective areas of expertise and experience. My thanks also to the following authors whose writing enriched my understanding:

On jungle and missionary life:
Michael Dawson, *Growing Up Yanomamo: Missionary Adventures in the Amazon Rainforest*
Clarence Wilbur Hall, *Miracle on the Sepik*
Joel P. Kramer, *Beyond Fear: A Harrowing Journey Across New Guinea Through Rivers, Swamps, Jungle, and the Most Remote*

Mountains in the World

Peter Matthiessen, *Under the Mountain Wall: A Chronicle of Two Seasons in Stone Age New Guinea*

Candice Millard, *The River of Doubt: Theodore Roosevelt's Darkest Journey*

Mark Andrew Ritchie, *Spirit of the Rainforest: A Yanomamo Shaman's Story*

On artificial intelligence:

Damien Broderick, *The Spike: How Our Lives Are Being Transformed by Rapidly Advancing Technologies*

Bill Joy, "Why the Future Doesn't Need Us," *Wired,* April 2000

Jay W. Richards, editor, *Are We Spiritual Machines? Ray Kurzweil vs. the Critics of Strong A.I.*

Eliezer Yudkowsky for his articles at the Singularity Institute for Artificial Intelligence, www.singinst.org

On future trends:

John Brockman, editor, *The Next Fifty Years: Science in the First Half of the Twenty-First Century*

James Canton, *The Extreme Future: The Top Trends That Will Reshape the World in the Next 20 Years*

Mike Wallace, editor, *The Way We Will Be*

50 Years from Today: 60 of the World's Greatest Minds Share Their Vision of the Next Half Century

PROLOGUE

April 3, 2088
"I see your neurons firing, Ray."

The voice was familiar, one Ray Caldwell had known for decades. Bryson Nichols's face came into view overhead.

I must be on my back.

He had no such sensation. He tried to turn his head to the right, then the left. It didn't respond. He tried moving his fingers. No sensation. Panic swept through him. He was paralyzed.

"I brought you back to consciousness to let you know about the procedure."

The procedure. On whom? There were no more procedures scheduled. Caldwell had canceled them all.

Nichols's face slid in and out of view as he hovered above and behind, wielding surgical instruments with which Caldwell was all too familiar.

No . . . He wouldn't . . .

11

Nichols spoke calmly as he worked. "I do so apologize for having drugged you. But it was the only way. You know how much I've valued our working relationship — our friendship — these many years. I'd never do anything to jeopardize that friendship.

"But you were acting nonsensically, Ray. Halting the procedures at this point was sheer madness. I told myself it was the onset of disease, that you weren't thinking straight. Or perhaps you were having cold feet about your own procedure. In any case, for your own good, I had to accelerate the schedule."

Nichols paused, his upside-down face fixed in Caldwell's line of vision, smiling. "Your alphas reveal your reluctance, but I do forgive your response, Ray. I know that, once the procedure is complete, we'll see eye to eye."

Caldwell examined Nichols's face as he spoke. He was calm, purposeful, self-assured. No trace of consternation concerning the crime he was about to commit.

"Oh, Ray, to be free at last from the constraints of biological intelligence. How I wish I were in your shoes!"

The room fell silent save for Nichols's movements and the methodical hum of neural scanners. Caldwell knew the routine.

He had performed it himself numerous times, though not to completion.

Think! He had to think. Within the hour he would be disconnected from his biological brain . . . forever. If only he could talk, he could dissuade Nichols from —

Nichols's face reappeared. The procedure was ready, Caldwell intuited. Now was his final chance to change his destiny.

". . . pat your hand, Ray. But I know you can't feel it. I want you to know that I'll be with you throughout."

Nichols leaned closer to Caldwell's face, his voice softening. "I have to admit, I'm envious. We had always planned on my being the one unveiled. And now it appears you will be the world-famous one — the first transhuman."

He straightened up. "I could be bitter, being supplanted by you in that regard. But of what value, ultimately, is the recognition we receive for our achievements? Is it not of minor importance compared to the contribution we make to the advancement of our species — of the evolution of the universe itself?"

Nichols glanced to his right. "I can tell by your scan that you still aren't in full agreement." He cocked his head slightly. "Ray, are your gammas spiking? I recognize that configuration. Are you trying to tell me something?"

He turned back toward his patient and shook his head. "You never cease to amaze me. I doubt any of our colleagues could manipulate their brain waves with such ease. That's why I teamed up with you so many years ago. Always amazing."

Nichols stepped away from Caldwell's sight, then reappeared. "I'm putting you back to sleep now, Ray. When you wake up, everything will be complete. Your misgivings, whatever they may be, will be alleviated. You'll be everything we have worked toward. Everything humanity has dreamed of for millennia. Our friendship, our partnership in this grand endeavor, will continue. Shortly you'll perform the procedure on me. The two of us will lead humanity into its greatest adventure." He smiled broadly. "See you on the other side."

With all his will Ray Caldwell commanded his arms to move, his legs to break free from the bands that held him to the surgical table. But it was no use. In a few moments he would lose consciousness. When he awoke, he would be missing the only thing that made life — existence itself, even — worthwhile.

Drowsiness stalked him. His mind began to swim.

Three hours and six minutes later Caldwell's new brain powered up. He awoke. Electronic impulses coursed through the silicon mass that his cranium now housed.

Terror seized him. He bolted upright and scanned the room. His gaze landed upon the smiling face of Bryson Nichols standing four feet away.

"O brave new world that has such people in it, Ray. How do you feel, my friend?"

Past Nichols, in a glass jar, he spotted the three-pound mass of gray matter that had been extracted from him. His terror subsided into resigned grief. What he had feared most had come to pass.

It was gone. Utterly gone. He had lost his connection.

1

Three weeks later

I always expected to teach history. I never expected to make it. Making history is the stuff of inventors and politicians and astronauts. Not professors. Especially not those with both feet in the past.

Visitors to my office — and they are few, since no one is on college campuses anymore — are always struck by what they regard as the antiques. The brass doorknob that requires a physical key. The mechanical clock. The metal nameplate with "Creighton Daniels" etched into it. The sea of books.

Meeting me in my virtual reality office (identical to my physical one), students are always surprised by two things: the books and the smell. They are one and the same, of course. Have enough old books on hand, and you get a musty smell. No one knows that anymore, because no one owns books.

With the exception of the door and a large

window directly behind my desk, my office walls are covered by floor-to-ceiling wood bookcases filled to overflowing. "Where'd you get all these books?" students ask. The less polite ones add, "And why do you have them?"

I like being surrounded by books. Always have, even as a kid. I used to visit my grandparents' house and climb up in the attic and dig through dusty boxes looking for old kids' volumes. *Alice's Adventures in Wonderland,* Harry Potter, the Planet Nine series . . . the classics.

"Why don't you just experience those stories in virtual reality like the other kids?" my father would ask. He worried I'd fall behind the times technologically. Which I did. But I also cultivated a love of books and, with it, a love of learning.

By the time I finish explaining why I'm a bibliophile, most students scrunch their noses and ask, "What is that smell?" At which point I expose them to the delights of holding old books: the feel when you take one off the shelf, the aroma when you open it, the hint of mustiness. There's nothing quite like it.

This particular Wednesday I walked down the deserted third floor of McMinnus Hall to my office and started my morning routine. I grabbed a cup of coffee, sat at my desk, took a bite into a toasted cranberry bagel, and pulled up my Grid interface.

"Good morning, Alistair."

Alistair appeared in one of the two chairs across the desk. "Good morning, Creighton. How did you sleep?"

"Well, thank you. Access CulturePulse, please."

Alistair frowned. "You still have seven dissertations to review before the end of the term. I can access the current one for you."

I sighed. Dissertation reviews. The bane of my profession. Having neural implants that enhanced reading speed and comprehension by a factor of eight didn't make five hundred pages of "National Stereotyping in Virtual Reality Programming and Its Effects on Preadolescent Cross-Cultural Relationships" any more enticing.

I did what I always do when faced with an unpleasant task.

"CulturePulse first, Alistair."

A hundred electronic images appeared in the air above my desk — the cultural items that received the most hits on the Grid in the previous twenty-four hours.

"Number one, please."

The image on the far left moved to the chair next to Alistair. It was an attractive young woman with short brown hair, dressed in a blue sundress and sandals. Her name was Jade, from Auburn, Michigan. She'd had a dream in which Jesus appeared to her.

The second image appeared, a young man dressed in a beige T-shirt and jeans. He'd had the same dream. I scanned the remaining images. Twenty-two of the ninety-eight were the identical story.

I picked up my coffee cup and leaned back in my chair. *How did all these people have the same dream? And why are they all from North America?*

An audio-only tap interrupted my thoughts. City of Champaign Police Department. *This can't be good news.*

"This is Creighton Daniels."

"Mr. Daniels — is it 'mister' or 'doctor'?" The voice was low, the speech slow.

"Either is fine. Is anything the matter?"

"Mr. Daniels, the Grid lists you as the primary contact for your father, Eli Daniels."

I sat up straight in my chair. "That's correct. Is he all right?"

There was a pause. "I'm sorry to have to tell you. Your father has committed suicide."

The police officer climbed out of his car

when he saw me pull up in front of my dad's place. "Mr. Daniels? Officer Stefan Hixon."

We shook hands.

"You went to the morgue to identify him?" I nodded.

"A crying shame, a man that young, in his eighties. At least it was painless. Did he give any indication?"

"No. Not to me, at least. They said he left a suicide message."

"Yeah, I need you to look it over and check out his place. This is all just a formality since they've done the autopsy."

We walked through the front door into the modest, sixty-year-old house where my dad lived his last two decades. Though we visited in virtual reality once or twice a month, I hadn't been to his house in eleven years. It looked the same: immaculate. My dad was a neat freak, a gene he had failed to pass along.

The officer started the visual. Dad was sitting at his desk at home, expressionless. But he was always expressionless. "This is just a simple message for those I leave behind," he said. "I'm fortunate to have had so many good friends and family, especially my university colleagues. I've appreciated you all. But now it's time for me to say good-bye. I've been diagnosed with CJD, which has no cure. I haven't told anyone this, not wanting to burden you with my troubles. The doctors give me only a few months of rapid deterioration. I don't want to go out that way, and I don't want to be remembered that way. This is better for all of us. My fond farewell to you all."

That was it.

Why didn't he tell me? And why didn't he have more to say than a fond farewell?

The officer shook his head. "That's rough, man. I'm sorry." He glanced around the living room. "Well, I just need you to make sure everything seems normal. It's just you, I take it? No brothers or sisters?"

"No."

"A life partner?"

"His last one was years ago."

"Parents?"

"They're in Washington State. I don't think he's talked to them in years."

He nodded. "I get this a lot — only children having to do everything themselves. That's the way it is anymore, I suppose." He paused, then motioned toward the door. "I'll just wait over there. Take your time looking around. Just don't remove anything for now."

I walked slowly around the living room, kitchen, two bedrooms, and bath. Everything looked normal, but I wasn't exactly the best judge. I drifted into my dad's study and sat down at his desk. Everything on the desk top was in perfect order. I opened a drawer and glanced at some electronic accessories, neatly arranged. I opened another and pulled out a disheveled stack of papers. I wasn't sure what surprised me more, the papers or the disarray. Dad never kept things that way. I flipped through them. None seemed particularly important.

I looked in the bottom drawer. A bowl. Dad always ate popcorn at his desk. An old model electronic writing pad. I opened it. It was dusty — probably hadn't been used in years. I started to close the pad, then noticed that something had been tucked inside the cover pocket. I pulled out an old-style digital storage device. No one had used these for two decades.

I glanced toward the front of the house. The officer had momentarily gone into virtual reality.

I slipped the device into my pocket.

2

Nine days later

Abigail Caldwell's eyes blinked open. Painfully she lifted her head off the wood bottom of the dugout canoe and glanced at the sun shining between the endless colonnades of trees overhanging both sides of the river.

Early afternoon. I'm heading east.

She sat erect and looked at the jungle on both sides, then at the bends in the river fore and aft. Nothing was familiar. She reached for her oar and began to row, the handcrafted paddle cutting swiftly through the water. Her arms and shoulders felt stiff. She focused on the mechanics of her stroke. Back straight. Arms relaxed.

Mosquitoes, stirred by her awakening, returned. Swatting them occupied her arms full-time, bringing her rowing to a halt — a luxury she couldn't afford. She let the mosquitoes feed.

She was so hungry and thirsty. She hadn't

eaten in two days, had no time to stop and forage for food, and didn't want to risk venturing alone into unfamiliar jungle. She slid her hand over the side of the canoe, cupped some brown water, and drank. It was rancid, but the liquid felt welcome on her tongue and her lips.

At least she had slept. Prior to leaving in the canoe, she hadn't slept for two nights. She had been too much in demand, tending the sick. Her body craved more sleep now. She could feel the heaviness in her head and muscles, but she couldn't indulge it. She had to keep going.

The sun drifted downward. Her canoe traversed an endless series of switchback curves — at this moment east, at this one west. She pressed to push the oar through the water at a consistent pace. She noticed her posture failing and straightened. Ten minutes later she straightened again. Finally she resigned herself to a permanent, aching slouch.

Night fell. The jungle erupted into a cacophony of hoots, grunts, wails, and caws. A guttural scream brought silence to the entire rain forest. She jerked her head and stared into the blackness. Her own hand was invisible to her.

She fought a growing panic. Could she

survive another moonless night on the river? Proceeding was terribly risky. At any moment the canoe might crash into a fallen tree, a boulder, or a low-lying bridge, spilling her into water infested with crocodiles and river sharks. Worse, she didn't know when the river might turn into rapids that could send her swirling beneath the brackish water.

The danger was unavoidable; she had to reach the coast. If she failed, the village — everything she had ever known — would die.

Hour after hour, she rowed. Exhaustion overcame her. She finally stopped rowing and let the current carry her. She closed her eyes. She slept. She dreamed. A dark-skinned little girl approached her with a white rose of Sharon.

"Where did you find this, Miraba?"

"By the river."

"This flower doesn't grow in our jungle."

"There was only one."

The girl placed the flower at her own feet. It grew, slowly enveloping her.

"I'm going for help, Miraba. Hold on."

"Xén, bi náana 'nû ten la." My heart is with you always, Mama.

She woke when her face hit the water. She gasped and sucked in a mouthful of black liquid. She tried coughing it out but only sucked in more. Her feet thrashed, and her arms flailed, and she moved through the water — whether up or down, she didn't know. Her head smashed into something solid. She stopped momentarily, dazed.

I have to breathe!

She raised her hands above her head and felt an object. The canoe. She thrust upward to her right, her head finally breaking the surface. She gasped, retched, and reached for the canoe. She touched it and clung to it and coughed up black water. She wanted nothing more than to hold on and simply drift downstream. But that was likely fatal. She had to get back into the dugout.

Hand over hand, she silently made her way to the stern. She placed one hand on each side of the canoe and lunged upward, lifting her torso out of the water and onto the craft. She lunged again, her waist straddling the stern. The canoe tipped precariously. Guardedly, she dragged her legs onto the canoe and collapsed inside.

In sudden desperation she ran her hands along the inside of the canoe. *Where is my paddle?* She felt something move under her palm and grasped it. The paddle. She briefly breathed a sigh of relief, then resumed a frantic search of the canoe but failed to find her other vital possession: her knife. She was defenseless.

Abby bit down on her cracked lip, feeling the split widen and tasting the blood. She stared into the darkness and thought about what to do next. She picked up her paddle. Row. She could only row.

When her arms gave out and she felt barely conscious, she lay down again in the dugout and slept. She woke with the sun, moving her hands to scrape away the feasting mosquitoes. Her arms throbbed. She reached to the back of her head and felt a knot. Her hair was matted with dried blood.

She sat upright and surveyed her surroundings. She had entered a new river: wider, lazier, the color a milky brown. On its sides the trees overhung the water in sweeping arches. Vines, branches, and epiphytes twisted together to form intricate tapestries, often so thick that the bank was hidden from view.

Midmorning the terrain changed. She passed a series of cliffs straddling the river. The current grew swifter. She heard a noise ahead — one foreign to the jungle. The hum was mechanical, an engine of some kind. Whatever it was, she wanted to avoid an encounter with those producing it. She had no idea what tribe inhabited this part of the river or whether they would allow her safe passage.

She steered the dugout to the far side of the river. Looking back across the water, she saw the source of the noise — a motorized boat with two men, idling next to a pier. Behind the pier lay a village of perhaps a hundred wood houses on stilts. Spanning the river, past the pier, was a wooden bridge. She guided the canoe between the riverbank and the curtain of vines overhanging it. The flora would hide her long enough to reach the bridge.

Once she was behind the curtain, vine after vine scraped against her. She heard a thump in the stern and jerked her head around. She heard another thump in the bow and turned back. Two death adders had joined her. She raised her paddle and brought it down upon the second one, killing it instantly. The first flared and struck, biting her left leg. Abby spun around and cried out, the pain searing through her calf. She grabbed the creature, pulled it out of her flesh, and flung it into the water.

She had to get out from behind the vines, but there were no easy exits. She aimed the canoe straight toward the tapestry, bent down low, and crashed through. The impact knocked her on her back. She raised her head and scanned the dugout. No more snakes had joined her. She turned to examine her leg, which had already begun to swell. If she'd had a knife, she would have cut it and sucked out the venom. She bent down and drained as much as she could, wincing and clenching her jaw in efforts to stay quiet.

She grabbed the oar just as she heard voices from the other side of the river. She looked up. The villagers had spotted her. Several men and boys were running toward the bridge on the far bank. Others motioned to the two men in the motorized boat. She glanced upstream and saw the men untying the craft. They backed the boat away from the pier and aimed it toward her. She rowed with all her strength toward the bridge. The villagers had reached it and were crossing toward her. She imagined the shower of arrows that might rain upon her at any moment.

The motorized boat was gaining on her. The men were gesturing frantically, signaling, she thought, the men on the bridge, who were shouting and waving their arms. She didn't see weapons, but that didn't assuage her fear.

She ducked her head as her canoe shot under the bridge and out the other side.

She looked back. The villagers were still screaming and waving, but none made hostile movements. The motorized boat slowed and stopped next to the bridge.

She breathed deeply. She had survived.

Slowly she turned her face downstream. The current had picked up considerably. She heard a low, rumbling noise like the sound of an approaching drenching rain. The roar grew. Despite her furious attempt to paddle to the shore, the river pulled her inexorably forward.

She entered the rapids between two large boulders on the left side of the river. It took all her fading strength to steer the canoe bow-first down them. The waters churned beneath her as countless rocks passed by.

She spotted a small island ahead. At its tip was a boulder twice her height. She paddled furiously to the right, where the rapids had ebbed, to no avail. The current pulled her to the left. She paddled with all her might as the rock came upon her. The bow of the canoe struck it and flipped her to the left.

Her craft sped horizontally down the rapids. *I have to straighten it.* She dug her oar into the water. The dugout began swinging to the left, stern first. She thrust her paddle to parry an oncoming boulder. The

31

paddle struck it with such force that it tossed her into the bottom of the canoe and her oar into the air. She bolted upright only to see it hit the water and disappear down a ferocious whirlpool.

Now she was impotent.

She turned to face the onslaught of the river. The canoe bobbed and weaved in the rapids, sprays of water assaulting its passenger from all sides. She became aware of another low, thundering noise. Ahead she saw a violent churning beyond which the river seemed to disappear.

Terror overcame her. She planted her face near the floor of the dugout and endured the battering of rocks, wondering if the canoe would be smashed to pieces even before the falls.

The bottom of the canoe fell beneath her. She grabbed its sides as she floated down with the plunging water. She caught a glimpse of a plume-covered lake below, then ducked her head just before the canoe hit the water.

The impact knocked the breath out of her, and she was thrown from the canoe. She floated in the depths for a moment, then gathered her strength for a surge to the sunlight. She kicked her right leg with all her might — the snakebite had rendered her left one useless — and thrust down with both arms.

She opened her mouth and gasped for breath, sucking in large quantities of water.

This is the end of us all. Miraba . . .

Sunlight broke upon her eyes, and misty air surrounded her head. She coughed violently, breathed deeply, coughed some more. She looked upriver. She was a considerable distance from the falls, floating lazily downstream. She glanced to her right, then to her left. Her canoe, capsized but intact, was floating parallel to her, ten arm lengths away.

She kicked over to it, grabbed its hull, and laid her head upon it. *I have to get it upright.* But she didn't have the strength. She thrust her arms against the hull and lifted herself a few inches onto it. She tried repeating the maneuver but fell back into the water, grasping for the canoe.

She hung on to the boat. She floated. She gathered her waning strength and pushed herself upward again. Six attempts later she straddled the bottom of the boat, feet dangling in the water.

She laid her head on the boat's hull and lost consciousness.

3

Abby Caldwell opened her eyes to a place unlike any she had ever seen. She was lying on a soft bed. All was white around her. A long, thin plastic tube was attached to her right arm. Metal boxes with lights surrounded her.

A dark-skinned woman in white clothing entered the room. She looked at Abby, then at the metal boxes. She smiled and said something in a language Abby didn't recognize.

"*¿Neen jné?*" Abby responded.

The woman looked at her, clueless.

Abby tried English. "I'm sorry . . . I can't understand you." The words came haltingly. Though she was accustomed to thinking in English, she hadn't spoken the language in years.

The woman answered in English. "Are you feeling better?"

"Everything hurts."

"You are a lucky one. I'm told you were drifting in the Sepik when they rescued you."

Abby groaned and tried to sit up. "Where am I?"

"Easy." The woman moved to help Abby lie back down. "You are in the Meridian Hospital in Lae. I'm Somare, your nurse. You're under the care of Dr. Kate Sampson, so you're in very good hands. Can you tell me your name?"

"I need the doctor."

The nurse glanced at a schedule above the bed. "She should be here in about two hours."

Abby grabbed the nurse forcefully with her left arm. "No! I need the doctor now! It's an emergency."

The nurse spoke in a measured tone but didn't pull away. "You were dehydrated and suffering from an adder bite. But you are all right now."

"No, not me. My people — they're dying! Please." She loosened her grip on the nurse's arm.

The nurse looked into her eyes. "I'll tap her."

Five minutes later a woman dressed in blue scrubs entered the room. "I'm Dr. Sampson. I'm glad you're awake. You're doing amazingly well considering how you got here." She glanced at the electronic pad in her hands. "You were dehydrated and suffering from heatstroke, you had a concussion from that knock on your head, and you had an adder bite. We gave you antivenin for the bite, and the swelling has receded. The IV fluids have rehydrated you. We are monitoring the concussion, but you appear to be recovering nicely."

She looked at Abby and smiled. "You must have had quite an adventure. How long had you been in the canoe?"

Abby didn't answer but just stared at the doctor's face.

"Maybe we should back up a little. Can you tell me your name?"

Abby shook her head and finally spoke. "I'm sorry. I was just . . . You're Caucasian."

The doctor had a quizzical look momentarily, then a softer expression. "Yes, I am. I'm from the United States. You must not be accustomed to seeing Caucasian faces."

Abby shook her head again. "Except for a man on the river last week, not in the last eight years."

"Eight years? You must not travel out from the interior often."

"No. Never."

The doctor raised her eyebrows. "Never?

How did you get to the interior?"

"My parents. Please, can you help? They're dying."

"Your parents are dying?"

"No, my parents are dead. My village is dying. Can you come?"

Kate Sampson felt a knot in her stomach the minute she instructed her Grid interface to tap the health minister. Their last encounter, a face-to-face one, hadn't ended on the best of terms. A New Guinean with a receding gray hairline appeared on her visiscreen.

"Dr. Poon."

"Dr. Sampson. Are you still in our country?"

He knew perfectly well she was. Hers was the only hospital in the country's second largest city, and she was the internal medicine department. She let the remark slide.

"I need your approval for a medical mission."

"In your position you are free to travel as necessary, Doctor."

"These patients are Inisi."

Poon's eyebrows rose. "Inisi? You've been in touch with Inisi?"

"No. An American woman living in an Inisi village was found unconscious on the Sepik yesterday. She says her village is dying of some disease."

"All outsiders are banned from contact with the Inisi."

"Yes, I know that. She says that, at the request of the tribe, her family was given permission years ago to remain with them. She came out seeking medical help for her village."

"What disease?"

Kate shrugged. "I don't know. She describes the symptoms as headache, disorientation, dizziness, vomiting, and loss of memory, then coma. It doesn't match any of the jungle diseases."

Poon shook his head. "No, it doesn't. How many have died?"

"Four as of the time she left."

"How long from onset to death?"

"Three days. Maybe less."

"Is she symptomatic?"

"No. And we've run all viral tests on her."

"Negative?"

Kate nodded. "Dr. Poon, I need your authorization."

He shook his head vigorously. "I can't authorize that. Not to the Inisi. The Interior —"

"It's my understanding that you can authorize it to contain a contagious disease." They stared at each other a moment. "Isn't that true?"

"Dr. Sampson, we don't know how contagious —"

"It's infected an entire village and killed at least four. Dr. Poon" — she stepped closer to her visiscreen — "this woman, my patient, is desperate. She canoed all the way out to save her village."

"Then she possesses both endurance and patience. She can wait until I obtain permission from the Interior Ministry. Good day, Doctor."

His image disappeared. Kate sat fuming. After a few moments she accessed the interface with her assistant, who appeared on the visiscreen.

"Yes, Dr. Sampson?"

"Amu, secure the helicopter."

"For what time?"

"Immediately."

Kate looked across the passenger compartment of the medical helicopter. By the terrified look on Abby's face, Kate could tell the takeoff had been rough on her. But she had adapted quickly. Since the helicopter had leveled off shortly afterward, Abby hadn't stopped looking out the window. From time to time on their headsets, they heard the pilot note their location. "Thank you," Abby would always respond.

The truth was, they didn't know exactly where they were headed. Up the river Abby had traversed, the Sepik. Then up a major tributary, the Yuat, off which the Inisi tribe lived. After that, who knew? Abby couldn't name the smaller tributary where her village was situated. *Jmîî juee'*, they called it. *The River.* Satellite mapping was useless; the Inisi were spread over a wide area. Finding one village might take all day.

The effort was worth it to her. Approval or no approval, Kate wasn't about to place the survival of an entire village on the desk of some bureaucrat in Port Moresby. She had come to Papua New Guinea four months before with Matt, her life partner and fellow physician, to save lives, not wait on pencil pushers. The government had started a new health program, providing critical care and medical maintenance to tribes via boat and helicopter. It was exactly the sort of adventure she sought: bringing healing to the true wild, the still untamed interior of the vast island.

It hadn't worked as planned. Two months after their arrival, the government canceled the program. A week later Matt returned to the States to think things over. Shortly thereafter the relationship ended.

40

For her part, Kate had become enamored with Papua New Guinea — both its spirited people and its forbidding terrain. She had decided to stay, landing a job as head of internal medicine at Meridian.

Traveling to the Inisi — a tribe the government had placed off-limits decades before to preserve its cultural integrity — could get her fired. She expected a reprimand instead. Where were they going to find a replacement? Prior to her arrival, her position had been open for fourteen months. Besides, her request would likely be approved — though too late to save anyone. One thing was certain: the disease spread rapidly and could be fatal. Such a pathogen, if not contained, could threaten not just the Inisi but the entire interior and beyond.

The only misgiving Kate had about the trip was the presence of her patient. Given her condition upon arrival at the hospital two days before, Abby had no business flying on a medical rescue mission. But once rehydrated and treated for her snakebite, Abby had shown amazing resiliency. Nevertheless, Kate insisted on checking her vitals every two hours on the trip.

The helicopter reached a large tributary.

"We are heading up the Yuat," the pilot informed them.

Down below, Kate saw a blackish river intersecting a larger, milky brown river. The sediment of the former created a weaving of black and brown for several miles downstream.

They proceeded upstream at a height of four hundred feet. Every five to ten minutes they would approach a smaller tributary, one of which, they assumed, Abby had traveled down. But Abby had no idea which one. The only marker she could describe was a long, dark brown sandbank that was a forty-five-minute walk from her village.

The pilot took the helicopter ten minutes up each tributary. They found nothing.

"Is it possible the trees overhang it?" Kate asked Abby.

"No. It's open to the sunlight."

They kept on looking. Ten tributaries. Fifteen.

"We're going to have to head back soon," the pilot warned. "We're almost to the return point on fuel."

Abby looked worriedly at Kate, who forced a smile. It was little consolation, she knew.

They scouted two more tributaries. No sandbank.

"That's it," the pilot announced. "We're heading back to base." The helicopter banked sharply and turned to the east.

"No!" Abby shouted into her headset. "Not yet. We have to keep looking."

"Sorry, ma'am. My fuel light just came on. That means we have just enough to make it back."

"Can we do one more?"

"Don't you have an additional fuel reserve?" Kate interjected.

The pilot shot a look at her. "All right. One more."

He flew back up the Yuat. They found another tributary in six minutes and followed its twists and turns. After five minutes the tributary became a mountain stream.

"We're heading back," the pilot said. He turned to the east again.

Kate looked at her patient. "I'm sorry, Abby."

Abby nodded but didn't turn her way. She was still glued to the window, tears dripping off her cheeks.

4

They tried again the next day. Having logged their last position from the day before, the pilot flew straight up the Yuat and to the next tributary. They ventured up two with no success. On the third they flew upriver seventeen miles before Kate spotted a sandbank on the left. "What's that?" she asked, pointing.

Abby threw off her safety belt and flew across the passenger compartment. "Yes! That's the bank!"

She adjusted her headset and shouted into it. "That's it on the left."

The pilot was already turning the craft and taking it down. He skimmed the surface of the river for two hundred feet before hovering over the bank.

"Can we land?" Kate shouted.

"Not sure. How soft is that sand?"

"It doesn't leave a deep footprint," Abby responded.

"Why don't you check it out, Dr. Sampson? I'll hover and let you drop down."

He positioned the copter five feet off the ground. Kate grabbed the safety latch, unlocked it, and pulled the hatch open.

"You can lower yourself down with the rope."

"That's okay. I'll jump."

"Suit yourself. Just throw the rope over with you. You'll need it to pull yourself back in."

Kate tossed one end of a thick rope overboard, then jumped onto the sand below and fell to a knee before returning to her feet. She bent low and circled the helicopter, stamping her boots on the sand as she went.

"It's pretty firm," she shouted into her headset. "I don't think you'll sink."

"We'd better hope not."

Kate looked at the river to her left and the jungle to her right. She walked twenty yards down the bank to make space for the helicopter, keeping an eye on the river. New Guinea has no large jungle predators, but crocodiles are another story. The helicopter descended onto the bank, sinking a couple of inches into the sand before the pilot cut the engine. He turned, looked at Abby, and spoke into his radio. "Are you sure I'll be safe here?"

Abby didn't respond. She was already leaning out the hatch. Kate approached the exit, stuck out her hand, and helped her off. "How far a walk from here?"

"Less than an hour. We hike the beach, and then we take a trail in the forest. That leads to the village."

Kate noticed that the desperate look in Abby's eyes had turned to fierce determination. She looked her patient up and down. "Are you up for this?"

"Yes."

"Let me take your vitals before —"

Abby shook her head. "No time. You can do it there."

Kate shrugged, slung her backpack between her shoulders, and picked up her med kit. "You lead."

The two women walked silently along the bank. Though in good shape, Kate struggled to keep up. The late-morning heat was already suffocating. No breeze came off the river. Overhead she heard a strange symphony of bird calls and animal noises. Kate jerked her head upward at every shrill shriek. Abby seemed to ignore them all.

Within five minutes the sand along the river's edge narrowed and then disappeared altogether, with trees and underbrush now coming all the way to the water's edge. Abby stopped and waited a moment for Kate to catch up. "Watch for adders here."

She pushed through some undergrowth and disappeared into the jungle. Kate glanced warily at the foliage in front of her, then followed, catching her shirt in three places on the branches.

Once past the curtain of flora, she found herself on a jungle path suitable for single-file passage. Abby walked swiftly ahead. Kate jogged to catch up, tripping repeatedly on roots that Abby navigated effortlessly. Often Abby would disappear into what appeared to be dense undergrowth. When Kate followed, however, she always discovered they were on a new path.

The path veered to the left and right without discernible intent. It intersected another trail, and Abby strode to the left. Kate checked the time. Half an hour gone.

The closer they got to the village, the faster Abby walked. Kate finally broke into a continuous jog just to keep pace. Sweat poured off her face in rivulets. She looked down and saw red stains on her socks. Leeches were getting their fill. She stopped to pick them off, then ran to catch up, fearful of Abby's disappearing through a hedge onto another hidden path.

The trail broadened slightly, straightened, and broke into a clearing that revealed two dozen thatched-roof huts surrounding a larger thatched structure. Abby had stopped at the tree where the path ended. Kate arrived, panting, beside her.

The two women looked at each other. They already knew the answer they had come to discover. The stench told them.

Abby started quickly toward the huts.

"Stop!" Kate grabbed her by the arm. "We need masks. And gloves."

Abby hesitated, then complied. Kate opened her med kit and pulled out surgical masks and gloves. She placed them on Abby and herself. She had considered bringing biohazard suits but had decided against it. She didn't want to make this woman feel too much like an alien in her own village. Now she was kicking herself for that decision.

"Abby, even with these on, we need to be careful not to let anything come in contact with our bodies. We don't want to risk contracting the disease. We need to proceed slowly."

Abby didn't proceed slowly. She ran past the first four huts and entered the fifth. Kate followed. No one was inside. They went to the next hut. Abby looked in. *"¡¿'Ee hua 'noo. Jiaa' mîoo lajîn te' dsa?!"*

She entered and knelt beside the bodies of a baby and three children wrapped in burial shrouds, lying on the dirt floor. Next to them were the bodies of a man and a woman on a straw mat. Abby reached out to stroke the head of the baby.

"Don't touch the bodies!"

Abby looked up at Kate, her eyes pleading for leniency. Slowly she raised herself off the floor and went to the next hut.

Every hut was the same. Mercifully, the children had died first. They were all wrapped in burial shrouds, only their faces showing. Kate watched as Abby, her lean shoulders set in determination, moved ahead through the village. She paused at each doorway, glanced at the faces of the children, and with the force of her will seemed to repel the waves of grief as she moved from one enclosure to the next.

They came to the last hut. Two adults lay dead on the sleeping mat. Four children were wrapped in burial shrouds. Beside the two adults lay a dark-skinned child, unwrapped. Abby ripped off her mask and rushed to the deceased child.

"Abby, no!" Kate cried out.

But it was too late. Abby cradled the child and was clutching and rocking her, sobbing.

"¡Miraba! ¡Xii' mî bi 'náana, Miraba!"

Her sobbing turned to wailing, then finally to quiet moaning. Back and forth she rocked the child, minute after sorrowful minute.

Kate gave her space. There was no use asking her to put the child down now. After many minutes of standing silently, she stepped to Abby and placed her hand on her shoulder. "I'm so sorry."

Abby caressed the girl's hair. "She was my daughter."

The revelation raised numerous questions; the girl was clearly a tribal native, not half-Caucasian. But Kate exiled the questions to the back of her mind.

Abby laid the girl down. *"Rîgüe'na co' ca'ee cî,"* she said to the child. *I'll be back shortly.*

They went outside. Abby walked to a large flat rock at the entrance to the community hut and sat. She started to place her head in her hands, but seeing the plastic gloves, she simply put her head between her knees and wept. Her body shook from the waves of grief.

Kate sat beside her and put her arm around Abby. Comforting patients was never her strong suit, but Abby needed her. "I wish I knew what to say."

Abby's body slumped into her, and Kate held her tightly as she sobbed in heaves. Gradually the heaves gave way to quiet crying. Finally Abby dabbed her eyes with her sleeve. "I loved them. All of them."

Kate felt tears pooling in her own eyes.

After a time Abby leaned forward, her face full of regret. "We were too late. If only . . ."

"Abby, no. This isn't your fault. Don't believe that for a second. You did everything you could."

They sat on the rock a few more minutes. Kate checked the time. "It's two thirty. We need to head back."

"Head back?"

"To Lae."

Abby shook her head. "I have to stay."

"We can come back tomorrow. They'll fly in men to take care of the bodies and the village. You need —"

Kate watched Abby lift her head, her mouth set in a hard, sad line. "How will they take care of the bodies?"

"They'll burn the bodies and the village. I know it sounds —"

A look of horror came over Abby's face. "Burn? No! They can't be burned. They must be buried."

"Abby, these people died of a communicable disease. The bodies must be destroyed

51

to prevent its spread. I'll take one back with us and do an autopsy. The others must be burned."

Abby stood. "They have to be buried. It's their way."

"But we can't risk spreading the disease. What if someone disturbs the graves?"

"No one would do that. It would invite evil spirits."

Kate looked at her for a long moment, then shrugged. "All right. We'll bury the bodies. But we have to set fire to the village."

Abby glanced around at the huts. "Okay. The village."

"So we're agreed? We'll come back tomorrow."

"I'm spending the night here, Dr. Sampson."

"Abby, you can't stay here."

"I have to." She extended her arms in a sweeping motion. "These are my people. I can't abandon them."

Kate looked around the village and sighed. She contacted the helicopter. "Saperi, everything all right there?"

She heard silence on the other end, then a voice. "Still here. What did you find?"

"The villagers have all died." She looked down at Abby, who met her eyes. She continued, "I need you to arrange for men to bury the villagers and burn the village tomorrow."

"What are you going to do?"

"We're going to spend the night here. You can go."

"You're staying? Is it safe?"

"No, it's not. I don't know what the disease is or how it's transmitted. But Ms. Caldwell won't leave, and I won't leave her here alone."

There was a long pause. "Do you want me to stay with you?"

That was the last thing he wanted to do, Kate knew. "No. Just make sure you're back here with help tomorrow."

They went back to Abby's hut, the first they had entered. Kate walked to the other huts and took blood samples from the bodies. By the time she returned, Abby had gathered wood for a fire. The sun set, and Kate pulled some food and water from her backpack. Despite her entreaties, Abby wouldn't eat, taking only a bottle of water.

They lay down to sleep on the bare ground. The jungle erupted into a terrifying series of shrieks, howls, grunts, and calls that kept Kate awake for hours until finally she could no longer open her eyelids at even the most hideous noises. She had never been so glad to have someone sleeping next to her.

The next day eight men arrived via helicopter. Abby and Kate watched them start the burials.

"Abby, we'll need to take one body back with us to perform an autopsy, but the morgue at my hospital is closed. We'll have to send it to Port Moresby."

Abby thought for a moment, then quietly replied, "The chief's. He'd want to sacrifice his body for his people."

The men took until midafternoon to bury the bodies. When they were done, Abby spoke a eulogy over each one and said her final good-byes. Her daughter, Miraba, was the last. Abby knelt beside her fresh grave and wept. She reached to the sides of her head to remove her medical mask.

"You must keep your mask and gloves on, Abby," Kate instructed.

Abby didn't seem to hear her. She removed the protective items, placed her fingers to her mouth, kissed them, and placed them on the dirt. *"Rîcuaa'nu 'nû quia'nu jné ten la, Miraba. 'Ajia' huøø rîcuaa'na núu." You will always be my little one, Miraba. Our time apart won't be long.*

She bowed her head silently for several

54

minutes, then finally rose. "I'm ready to pack my personal things."

Kate handed Abby her mask and gloves. "One of the men already collected them."

Abby walked to her hut and looked inside the mostly bare enclosure. "I want to stay here another day or two."

"The helicopter pilot needs to return to Lae now."

"Ask him if he can come back in two days."

"He'll say no."

"Please, Dr. Sampson." Her whole body sagged from the weight of her heartbreak.

"Okay," Kate answered.

She contacted the helicopter, spoke to the pilot, and turned back to Abby. "He says he can't come back a third time. The men say we must all leave now. They're going to set fire to the village immediately."

Abby walked to her doorway and looked out at the village. She spoke softly. "All shall be well, and all manner of things shall be well, and everything shall be well," she said softly.

"What is that?"

Abby turned back to Kate. "An old saying. I'm comforted by it sometimes."

The two women walked through the jungle as the men set fire to the village. They waited at the helicopter while the men ensured no flames spread. At twilight the helicopter rose with all aboard. Abby looked down at her village. Her entire history was burning in two dozen smoldering orange rings. Behind her, nighttime had fallen. Ahead, the sun would rise on a world she had never known.

5

Damien Cleary sat on the back row of a thousand-plus crowd crammed into the ballroom of Chicago's Hotel La Salle. He wasn't fond of large gatherings in physical space. He had argued against having people physically present for the unveiling; it always increased the risk of the unexpected. But Bryson Nichols had insisted. And this was Nichols's show.

Nichols hadn't physically appeared before the Foundation for the Advancement of Transhumanity since starting the organization fourteen years earlier with a handful of technological visionaries and philanthropists. Now almost every scientist of note in the fields of artificial intelligence, robotics, and genetic engineering was a member, as well as a bevy of do-gooders who financed the nonprofit side of Nichols's endeavors.

Not that Nichols needed the money. As founder and CEO of Nichols Technology

Inc. (NTI) and the leading artificial intelligence innovator of his time, he could easily launch and finance any project he wished. It had been Nichols's plan all along, however, to involve the nonprofit and governmental spheres. His vision wasn't simply the development and marketing of a fantastically profitable new AI technology; he sought the transformation of humanity itself. To date, the plan had worked like clockwork. Which didn't surprise Damien Cleary. Everything Nichols touched worked like clockwork.

Cleary disagreed with Nichols's approach. He was contemptuous of the foundation's nonscientists — sycophants who felt important by hob-nobbing with the world's scientific elite. Such a technological leap as he and Nichols had achieved, Cleary believed, would create its own momentum. Given sufficient motivation, the world would follow their lead into humanity's next stage.

Despite his misgivings, Cleary wasn't about to miss this event. He, Nichols, and Ray Caldwell had been the brains behind the accomplishment to be unveiled. Only a few in the audience knew of Cleary's key role, perhaps most notably Hutch Hardin, a political operative and consummate Washington deal maker whom he had befriended in the early days of the foundation. To most, Cleary was just another face in the crowd.

As head of the Contingency Planning Unit at NTI, Cleary worked in the shadows. He aimed to keep it that way. "Contingency planning" was an antiseptic way of saying, "What if we lose control and our work ends up threatening the planet?" No one wanted to acknowledge that such questions even had to be addressed.

With NTI on the cutting edge of self-replicating nanotechnology, Cleary's job was twofold: first, to ensure that the company's cell-sized robots didn't replicate out of control, producing a doomsday scenario in which exponential replication would consume all the planet's resources within days, and, second, to work with transgovernmental agencies to develop worldwide immunity systems guarding against such a threat (intentional or not) from others. Bryson Nichols would entrust such a job only to a close associate. Cleary had been that since they had roomed together as freshmen at Cal Poly.

Cleary eyed the ballroom. There was an air of expectancy. People hadn't been asked to don their tuxes and formal gowns just to hear the latest annual report. The last patrons took their seats, champagne and hors d'oeuvre still in hand.

Cleary accessed the time on the worldwide Grid. Six fifty-eight. Nichols would appear in two minutes; the man was punctual to a fault. He heard the ballroom doors behind him close. The overhead lights dimmed. A hush swept the audience.

Seven o'clock. From the left of the stage, a door opened. Bryson Nichols walked out, climbed onto the stage, and strode to the podium. He gave a confident smile — Cleary called it Nichols's smirk — and glanced left to right across the audience.

"Gentlemen, ladies. The moment that our foundation has been striving toward — the moment for which the universe brought us forth — that moment has finally arrived. The Singularity is here."

The room broke into sustained applause. Three attendees in the front row stood. Those behind them followed suit until everyone was standing. Nichols basked in the ovation, smiling broadly, nodding, and pointing to select individuals in the crowd until he finally held up his hand. The applause subsided, and people took their seats.

"Thank you. Literally . . . thank *you*. For truly this is an accomplishment that came to fruition only through the dedicated effort, support, and unwavering faith of this august body of believers. You believed that human intelligence and its creation, techno-logical intelligence, could be merged, that *Homo sapiens* could within our lifetimes be supplanted by the next step in the evolution-ary chain. I stand before you to announce that we have achieved that next step. *Homo technicus* is a reality."

The crowd rose and applauded once more. Nichols beamed. He waited a full minute, then motioned for them to sit.

"Not long ago the idea of humans merg-ing with technological intelligence was sci-ence fiction. As Arthur C. Clarke once said, 'Any sufficiently advanced technology is indistinguishable from magic.' And, indeed, to those alive a hundred years ago, what I'm about to unveil would seem magical.

"But the road to this point is one our predecessors should have known would be traveled. That road is the exponential curve of technological progress that humanity has trod for millennia."

Above and behind Nichols appeared a holographic projection of a two-axis graph with an exponential curve sloping up to the right. Along the horizontal axis, markers for each of twenty-one centuries appeared.

"Technological progress is never linear. It is exponential. That fact wasn't apparent for most of human history, because humans were living on the flat part of the curve. But because human knowledge builds upon itself, the rate of change is always accelerating. The twentieth century saw as much change as had occurred in the previous five centuries combined. The first two decades of this century saw as much change as the entire twentieth century. At this point we are experiencing that amount of change in a single year. Within fifty years human knowledge will be advancing along a slope approaching vertical."

Cleary glanced around the large room. No one stirred.

Nichols continued. "We can't place too much blame on our intellectual forebears for not anticipating the Singularity. Our accomplishment results from the convergence of revolutions in three fields that were unknown as late as 1950: biotechnology, nanotechnology, and artificial intelligence.

"The average person in the year 2000 had no idea that the foundation for this event had already been laid. The entire human genome had been decoded. Primitive artificial intelligence was already in use, as were early neural implants. We had already taken the first step in building an artificial brain: the construction of artificial neural clusters

62

that could work in tandem with biological clusters."

Nichols was speaking faster now. Cleary knew he loved recounting the path of AI development.

"By 2020 we had fully mapped animal brains and modeled extensive regions of the human brain. Millions were using neural implants for hearing and sight loss. First-stage virtual reality was commonplace in the military and in industry.

"Moore's Law was still operating: computing power was doubling every eighteen months. By 2030 a standard personal computer equaled the processing power of the human brain. We didn't have the software to emulate the brain yet, but in pure processing power we had arrived.

"By 2035 advanced speech recognition software terminated computers as separate objects. Keyboards went the way of manual typewriters. Full-immersion virtual reality had been achieved, with visual and auditory input channeled directly to sensory neurons. The old Internet was replaced by the world-wide Grid, a thousandfold improvement in cyberspace.

"By 2045 the first molecular assemblers made nanotechnology a commercial reality. Nanites enabled us to map the human brain through internal scanning at the neuron and synapse level. This catapulted our efforts to reverse-engineer the brain and develop a functional software simulation.

"The Nuclear Depression slowed progress considerably, of course. But the exponential curve continued on its unrelenting path. By 2060 nanotechnology had exploded: molecular assemblers were commonplace, producing industrial and consumer products from base materials. Neural implants to enhance brain speed, analytic ability, and creativity meant that human intelligence, even for ordinary citizens, approached what once would have been labeled genius."

Cleary glanced at the attendees seated to his left and shook his head. *Not sure I'd call these people geniuses.*

"In 2063 NTI entered the artificial intelligence marketplace with the introduction of neural implants that enabled direct brain connection to the Grid. Overnight we assumed the worldwide lead in AI technology.

"Nine years later came NTI's next revolution: memory streams. In 2072 we unveiled technology by which individuals with our neural implants could record, electronically store, and subsequently access in virtual form all waking and nonwaking memories. Demand was insatiable. Within three years

82 percent of North Americans and 43 percent of the worldwide population were saving their memories.

"While we were advancing brain function, others were leaping forward in health management and life span. By 2060 genetic engineering had cured the majority of diseases for the majority of people. Advances in biotechnology extended the average life span to more than one hundred ten years. It was speculated that death, postponed by more than thirty years compared to the previous century, might see its end before 2100 CE.

"But though most cells are reparable almost indefinitely, the brain has proven more resistant. Despite years of research, little progress has been made on brain cell repair.

"Humanity's ageless quest for a never-ending existence, so promising thirty years ago, was postponed — perhaps, it appeared, indefinitely. The fragility of the brain itself, that marvelous yet imperfect creation of biological evolution, had become the final and insurmountable barrier to humanity's ultimate leap."

Nichols paused — for dramatic effect, Cleary knew.

"But evolution never stops. It is the

progressive arrangement of matter into ever-higher levels of order, capability, and meaning. Through humanity — through us in this room — the evolution of life on this planet has changed mediums, from the infinitesimally slow pace of biological change to the exponentially quickening pace of technological change. For we are this universe's creation, and what human intelligence creates is the realization of the universe's purpose, the culmination and continuation of the universe's evolution."

Nichols's voice was moving toward a crescendo.

"Our intelligence isn't now — nor was it ever destined to be — purely biological. It is now the merger of the biological and non-biological, the human with the artificial. We stand on the precipice of limitless intelligence."

Nichols's arms had levitated to a position alongside his shoulders, elbows bent, hands forcefully gesturing, as if his body itself prepared for the announcement to come.

"Intelligence, the product of a life-creating universe, can't be denied. I stand before you tonight to announce that eternal life has been achieved. We can not only solve this planet's mundane problems — food and water allocation, environmental degradation, international conflict, and the like. We can now solve humanity's ultimate limitation: death."

Cleary looked over the audience. They sat spellbound, awaiting the unveiling.

"Two years ago, in a revolutionary breakthrough unannounced until now, NTI successfully uploaded an entire human brain into a functioning software form. We can now take the essence of any individual human being — his or her thought patterns, memories, proclivities, the entire operation of the neural network — and re-create it in software. That constituted phase one.

"Seven months ago we operationalized phase two: the downloading of the software into a nanite-assembled permanent silicon substrate that parallels the functioning of the biological brain. Once activated by the software, this silicon brain replicates the operation of the host's biological brain.

"Tonight I am proud to announce the completion of the third and final phase. We can now transplant the new silicon brain into the human skull, providing the host with, in essence, a limitless span of brain life. We have achieved the merger of human and technological intelligence.

"We can now fulfill our ultimate purpose, the destiny that the cosmos itself has assigned us. We can seed the universe with intelligence, bringing into conscious awareness the very universe that gave us birth.

"Ladies and gentlemen, I present to you . . . the first transhuman."

As eyes scanned the stage for the announced spectacle, Nichols reached both hands up to the sides of his skull. He worked his fingers momentarily under his hair, then placed his palms alongside his head. He appeared to start pulling his head upward, but his true action quickly became evident. Nichols was lifting the top half of his skull away from his head.

Several women near the front shrieked. One fainted. The ballroom erupted into a cacophony of shocked exclamations and then quieted once more.

Nichols finished lifting the artificial skullcap off his head and held it to his side. He stood, sans the top of his skull, and smiled.

The hushed crowd beheld the metallic gray device that was Bryson Nichols's brain.

"We didn't find anything."

Kate stared at the image of the hospital's lab supervisor, unbelieving. "What do you mean you didn't find anything?"

The man shook his head. "We ran the tests twice. We found nothing. No viral or bacteriological agents beyond those that are common to humans on the island. They pose no inherent threat of illness."

"In any of the village samples? You're saying these people weren't infected with anything?"

"There was nothing in the samples that would produce a pathogenic response. As far as we can tell, these people's blood was perfectly healthy when they died — as healthy as can be expected, given their living conditions. If there's a pathogen there, it's something we've never seen before — something we don't know how to look for."

Kate thought for a moment. "You did the tests on Abigail Caldwell's sample again?"

He nodded. "Same thing. Nothing. Clean bill of health, just as before."

Kate breathed a sigh of relief. She had only known Abby for four days, and already she felt attached to her. "Thanks, Yopi. I'd like you to do one more thing for me. I'd like you to overnight the samples to Port Moresby. I just want the results confirmed."

"I'll send them right away."

The supervisor's image disappeared. Kate leaned back in her chair. Abby still wasn't carrying anything in her blood. That was the good news. The mystery was that no one else from her village was carrying anything, either. So what killed them?

A puzzled expression crossed Abby's face as she paced the hospital room. "They didn't find anything?"

Kate sat in a chair by the wall. "No. All the samples tested negative. We have no idea what killed them. Whatever it was doesn't appear in their blood, as far as we can tell."

"How can that be?"

"Abby, I have no idea. It doesn't make sense."

"And my test results?" She stopped pacing, lifting her eyes from the tiles to meet Kate's. She didn't seem afraid, Kate noted, just wanting answers.

"Still negative as well."

"So now what?"

"Now I have to schedule an autopsy on the chief."

Abby's brows rose. "Today?"

Kate shook her head. "Unfortunately, no. Several days at least. The morgue in Port Moresby is understaffed and backed up, as always."

"Do I need to stay here until then?" She gestured at the white walls as if pushing them away from her.

Kate smiled at her. "No, hardly. I'm releasing you."

Abby broke into the first real smile Kate had seen on her. "Releasing me?"

"Yes. Your injuries are healing, there's nothing in your blood, and you have no symptoms of the village illness."

"So where . . ." Abby fell silent and looked out the window.

Kate stood and took a step toward her. "Where do you go now?"

Abby nodded.

"The government has agreed to fly you back to the Inisi at any time. Same stipulations as before — you can't go in and out. But if you want to remain in Lae a few days —"

"Dr. Sampson," Abby exhaled, "I don't have anyplace to stay."

"You have a friend you could stay with."

"Who?"

Kate smiled. "Me."

6

I had barely opened my eyes before Alistair's voice penetrated the silence of my bedroom. "Creighton, you may wish to access the Grid immediately this morning."

"A disaster?"

"No. A scientific breakthrough."

I swung my feet to the floor. "Very well." I yawned. "Access it here."

"Full recording or summary?"

"Full."

I watched Bryson Nichols deliver a speech to his nonprofit foundation and then remove the top part of his skull. I sat speechless.

Artificial brains were now a reality. How long before they became ubiquitous in the population? And if, as Nichols asserted, a person could be endlessly downloaded into successive silicon brains, how would that affect people's view of life — to know that they need never die? Take away life's end point, and suddenly how we plan and conduct our existence are irrevocably changed.

But beyond that, for one's brain to both possess and process almost limitless volumes of information . . . What could a person — to say nothing of all humanity — accomplish with such abilities? *Perhaps more to the point, what could I accomplish?*

My students quickly got the word. Half a dozen tapped me before ten o'clock. I tried to underplay my reaction as much as possible. Yes, the achievement is amazing. Let's wait and see how it plays out in society at large. But I already knew. Overnight the world had been transformed.

I resisted the impulse to spend the morning monitoring Grid chatter on Nichols's breakthrough. I had other tasks. Perhaps if I had an artificial brain, I could do both, but . . .

"Alistair, tap the supply supervisor at the university."

A moment later I was in virtual reality at the desk of a gregarious man I'd met once before.

"Professor, good to see you again." He smiled broadly and we shook hands. "What can I do for you?"

I pulled from my pocket the electronic storage device I'd retrieved from my father's place. "I want to see if any files are stored on this thing. Do we have a machine that can read it?"

He reached over, lifted it out of my hand, and stared at it. "Hmm. I haven't seen one of these in twenty years." He looked up at me. "No need for them since everything's stored on the Grid now."

"Yes, I know. It was my father's. I just wanted to see if I could access it."

He looked at it again. "Well, someone should have one, for sure. Maybe we do. Let me check and tap you back."

Two hours later I received the tap.

"Found one. We have a bunch of old electronic gear in the warehouse. No one uses the stuff; it just sits collecting dust. I think the last time —"

"So can I come by and pick it up?"

"Sure. I can set you up right here in my office, if you wish."

"I'd rather take it to mine."

"Whatever suits you. I can show you how to use it when you get here."

I exited VR.

"Alistair, I need a car to go to campus."

Within an hour I was inserting the storage device into a small piece of electronic gear that I'd placed on my office desk. I connected the machine to the Grid.

"Alistair, please show me the saved files on this device."

"There is only one file."

"One file? Are you sure?"

"Quite sure."

"What is it?"

"A video message. But the file is corrupt. Only the audio is functional."

"From what source?"

"Only a Grid address is listed. It is Ray4306."

"No name is attached?"

"No."

"Please play the message."

I sat back and listened. The man sounded older, in his eighties perhaps. "Eli, I wanted to meet with you in VR and say this face to face, but I'll leave you this brief message. I'm sending parallel messages to Sam and Lauren. I hope somehow he is able to receive his, and I hope after all these years she is willing to respond. I don't know if I can trust her, but my options are few. I realize we only recently reignited a friendship that began decades ago, but I *do* trust you.

"I've never been an alarmist. But now I am alarmed. I'm afraid I've made a grave mistake in my involvement here all these years. My associate is willing to go to extremes I never envisioned to accomplish his objective. I fear humanity itself is about to be led down a tragic path, one from which there may be no escape. And I've collaborated in it."

There was a pause, then the message continued. "This has something to do with what you and I have been discussing. I apologize if all this sounds like the ramblings of a madman. I didn't intend that. But events have given me the clarity I've been missing all along. Please tap me as soon as you get this."

I leaned back into the office chair and exhaled deeply. Who was this man? I didn't recognize the voice. My father had known him for decades? What was my father's association with someone like this? The man did indeed sound, if not demented, at least mildly paranoid.

"Alistair, in what year was this message sent?"

"This year."

"This year? On what date?"

"April 14."

A week before my father died.

Kate turned off the fan over her stove and dished two servings of linguine and pesto sauce onto plates. She cocked her ear to the side. What was that noise? She followed the sound to her bathroom, where Abby had gone for a moment before dinner. She could hear water running inside. And Abby crying.

"Abby? Are you all right?" She knocked gently on the door. "Abby, it's Kate. Are you okay? May I come in?"

There was a pause. "Yes. Come in."

Kate opened the door. Abby was leaning over the sink, trying with her hands to plug the water pouring from the faucet. Water was spraying everywhere.

"What's the matter?"

"I just . . . I don't know . . . how to stop . . . wasting this water."

Kate stepped to the sink. "You wave your hand in front of this motion sensor."

The water stopped. Abby stood in the middle of the bathroom, drenched. "Kate, I'm so sorry. I've never wasted so much water. How can I ever —"

Kate reached for a bath towel and handed it to her. "Abby, it's okay. There's plenty of water."

"There is?"

She smiled. "Yes. All you want." She looked Abby up and down and put her hand to her mouth to stifle a giggle. "Well, I think we'd better put you in a different dress."

Abby smiled back, tugging at her soaked

clothing. "You don't think this'll do to-night?"

Kate laughed and shook her head. "I'll get you one of mine. It'll be a little short, but it will fit. Tomorrow I'll take you shopping for some new clothes."

"But I don't have any money."

"That's okay. My treat."

Abby changed, and they sat at the dinner table. They chatted about clothes and food and Kate's home décor, which intrigued Abby. Kate didn't want to ignore the trauma Abby had just been through, but she thought some conversation on other topics might be a nice distraction. When they adjourned to the living room after dinner, Kate thought the time was right to inquire about Abby personally. "How are you doing? Emotionally, I mean. Coming from the jungle, you're probably going a bit stir-crazy."

Abby paused a moment before she answered. "I'm better. But . . . I don't see how you can stand being inside all the time. It's so . . . lifeless. Just the opposite of the jungle — the sounds, the smells, the wildness, the sense of life that it brings. I miss that."

Kate couldn't help feeling a bit envious of this woman who had lived an extreme version of what Kate had come to Papua New

Guinea to experience. True, Abby's life had a strong religious component that Kate couldn't relate to. But neither was she offended by it. She had come here expecting to encounter people of all different beliefs. Meeting an American living with the Inisi is what surprised and intrigued her.

"What else do you miss?" she asked.

"My village. They're my family. And my daughter." Abby swallowed hard. "I miss Miraba terribly." Her eyes teared up when she spoke her name.

Kate gave her a moment to compose herself. "Miraba . . . was she your natural child?" The girl had looked too dark skinned for that, but she didn't want to presume.

"Oh no. I adopted her when she was just three."

"What happened to her parents?"

"Malaria. Miraba's grandmother died too."

"So the village was okay with your taking her in?" Kate hoped her curiosity wouldn't upset Abby further.

"They were thrilled that they didn't have another mouth to feed. The village always lived on the edge of hunger."

"So you raised her alone? Without a male partner?"

"A husband?" Abby smiled. "No, no husband."

"Why does that make you smile? There was never a man you were interested in?"

Abby shook her head, her mood lightening. "The other way around. There was never one interested in me. The men figured I wouldn't be the kind of wife they wanted. Which was true."

"And what kind of wife did they expect?"

"One who would do the hard work. Women gather the food, except for the meat. They fetch water from the river, prepare the meals, care for the children. They weave the baskets, make the clothes, mend holes in the huts —"

"What do the men do?"

"They hunt, mostly. And fish. And train the boys."

"So the men go hunting every day, and the women do everything else."

Abby laughed. "Pretty much. Inisi men have one set of tasks, the women another. For the Inisi, that's what marriage is about."

"What about . . . you know, love?"

"Tribal marriages aren't about love. Well, a few started to be, after watching my parents. Their marriage was . . ." Abby thought for a moment. "Tender. That's the best word to describe it. Fun. Dad and

80

Mom laughed a lot.

"Seeing them, a few of the younger men started to woo girls romantically — what they considered romance, in any case. But marriages are still primarily for subsistence. That arrangement never appealed to me, not after seeing what my parents had." Abby glanced around. "This house is big. You live here by yourself?"

Kate smiled. "It's not so big. Until a couple of months ago, my partner, Matt, lived here too. But he moved back to the States."

"He was your husband? Why did he leave his house?" Abby looked truly perplexed.

"No, he wasn't my husband. He . . ." How to explain Western social mores? "We both owned this house. When he left, I bought his share."

"Oh." Abby seemed like she might have other questions, but Kate rose and began clearing the table. She didn't know if she could talk to Abby about Matt — it was so complicated. She insisted that Abby relax on the couch while she straightened the kitchen.

When Kate entered the living room, she found Abby curled up with a large, old book. The binding was fragile, but Abby seemed to be tender with the antique. "I see you found my photo album. My grand-mother put that together sixty years ago."

Abby gingerly turned a couple of pages. "These are your sago drawings."

"My what?"

"To remember family members when they die, the Inisi cut a long piece of wood from a sago palm and carve drawings to tell that person's life story. They hang the wood in their huts. If you visit them, they'll point to the drawings and say, 'This is my mother's story. This is my grandfather's. That's my sister's.' " Abby closed the book. "Do you have recent photos from the States?"

"Of course. I can pull them up on a visi-screen."

"A visi . . ."

"Visiscreen. It's the way I see things on the Grid. You don't need it if you have a neural implant, but I don't." Abby looked confused, and Kate didn't want to throw too much at her too soon. "I'll explain later. Did you have Grid access in the jungle?"

"We lost it when I was little."

They flipped through several dozen im-ages.

"That's my mother," Kate noted. "She lives in Indiana. And this is my father. He's in Arizona."

"Are they no longer married?"

Kate smiled. "They were never married. Abby, people don't get married much anymore."

"Oh."

She went to the next image. "That's Matt."

They both examined the image for a moment.

"Do you miss him?"

Kate inhaled deeply, then looked at Abby. "Yes, quite a bit. I thought we'd be together a long time." She pulled up the next image. It was a side view of Kate, obviously pregnant. She felt her airway constrict, her chest suddenly tight. How could she have forgotten the photo was in this file?

Abby sat up straighter. "You have a baby?"

"I meant to delete this picture." Her words were just above a whisper.

"Why? Did you . . . have a child?"

Kate shook her head. "I . . . I had a stillborn child. A little girl, a year and a half ago."

"With Matt?"

She nodded, not taking her eyes off the image. They sat quietly for several moments. When Abby spoke, her voice quavered with grief. "I'm so sorry, Kate. I've seen many stillborns. It's very painful, I know."

Kate turned toward her, her eyes moist.

"How have you seen so many?"

"Midwifing for the Inisi. It's common."

"Not in the States. No one understands what it's like." Kate wiped away a tear. "I'm sorry, I didn't mean to get emotional."

"No, it's okay." She placed her hand on Kate's, tears tracking down her face as well. "I know what it's like . . . to lose a daughter."

Kate looked at her and smiled gently. "No one's ever called her my daughter before."

7

I spent the afternoon actually doing what the university employed me to do. Dealing with my father's death had put me hopelessly behind. After tinkering with a new lecture for an hour, I took the easy way out. The students in my American Cultural History Since 1900 class would construct cultural-impact questions regarding four mid-twentieth-century events (the bombings of Hiroshima and Nagasaki, the Kennedy assassination, the Vietnam War, and the civil rights movement), and we would discuss them. Lesson planned.

I returned home and accessed taps that I had been ignoring all afternoon. Several more students wanted my reaction to the brain transplant story. This news could be a defining moment for their generation.

I sat at my desk and returned to what had actually been on my mind all day: uncovering the identity of Ray4306. Fortunately, as the executor of my father's will, I had obtained his Grid password. "Alistair, access the Grid messages of my father. Password: adt36w48."

"Accessed."

"Please display all message listings this year from Ray4306."

"There are no such messages."

I was confused. "What do you mean there are no messages? What about the April 14 audio message?"

"That message isn't listed."

Not listed? Every message is retained on the Grid, either in active status or in archives. "List all messages from that source for the last five years."

"There are no messages from that source."

I was exasperated. "The last twenty years."

"There are no messages from that source."

That was impossible. Unless my father had deleted every such message. That seemed unlikely. Why would he delete them on the Grid but save one on an anachronous storage device?

I considered the other possibility. Someone else could have deleted the messages — a technically difficult process without the password and highly illegal. There was one way to find out. "Alistair, record a message, please. Audio only."

"Recording."

"Sir, my name is Creighton Daniels. I'm the son of Eli Daniels, who received an urgent message from you dated April 14. I regret to inform you that my father passed away on April 21. I'm responding in his stead. I'd appreciate a reply at your earliest convenience. End message."

"Would you like to review the message?"

"No. Grid destination Ray4306. Please send the mes . . ."

I paused.

"Did you say 'send the message,' Creighton?"

If someone didn't want Ray4306's message discovered . . . it was likely they were monitoring his Grid address.

"Creighton, did you —"

"Alistair, delete the message."

"What is Inland Tribes?" Kate placed a cup of tea on the breakfast table in front of Abby.

"That's the mission organization my parents were with. Why?"

"You have a message from them. The hospital just forwarded it to me. Do you want to take a look?"

"Yes, of course."

The image of an African man sitting at a desk appeared on a visiscreen in front of them. "This message is for Abigail Caldwell. Abigail, my name is Umtobo Ogunji. I'm the office manager at Inland Tribes. Your appearance in Lae was brought to my attention by one of our staff members. I looked over your family's file, and I discovered that we have a very old communiqué that has never been delivered to you. We apologize, but of course we had no way to send messages to you in the interior. We were saddened to hear of your parents' deaths, but we are heartened to hear you are well. God's blessings upon you."

Kate turned to Abby. "Do you want me to pull up the old message? It's from . . . wow . . . sixteen years ago."

Abby nodded, leaning toward the screen as if encouraging the message to materialize. Kate accessed it. Two older people sat on a couch in an American-looking home. Abby started when she saw them. "Nonny and Poppy! Those are my grandparents."

Her grandfather began to speak. "Our precious Abby. We so wish we could speak these words to you face to face. But that hasn't been possible since we last came to visit you in Papua New Guinea, when you were just a baby. Even though we weren't able to return, our hearts have always been with you, and we have prayed for you daily. After

88

your tribe was declared off-limits, we lost communication with your parents, but we trust that at some point Inland Tribes will be able to deliver our message."

He glanced over at his wife and smiled. "Abby," her grandmother began, "we have chosen your eighteenth birthday to record this message because, in America, eighteen is when most young people begin to make their own path in life. I guess, if you were here, Poppy and I would be pestering you with all sorts of advice as you become a young woman. But you have certainly not had a typical teenager's life, and we're sure your parents have prepared you well."

She looked at her husband, squeezed his hand, and continued. "So, instead, we'd like to use this message to talk about something else — something quite important. I know this is going to sound a little overwhelming, but we need to talk about the future — yours, ours, and, in fact, our entire country's."

She turned to Abby's grandfather. He appeared more serious as he started speaking again. "Christianity as we once knew it — and hopefully as you still experience it there on the mission field — has practically disappeared in America, Abby. Though it prospers in many parts of the world, the

U.S. has followed the path Europe took into secularism. Our faith isn't outlawed, but the preaching of the gospel is regarded as hate speech and prosecuted. Not that it matters much anymore — few are left who would proclaim it. That's how bad it's gotten.

. "Things will get even worse before they get better. God has made that clear to us, both in our spirits and lately" — Abby's grandfather leaned forward on the couch, and his tone changed — "in our *dreams*. I never thought God would speak to me in dreams, and at first I ignored them. But your grandmother started talking to me about her dreams, and we found that, sometimes, we have the *same* dream. It has to be from God, Abby. There's no other explanation."

He leaned even closer. "We believe God has let the Christian church die here for a reason. Everything God does has a purpose. He has a plan for bringing the faith back.

"You're probably wondering what this has to do with you. We know how strange this may sound, but in our dreams Nonny and I believe God revealed to us the person he will use to rebuild the Christian church in America. We don't know how this will happen, or when, or why this person has been chosen for such a hard task. But God's

90

choice is clear to us. That person is you, Abby."

Kate looked over to see Abby's jaw drop.

"We believe Jesus has destined you to reignite Christianity in the States. I wish we could tell you more. I wish we knew more. But this is all we have, and God has a good reason for that. I'm sure he wants you to look to him to direct you."

Her grandmother spoke. "Abby, life is full of possibilities and challenges, some of which seem overwhelming at the time. No matter when you view this message, I'm sure our words will sound crazy. But please . . . talk to God about it. He knows how he'll use you. Lord willing, we will be at your side at that time, feeling very privileged to share this journey with you."

Her grandfather smiled warmly. "You always have our deepest love and daily prayers for your safety and for your closeness to God."

Her grandmother added, "We love you and can't wait for the day when we can give you big hugs, darling girl. Bye-bye."

The message ended. Abby sat silently, a stunned look frozen on her face.

"Wow . . . what can you possibly say after that?" Kate said, then immediately regretted saying anything at all.

Abby slowly shook her head. "I don't know . . ."

Kate turned off the message; the image of Abby's grandparents disappeared. For a moment Abby seemed ready to cry.

"Are you okay, Abby?"

Abby didn't respond. Her face seemed unusually pale. When she finally spoke, there was both resignation and resolution in her words. "I have to go there," she said, nearly in a whisper.

"Where . . . to the U.S.?"

Abby nodded.

"Abby, that message is sixteen years old. How do you . . . Well, how much did you know about your grandparents when you were growing up?"

"I don't remember meeting them. I just remember the packages Nonny sent before our village was closed. I was very small, but I loved a fuzzy pink bear she sent, and I slept with it for years." She seemed lost in the past for a moment. "Mostly, I knew they were strong Christians. My father talked about what it was like being raised by them, how God and the Bible were central to their family. My father was close to his parents, and he trusted them completely." She shrugged. "My grandfather was some kind of scientist, but I never knew exactly what he did. Beyond that . . ."

Kate leaned toward her. "Don't you think it would be best to talk to your grandparents before leaping into anything?"

Abby brightened. "Can I do that from here?"

"Of course. We only have to look them up on the Grid. What are their names?"

"Ray and Giovanna Caldwell. But . . . they might not even be alive. They'd be in their nineties."

Kate smiled. "I know your parents and brother died early. In the jungle they didn't have access to medicine. In the States people often live past a hundred and twenty."

Abby sat up straighter on the couch. "How do we look them up?"

"We only need to input your information on the Grid. Your full name?"

"Abigail Elizabeth Caldwell."

"Your date of birth?"

"March 13, 2054."

"Place of birth?"

"Here."

Kate looked at her. "In Lae?"

Abby nodded.

"At the hospital?"

"Yes. My mother had complications in

pregnancy, so they traveled out for the delivery."

"Well. Small world." Kate looked at the Grid projection in front of her. Unlike most people, who named their interfaces, she preferred relating to the Grid impersonally. "Grid, show us a three-generation family tree of Abigail Elizabeth Caldwell, born March 13, 2054, in Lae, Papua New Guinea."

A new image appeared before them. Kate shifted forward. "Your mother's parents are alive and living in Hamburg, Germany."

Abby shrugged. "I never knew them. Or even knew about them, really. They didn't agree with our coming here, and they didn't stay in touch even before we were cut off."

Kate glanced across the image. "Your father's parents . . . Giovanna . . ." Her voice quieted. "Abby, your grandmother died six years ago. And your grandfather Ray . . ."

Abby stared at the image. "Is he dead as well?"

Kate placed her hand on top of Abby's. "Abby, I'm sorry."

Tears trickled down Abby's cheeks. "No, it's okay. I just . . . They were who I really wanted to see. Even before that message . . . I had been imagining what seeing them

94

would be like."

"It sounds like you had a lot in common with them."

Abby wiped her cheeks and straightened up. "When did he die?"

"This year, it appears," Kate said. "Grid, specify date of Raymond Caldwell's death."

"April 16, 2088."

Abby looked at her. "That was just three weeks ago."

8

Lauren Caldwell hated Washington receptions. Pasting on a three-hour smile and making political small talk with the capital's in-crowd wasn't the thrill she had expected it to be when she was elected to represent Texas's Fifth Congressional District eleven years before. Attending the Washington Media Club's annual gala wasn't optional, however. Not for a candidate for the U.S. Senate.

Caldwell glided through the hotel ballroom with her requisite smile. She was a striking woman — tall, stately, with a raspy, commanding voice — the kind of woman everyone pretends to admire in Washington.

"Lauren!"

She turned to see the chiseled face of Ethan Norwood, an online political commentator and frequent nemesis. She broadened her smile. "Why, Ethan, I thought you were in the Caribbean on vacation."

"Cut it short. Election cycle. Never seen an off year like it. Where's Sabin?"

"At home. Deadline on some hologram he's designing, as usual. So it sounds as if Rodney has you pulling overtime too."

"He wants me to do a feature on the American Party's chances."

"And what do your instincts tell you?"

"That you'll lose seats in the House but might hold on to the Senate. Counting your seat, of course."

"It's not my seat yet. But thanks for the vote of confidence."

He stepped closer and lowered his voice. "Lauren, our latest polls show the Democrats pulling even with the AP in national party affiliation. And they're ahead in Texas. Do you really think you can hold your lead?"

"Well, without a viable Republican in the field . . . I assume this is off the record."

"Of course."

"We're figuring on forty percent of the Republican vote. And with Governor Menendez working for us . . ."

He shook his head. "With the economy going south, I just wonder how you're going to turn the tide." He took a sip from his drink. "After five years in the White House, the AP — look, I hate to say it — you guys look stale."

"If we look stale, it's not the first time you ingrates have created a false impression." Lauren laughed. It was a forced laugh but moderately convincing. She wanted to keep Norwood honest, but she also needed to stay on friendly terms with him.

Norwood was right. With the economy faltering, things weren't breaking the American Party's way. It wasn't the fault of their policies. War in south Asia had caused shortages and price spikes in several technology sectors, fueling inflation and creating market jitters. Economic growth was slow, and unemployment was up. The trajectory of the American Party — a centrist third party that had overtaken both the Democrats and the Republicans and captured the White House and Congress — was for the first time downward. They were no longer the up-and-comers; they were in power, and they were being blamed for the nation's woes. That's how the game worked. The party needed an issue it could latch on to. Lauren needed an issue that would create movement in the Texas polls.

Lauren's audial implant alerted her to an incoming message. "Excuse me, will you, Ethan? My assistant is tapping me."

Lauren stepped aside and entered virtual reality, a glazed look overtaking her face. A moment later she returned to physical reality. She turned to see a congressional colleague, Clara Barnes, standing in front of her.

"Are you okay, Lauren? You look like you've just seen a ghost."

"No," she answered unsteadily, "but I'm about to."

"Crisis, Lauren?"

Lauren Caldwell turned to the familiar profile of Hutch Hardin. He was studying the pastries at the front counter of Sal's Seaside Café. Overlooking the pure blue waters and pebble beaches of the Adriatic Sea's far north coast, the café was the favorite virtual reality meeting spot for Lauren and her political mentor.

Unlike days past, when meetings at Washington watering holes were common among pols and provided fodder for the morning political gossip pages, virtual reality meetings were untraceable through normal channels. Any twosome or group could meet without fear of legal detection. Even illegal detection could be precluded by a sophisticated VR consultant.

"Everything between us is a crisis, Hutch. But nothing that some coffee and a pastry wouldn't solve."

He ordered croissants and coffees. They strolled to a table close to a railing separating them from a fifty-foot drop to the beach below. Lauren sat and gazed at two white yachts heading out to the open Adriatic, then turned toward her mentor. "Why, Hutch, I do believe you've lost a few years. And added even more hair."

Hardin had, as usual, chosen a VR image of himself twenty years younger and ten pounds lighter than his actual body. "Considering making my own Senate run," he deadpanned. "Do you think the voters will go for this look?"

"That'll be the day, you running for Senate. Voters do like some sort of track record in the people they elect, you know. A public record, I mean."

"Nothing would get done in this town without people like me."

She smiled. "Which is why you've never run for office, isn't it? No use taking a step down in actual power."

"No. The political games we play, Lauren, are much too entertaining."

A waiter appeared at their table, welcomed them with a distinct Croatian accent, and set their order in front of them.

Hutch took a bite of his pastry. "So tell me about this cousin of yours."

"She's actually the daughter of my first cousin, Sam Caldwell. I didn't know him very well growing up. He was a religious activist. In their late twenties, while I was in high school, Sam and his wife, Emily, signed up with an organization that proselytized tribal people with the message of Christianity. They went to work with a tribe in New Guinea that was still cut off from the civilized world."

"There were still tribes like that? What year was this?"

She sipped her cappuccino. "In the forties. My understanding is that this was the last such tribe, at least in New Guinea. And the government there finally declared them off-limits to the outside world, wanting to preserve the tribe's cultural integrity."

"But your cousin and his wife were already there."

"Correct."

"They didn't have to leave?"

"The tribe wanted them to stay. So the government agreed, stipulating that Sam and Emily cease all contact with the outside world. That was the last anyone heard from them."

"How long ago was that?"

"It was 2052, the year I graduated from Swarthmore."

Hutch leaned back in his chair. "So this Abby was born there."

"Right. They had a young boy when they went in. The family . . . we just assumed they died at some point since so many years passed."

He drank some of his espresso and set his cup down. "What do you know about her religious beliefs?"

"I think we have to assume she believes as her parents did."

"I agree." Hutch stared into his cup. "Her arrival isn't the best news we've had."

"No, hardly."

"What's the plan at this point?"

"I'm having her fly in to Dulles."

He gave her a hard look.

"What was I going to do, refuse to bring her over?"

He shook his head. "No."

"She'll stay at our place."

"And then?"

"I don't know." She looked anxiously at him. "Any suggestions?"

He took a bite of his croissant and had another sip of espresso. "I suggest we get her out of here as soon as possible. The media will find her, and she'll be painted as a Christian missionary. You'll either have to defend Christian proselytizing or distance yourself from a hapless, homeless family member. Either way, you lose."

Lauren sighed. "Agreed."

He leaned forward. "Lauren, voters will forgive many things, but being tied to a religious zealot — you'll lose a point or two on that one. Your margin in this Senate race is razor thin. Get her back on a plane to the jungle before she torpedoes everything you've worked for."

Several days of investigation had brought me face to face with the tap I loathed making. I had tried every other route of identifying Ray4306. Alistair had scanned my father's messages for anything from the two other recipients of Ray4306's message and had found nothing. He had checked for any Raymonds on the University of Illinois faculty. He had scanned the faculties of every neurology department in the world. Of three Raymonds, none knew my father.

As a next-to-last resort, I contacted Gwen, my father's last life partner. Their relationship had ended seventeen years before. Although we had always been on good terms, I hadn't spoken to her since. She was sorry to hear that my father had died. No, she didn't recall any Ray he had known.

I sat at my home desk and placed my last

tap. I would have preferred audio only, but that seemed too impersonal. I descended into VR. I stood next to a table at a bistro in Paris. Sitting at the table was a woman in her eighties with gray hair and a wide smile.

"Hello, Creighton. How long has it been — ten years?"

"Hello, Mother. Eleven, I think."

I'm not certain why my mother and I had a falling out. An argument over something, I'm sure. We didn't speak for a year, then two, and after that it simply felt too uncomfortable to tap. What do you say when you haven't tapped for four or six or eight years?

Our circumstances weren't unusual. Many people didn't keep up with either parent anymore. The parents of my generation had never married and hadn't contracted to stay together more than ten years. Parenting had become a life stage, not a permanent commitment. Still, it felt awkward to sit at a table and catch up with the woman who had given birth to me.

"Mother, I need to tell you something," I said when the small talk waned. "My father is dead."

A look of sadness and what seemed like genuine concern crossed her face. "He is? How?"

"Suicide, apparently."

"Oh, Creighton, I'm so sorry." She paused and looked into my eyes. "How are you doing?"

"It's . . . I'm all right. I've been going through his things, taking care of his affairs. That's what . . . well, what gave me the excuse to tap you."

"How so?"

"He had a somewhat unusual message from a friend of his — someone named Ray. Supposedly, they'd known each other for decades. Do you remember any associate of my father's by that name?"

She shook her head. "It's been so long. Almost forty years since Eli and I were together." She sipped some wine and concentrated a few moments. "No. No, not that I can recall. I knew some of his associates, but others . . . I don't remember anyone named Ray. Was the message important?"

I pasted on a smile. "Probably not. I was just curious, and it provided an excuse to tap you. I apologize for waiting so long."

She smiled back. "No apology necessary. Maybe we can stay in touch better this time."

"Yes, that would be nice, Mother."

I exited VR. I reached for a lukewarm cup of coffee and spilled it.

"Shall I summon your homebot, Creighton?"

"No, Alistair, thank you. I'll wipe it up myself." I retrieved a towel and a doughnut from the kitchen — anything to divert my attention from seeing my mother and from the dead end of my pseudo-investigation.

"Alistair, what do you have on CulturePulse for me?" Recent events had placed me several days behind in what was normally a daily review. Summaries with images appeared. A few more dreams about Jesus. People signing up for brain transplants. I'd wait a year or two if I were they. Let someone else be the guinea pigs and get the kinks out of the system.

Then I noticed an unusual headline on a written news story:

American Emerges from Last Indigenous Enclave

An American citizen, Ms. Abigail Caldwell, emerged into civilization last week for the first time in her life, traveling by canoe via the Sepik River from the interior of Papua New Guinea. Ms. Caldwell has lived for 34 years with the Inisi, the last remaining isolated people group on the planet.

She was born in Papua New Guinea to American parents who were missionaries of the Christian religion. Ms. Caldwell's family chose to remain with the Inisi when the government closed the tribe to outsiders. Her parents having died during the 2070s, she is the only outsider reportedly living with the tribe.

Found unconscious in her canoe last Sunday near the town of Dagua on the northern coast, Ms. Caldwell was transported to the hospital in Lae, treated for minor injuries, and released. The U.S. Embassy has arranged for a visit to the U.S. to meet her cousin and closest relative, U.S. Congresswoman Lauren Caldwell of Texas.

Christian religion.

Most readers of the story would naturally wonder about her reaction to encountering civilization for the first time. She probably had no Grid access. Certainly no neural implants. How could she even remotely function in the modern world?

I knew that those issues were secondary. Travel to a new country, and you can adjust to unfamiliar technologies and lifestyles — as long as you can find people with a similar belief system through which to interpret the experience.

But this woman would find no one of a similar mindset. Not in America.

9

Visitors typically expressed surprise upon their first visit to Bryson Nichols's personally designed VR getaway. They expected one of the world's leading innovators to prefer cutting-edge twenty-first-century décor. What they discovered instead was a nineteenth-century English bar that Nichols called the Library.

Fine oak bookshelves lined the walls, each filled with signed first editions of classic English works from the previous six centuries. An original of the Magna Carta hung on one wall, bearing the royal seal of King John. Dark brown leather easy chairs were separated by mahogany end tables. Oil lanterns provided low lighting. A haze of pipe smoke floated near the ceiling, its aroma permeating the room. Holographic patrons provided background chatter.

As Nichols explained to his guests — he rarely hosted more than one individual at a time — though his vision was toward the future, he was a man whose roots lay in the past. There the human creature had emerged from millennia of tribal warfare and despotic rule to shape the beginnings of an enlightened world.

The light had finally shone in thirteenth-century England with the signing of the Magna Carta. For the first time in recorded history, the authority of the king was curtailed. Subjects had rights. A revolution in political history, one corresponding to the Copernican revolution in scientific history, had begun. Within six hundred years Thomas Jefferson would pen the words "We hold these truths to be self-evident . . ."

Nichols saw himself continuing the line of Hume, Jefferson, and Lincoln, inexorably marching humanity toward its rightful destiny. They had set the stage for humanity's political future. He was setting the stage for the future of human intelligence — a future free from the stultifying constraint of biological decay and death. Sitting in his nineteenth-century English pub, Nichols had mapped humanity's course not just for the upcoming decade or century but for millennia to come.

The image of Lauren Caldwell appeared at the doorway. Nichols signaled to her.

Lauren scanned the pub's patrons, crossed the room, and sat at Nichols's table.

"Good evening, Lauren."

"Good evening, Bryson." She glanced at the top of his head. "Congratulations on your announcement."

"Thank you. I couldn't have done it without you. Or I should say, I can't do it without you, Congresswoman."

"Indeed you can't."

Nichols motioned to the bartender. "So what should we discuss first — your campaign finances, the hearings, or your cousin?"

"We're holding a seven-point lead in the polls —"

He shook his head slightly. "I've kept up with the race. I just need to know how much money you need."

"For the duration of the campaign?"

He nodded.

"Sixteen million."

"I'll have it transferred tomorrow." He leaned forward and looked her in the eye. "I'm counting on you to win this one, Lauren."

She cleared her throat. "I am as well."

He leaned back and smiled. "So tell me about the hearings. Has your good chairwoman scheduled them yet?"

"It's looking like they won't happen until the fall."

"Fall? Lauren, the momentum is now, not in the fall."

The bartender set a drink in front of Lauren. She picked up the glass. "The Technology and Innovation Subcommittee is largely booked until the August recess. And this isn't on her priority list. If your schedule hadn't moved up . . ."

He sighed. He was used to the corporate world, where a CEO could actually get things done. The political arena, with its perpetual give-and-take, frustrated him. "We need to keep pressing for an earlier time. How many days of hearings are we counting on?"

"Three."

"How much can we accomplish in that time?"

"You mean can we generate enough public pressure on the administration to force them to cover your transplants?"

"Precisely," he responded.

This was why Nichols gave Lauren Caldwell the time of day, much less tens of millions to finance her political career. He needed someone on Capitol Hill to champion one small cause: getting brain transplants paid for by the government under the national health plan.

Nichols knew that the demand for brain transplants would be high but also that their cost would be prohibitive for all but the wealthy. The only way to achieve high market penetration was to have the government finance the procedure. Politically, that was tricky. Congress could pass a law mandating the coverage, but garnering sufficient support for such legislation would take at least a year — probably two. Health Services could circumvent that by extending such coverage themselves.

Perpetual budget shortfalls, however, kept Health Services in a mode of cutting coverage, not expanding it. A groundswell of public opinion could force the administration's hand. Nichols's own unveiling of the transplant procedure had started that process. The second step was to hold widely publicized Congressional hearings.

Lauren shrugged. "In this business . . . Let's just say the hearings will move the ball further down the field. Whether we score this year or not . . ."

"If we don't, you can carry the ball in the upper chamber."

She smiled. "That's what I'm here for, isn't it?"

They both sipped their drinks.

"So," Nichols continued, "your cousin."

"My cousin."

He put his glass down. "We haven't spoken again of the message you received from Ray."

"Perhaps we should."

"It would benefit neither of us if she became aware of that message."

"No, of course not."

"Nor for her to stay in the country too long."

"Agreed."

Nichols lifted his glass. "To our continued partnership, Lauren."

Abby stared at the open suitcase, her meager belongings not quite filling one side. She picked up the toiletries bag, unzipped it, fumbled for the new toothbrush, then walked over to the sink to brush her teeth for the second time in the past ten minutes.

Within the hour she'd be heading to the airport, climbing aboard a plane, and heading off on an adventure that somehow seemed riskier than any she had yet known. But what choice did she have? The certainty of her grandparents' message had unnerved her — not because she didn't want to do God's will, but because she couldn't imagine she could be the one woman to make a difference. How could someone who had never traveled beyond a handful of Inisi villages hope to start a spiritual revolution in America?

Despite the odds, Abby felt compelled to move forward. Her parents had brought the message of Christ to the Inisi. Now God was asking her to bring the same message to her parents' homeland. It was simply another mission field. A huge one.

"Abby, are you ready? We probably should be heading to the airport."

"Just a moment," she called. She faced her reflection, inhaled deeply, and voiced the question that had been foremost on her mind. "God, you know what you're doing, right?"

She looked down at the toothbrush, stuffed it in the toiletries bag, and closed the suitcase. She walked into Kate's living room. "I'm ready."

"There's your plane." Kate turned away from the plate-glass window and faced Abby. "Are you sure you want to go through with this? Going to the States will be a bigger shock than waking up at my hospital and seeing a Caucasian face."

Abby nodded. "I'm sure. I'm apprehensive, but I'm sure." She touched Kate lightly on the arm. "Kate, I can't tell you how much I appreciate everything you've done for me. You've —"

Kate shook her head. "It's been my privilege. When you return, remember that my place is your place. You're welcome to stay with me as long as you wish."

"Thank you."

Abby turned and looked at the windows on the other side of the concourse that faced the highlands. "I'm going to walk over there one more time."

"I'll go with you."

Abby picked up her bag, and they crossed the concourse. They stood looking toward the island's interior. Abby reached her hand out and touched the glass with all five fingers. "I wish I could stay for the chief's burial."

"I'm sure he'd understand."

"After you do the autopsy, the government will fly him back and bury him in the village, right?"

"Yes. They've committed to that." Kate hesitated. "Abby, I can fly back to the village with him if you like."

Abby turned and smiled. "Oh, Kate . . . thank you. That would mean a lot to me."

"I'll do it."

Kate heard the first call for boarding.

116

"They're calling for your plane. We'd better go back."

Abby looked out at the jungle again for several moments. "Good-bye, Miraba," she whispered.

They turned and walked to the gate.

"You will keep in touch, won't you, Abby?"

"Of course." She shrugged. "You're the only person on the planet I know."

Kate hugged her. "That will change soon. You remember how to contact me on the Grid?"

"I have it written down."

"Anytime. Don't worry about the time difference."

"Okay." Abby looked at the boarding line, squared her shoulders, then glanced back at Kate. "Thanks again for all the clothes and personal items you bought for me."

"Just trying to help you blend in." She put a hand on her shoulder and smiled. "Wouldn't want anyone knowing you hadn't grown up there." Kate paused before she spoke again. "Remember, if you get to Washington and your ride isn't there to pick you up —"

"I know. I have the instructions to tap you. I'll be fine, Kate."

They hugged each other again, a tight,

long hug. Abby bent down, picked up her bag, and stepped to the end of the line. She paused at the entrance to the jet bridge, turned, and waved. Kate smiled and waved back. She watched Abby disappear, then wiped the moisture from her eyes.

What awaited this resilient woman in the States? Abby encountering America — an alien from another planet would have almost as much to relate to. But Abby was smart, and strong. Stubborn even, Kate thought, remembering how Abby had handled things at the village. She'd adapt to America. She'd have to.

The workers closed the jet bridge doors. Kate turned and walked back up the concourse. She needed to get to the Port Moresby morgue. She had an autopsy to perform.

Kate turned away from the body and threw up. Though she rarely performed autopsies, she expected to get used to the smell of corpses. It hadn't happened yet. She looked over at the morgue's head pathologist, Dr. Jonathan Mandoha. "I apologize. I can't believe I still do that."

The pathologist didn't raise his eyes off the body. "You're not the first." He turned to an aide. "Pyande, get someone in here to clean that up, will you?"

Mandoha performed a visual scan of the village chief's shaved head. Kate was glad she had refused Abby's request to attend the autopsy. No one should attend the autopsy of someone they knew.

Kate leaned close and let her eyes follow Mandoha's over the head. There were no identifiable punctures or incisions.

The pathologist spoke. "No external abnormalities. Are we cutting into the cranium, Dr. Sampson? If so, I need my technician to set up the equipment."

"I'd like to do some brain scans first. I want a full neural imaging workup."

In the States, of course, everything was done with imaging. But brain disease wasn't a major health concern in New Guinea, not relative to the many others, and the neural imaging equipment here was decades behind the times, so they would have to cut. Nevertheless, it made sense to first see what they could with the available imaging equipment.

They placed the scanner around the corpse's head. The scan took ten minutes, during which time Kate checked her taps on the morgue's Grid access. The technician glanced over at her as she was watching her last message.

119

"Done, Dr. Sampson."

"Transfer it over here, will you?"

A 3-D hologram of the chief's brain appeared in front of her. Mandoha walked across the room, and they both looked at it quizzically. He spoke to the technician. "Pyande, what happened to the rest of this image?"

"What do you mean?"

"Here." He pointed at the lower left section of the cranial cavity. "There's nothing here. Where's that part of the image?"

"I don't know."

The technician retraced the steps he had taken to project the image. "Everything looks right. Perhaps we should try another scan."

Ten minutes later he projected a second image on top of the pathologist's desk.

"Same thing. Why isn't that part of the brain imaging?" Mandoha looked more closely at the image. "And what is this gray substance by the — where the hippocampus should be?" He glanced at Kate. "I've never seen this."

She looked back at the corpse, then at the technician. "Do you have a backup scanner?"

The technician repeated the process with a second scanner. The image looked the same. Mandoha turned to Kate. "Well?"

"Let's cut him open."

Within minutes the pathologist was lasering through bone. He put down his laser and placed his hands above and below the skullcap. He pried it apart, and both physicians conducted a visual examination of the brain's exterior.

"Nothing so far," Mandoha remarked. "Would you like to take some slices for examination?"

"No, not yet. I want to get to the part where we had no image."

He continued lasering until he had split apart the lower back side of the skull. He removed the left section.

Kate's jaw dropped. Her eyes fixated on the area where there had been no image. She picked up a hemostat and poked at a silver goo oozing out of the area. It adhered to the instrument like motor oil.

"What the —"

10

Abby emerged from the vehicle nauseated and shaking. Riding in a car with Kate in Papua New Guinea had been unnerving, but this was much worse. The cars in America had no drivers. She felt so powerless. Every oncoming vehicle seemed headed right for her, and she'd shriek and duck down in her seat. She finally resigned herself to a permanent reclining position, eyes closed, until the car had stopped and instructed, "Please exit the vehicle."

Abby set her suitcase on the sidewalk and watched the vehicle drive away. She stared at the house in front of her. For the second time in twenty-four hours, an unfamiliar feeling gripped her: panic. She had felt it first on the plane — not just on takeoff, with the terrifying roar and speed. Anxiety overcame her midflight when she realized how unprepared she was to handle even simple tasks outside the jungle.

Kate had done her best to prepare Abby, but who could have remembered to explain the myriad of gadgets, rules, and customs attached to just one activity: airplane flight? How was she supposed to know the way to lock the bathroom door, much less flush the toilet? How was she supposed to know that at various times passengers were restricted to their seats? Or that strangers were unaccustomed to being greeted by someone walking down the aisle? She found it frustrating, encountering her own ignorance at every turn.

Now she stood in front of a house allegedly belonging to her closest relative in the world. What if this situation didn't work out? Her father had taught her, "Have a plan B." She adhered to his advice fiercely in the jungle, but there was no plan B here. She wasn't even sure of plan A.

She said a quick prayer, picked up her suitcase, climbed the steps to the front door, and knocked. No one answered. She knocked again, and the door swung open. In the doorway stood a man, perhaps forty to forty-five, slightly taller than she, with a welcoming smile.

"You must be Abby. I'm Sabin Wright, Lauren's partner. Lauren will be here shortly. Come in. Let me get that for you."

He leaned forward and picked up the suitcase. They walked into a large living room with two sofas.

"How was your flight? You must be exhausted. Can I get you something to drink?"

"Some tea would be nice."

Sabin disappeared into the kitchen.

Abby looked around the room. It was painted olive, with two woven tapestries adorning one wall. Between large windows on the opposite wall hung a painting of an old man walking his bicycle up a sharply inclined cobblestone street. Atop a wood credenza behind a sofa stood a picture of a dog. Next to it were a small antique globe and a bronze statue of a bull.

Through her conversations with Kate, she felt like she understood better what purpose décor served, but the room still felt desolate to Abby. She was saddened not to see any family pictures, having hoped for one connecting this home to her grandparents. How could you not have photos of the ones you loved? She'd have given anything for a picture of Miraba.

Abby felt a moment of panic. She had no pictures of Miraba. Would a time come when she couldn't recall her beautiful daughter's face?

Sabin returned. "The tea will be ready in

a minute. Please, have a seat." He motioned to one of the sofas and sat on the other. "So tell me about your flight. It was your first?"

Abby attempted a smile, thinking of how to couch her words. "Well . . . it was loud. And yet people fell asleep the moment they got on the plane and didn't wake up until the plane landed. I wasn't able to sleep as well, so I'm tired."

He laughed. "They weren't asleep most of the time. They were in VR."

"In what?"

"Virtual reality."

The teapot whistled.

"I'll explain later. VR is what I do. Professionally, I mean."

Sabin got up and crossed to the kitchen. Abby heard a sound at the front door and stood. An immaculately dressed woman in a blue suit and high heels entered the living room.

"You must be Abigail." She stepped down and stuck out her hand formally.

"Yes, Abby."

"I'm Lauren. Welcome to the United States."

Sabin returned with two cups in hand. "Lauren, I just made some tea. Let me get you some."

"No, thank you. I'd like to freshen up."

She turned to Abby. "So how was your flight, dear?"

"It was . . . different. When I got on the —"

"I assume you met up with my assistant easily enough at the airport gate?"

"Yes. But we went the opposite direction of everyone else who got off the plane. Was that okay?"

"Diplomatic privilege. Since I'm a member of Congress, my official guests don't have to go through customs." She took a step toward the kitchen. "Let me give you a quick tour of the house. We want you to feel comfortable during your brief stay."

In a few minutes the three of them were walking up the stairs, Lauren leading the way. "I'm just sorry you couldn't visit under more pleasant circumstances, Abigail. I'm sure you're eager to get back to the jungle and start over with a new village."

"Yes, well, I'd like to go back, but there are some things I need to do here first."

Lauren didn't seem to be listening. "Here's where you'll be sleeping," she said, pointing to a guest bedroom. It was moderately sized with a bed that sat high off the floor, several pieces of dark wood furniture, and two windows with white shutters. "I wouldn't open the windows, dear. It doesn't

126

cool down much in DC in the summer. We'll get acquainted in the morning. If you want a snack or meal before bedtime, you know where the kitchen is."

"Right now I need to use the bathroom, if that's okay."

Lauren motioned down the hall. "Of course. You do know how to use them, don't you?"

Lauren was treating her like an idiot, Abby thought. *I've been out of the jungle more than a week. Of course I know how to use a toilet.* She tried not to show her displeasure. "Yes, I believe I do."

Abby walked down the hall. She overheard Sabin's voice as she reached the bathroom.

"Don't you think you're being a little cold?"

Abby paused at the bathroom door.

"We've already discussed this, Sabin," came Lauren's response. "We didn't invite her here. She invited herself. And she's a potential liability."

"To you."

"To both of us, if you care to live the life we've been living."

"Yeah, about the life we've been living —"

"Don't start on that again."

"You're so obsessed with your Senate run we hardly see each other anymore."

"This isn't the time or place to talk about that, Sabin."

There was silence. Abby quietly closed the bathroom door behind her. In a few moments she returned to the bedroom. Lauren smiled tautly. "Is there anything else you need tonight?"

Abby looked at the bed. "Do you have a mat?"

"A mat. To wipe your feet on? I'm sure your shoes are fine."

"No, a straw mat — to sleep on."

"A . . . straw mat." Lauren glanced at Sabin, not hiding her frustration. "No," she answered, "we would not have a straw mat. But I'm sure you'll find your bed quite comfortable." She turned and walked out the door. "Good night, dear."

Sabin looked at Abby. "I'm sorry about Lauren. She's under a lot of stress these days. Her campaign. We're — I'm glad you're here. I'll let you get some sleep. See you in the morning."

"Good night."

Abby listened to his footsteps on the stairs. She sat on the bed and looked around the room. It had beauty but no warmth. She pulled the comforter onto the floor and lay on it. Within a minute she was asleep.

■ ■ ■ ■

Damien Cleary sat at Bryson Nichols's table and scanned the Library's clientele. Nichols chuckled at his associate's surveillance. "Damien, have you ever spotted someone in here that didn't belong?"

Cleary finished scanning the room. "It's hard to say. Why do you bother having all these characters in this place of yours, Nichols? It increases the security risk."

"I trust my security man. Besides, sitting in here by myself would be a dreadful bore."

Cleary motioned toward the VR patrons. "Yes, these gentlemen are quite entertaining."

The bartender arrived and placed Cleary's drink in front of him. Nichols signaled him to bring some cigars.

"You think history began with the Internet, Damien."

"No, civilization began with the Internet."

Nichols shook his head. "No appreciation of the progress we've made. Ten thousand years ago we were hunters-gatherers being savaged by saber-toothed tigers."

"Maybe you should have a head on the wall here."

"Indeed." Nichols sipped his vermouth

and rum. "So, speaking of conversation pieces, what did you think of my talk the other night?"

"Brilliant. Just as I expected."

"What was the reaction among those around you?"

"Incredulous. Astounded. You had them in your back pocket, Nichols. Or, rather, you have them in your back pocket."

Nichols smiled. "I must say, even I didn't expect such a successful launch. Have you seen all the publicity?"

"Of course. You're headline all over the world." Cleary leaned forward. "Nichols, I've doubted you in the past. I always thought you should take the wraps off this thing sooner. But you were right. And now, within ten years, the whole planet will be transhuman."

Nichols laughed. "Ten years? I'd be happy with fifty."

The two men's eyes locked, and they exchanged a knowing look of achievement and triumph. Cleary raised his glass. "To fifty years."

Nichols followed suit. "To fifty years, my friend."

They drank slowly and savored the moment quietly. Cleary finally broke the silence. "So we have a potential glitch."

Nichols settled back in his chair. "A minor glitch."

"You saw it on the Grid?"

"Of course. I don't miss anything, Cleary. Especially not now."

"All right. Don't get bigheaded on me. Or should I say silicon-headed? I'll be catching up to you shortly."

"When is your transplant scheduled? Next week?"

Cleary downed some of his bourbon. "Correct. And none too soon. In the meantime have you spoken with the congresswoman?"

"Yes."

"Is she going to be a problem with this cousin of hers being here?"

"No."

"How much of a threat do you think the New Guinea woman might be?"

"If she returns home quickly, none. If not . . ."

Nichols glanced around the room and instinctively leaned forward, lowering his voice. "If she finds out about Ray, that would be a problem. A huge problem. Damien, I'm going to leave it in your hands to make sure that doesn't happen."

"And how far would you like me to go to ensure that?"

"Track her, assess her, redirect her. Keep her in the dark."

"And if that doesn't work? What's more important, this one woman or the project?"

Nichols let out a long sigh. "I hope never to face that decision. I do know this: we can't let Abigail Caldwell jeopardize everything we've worked toward for twenty years."

Since I was the only heir, handling my father's will was a breeze. Disposing of all his possessions was another matter. My father was both tidy and sentimental, meaning he had amassed a substantial collection of personal treasures, all meticulously organized. A box of photographs he'd inherited from his parents. Two boxes of his science fair trophies and ribbons. Two boxes of my scribblings from elementary school. Wading through the rest of it at his place was too large a task. I had it shipped to Dallas, where, although it took over my living room, I could rummage through everything at a reasonable pace.

I had whittled the task down to three boxes. I sat on the floor and spent twenty minutes on the first, sorting through written reports — paper reports — from his college days. I reached for the second box and opened it. I stared at the object sitting on top of a pile of electrical cords. It was the same type of machine I had borrowed from the university to read the message sent to my father.

"Alistair, visual please."

Alistair appeared.

"Are my father's personal purchase records still available in his system?"

"Yes, they are."

"How far back do they go?"

"The archives go back ten years."

That probably wasn't far enough for a device like this, but it was worth a shot.

"Can you tell me when he purchased this item?" I read him the product name and number.

Momentarily, Alistair responded. "That item was purchased on April 17."

I rolled my eyes at him. "Which year, Alistair?"

"This year, Creighton."

I froze. *This year.* My dad had tracked down this device for the sole purpose of saving one file. Why?

11

The tap came just as another groveling constituent asking for a legislative handout left Lauren's office. It was Sabin. She entered their favorite VR meeting place, in Yosemite. Sabin kissed her. "Abby and I are in town. Would you like to join us for lunch?"

Lauren accessed the time on the Grid. "Eleven forty-five." She hesitated. "I have a committee meeting at one o'clock. How close are you?"

"Downtown."

Lauren was surprised. "What are you doing there?"

"Getting an evening gown for Abby."

Lauren furrowed her brow. "For what?"

"The dinner party tomorrow night."

"Dinner party?" She looked at him incredulously. "She is not coming to the dinner party."

"Lauren, she has to. She's your visiting

relative, and all the guests know she's staying with you. They'll expect to meet her."

"Sabin, she'll say things that will mortify me."

"She'll say exactly the kinds of things this group would expect her to say. They'll dismiss them. It won't reflect on you. They might even find her quaint."

"Quaint? Are you kidding?" She stood simmering.

"So . . . what's your decision on lunch?"

Her glare provided the answer.

It was midnight when Kate's old battery-powered Volvo pulled up in front of her house. She got out of the car, climbed the four steps to her front door, dropped her belongings in the entryway, and crashed onto her bed. Around three thirty, an incoming tap on the Grid integrated nicely into a dream she was having about Matt. By the time she awoke, the message was over. She glanced at her antique digital clock. Taps at this hour were never good news.

"Grid, who just left me a message?"

"You received a message from Abigail Caldwell."

Abby. She was sorry she missed the tap. Abby probably could use a familiar face right about now.

"Please play the message."

Abby's image appeared on a visiscreen across the room. She was sitting on the side of a bed in a nicely decorated room. She looked tired.

"Hi, Kate. This is Abby. Maybe it's too early to tap you. I apologize if I woke you up. I just wanted to let you know that I arrived here safely and have settled in at Lauren's place. It's quite nice. I guess everything here is quite nice. But I . . ." She glanced at the room around her. "I'm lost here. I don't know what the next step is. I'm not sorry I came . . . It was the right thing to do. My resolve hasn't softened, but I miss my village. I miss Miraba."

Abby shivered. "It's cold here. I always feel cold indoors, even wearing the sweater you got for me." She gave a slight smile. "I miss the warmth of the jungle."

She looked down at the floor, then back up. "I haven't done much here yet. I'm getting to know Sabin — that's Lauren's husband, or life partner, I guess. He's offered to take me to the National Mall and see the government stuff. I'm not sure I want to get back into one of those automated cars yet."

Kate smiled. Automated cars. She didn't

like them either.

"I thought there might be quite a few books to read here. But they don't have any books; everything is on the Grid. I've tried it, but it's not the same as curling up in a hammock with a book."

Abby stood up and started to pace. "I haven't gotten to know Lauren very well yet. She's busy with her work. Everything here seems very busy. I miss how, in the jungle, someone would come from another village, and we'd spend the whole afternoon just sharing stories. Things aren't that way here."

She stopped pacing. "Last night I dreamed that my village was burning, like it was when we flew away in the helicopter. Except I and everyone else were still there. I heard Miraba screaming, and I kept running into the huts, but I never could find her." She paused. "I've had several dreams about Miraba and my village dying. Maybe it will help when you hear something from the lab about the disease. Let me know if you've heard anything, okay, Kate? And has the chief been buried yet?"

The chief. Kate was loath to admit to Abby that the chief was still lying on a steel slab in a morgue. Maybe by the time Kate heard back from the lab, she could say that arrangements had been made for his burial.

Abby sat down on the bed, and Kate thought she could see her blinking back tears. "Kate, when I get back, maybe you could go to the jungle with me . . . help me settle in a new village. I'd like to take you to the places I loved growing up. There's a stream that leads into the river that ran by our village. We used to sit on logs in the water, thinking, talking, listening to the macaws, looking into the sky. I'd talk to God there. I know you'd enjoy that spot."

Abby rose off the bed. "Well, I guess I'll tap you again in a few days just to check in. Thank you again for all you've done for me."

The message ended.

Abby was lonely. And bored. And discouraged. Kate found herself wishing she had taken time off to accompany Abby to the States. Being there alone — how would she possibly cope with life in America? Still, Abby had traveled down the Sepik in a canoe to save her village. Somehow she'd find a way.

Abby's parents had quickly learned an essential fact while living among the Inisi. The key to a village's spiritual heart was the village chief. Persuade him to become a Christian, and the villagers would follow. Persuade the chief of an entire subtribe — there were six clans among the Inisi — and the entire clan would follow.

Dressing for the dinner party, Abby felt both the weight and excitement of the door God had opened for her. She'd be meeting some of the most important governmental officials in the United States. Win them to Jesus, and there was no telling how many Americans would follow.

She slipped on the red evening gown and high heels that Sabin had bought her for the occasion. She took a step toward her bedroom door, wobbled, and fell to the floor. How could anyone walk in these shoes? She tried to imagine running through the jungle and chasing a wild pig in them. She started to giggle. It felt good to laugh.

She decided to practice walking before venturing downstairs. Fifteen minutes later she emerged from her room and gingerly navigated the staircase, both hands on the railing.

Sabin was waiting at the bottom, drink in hand. "You look stunning."

Abby grinned. "You think so?"

The sound of a spoon on a wineglass called the gathering to attention. Lauren lowered the glass. "Welcome, everyone. May I introduce to you my cousin, Abigail

Caldwell. Abigail, as you know, joins us after spending her entire thirty-four years with the Inisi tribe in the New Guinea jungle. I invite all of you to take your seats at the dinner table."

Abby was seated near one end of the table, next to Sabin. Lauren sat at the other end. Abby glanced at Lauren, who was glaring at her.

The guests near Abby wasted no time in peppering her with questions. She felt bombarded but exhilarated as well. She could do this; she could earnestly talk with them about her life and faith. Responding to a question from Colorado Senator Blaine Carlson about the Inisi culture, Abby explained the cycle of war and revenge killings that had characterized the tribe before her family's arrival and related how that eventually changed.

"Your parents sound like miracle workers," the senator replied.

"Well . . ." Abby looked around at her small audience. "I think it was Jesus who was the real miracle worker there."

Adela Ruiz, partner of the Puerto Rican congressman, leaned forward. "Tell us how Jesus did that."

Abby turned toward her, surprised but heartened at her interest. "Well, the teaching to forgive comes from Jesus, of course — the Sermon on the Mount. Jesus said if someone takes your shirt, give him your coat also." She glanced down the table and caught Lauren's eye once more. *Surely she can't hear us down here.*

Rebecca Billups, former secretary of education, spoke. "But didn't all the religions teach forgiveness?"

"I don't know," Abby answered honestly. "I'm not exactly an expert on religions. But what Jesus taught about forgiveness was backed up by what he did on the cross. God tells us to forgive because he is forgiving, which he showed by sending Jesus to die for our sins."

"And why would that enable us to be forgiven?"

"Because Jesus paid the price for our sins."

"The price of . . ."

"Death. The wages of sin is death, the Bible says. Someone had to pay that price. That's what Jesus did. He paid the price, so if we put our trust in him and believe that he died for us and rose from the dead, he will forgive us, and we can live forever in heaven with him."

Abby breathed deeply. She had been speaking rapidly, as if she didn't want anyone to sidetrack her while she was

141

delivering the meat of her message.

Everyone was silent for a moment. Billups turned to Senator Benjamin Claymore of Virginia. "Ben, what do you make of that?"

The senator leaned back against his chair. "Very heartfelt. Very sincere, young lady. But — not to impugn your beliefs, of course — it seems to me that the kind of forgiveness you attribute to Jesus, I mean the people-to-people kind, we achieve in our secular society very nicely."

Sara Raynes, his partner and a professor of literature, agreed. "I understand what Abby's saying — most societies go through periods when people stop shooting one another over differences and, instead, embrace the more positive aspects of religious expression. It sounds as if, for this tribal society, those beliefs have served quite well. In our society, of course, we have advanced beyond the need for such beliefs. We're a peaceful society without them."

The conversation wasn't developing at all as Abby had anticipated. "But it's not just about a peaceful society. It's about being at peace with God. That's something that only Jesus can bring — because of his death on the cross."

Ms. Raynes set her fork next to her plate. "It seems ghastly to believe in a God that would require anyone to die just because they didn't keep certain rules. What kind of a God would do that?"

"I tend to agree." Everyone turned toward Secretary Billups. "No offense to you, Ms. Caldwell. Such a God does seem to be related more to the revenge killings that your tribe rejected than the forgiveness that Jesus taught."

"To be honest," Ms. Raynes interjected, "the whole idea of forgiveness with God doesn't make sense to me. Even if there were a God, what would he or she have to forgive? Frankly, if there were a God, I think he or she is the one who would need to ask forgiveness for leaving us in such an unenlightened state for so long."

The others laughed. Abby glanced at Sabin. At least *he* had refrained.

Senator Carlson spoke. "One can take Jesus's teaching on forgiveness as valid without embracing all the rest of it. The important thing is that people have the freedom to believe what they want, isn't it, Abby? Without causing offense, of course."

She jerked her head toward the senator. "I'm sorry. I was still thinking about . . . You were saying?"

He smiled patronizingly. "Never mind. We appreciate your sharing your views with us.

Quite informative."

Abby felt disconnected for the remainder of the meal. She responded when spoken to but remained mostly quiet.

The guests left. Lauren retired to her bedroom. Abby trudged up the stairs and opened her bedroom door. Footsteps in the hallway caught her attention. She turned to see Sabin.

"Hey," he said, "are you all right? You seemed a little distant at dinner."

They went into her room. Abby slumped into a cushioned chair. "That was a complete failure."

"A failure how?"

"In . . ." Abby hesitated, not wanting to jeopardize the only connection she felt with anyone in the States. "In sharing the gospel with those people."

"The gospel?" Sabin looked perplexed.

"The good news about Jesus." Abby sighed. Just as at dinner, she spoke the same language as the other guests, but no one seemed to understand her.

"Oh." He crossed the room and sat down on the bed. "Well, you presented your views. I thought you did fine. It's not like you were going to change their minds — not that group. Chalk it up as a learning experience."

She shook her head. "But everything got

144

so tangled up when they started giving their opinions, and I couldn't answer their arguments — not very well. And that was probably my best shot at accomplishing what I came here for."

"Which is what?"

Abby looked down at the floor. She hadn't planned on telling anyone exactly why she had come; she knew that could cause her problems. But Sabin had proven quite supportive since her arrival. "When I was in Lae, I got a message from my grandfather, Ray —"

"But he died before then."

"Yes, I know. The message was sixteen years old, from him and my grandmother."

"You got a sixteen-year-old message?"

"My parents' mission agency forwarded it to me when they heard I was in Lae." She crossed the room to her suitcase. "Kate left me instructions on how to access it. It's probably easier if you just see it for yourself."

Sabin took the instructions from her. "Do you want me to?"

She hesitated. She'd either gain an ally or an enemy . . . "Yes. Yes, I think so."

Sabin accessed the message, and they watched it together. When it ended, Sabin kept staring at the space where the image had been projected.

"Wow," he finally said. "That's not what I was expecting." He turned toward her. "You believe God is asking you to restart Christianity here?"

She nodded, waiting for Sabin to laugh at her. Instead, his expression softened. "Well, that's certainly ambitious. I give you credit for aiming high. I'll be honest with you, though. Americans aren't very interested in religion these days."

Abby let out a deep breath. "I never thought it would be easy."

12

"Abby, you have a tap."

Abby closed her Bible and looked up at Sabin from the living room couch. "A tap? How can someone tap me?"

"They tapped the house, actually. I have them on hold. Do you want to talk?"

She shrugged, wondering who, outside of Kate, would want to speak to her. "I suppose."

He projected the image onto a visiscreen in front of Abby. She watched as a blond woman in a blue dress appeared in the middle of the living room. The woman spoke swiftly. "Hello, Abigail. My name is Pamela Murphy. I'm with *Global Sunrise* in New York."

"Excuse me," Abby interrupted. "What is *Global Sunrise*?"

The woman smiled. "We are a news program. I'm contacting you, Ms. Caldwell, to ask if you'd be available for an in-studio interview tomorrow."

Abby scrunched up her face. "An in-studio —"

Sabin interrupted. "Hi, my name is Sabin Wright. I'm hosting Abby here in DC. Can I have a word with her?"

"Of course," the woman answered.

Sabin put the tap on hold and turned to Abby. "I'm guessing *Global Sunrise* wants to interview you about your life in New Guinea. You'd be interesting to their audience."

"Their audience?"

"The people who watch the program on the Grid. Millions of people watch."

Abby's face brightened, and she sat up straight. "Really? Could I say whatever I want?"

"Well . . . yeah. They'd ask you questions about yourself, and you'd answer however you wanted to."

"And all these people would be watching . . . on the Grid?"

Sabin laughed. "Yes, they would. It would be a tremendous platform for you to share that good news of yours. Probably the biggest opportunity, if that's what you're here for."

Abby nodded enthusiastically. "Then I'll do it."

■ ■ ■ ■

Lauren breached the threshold of her front door, swung her suit jacket over a coatrack, and greeted Abby as she strode across the living room. "Hello, Abigail. We need to discuss flight arrangements for your return home. I did tell you that Sabin and I are heading to Texas for a campaign swing late in the week, didn't I? That's probably a natural time for you to —"

"Sabin invited me to come with you."

Lauren stopped short at the kitchen and turned around. "Did he? What other arrangements have been made in my absence?"

"Well, I'm . . . I'm going to New York tomorrow."

"You're what?"

Abby seemed uncomfortable. "I'm going to New York."

"What in the world for? With whom? How are you getting there?"

Abby looked taken aback, which was fine with Lauren. She wanted to convey who was in charge.

"I'm taking the train. They said it was the easiest way."

"Who is 'they'?" Lauren asked brusquely.

"The . . . program people. Lauren, have I done something wrong? In the jungle when we decided to go to another village, we just got up and —"

"What program people?"

"There's a . . . program. *Global Sunrise.*"

"You're going on *Global Sunrise*?" Lauren practically shrieked.

Abby crossed her arms in front of her. "They invited me to speak to them about my life in Papua New Guinea. Is that a problem?"

Lauren collected herself, walked over, and sat on the opposite end of the couch from Abby. She managed a smile. "No, dear. It's just that . . . I was concerned about your safety. New York is such a big place for someone new to the country."

"I'll be fine. Sabin's going with me."

"He is?" Lauren could feel her face tense further. "Well. Perhaps tonight we can discuss your interview."

"I think they're just going to ask me questions about my life in the jungle. They seemed quite interested in it."

Lauren nodded. "I'm sure. They might ask some other questions as well, though. Perhaps it would be good to prepare in advance. They may ask you about your religious faith, for instance. It's best not to

150

say too much about that."

Abby frowned. "I plan to talk about my faith, Lauren. That's why I want to go."

"Yes, of course. But it might help if I coach you a bit."

Lauren rose and walked toward her bedroom. Abby on *Global Sunrise,* flaunting her religious fanaticism for all the electorate to see. That could be a political disaster. She opened her bedroom door and spotted Sabin at the bathroom sink. She closed the door behind her.

"Sabin, we need to talk."

"Dr. Sampson, I apologize for the delay in getting back to you with your lab results. We had some equipment difficulties, and then we had two teams examine the sample . . . twice."

The man, a middle-aged New Guinean in a white lab coat, appeared so genuinely apologetic that she resisted the urge to vent her frustration. The National Lab had had the tissue sample from the autopsy for days. Kate didn't want an explanation; she wanted the results.

"And what did you find?"

"The specimen you sent us consists of two substances. The first is broken-down organic material, primarily amino acids. Based on where the sample was obtained, we suspect this material comprised the bulk of the hippocampus, but it's impossible to say for certain."

"What possibly could have broken it down into molecular form?"

"The second material may hold the answer to your question," the man said. "It consists of inorganic molecules arranged in a prefabricated matrix."

"Which means what?"

"They are molecular machines — nanites, as they are commonly called. Nanites, of course, may have the potential for self-replication, but we didn't see evidence of that currently occurring. These appear to be inoperative."

Nanites? How could nanites find their way into the bodies of a completely isolated tribe?

"I'm forwarding a copy of our report. Would you like us to return the sample to you?"

"Yes, please." She hesitated, wondering if somehow the man could provide more answers. But he had done his job. "Thank you."

Kate slumped back in her chair. Nanites. The infection that had eaten away the villagers' brains was artificial. There was no new jungle virus that had to be contained. That was the good news.

It seemed small consolation compared to the bad news. Someone had programmed microscopic machines to invade the human brain and eat it from the inside out. They had infected the villagers with these machines, for what purpose she didn't know.

Three hours later Kate watched as a familiar face emerged on her visiscreen.

"Kate! What a pleasant surprise!"

Dr. Rich Godwin, her advisor at the University of Washington School of Medicine, had always greeted her warmly. He does that to everyone, she told herself back in school. But Kate knew she was one of his favorites. She felt guilty that she hadn't been in touch for three years and that now she was tapping only because she needed a referral. Whatever the circumstances, she was genuinely glad to be in touch. He seemed glad as well.

"I've thought about you so often since we last saw each other, Kate."

She smiled. "Thank you, Rich. I wish I had been more faithful about keeping in touch."

He shook his head. "No offense taken. We're all busy. So what can I do for you today? I take it you didn't tap just to chat."

"I wish I could say I had. But I do need something — a recommendation from you."

For a computer program, Alistair has the uncanny ability to read me like a book. When Alistair saw that the woman from Papua New Guinea had been scheduled to appear on *Global Sunrise,* he assumed I might be interested. He couldn't have been more correct. This woman was potentially a gold mine of cultural research.

I sat in my living room recliner and accessed the Grid to watch. The program began with a brief background piece on the jungles of New Guinea. The host, Gabrielle Marshall, described Abigail Caldwell's harrowing journey to civilization and the tragedy of her village's dying. Then Marshall turned to Abby, seated next to her on the *Global Sunrise* set. She looked older than her thirty-four years, had an attractive, tanned face, unusually muscular arms, and straight, near-black hair.

"What a story. What a life," Marshall commented. "Are you glad to finally come home to the United States?"

Abby stared at her with a classic deer-in-the-headlights look.

"Abby, are you glad to be in the States?"

She snapped out of it. "It's good to visit. But Papua New Guinea is my home."

"Of course. I understand you're staying with your cousin, Congresswoman Lauren Caldwell of Texas."

"Right now I'm at the Omni Hotel. In Washington I'm staying with Lauren."

Marshall smiled at the camera. "And how was your train trip to New York? What's it like seeing things you've only heard about before?"

"It was fascinating. I can't believe how many animals you have in the countryside. My tribe would be amazed. The horses and cows — they're bigger than I expected."

"You'd never seen a horse or a cow?"

"No . . . we don't have those in the jungle."

This had started as the worst interview I'd ever seen. How educated was this woman?

"So your parents, Sam and Emily, were missionaries of the Christian religion to the Inisi tribe, correct?"

"Yes."

"And you were born in the jungle?"

"Yes."

"But you are the only surviving family member?"

Abby pressed her lips together before

155

speaking. "I'm the only one, yes. My father and my brother, William, died from a virulent strain of malaria when I was nineteen. My mother died eight years ago."

Virulent. The uneducated didn't use the word *virulent.*

Marshall's expression transitioned from supportive friend to "serious" journalist. *Do these people practice their expressions?*

"Did your parents ever consider that their presence and the religion they brought would irrevocably change the Inisi?"

I imagined the guest was too naive to realize the question was a setup.

"There was no guarantee that my parents' mission would succeed. But they worked and prayed hard, and God honored their prayers."

Marshall smiled condescendingly. "Let me rephrase the question. Did it bother your parents that what they were doing might destroy the Inisi's natural way of life?"

Abby stared at her for a moment. "Oh. I see what you're asking. Did my parents hope that by being there they would teach the Inisi to change some of their ways? Yes, of course."

"And they decided that the Christian religion was the way to do that."

"They knew that only Jesus could set

these people free."

"How would you characterize your family's attitude toward the Inisi? Since you came preaching Christianity, was it hard not to be disdainful of them?"

Abby looked surprised. "Disdainful? No, not at all. We grew to love the Inisi. I adopted an Inisi girl as my own daughter. My parents' goal was to preserve their culture by teaching them Jesus's way of love and forgiveness instead of hatred and war."

"Didn't the Inisi have their own religion?"

"You mean did they have a connection with the spirit world? Yes, their whole lives were dominated by the spirit world. They lived in constant fear of the spirits, whom the village shaman would try to appease in various ways."

"It never occurred to your parents to introduce the Inisi to various other religions or worldviews?"

"Such as what?"

"Islam. Judaism. Hinduism. Or simply the acceptance of the universe as it is."

Abby looked confused. "No. Why would they? None of those is going to lead you to God."

Marshall perked up noticeably. "Really? Why would you say that?"

"Because Jesus is the only way to God.

Only he died and was resurrected to redeem humanity from its sin."

"And what about Judaism?"

"You mean in the Old Testament?"

"No, in the modern world."

"There's no point in being Jewish if one doesn't accept the Messiah, is there?"

Marshall seemed uncomfortable with the response. She shifted in her seat. "And what about Muhammad?"

"Muhammad is a false prophet. I feel terrible for all the people who have followed him all these centuries."

"And the Eastern religions — Hinduism, Buddhism . . ."

"Are all false. They all claim that salvation comes through enlightenment. But enlightenment doesn't save anyone from their sins. Only Jesus does."

"And what if there is no God?"

Abby laughed. "Some people do believe that, I understand. I don't know how, though. It's silly."

Marshall turned to the camera. "Well, some strong opinions coming from the jungle in New Guinea." She turned back to Abby. "So, Abby, do you plan to return to New Guinea?"

"Yes, of course I'll return to the Inisi. They're my tribe."

"I can tell. It must feel strange being in a country where no one practices Christianity anymore."

"Yes." She hesitated for a moment, a look of disbelief passing over her face. "Is that really true — that no one believes in Christ? My grandfather Ray —"

"Christianity is a dead religion here."

Abby seemed unnerved, fidgeting in her seat. The host looked at the camera. "So many surprises when you emerge from the jungle." She turned back to her guest. "Abby Caldwell, thanks so much for joining us this morning."

Alistair was right. The woman was a fascinating sociological study, perhaps the only one of her kind. "Alistair, disconnect with —"

And then it hit me. *My grandfather Ray.*

"Alistair," I said hurriedly, "replay the interview."

"Starting at what point?"

"Starting with . . . the first proper name mentioned."

Gabrielle Marshall spoke. "I understand you're staying with your cousin, Congresswoman Lauren Caldwell of Texas."

Lauren Caldwell. Ray4306 had sent his message to a Lauren.

"Alistair, next name."

Abby spoke. "Right now I'm at the Omni Hotel."

"Next," I instructed. "People only."

"In Washington I'm staying with Lauren."

"Next."

"So your parents, Sam and Emily, were —"

"Stop. Discontinue program."

Ray 4306 had sent his message to a Sam as well. Sam. Lauren. Grandfather Ray. The message my father had received concerned this family. It had to be. The names couldn't be coincidental. Grandfather Ray had sent the message to my father, Abby's father, and Abby's congresswoman cousin.

I had to find Abigail Caldwell.

Lauren received a tap within seconds of the interview. She entered Sal's Seaside Café and walked to Hutch's customary table by the railing.

"So what do you think?"

She pulled out a chair and sat. "About the interview?"

Hutch nodded.

"I think she could go to jail," she answered.

"Why?"

"She violated the Tolerance Act."

160

"How so?"

"In her interview she was overtly critical of others' religious beliefs."

"So?"

"The Supreme Court has explicitly ruled that to be a violation of the Tolerance Act. *United States v. Gadney,* 2039."

Hutch smiled. "Okay. Just seeing if we're on the same page. We are. So what do we do about it?"

"We tell her that either she leaves the country or the attorney general will begin prosecution."

"We'd have to contact him beforehand to verify. I'm not sure he would actually pursue it."

"But this was *Global Sunrise,* Hutch. Millions saw it. It's not like the AG can look the other way."

"No. But it does the president no good politically to be seen as picking on helpless newcomers."

"Even if they're religious fanatics? I think that could benefit him."

Hutch paused to think. "Maybe. Hard to say. I think if we press it with the AG, he'll be happy to simply have her leave. That solves our problem. She disappears, and no one remembers the *Global Sunrise* interview. Her presence here is just a blip on the screen — old news. In a month no one will care." He leaned forward. "Let me ask you this, though. Are you sure she'll leave?"

Lauren nodded. "In the face of prosecution? Absolutely. She doesn't like it here, anyway. Let me assure you: Abby Caldwell will take any excuse to return to the jungle."

"You have some taps."

Abby lifted her face from the hotel room sink and wiped off her stage makeup. She didn't feel like responding to taps. The interview had been a disaster, and she just wanted to hide. She walked out of the bathroom, sat resignedly on the bed, and looked at Sabin. "Who tapped?"

"I don't know. I don't recognize any of the Grid addresses. There are 338 of them, though."

"Oh dear. That many people have contacted me? How do they know I'm here?"

"You mentioned it in your interview, Abby."

"Oh." She sighed. "I don't really feel like talking to anyone, but I suppose it won't hurt to play them."

"Sure. Why not? Maybe some people are interested in what you had to say." Sabin had been trying to encourage her since the interview finished.

He played the first tap. The image of a middle-aged man appeared, his demeanor combative. "You imbecile! What gives you the right to come to our country and dump your intolerant beliefs on us? Go back to your jungle where the neanderthals believe whatever you trained them to. We aren't so gullible anymore, you cretin!"

Abby's hand covered her mouth. The image disappeared.

Sabin shook his head. "He wasn't exactly welcoming."

"No, he wasn't. Maybe the next one will be better."

Sabin played the second tap. A young woman appeared, her face filled with anger. "I hope they throw you in jail for what you said this morning. How dare you come here and say that what you believe is superior to what anyone else believes. We did away with that kind of narrow thinking a long time ago, sister."

Sabin walked over and put a hand on Abby's shoulder. "Abby . . . I'm sorry. I don't know what's wrong with these people."

"No, they have a right to their opinion. That's America, isn't it?" Out of shock and curiosity, Abby encouraged Sabin to go ahead and play a couple more. They were worse.

"It looks like the next one is from some professor. Abby, I think we should stop. There's no use —"

"You're right." Abby sat down on the side of the bed and stared blankly at the Manhattan skyline. "I think that's enough."

Damien Cleary sat down at Bryson Nichols's favorite table at the Library and picked up a copy of the May 12, 1859, London *Times*.

"How did people manage to keep up with the world by reading these things?"

Nichols sipped his vermouth and rum. "You think people are better informed today, Damien?"

Cleary put the paper down. "Soon enough people will know more than they ever dreamed. Speaking of news, I see our visitor from New Guinea has managed to make some."

"Yes. To our great benefit. I predict she'll be out of the country within two weeks."

"Out of the country, not under indictment?"

Nichols shook his head. "It does the attorney general little good to indict her. She's too easy a target, coming from the jungle, not knowing our laws. But they will threaten indictment, and she will leave. I believe she'll find life in America ill-suited to her tastes, anyway. Going back home will seem preferable to her, if my guess is correct. We will, of course, have to continue monitoring."

"And if the AG doesn't take care of her?"

"If you recall, when he was NTI's chief counsel, Tad Knowles didn't go to the john without my approval. Let's just say he knows who got him appointed to his current position."

13

"This is officially my place," Sabin noted as he and Abby walked through the front door of a Fort Worth town house. They set their bags in the foyer.

"You mean the one in Washington isn't? I thought . . . since you're the husband . . . sort of . . ."

Sabin smiled. "Life partner. It's only a ten-year contract. And, no, being the male doesn't make any difference. Lauren owns the place in DC. Having two homes gives us some time apart. Every relationship needs space, right? Let me show you around."

They walked through the house. "This is the master bedroom. The guest room is upstairs — you can put your stuff up there. Here's the kitchen. A bit out of date. Well, not for you." They smiled at each other. "The breakfast room. The utility room behind here." He opened a door into it.

"And through here" — they walked through a pair of swinging gates — "the living room."

Abby stared at a teenager lying on the couch. She appeared to be asleep, but Abby guessed she was actually in VR.

"Who's that?"

"That — that is Lauren's daughter, Chloe. She's staying here for the summer while we go back and forth to DC."

"Lauren has a daughter? She didn't mention that."

"Yeah. Sometimes she doesn't. She had her with her previous life partner."

Chloe opened her eyes, startled. "Hey. You made me jump."

Sabin walked inside the room and took a seat. Abby followed him.

"Chloe, this is your . . . your cousin, actually. Abby Caldwell."

Chloe looked at her but didn't speak.

"Hi," Abby said. "Pleased to meet you."

"Uh-huh."

Sabin shook his head. "Were you working on your final project for biology? That's due soon, right?"

Chloe shrugged her shoulders. "I was having sex with Jerod." She looked at Abby. "My boyfriend."

Abby felt appalled. The girl looked so young and innocent. Young women in her village were married off at an early age, but this . . . this felt different.

She watched Sabin shoot Chloe a look. Chloe made a face in response. "What? It's nothing to hide."

"Lauren and I have asked you not to do that in the living room."

Chloe sat up. "What difference does it make? It's not like you can see anything. You can't even tell what I'm doing."

Sabin sighed. "All right. Let's move on. Chloe, would you take Abby's suitcase upstairs?"

"Why can't she take it?"

"Because she's our guest. Would you do it, please?"

Chloe rolled her eyes. "All right." She walked to the foyer.

Abby watched her trudge upstairs with the suitcase. She turned to Sabin. "How exactly do people touch and hear and taste things in virtual reality?"

"It's not that complicated. I mean, the technology is, but the concept isn't. We all have neural implants that receive input from the Grid's VR programming. It causes our motor neurons to experience the same sensations we experience in the physical world. The neural messages are processed exactly the same way. Actually, the sensations are even more pure in VR. Everything is a bit enhanced: the tastes, the smells, the touch. That's why most people would rather do things in VR. Especially something like sex."

Abby's voice caught in her throat. "But she's just a . . . How old is Chloe?"

"I realize this may seem strange to you. Kids are usually granted access to VR sex at thirteen. Chloe's fourteen." He paused. "I apologize if Chloe embarrassed you."

She shifted in her chair. "No, that's okay. It's your house. I want you to do . . . well, whatever you usually do. It all just takes a bit of getting used to."

Sabin nodded. "I'm sure."

"I set something up on the visiscreen for you." Sabin cleared Abby's dinner plate from the table. "An interview Bryson Nichols did today on the Grid."

"Bryson Nichols?"

"He's the head of NTI. Your grandfather was their chief neuroscientist. He and Nichols were the primary creators of NTI's latest invention."

"Which is what?"

"You haven't heard? An artificial brain."

Abby looked at him, dumbfounded. "An artificial brain? My grandfather was involved in creating artificial brains?"

"He was one of the leading neuroscientists in the world. He and Nichols had been working on this together for twenty years."

"How do you know?"

"Through Lauren. Nichols is her primary political benefactor."

"Which means what?"

"It means he pays for her seat in Congress." He walked into the living room and pulled up a visiscreen. "So do you want to watch the interview?"

"Yes, definitely."

Two people appeared on the screen. Meredith Norby, a science reporter, introduced Nichols. "You are literally not the same person you were a month ago. Explain what has happened to you," Norby began. She was, like everyone else in media, slender and well dressed, with an air that toggled between confidence and arrogance.

Nichols looked relaxed, as he always did during interviews. "I haven't changed, actually. I'm still just as much Bryson Nichols as I've ever been."

"Some would argue that the alteration you've undergone makes you no longer you."

Nichols smiled coyly. "Well, Meredith, we can't control what others may think, can we? What makes us ourselves isn't the particles that compose our physical beings at any given moment. Those particles are constantly changing. All the molecules in our bodies turn over every month or so — even the ones in our brains. Yet we remain the same people. Why is that?"

"You tell me."

"Because what makes us ourselves are the patterns of information that compose us, originally found in our DNA. That's what NTI's new technology does; it preserves the patterns of information while replacing our biological neurons with a silicon neural net. None of my essence has been lost. I'm going to live forever."

The interviewer leaned forward, her brow furrowing. "But how do you know that your silicon brain will take the same path or make the same choices as your carbon-based one would have?"

Nichols shook his head. "I don't. But neither did I know how my carbon-based brain would react to any given circumstance. Brains operate on quantum-level algorithms that are inherently unpredictable. Saying what a brain would have done is impossible. So it's inaccurate to say I'm altering what would have been my future. That future never existed. What might have happened is only one of myriad possibilities. Even now with a silicon-based brain, there are too many quantum variables to say how I'll respond. Having a silicon brain doesn't make me less than human. Silicon brains aren't programmed like a robot's; they're structured like carbon-based brains."

Norby glanced down at her e-pad. "Other than the fact that it declines in later years, what's wrong with the way the biological brain works?"

Nichols chuckled. "Well, that's a substantial problem, don't you think — the brain's becoming diseased and dying? We have ameliorated that.

"But to get to your question, nothing is wrong with the way the brain works, assuming you are a hunter-gatherer circa 50,000 BCE. The brains we inherited are great at some things — facial recognition, for instance, a quite complex task that was once critical for survival. They're lousy at other tasks, such as processing large amounts of financial information quickly, which our mastodon-hunting ancestors rarely had to do. The only way for us to transcend these limitations is to merge with technological intelligence. We all have neural implants already. Our new technology is simply the next step."

Norby shifted in her seat. Sabin could tell she was enjoying this interaction, but she continued acting as devil's advocate. "How could we meet the resource needs of an earth on which no one ever dies but new persons are constantly being added?"

Nichols smiled. "Your question presumes that everyone will have physical bodies. Once people's brains are uploaded into computer substrates, I believe many will choose to live in virtual reality."

He leaned forward and had a sip of water. "However, I'd venture to say that transhumanity's vastly superior intelligence will solve that problem rather easily. Not only will earth support a virtually limitless population, but Mars and the moon will be habitable for large numbers. In addition, colonizing other solar systems will for the first time be feasible. Anyone uploaded into a computer substrate could make the trip in VR and download themselves into a nanite body upon arrival." Nichols spoke with an extra gleam in his eye when he talked about space travel.

Chloe walked into the living room and sat on the couch. "Why are you watching something on a visiscreen?"

Sabin frowned at her. "For Abby. Quiet, please."

"But why remove your biological brain now?" Norby asked. "Why not upload your brain into software form, store it, and do the transplant when your biological brain has worn out?"

"That's an excellent question. There are two primary reasons. The first is a sense of continuity of one's personhood. If you stored your brain, waited ten years, then did the transfer, you'd lose the intervening years."

"But what if you constantly updated the software upload, say, weekly?"

Nichols shook his head. "That would require a full brain scan, which is time-consuming and expensive. No one would even do it monthly. The better option is doing the complete brain transfer now.

"Which leads us to the second reason. The silicon substrate simply provides a better brain — much faster, with more connections, providing much greater intelligence than even the most enhanced biological brain."

Norby leaned back in her chair. "There are critics who would say you're nothing more than a robot, not a human."

"If your definition of 'human' is limited to a chemical-based brain tied to a decaying carbon-based body, you may have an argument. But my definition is much broader than that. I think the core of humanity is the intelligence, the creative spirit, and the ability to adapt that evolution has produced in us. That's the key to being human, not the physical molecules that make up this body on any given day. The process we've invented doesn't dispose of our humanity. Rather, it elevates our humanity. It enables us to fulfill our true destiny."

"And what do you see as that destiny?"

Nichols grinned broadly. "To spread our intelligence to all corners of the universe."

"Literally? The universe?"

"Absolutely. The most powerful force we know, the one with the greatest effect on existence, is intelligence. By merging the biological and nonbiological, we have no limit on how vast our intelligence can be."

"Some people will say you're taking nature's plan into your own hands."

Nichols seemed impatient with the question. "We *are* nature. We are the product of natural evolutionary forces. Now, through us, evolution shifts mediums. It's not simply biological. It's technological."

"Bringing us back down to earth for a moment, what if some people don't want to go along with this?"

"No one will force them to. But why

would anyone want their existence to cease when, for the first time in human history, they can prevent it?"

"But are you just setting up another haves and have-nots situation? Some people get perpetual life; most around the world do not."

He nodded. "But that's the case with any new technology. At first it will be available, affordable, to some. Eventually, to the entire world. My goal is for us to end death as we know it on earth within fifty years — for the essence of every person to live perpetually in an uploaded state. It will require the combined global effort of government and private sector, but we can do it. We will do it. The transhuman age has dawned."

The program ended. Sabin looked over at Abby, who sat silently. "So what do you think?"

"I still can't believe my grandfather helped invent this."

Chloe scowled. "Why not?"

"I think it's . . . unnatural."

"You think it's better to die?"

"No." Abby looked Chloe in the eye. "I think it's better to have faith in Jesus."

Chloe stared at Abby for a moment, then looked at Sabin and laughed. "Okay. Whatever."

"Find anything interesting in there?"

Abby swung around and looked out from the closet into the bedroom, toward the voice. Sabin was standing over her. She smiled and nodded toward a low-hanging shelf. "I was just looking through these framed photos that were stacked in here. They look like family pictures. I was hoping to find one with my grandparents."

He sat on the floor next to her. "Yeah. That's unlikely." He picked up a frame and glanced at the photo.

"Why wouldn't Lauren have a picture of Poppy? He was her uncle. It seems odd, given her association with Nichols —"

Sabin shook his head. "She had a falling out with him when she was a teenager, I think. It never got repaired. I thought that might change when Lauren got involved with Nichols, but it didn't. She can be pretty stubborn."

Abby lifted a final frame off the shelf and looked at a picture of people she didn't know. "I can't stop thinking about that interview with Bryson Nichols."

"That he invented an artificial brain?"

She frowned. "No, I just can't believe my

grandfather would be involved with that type of work."

"Why?"

"Because of his faith."

"His faith . . . in . . ."

"God. You didn't know that he was a Christian?"

Sabin looked surprised. "No. He really was? He must have kept that under wraps."

Abby's brow furrowed. "I wouldn't think so." She began stacking frames back on the shelf. "How did he die, exactly?"

"Brain aneurysm, I believe. Kind of weird since he was a neuroscientist. You'd think he would have had his own brain scanned regularly. Apparently he didn't. It's a shame you missed meeting him by just a few weeks. Given all you had in common, I'm sure that would have meant a lot to you. And him."

Abby lifted the last frame off the floor and placed it back. She slowly ran her hand over its edge. "I never really knew him, but I miss him. I feel like he's the one person here I really would have connected with."

"Chloe, do you know if you have any unleavened bread?"

Abby watched from the kitchen entrance as Chloe shut the refrigerator door and

178

looked at her. "Any what?"

"Unleavened bread. It's . . . made without yeast."

"You can't make bread without yeast."

"Yes, you . . ." She paused. Getting into a disagreement with Chloe was the last thing she wanted. "Can you point me to some bread — any bread?"

"In the pantry." She motioned across the kitchen.

Abby decided to gamble on another request. "Do you have any juice made from fruit?"

"Mango in the fridge. And orange." Chloe walked past her and up the stairs.

Abby gathered the bread and juice and headed to her bedroom. In a few moments she heard a knock on her doorpost. She looked up and saw Sabin leaning against the door.

"You've had some more taps."

Abby's shoulders slumped. "Same as before?"

"A few hate ones. I'm not sure how they tracked you here. But also a college professor in Dallas keeps tapping. He says he'd like you to come speak to his class."

"College students? Why would anyone want me to speak to college students?"

"I suppose he finds your story interesting."

She moved a glass and a plate in front of her on the floor. "I don't think so, Sabin. It seems I've made one public appearance too many as it is. Besides, you're already spending too much time deleting angry messages for me. No need to add to them."

He grinned. "It couldn't possibly go as badly as the *Global Sunrise* interview."

She rolled her eyes. "Unless they start throwing things at me this time."

He slipped inside the door and sat in a chair. "Look, I'm not sure it's the best idea, but the venue isn't so public, and it is another chance to deliver your message. I'd be careful about criticizing others' beliefs, but beside that, isn't this just the sort of opportunity you're looking for?"

She considered that for a moment. She wished she felt more confident in her answer. "Yeah. I guess it is. I'll go."

"If you want, we can tap him back tomorrow morning."

"That would be good. Thanks."

Sabin looked at the food she had gathered. "Late-night snack?"

"Um. No. I'm taking communion."

"Which is what?"

"A remembrance that Jesus gave to his

disciples."

"Disciples?"

"His . . . closest followers."

Sabin leaned forward. "This remembrance, you do it alone?"

Abby smiled slightly. "I never have before. In the jungle the whole village did it together. I don't have anyone here to do it with, but I'm used to doing it every week, so . . ."

"I have time if you want some company."

"That's nice of you, Sabin, but —" She stopped, not sure how to explain.

"But what? You said you do it with other people, right?"

It ran contrary to all the theology her parents had taught her. Communion was only for believers in Jesus. But she didn't have it in her to say no to the only person in America who seemed to be on her side. Besides, maybe God would use it somehow.

"Okay," she replied. "That's nice of you to offer."

Sabin joined her on the floor, legs crossed. Abby picked up the juice. "The night before Jesus was crucified, he was having the Passover meal with his disciples."

"The Passover meal?" He shook his head. "I'm sorry. I'm asking too many questions."

"No, it's all right. I don't mind. The

181

Passover meal was a Jewish feast. It celebrated God delivering the Jews out of Egypt. Jesus was Jewish."

"Yes, I do know that."

She smiled sheepishly. "So . . . Jesus was saying his final words to them."

"Before he was crucified."

"Yes. And he took the bread and said, 'This is my body, broken for you.' And he passed it around the table. So we take the bread . . ." She pulled a small piece of bread off the slice and handed it to Sabin, then pulled one off for herself. "And we thank Jesus for giving his body for us." She bowed her head. "Jesus, thank you for giving yourself on the cross for our sakes." She looked up. "And we eat the bread." She placed the piece in her mouth and swallowed. Sabin copied her.

"And what is the juice?"

"It stands for the blood of Jesus. At the Passover meal it was wine, but we didn't have grapes in the jungle, so we used kwa juice."

"We have wine if you want it."

"You do?" Abby asked excitedly. "Is it . . . Could we use it?"

Sabin smiled. "Of course. I'll get us some."

In a minute he returned with two small glasses of wine. "If you've never had wine, this may have quite a bite."

"That's okay."

She couldn't have been more eager to have real wine with communion. Sabin handed her the glass. Abby meditated quietly for a moment, then spoke. "Jesus said, 'Do this in remembrance of me.' Thank you, Jesus, for shedding your blood for the forgiveness of our sins." She raised the glass to her lips and drank. She grimaced and smacked her lips. "That's wine?"

Sabin laughed. "I told you it would have a kick."

"It tastes . . . awful." She started to laugh. "And all these years I've wanted to try it."

"It's an acquired taste."

Sabin held out his hand, and Abby handed the wineglass back to him. "So what do you do next in this remembrance?"

"That's all."

"That's a very short ceremony."

Abby nodded. "It's a reminder of what Jesus did for us."

Sabin looked at the wineglasses. "You believe this stuff deeply, don't you?"

"Yes, of course."

"What's it like, believing in something that much?"

She shrugged. "I never really thought about it in those terms. Isn't there anything you believe in?"

He shook his head. "Not in that way."

"Hmm." She looked to the floor, lost in thought, then back at Sabin. "It's . . . comforting. To know I have someone who hears when I pray."

"Do you really think there's someone up there, listening?"

"I know there is."

He set the glasses on the floor and looked at her. "Abby, do you feel lonely? In the States, I mean."

Abby hesitated, then nodded. "I guess I do. Nothing is familiar, and I'm not close to anyone. But God is always with me."

Sabin regarded her a moment. "I can't relate to what you say about God." He smiled warmly. "But I'm glad you're here, Abby. I'm certainly learning some interesting things."

Abby smiled back. "I'm glad too, Sabin."

14

I had almost given up hope of hearing from Abigail Caldwell when the tap came. She was using a visiscreen, but her image, of course, was transmitted directly to my neural implants. Even more than I had noticed on *Global Sunrise,* I was struck by this woman's presence — her arresting black hair, her striking face, her athletic body. I pushed those thoughts out of my mind.

"Hello, Ms. Caldwell, my name is Creighton Daniels. I'm a history professor at the University of the South in Dallas. I saw your interview on the *Global Sunrise* show, and I wanted to invite you to do a question-and-answer session with one of my upper-level classes, American Cultural History Since 1900."

She arched a brow. "A question-and-answer session?"

"Yes. I'd brief my students on your story

and ask them to prepare questions for you to answer."

"In person or in writing?"

"I'd love for you to appear in person here at the university, if you're willing." I didn't tell her that the class met in VR and we could project her in from any location. I wanted to meet her in person.

"Mr. Daniels, why would your class be interested in asking me questions?"

I took her queries to be a positive sign. If she had no interest, she would have rejected me out of hand.

"We will soon be discussing the de—" I started to say *demise*. ". . . the history of Christianity in the U.S. during this century, and I think it would be instructive for them to interact with a practicing Christian. There aren't many around here to choose from."

"Yes, I've been informed of that."

"I thought they would find your story particularly intriguing."

"How many people would be viewing this conversation?"

"Just my students. That's about sixty people."

"It wouldn't be available worldwide?"

"No. Only to my class." *And anyone they cared to show it to.*

"I could speak about my faith?"

"Of course. I would want you to."

She paused, seemingly considering my invitation. "Yes." She drew the word out as if convincing herself. "I think I would like to do that. On what day?"

"How about a week from Monday?" I hated waiting so long, but I didn't have much choice. I couldn't bring her in during the upcoming week's midterms. "I'll send a car to pick you up. I can even give you a tour of Dallas."

"That would be fine. Thank you for inviting me."

She turned, asked someone how to end the communication, and disappeared from my view.

I leaned back against my office chair. I wanted desperately to dash to Fort Worth and show her the message my father had received from her grandfather. But that, I had concluded, wasn't prudent.

One step at a time. I had to win her trust. And, in truth, I did look forward to having her in my class. She was a cultural specimen my students would never encounter again: a living microcosm of the world of faith, raised apart from the modern world.

I picked up my cup of tea. "Alistair, what can you tell me about the Inisi tribe from

Papua New Guinea?"

The next morning Sabin opened his front door to find two men in business suits. In an age of virtual reality, people rarely visited others' actual homes; dropping by unexpectedly was unheard of.

"Is Abigail Caldwell at this address?"

He regarded them suspiciously. "Who's asking?"

"We're from the U.S. Department of Justice. Is she at this address?"

"Is there a problem?"

"We need to discuss that with her, sir."

Sabin frowned. "One minute."

He called upstairs. Abby came down, barefoot, in khaki shorts and a T-shirt.

"Abby, you have visitors."

Her face brightened. "Really? Who?"

"Federal agents."

They sat in the living room. Sabin offered the men coffee; they refused. The taller agent, a man with a five o'clock shadow, started the questioning. "Are you aware of the legal ramifications of what you said on the *Global Sunrise* program on the morning of May 17?"

"What legal ramifications? Did I say something wrong?" Abby looked over at Sabin, who shrugged.

The shorter agent spoke. "What you said would in most quarters be construed as hate speech."

"Hate speech?" Abby looked floored. "What did I say that was hateful?"

"Your statements concerning non-Christian religions."

"But I was only saying what was true — what the Bible says. I thought there was freedom of speech in this country. And freedom of religion. That's what my parents always taught me."

The first agent shook his head. "Under the Tolerance Act of 2036, what you said is illegal."

For the first time, Sabin heard anger in Abby's voice. "So are you here to arrest me? Is that what you're saying?"

"No, Ms. Caldwell. The attorney general would prefer not to prosecute. But your violation was in a very public forum. He can't postpone taking the matter to a federal grand jury."

"And then what would happen?"

"You'd be indicted, and once that occurs, you wouldn't be able to leave the country before standing trial or working out a plea bargain with the court."

Abby narrowed her eyes and when she spoke, her words were clipped. "Are you saying I could actually be thrown into prison for what I said?" She turned again to Sabin. "Can they do that here?"

Sabin nodded.

The first man responded. "You run that risk, Ms. Caldwell. It depends on whether a jury finds that your language was an incitement."

Sabin spoke. "And so for Abby to avoid being prosecuted —"

"You'd have to leave the country. That's what the attorney general would prefer. That way the matter wouldn't have to be handled at all."

"And how soon would I have to leave?"

"Within two weeks."

The tap came from NTI. Kate put it on her visiscreen. The emotionless face of a woman in a lab coat appeared.

"Dr. Sampson, my name is Danielle Short. I wanted to contact you regarding the sample you sent us."

"Did you find anything in the nanites that might indicate their source?"

"Unfortunately, no."

"There are no identifiers at all? How is that possible?"

Short shook her head. "No, I'm trying to tell you. We couldn't run an analysis."

"You couldn't? Why not?"

"We had a mishap in the lab. It was minor. Unfortunately, your sample was contaminated and couldn't be recovered. Do you have any more of the material to be analyzed?"

It took a moment for the statement to sink in.

"Yes, of course." Kate couldn't hide her annoyance. "But this sets me back at least a week."

The woman shrugged. "I do apologize. We'll try to expedite the analysis when we receive the second sample."

Bryson Nichols and Damien Cleary strode through the north wing of NTI's neuroscience lab. It wasn't often that Nichols made a physical appearance at the lab; less frequently were he and Cleary seen together there. But Nichols felt it was important to appear in person every once in a while, if only to show his support for their efforts. He shook hands with people in two research departments before he and Cleary walked down a long hall.

"What's the latest sign-up figure for transplantation?" Nichols asked. He had reviewed the figure himself early that morning, but the question would gauge how closely Cleary was monitoring their progress.

Cleary strode quickly, trying to keep pace with the taller Nichols. "Fourteen hundred. And growing."

They turned left and walked through a pair of swinging doors, then opened another door and walked into a chamber that served as a recovery room. A neurosurgeon was speaking to an elderly man in a hospital bed who, it appeared, had just received the transplant. They walked over to the surgeon, and Nichols stuck out his hand. "Dr. De-witt. Good to see you again." He turned to the patient. "And whose life have we forever changed today?"

Dewitt beamed. "This is Alston Randolph. Former patient at Boston Neurological. Terminal condition. Was given four months."

Nichols shook the man's hand. "How old are you, Mr. Randolph?"

"One hundred twenty-three next week."

"And how are you feeling?"

"Could hardly feel better, except for some itching where they put the top half of my head back on. I challenged the doctor here to a game of chess, but he wouldn't take me on."

Nichols grinned. "I don't blame him. We

can reprogram your sensory input to help with your itch. Glad to see you're doing so well."

Nichols nodded at the doctor. He and Cleary walked into the operating room next door. Cleary sat on an examination table. Nichols sat on a swivel stool and started playing with some monitoring equipment. "The key question is whether our training regimen can keep up long term with the demand."

Cleary nodded. "The program that Holographics put together is working even better than we expected. Our first physicians have flown through it. As you said, it doesn't hurt that neurosurgeons typically have the best neural implants. It's taking them only three weeks on average to develop full competency with the transplant procedure."

"How many do we have performing actual procedures right now?"

"Six."

"How many a day?"

"Two apiece, two days a week. A little more practice, and they'll do three a day."

"That's almost two thousand a year, just with current staff."

"Correct."

Nichols swung around and placed his hands behind his head. "So, Doctor . . ."

Cleary shook his head. "Don't call me 'Doctor,' Nichols. I just work here."

Nichols smiled. "So how many of these things do you think we could actually do in a year?"

"Three million."

"Three million? How do you arrive at that?"

"I estimate fifty thousand neurosurgeons worldwide. Say we get twenty percent doing this procedure. That's ten thousand surgeons. They do three procedures a day, one hundred days a year. That's three million procedures."

Cleary's figure was higher than Nichols's by a factor of three, but it wasn't outrageous. "Three million procedures a year. So at that rate it would take two hundred years to cover the current U.S. population, to say nothing of the world."

"Of course," Cleary added, "we're unlikely to get more than ten or twenty thousand on the waiting list unless you get it funded by the government health plan."

"I'm working on that."

"Any progress?"

Nichols frowned. "Politics. The wheels grind slowly."

Cleary walked across the room, facing away from Nichols. "The whole conversion

194

process would speed up a thousandfold in a crisis."

"What kind of crisis?"

"A worldwide pandemic, for instance." He turned to face Nichols. "A worldwide flu epidemic deadlier than the one fifty years ago. People would rush to be uploaded before the flu hit them."

Replacement bodies, Nichols knew, could eventually be constructed from nanites. In the meantime, those uploaded would live in VR. "At what speed do you think we could do actual transplants en masse rather than just uploads? Assuming we had the unprogrammed substrates on hand, of course."

"It depends on how much of the procedure is done by robots."

"Which we won't know until we've written the software for it."

Cleary grinned. "Actually, we already know."

Nichols furrowed his brow. "How?"

"Because we've already developed the robotic software."

"You have?" Nichols stared at his compatriot. He was simultaneously thrilled to have such resources available and bothered that such large-scale activities were taking place without his knowledge. "I'm impressed. But don't you think you should have run this past me?"

Cleary laughed. "Nichols, you always say how much you value self-starting. That's what we've done. You're not complaining, are you?"

Nichols thought for a moment, then smiled. "No, I'm not complaining."

"So, to answer your question: we take half the surgeons on the planet — roughly a million — and provide them our training software. Allow two extra weeks for the non-neuros. The surgeons then supervise robots performing ten surgeries a day, six days a week. That's three billion surgeries. We could convert the entire planet in three years. Maybe less."

That was wildly optimistic, Nichols knew. But running the numbers was a thought-provoking exercise.

"Well." Nichols stood. "The chances of a pandemic are no longer as high as in 2039. Medicine has advanced a bit since then."

Cleary cleared his throat and slipped down from the examination table. "We wouldn't have to wait for a natural pandemic, of course."

Nichols looked at him.

Cleary continued. "What if, theoretically, an alien pathological element was introduced into the human ecosystem?"

"A disease," Nichols clarified.

Cleary nodded. "Specifically, a rapid brain degeneration disease, like the mad cow disease of the 1990s. Only highly contagious. With a sufficient mortality risk, the demand for transplants would be almost universal. The transition to transhumanity would, in the grand scheme, be almost instantaneous."

Nichols's brow creased. "Damien, you are quite mad. I will not be party to creating a worldwide pandemic just to promote my own technology."

"Not to promote your own technology. To advance the ultimate cause of humanity."

"And who would develop this disease?"

"There are already artificial pathogens available. You know that."

"None of which have been tested on real populations."

"Yes. Well, that wouldn't be difficult to arrange, would it?"

"No, it wouldn't. And we will not proceed down this road any further. Humanity will become transhumanity soon enough. I'm content to let the transition come at its own pace." He stared at his associate. "I trust you are as well?"

Cleary laughed. "Nichols, you're too serious sometimes. I'm just testing you."

"Testing what? My commitment to the transition? I think my commitment is beyond question. Or do we need to have me remove my skullcap?"

"Your commitment is beyond question, Nichols. I can't fault you on that."

15

"Sabin, I'm going back to Papua New Guinea."

Sabin finished pouring a glass of orange juice and walked to the kitchen table with a plate of English muffins and eggs. He sat and looked at Abby. "I guess you don't have much choice, given what the federal agents said."

Abby shook her head. "Prosecution or not, I'd stay if I were sure God wanted me to. I know my grandparents believed what they were telling me. And I've prayed about it. Maybe God does have a task for me here. I felt that way before I came. But . . . what have I accomplished? I'm out of place here, I don't know how to function in this culture, I'm lonely — that's not a comment on you, by the way —"

"No, I understand. We just met."

Her mouth turned down, and she continued. "Lauren is too busy for me. I know

I'm a sore spot between you and her —"

"Whatever issues Lauren and I have existed long before you arrived."

"Well, I don't want to make things worse. I just can't see how God can use me here. I feel like a failure." Abby pressed her hands to her eyes. "And the truth is, I miss Papua New Guinea terribly. I just want to go home."

Sabin handed her a tissue. She dabbed her eyes and pushed the muffins and eggs toward him. "Here, eat some of this before it gets cold."

He served his plate and pushed the food back to Abby. "If you go back, where would you go?"

"Ultimately, to the Inisi. But first to Kate's. She's invited me." She looked around the room as if searching for something. "I don't know why it's been so long since she tapped."

"Does she know you're here?"

Abby stared blankly at him. "I guess not."

"She has to have a place or a person to tap." Sabin accessed Papua New Guinea time on the Grid. "It's midnight her time. Do you want to tap her?"

"No, we can wait."

Sabin got up, brought the juice pitcher to the table, and poured both of them more.

He took a sip and looked over at her. "I'll tell Lauren. I assume it'll be a few days before you leave. I'm heading up to Colorado to do some hiking this weekend in the Collegiate Peaks. Would you like to join me? Might be your last chance to see the mountains here."

"I thought everyone did that sort of thing in virtual reality."

"Yeah, well, when it comes to hiking, I like the real thing."

She smiled. "I'd love to go with you."

"It's not Washington politicians who make this country what it is. It's the hard-working, honest, dedicated people of places like Grapevine who always have been, and always will be, the backbone of America."

Hutch watched as Lauren worked the local crowd. He didn't attend actual political events much, but it did him good to see real people get excited about something they thought was genuine.

"And as your senator, I want you to know that no matter how long I may spend representing you in Washington, my heart will never be anything but true Texan. And I promise you this: I'll never stop working to ensure that Texans can make their lives everything you always dreamed they could be!"

The crowd cheered. Piped-in music filled the high school gymnasium. Lauren pasted on a broad smile, waved at the crowd, and walked to the side of the stage, where several reporters awaited her. Hutch walked over and stood behind them.

"Congresswoman," one was saying, "it has been reported that your cousin, Abigail Caldwell, is staying at your residence in Fort Worth."

Hutch could see Lauren stiffen. "Temporarily," she answered.

"Are you in agreement with the views she expressed on *Global Sunrise*?"

"No, of course not."

A second reporter followed up. "It has been suggested that the attorney general will be forced to indict her for her statements. If that transpires, will you continue to support her?"

She stared at him icily. "I am not supporting her. I do not condone the expression of intolerant beliefs. I am simply extending hospitality to a family member who shortly will be returning to her own country."

Hutch was about to rescue Lauren from further questions when a tap came. He stepped backstage. When he emerged from

VR a few minutes later, Lauren was standing beside him.

"I thought you came over to rescue me from the wolves, Hutch, not desert me."

"Yeah, well, sometimes there are taps you have to answer."

She reached out and touched his arm. "What is it?"

"My dad."

"Is he sick?"

"He's dead."

Kate didn't look right. She was dressed in pajamas and had a disheveled appearance.

"Kate, are you all right?"

"Hi, Abby. Good of you to tap. Yeah, I'm fine. Just feeling a little under the weather this morning." She reached over and took a sip from a coffee cup. "I just need to wake up. So how are things in the States?"

Abby cleared her throat. "I've decided to come back to Papua New Guinea."

"You have? So soon?"

"Yes. I suppose the truth is that things here haven't worked out so well. My cousin Lauren is in the middle of her campaign, and her partner, Sabin" — she glanced at him across the living room — "he's been great, but I don't want to overstay my welcome. Mostly, I miss home. I miss the jungle."

"I understand. You were brave to go to the States in the first place. I saw you on *Global Sunrise.*"

"You did?" Abby cringed.

"I thought you did great."

"Thanks for saying that. Not everyone here agrees."

"That's too bad. Well, I'd be glad to host you here as long as you like. It's not the jungle, but it's close to it." She reached over to put her cup down but missed the table and spilled coffee on the floor. "Crap." She grabbed a cloth to wipe it up. "That's the second time this morning." She turned to the visiscreen. "So have you made arrangements to fly back?"

"Sabin is checking on flights. Does Thursday next week work for you? In the evening?"

"Yes, that's fine. Let me have my Grid interface put this down. You said you'd arrive . . . what day?"

Abby raised her brows and repeated herself. "Thursday."

"In the morning or at night?"

"In the evening. Kate, are you sure you're all right?"

"I'm just feeling a bit discombobulated."

"I'm sorry. I don't mean to bother you when you're not feeling well, but have you found out anything about the disease?"

Kate looked confused for a moment. "Oh yeah. The disease. It's not a jungle disease. We think the village died of an infestation of nanites — that's miniature robots. They ate away at the brains, we think."

Abby held her hand to her mouth and stared in disbelief at the visiscreen. Miraba and the villagers had their brains eaten away? "But how . . ." She felt tears welling in her eyes.

"I don't know. We're trying to find out. I sent a sample to a company in the U.S. for analysis. But they said it got contaminated, so I have to send another. Except it seems to be missing. We're still looking. I'm sorry for the news, Abby."

Abby pressed her palms against her eyes and gathered herself. She finally spoke. "And the chief? Have you been able to bury him?"

"Oh. Abby, I apologize. I forgot about the chief. I'll check on that today and make sure it happens."

Abby gave a weak smile. "Thanks." She hesitated, not knowing what else to say. "Well, shall I contact you about my flight in a few days?"

"That would be fine."

"I can't wait to be back in Papua New Guinea. Thanks again for opening your place to me."

"You're welcome. I look forward to it."

They disconnected. Sabin leaned forward. "I'm sorry for the news, Abby. That sounds horrible."

Abby sighed deeply. "At least . . . at least it's over now. For all of them." She looked at him and shook her head, puzzled. "Sabin, there was something wrong with Kate."

Two days later Hutch stood looking down into the casket of Thomas Hardin, his father. He had known for years that Thomas would die prematurely. One couldn't live the way his father had and last to a hundred and twenty. Or even a hundred, for that matter.

"He looks so peaceful," the people would say tomorrow. Truth was, he looked antiseptic and smelled that way too — the same smell he had every Sunday during Hutch's youth after he shaved, splashed himself with Old Spice, and put on a starched white shirt and a tie for church. "God doesn't countenance sloppy dressers," his father would say.

He had reeked of aftershave the morning he took Hutch's pirate set. "We're leaving,

206

Hutch. What's your toy, Hutch? You have to tithe a toy today for the gift boxes." Hutch looked around his room. He glumly walked over to his dresser and took a Matchbox car off the top. He held it out for his father.

"What's this?"

"A Matchbox car," he said.

"One little car? You think this gift is good enough?"

His father tossed it into a trash can.

"Daddy!" Hutch retrieved the car. He looked around the room and held back his tears. "Why does God want my stuff, anyway? Didn't he give it to me so I could enjoy it?"

"You selfish . . ." His father loomed over him with his hand pulled back, ready to strike.

"Daddy! Please!"

"How dare you talk about God that way. He wants our best. You can't even give him your worst." He lowered his hand and scanned the room. "It's time you learn that lesson." He started picking up pieces of Hutch's pirate set — ship, fortress, and men — and placing them in a large plastic bin.

"Daddy, not my pirate set! I'll choose another toy. Any other toy."

"Too late for that, Hutch. You should have chosen to serve God in the first place. 'If anyone serves Me, the Father will honor him.' John 12:26."

Hutch cried silently all the way to church. His mother remained wordless in the front seat. Once there, his father strode across the parking lot, into the foyer of the sanctuary, and dropped the set into a large container marked Love Gifts. Hutch shuffled behind him. His father grabbed him and dragged him to his Sunday school class. "Maybe here you'll learn to love like Jesus loves." He opened the classroom door.

"Good morning, Elder Hardin," the teacher intoned.

"Good morning, Judy." He smiled broadly. "The Lord blessing you this week?"

Hutch never forgave him, just as his father never forgave Hutch for leaving the church — and the faith — when he was seventeen. His departure forced Thomas to resign his prized eldership. He was now one who couldn't "manage his own household," as the apostle Paul had written, and he was therefore unfit for leadership.

Hutch left home and worked his way through college and law school, never accepting another penny from his parents. He saw them on holidays, observing his father's spiral from church elder to Sunday school teacher to pew sitter to a bitter man who stayed home Sunday mornings, watching football. In the end, of course, there were no churches to return to even if he had wanted. But by then his father had turned his back on God permanently — or God on him. Was there any difference? Religion was all a mind game, anyway.

16

Hutch looked around at the thirty or so mourners who had braved the central Texas sun: half a dozen longtime acquaintances of his father's, a few relatives Hutch hadn't seen in years, some locals, Lauren and Sabin, and Lauren's cousin, Abby, whom Hutch had suggested Lauren invite. He wanted to assess her for himself.

The funeral officiant walked to the casket and cleared her throat. "Welcome to all of you who are here to celebrate the life of Thomas Hardin. The very elements of his being, the atoms of his body, were given birth in the middle of distant stars eons ago. The universe itself gave him what we call life. Now his elements assume a different form in that universe, and we remember and celebrate the being we knew as Thomas.

"There was a time in his life, a darker time, when Thomas had fallen prey to the former myths of Western civilization, myths that upheld us and united us when we were young as a society but which we finally outgrew. Thomas outgrew them too. He emerged as a man who was whole, at peace with himself, at peace with life itself, giving himself to the betterment of society around him."

At peace with himself. The only time Hutch could recall Thomas Hardin at peace with himself was after he had downed a six-pack while watching a game. How many times had he spoken the words, "Dad, there's a cure for alcoholism now. You don't have to live this way anymore." But his father wasn't interested. "I'm not going to let some idiot doctor fool with my genes," he'd reply. Alcohol was one of two pleasures in his life.

"He was a faithful contributor to the Humane Society, a lover of dogs, and an active participant in the Brownwood Gardening Society. He constructed his own greenhouse in his backyard, a real one, mind you, not a VR one" — there was laughter among the attendees — "in which he grew a wide variety of flowers not native to this area of Texas. His greenhouse was a favorite stop on the annual gardening tour of Brownwood."

His other pleasure was flowers. From Hutch's earliest memories, his father had tended his flowers. Now his casket was surrounded by those very flowers. How could a man of such ugliness bring forth — and appreciate — such beauty? Hutch didn't know. *We are all mixtures of beauty and ugliness,* he supposed.

"Just as the annuals in his greenhouse lasted only a year before more seeds were planted and new flowers bloomed, so also we last only a certain time in this state that we call our lives. Then we return to the elements and make room for the lives of those who come after us. And though we miss Thomas Hardin, we have gained through him so much more than we have lost. To him and to the cosmos from which he sprang, we dedicate this time of remembrance and celebration."

Several friends and relatives stood in turn and recounted fond memories of Thomas. A woman from the gardening society read a poem about the sacred ritual of life. Then an eleven-year-old boy, one of Thomas's great-nephews, walked to the front. He read from an electronic pad.

"I'll miss Uncle Thomas because, of all the grownups in my life, I could count on him to just hang around and teach me what he knew. He taught me a lot about plants. He helped me start a garden at home, and when I grow up, I'd like to have a green-house like he did. He took me to baseball games and taught me strategy. He used to tell me about wars and presidents and old cars. I could have gotten all that stuff from the Grid, but listening to Uncle Thomas tell me was a lot better."

He looked up nervously at the audience, then back down at his pad. "I think Uncle Thomas was about as good an uncle as you could have. I'm glad he was alive on the earth for ninety-six years so I could know him. I wish he had lived longer. I know we'll never see him again, but I'll always remember him."

He paused, then walked briskly to his seat without looking up.

A flautist began playing a familiar song about the beauty of life and the naturalness of death. It was a fitting end to the ceremony, Hutch thought. His father hated the flute.

Abby left the funeral gathering, walked to a small creek she had spotted on the far side of the cemetery, sat down, and cried.

In a few minutes Sabin sat down next to her. "Abby, are you okay?"

Abby wiped tears from her cheeks. "I . . . You wouldn't understand, Sabin."

He reached out and put a hand on her shoulder. "You can try me."

Abby turned, looked into his face, and gave a hint of a smile. "I'm not sure this is going to make much sense to you. The talk the woman gave . . ."

"The eulogy?"

"Yes. It was awful."

"Why?"

"Because . . . because it had no hope. What a terrible statement to make at the end of someone's life."

"What do you mean?"

She looked down at the creek. "It was like the Inisi when my family first went to live with them. Funerals for them lasted a week or more — mourning the dead, I mean. I remember it as a child. There was loud wailing for days, and the mate and the parents of the deceased would cut their arms as a demonstration of their grief."

"I suppose that was their custom."

"Yes. But they had a good reason for the long mourning, for the grief. They believed loved ones passed to the realm of the dead, the realm of the spirits. And the spirits — they weren't on the Inisi's side. They weren't on *any* human's side. They were pernicious and unpredictable. And the Inisi's loved one was now in their hands. But there was noth-

214

ing they could do. There was no hope."

Sabin thought for a moment. "You said that was the case when you *first* went to live with them. What changed?"

"My parents brought them a message of hope. When someone died, they didn't have to be in the hands of the spirits. They could forever be in the hands of the loving God who created them and who came to earth to die for them so that their sins might be forgiven."

"And how did the Inisi react to that?"

"It took a while, but when they saw my parents living out the message they preached, they embraced that message as their own. They started putting their trust in Jesus. And after that, their mourning for the dead changed. They still mourned, because they missed them. But they didn't mourn without hope. They knew their loved one was in a better place."

Sabin shifted his body toward Abby. "So . . . I guess I'm not getting it. What does that have to do with this funeral?"

She gestured back toward the gathering. "That woman's message . . . There is no hope there. To say we're alive and then our molecules simply return to be elements in the physical universe — what does that say, not only about death, but about life? It takes away the meaning. If we are simply collections of atoms . . ."

"I don't know if she —"

"And then when that little boy got up and said essentially the same thing — to hear such a hopeless message about life coming from a young boy. He doesn't even realize how hopeless it is. This is what life is here now — even for children." She paused, shaking her head slowly. How could people live like this? "After everything I grew up believing about America, it's just so depressing. So frustrating."

"I'm . . . I'm sorry it upset you."

They were silent for a moment. Abby looked back at the creek. "My grandfather's funeral wasn't like this, was it?"

"I don't know. I wasn't there."

Abby was surprised. "You weren't? What did Lauren say about it?"

"She wasn't there, either. Some overseas trip suddenly came up."

Again Abby felt a pang for her grandfather. She couldn't help being unavailable for him, but she wished it had been different. "Who was there?"

"I can find out."

"Do you know if they produced a visual of the funeral? If they did, I'd like to see it."

Sabin shook his head. "We never received

one. Not that Lauren asked, I'm sure. She did get an inheritance check, though."

"An inheritance check?"

"All the heirs got . . . but I suppose you couldn't have gotten one."

"No."

"I wonder if you were in the will."

Abby shrugged. She knew money would be helpful if any had been willed to her, but the thought of her grandfather's lonely service still occupied her.

Sabin stood and motioned for her to follow him. They walked back to Lauren, who was concluding a brief interview with a local reporter. Sabin waited for the man to walk away.

"Picking up a few votes, Lauren?"

She shot him an exaggerated scowl. "The other side takes advantage of dead folks. Why can't I?"

"Abby and I were talking about Ray's death."

"Who?"

"Your uncle Ray."

"Oh yes. Him."

Abby felt like shaking her cousin. What was wrong with Lauren that she couldn't show basic respect for her own uncle?

"Who executed Ray's will?" Sabin asked. "Do you know?"

Lauren glanced over and called her assistant to her side. "Claire, do you remember the inheritance check I received from Raymond Caldwell?"

"Yes, Ms. Caldwell."

"Was there a letter attached to it from the executor of the estate?"

"Yes. The letter was from Bryson Nichols."

Abby felt the tension creep up her neck. None of this made any sense. She couldn't understand why the family wasn't involved with Ray's affairs, or why Nichols was. And why was Lauren so unfazed by it all?

Lauren looked at Sabin. "There you go. I don't know why he didn't use a family member. But he and Nichols were close. Ray always seemed rather standoffish to the family, anyway."

"I think it was the other way around," Sabin replied.

Abby felt relieved when Lauren was cornered for another interview. She didn't know how long she could maintain a cordial demeanor to her cousin. They all stepped aside as the cemetery workers started to take down the tent that had sheltered the service. Abby turned to Sabin. "Since Lauren is close to Bryson Nichols, do you think it would be possible to contact him about the inheritance — and to see if he has a recording of the funeral?"

Sabin shook his head. "Abby, the man is almost inaccessible. And since this brain transplant thing, the demands on his time are probably unbelievable."

"But you're Lauren's partner. If they are close . . ."

He sighed. "Okay, I'll give it a try. But don't get your hopes up."

"The granddaughter of my close friend Raymond Caldwell. Plus a woman of many adventures. It's not every day I have such a privilege."

In person — on the visiscreen, at least — Bryson Nichols exuded a personal warmth and charm that disarmed Abby.

"You know about me?"

"I saw your interview on the *Global Sunrise* show. May I say, you have an indomitable spirit."

She looked over at Sabin, who was sitting across his living room, and blushed. "Well, I don't know about that," she answered. "But thank you. And it's a great honor to have a minute of your time."

"It's my pleasure. Tell me what I can do for you."

"I'm told you were the executor of my grandfather's will."

"Yes, he and I were quite close. My condolences to you. I'm sure you loved him very much."

"I'm sure I would have if I had gotten to know him. I'm told he was a delightful man."

Nichols nodded. "He was that. So you have a question about the will?"

"My first question actually is, do you have a visual of my grandfather's funeral? I'd love to see it and get a sense of how he was remembered by those who knew him."

Nichols looked momentarily surprised, then smiled. "Of course. I don't have one personally, but funeral homes usually have that done. I'll have my assistant look into it for you."

"That would be great. And about the will, I don't mean to come off as disrespectful of my grandfather or greedy in any way —"

Nichols gave a small wave of his hand. "No, not in the least. You're wondering if you were named as one of your grandfather's inheritors."

"How did you know?"

"A reasonable question on your part. And not out of line at all."

"So . . . I don't mean to be a bother, but . . . is it possible for someone who works for you to check into that for me?" Abby watched Nichols carefully, hoping his body language would reveal something beyond his polished demeanor.

He shook his head. "Not necessary. I recall the wording myself, which was indeed more generic. You are an inheritor. There are still some undisbursed funds from his estate that I have the authority to direct. I'll make arrangements for a transfer to be made . . . Do you have an account?"

"An account?"

"A bank account. I'll have my assistant help you make arrangements to obtain one."

Abby sat back against the couch. Nichols was all business and didn't seem likely to divulge more personal information about Ray. "Thank you. Thank you so very much."

"It's my pleasure. I hear from your cousin that you'll be heading back to Papua New Guinea soon."

Abby nodded. "My flight is in six days."

"Then I'll transfer the funds promptly. I hope your visit to the States has been a pleasant one. My best wishes for your trip back home, Ms. Caldwell."

Abby watched Nichols disappear. The man was her closest connection to her grandfather. The thought left her feeling cold. And alone.

Sabin stopped to catch his breath. The trail had grown steadily steeper. He was accustomed to hiking to an altitude of ten thousand feet, but at twelve thousand he was feeling the diminished oxygen. He glanced over his shoulder. Abby had stopped thirty feet back and stood admiring the peaks of the Rockies that surrounded them. She had kept pace the entire way as the trail wound upward through aspen and blue spruce yet didn't seem as winded.

"How do you do this so easily?" he called over to her. "Do you climb mountains in Papua New Guinea?"

She smiled at him and sauntered over. "We do have mountains, but it would take days to hike to them, and they're outside our territory, anyway. I do a lot of hiking in the jungle. Plus, I'm just thrilled to be outside."

They remained mostly silent on the steep incline, taking in the scenery. Occasionally Abby would ask about some noise that Sabin hadn't heard. She seemed not only to hear but also to see things that, despite his best efforts, escaped him. She was completely in her element.

The trail leveled off after twenty minutes. Abby walked up next to him. "Sabin, I wanted to talk about something."

"Sure. Anything."

"I'm thinking about staying."

He turned and faced her, flabbergasted. "Wha—What do you mean? In the States?"

She nodded.

"I really don't think that's a wise decision. You could be in a lot of trouble if you stay. I think the federal agents made that clear."

She breathed deeply. "I know. But the more I've thought about all this, the more I see that these things that are happening have a purpose. God knew I'd face these obstacles."

"Abby, the attorney general isn't fooling around. You could be thrown into prison."

She shifted her weight from one leg to the other. "I realize that. But if God wants to use me there, he'll give me the strength to face it."

He shook his head. "Abby, think this through. Prison may not be as horrible as it once was, but it's no place for a woman like you. You belong in the jungle."

Abby shot him a puzzled look.

"Okay, that came out a bit harsh," he said. "What I mean is, as much as I like having you around, you don't fit here. Right? Isn't that what you said? And with these legal issues, it only makes sense —"

"Sabin, I can't ignore what I'm feeling. When I went to the funeral and heard that young boy —"

"Abby, excuse me for being blunt, but look at your reasons here. An old message from grandparents you never knew? Something an eleven-year-old boy said? Your feelings? Do those justify throwing your life away?"

"I know it sounds foolish. But this isn't something I'm taking lightly, Sabin. I just sense . . . It seems like God is telling me to stay, that he has a purpose for my being here. Like my grandparents said, to restart —"

He shook his head. "Lauren is going to explode when she hears this."

Abby's face hardened. "Is that what you're worried about? Is that why you're anxious to get rid of me? Because of how Lauren will react?"

"She simply made it clear that having you around was making life more difficult."

"Well, I'm sorry I'm so much trouble. I'll just have to find somewhere else to stay."

"Abby, I didn't mean . . ."

She didn't wait for his apology. Instead,

she stepped past him and stormed up the trail.

Sabin hiked after her. It was no use. Abby wouldn't turn around at his calls, and he was falling farther behind every minute. After fifteen minutes of brisk hiking, he settled into a maintainable pace. He'd catch up to her eventually. If she reached the top, she'd have to turn around and come back down.

After an hour of steady hiking, he came upon her. She was sitting on the grass just off the trail, surrounded by a glade of aspen trees.

"Are you okay?" he asked.

"Yes." Her anger seemed to have dissipated, but she was distant.

He caught his breath, then sat beside her. "Look. I'm sorry. I shouldn't have told you what Lauren said. It's just that . . . I've grown to care about you. I don't want to see anything bad happen to you."

Her countenance softened. "I appreciate that, Sabin. And I'm the one who's sorry for the way I responded. It wasn't your fault. I think maybe my own confusion was coming out as frustration toward you."

She looked back down the trail. "I don't know for sure what to do. It's true, what you said about my reasons. And it's not like anyone's interested in what I have to say. But after that funeral, I came away thinking how desperate these people are for the message of Christ. Now this inheritance thing comes up. Maybe God is providing funds for me to stay." She looked at him. "I know this sounds like nonsense to you."

He shook his head. "No, it makes a little sense. What doesn't make sense is why God — if he existed — would want to use you here rather than in Papua New Guinea. No offense. It just seems like you're a better fit there."

She stared at the ground. "I know. It seems that way to me too."

"Any word from God?" Sabin asked two days later.

Abby closed her Bible and watched as he crossed his living room and sat on the couch. He glanced at her Bible. "Well?"

She sighed. "I keep hoping for something in here to jump out at me — some concrete direction. A verse that says, 'Abby, do this next.' " She gave a half smile. "But the Bible doesn't really work that way."

"Maybe I have some direction for you."

Abby straightened up. "You? What is it?"

"Lauren's assistant just forwarded a message to you."

"From who?"

"Inland Tribes."

"Inland Tribes? Another one?"

"I'll retrieve it and let you watch it by yourself. No telling what God may want you to do this time." He grinned warmly at her. She smiled back.

Sabin accessed the message and gave Abby instructions on starting it. "I'll be back in a couple of hours. Good luck at that professor's class, by the way." He walked out the front door.

Abby started the message.

17

I sat at my desk, waiting. What I felt surprised me. Anticipation. When had I last so looked forward to an event?

McMinnus Hall was silent, as usual. People hadn't walked these corridors regularly for years. I heard footsteps far down the hallway from my third-floor office. They grew close, then stopped outside my door. I waited. The inevitable knock came.

"Come in."

The doorknob turned, and the door swung open. In the doorway stood a woman not only out of place but out of time. She was tall — five ten perhaps — and thin. Sinewy was a better description. Her face was weathered beyond her years — thirty-four, was it? — yet attractive, with high cheekbones sloping to a thin chin below a wide mouth and slender nose. I was struck immediately by her hair: long, almost black, perfectly straight.

She wore a red sundress that immediately caught my eye. Whatever her strict moral upbringing, she didn't dress in a Victorian manner. Her skin was dark, expected from life in a tropical climate, but more than just being tanned, she was radiant. I chalked it up to healthy living but couldn't deny it added to her appeal.

"You must be Abby."

"Professor Daniels?"

I stood. "Please, call me Creighton."

I motioned for her to sit in a chair across from my desk and got her a glass of water. We exchanged pleasantries. I told her how much I appreciated her coming to my class. I asked how her time in the States had been so far.

"It's . . ." She seemed to consider how open to be with me. "It's hard. Life here moves so fast. So many things that people try to accomplish each day. Life where I come from is slower."

"Yes, I can imagine." I noticed her looking around my office.

"You have a lot of books."

"A bit old-fashioned, I know. There's nothing here you can't access on the Grid."

"So why do you keep these?"

"I like books. I like the feel of them, the fact that you're holding something solid in your hands, flipping pages. There's intimacy in time spent with a book."

Her eyes met mine for a moment, then continued around the room. "I like books too."

"You had books in the jungle?" I immediately realized that was a stupid question. "Well, of course you had books."

"We had over a hundred books in plastic bags in our hut. I guess you could say those books were my college education."

"So what books did you have?"

"Some Greek classics. Early church fathers. The Reformers. Let's see . . . Shakespeare, Dostoevsky, Darwin —"

"Your parents had you read Darwin?"

"Yes." She paused, tilting her head. "You look surprised."

"I am. That seems unusual for parents like yours."

Abby shrugged. "They wanted me to be well read."

"You had a pretty hearty education — a classical one at that. Unheard of anymore. What did you read for fun?"

"Jane Austen."

"No, I meant children's books."

"Oh . . . I loved Lewis Carroll. The Chronicles of Narnia. The Little House on the Prairie books. I cried when my mom told me the United States wasn't that way anymore."

I laughed. "No, it isn't. Coming to the States, you probably feel as if you've tumbled down the rabbit hole with Alice."

Abby smiled. "Yes, you might say that."

I felt both sorry for her and envious of her. The wonders must never cease for her. But the emotional toll — both the culture shock and the recent loss of her village. I was surprised to find her seemingly coping so well . . . if it was so well. But she struck me as incapable of putting on a facade.

I checked the time. "I promised you a tour of the town. Shall we get going?"

"When did you decide on teaching history as a profession?" Abby asked as we hopped in the car.

"About sixteen."

"That's early to decide something like that, isn't it?"

"Yes. Many people have no idea what direction they'll take even after they get a degree."

We drove through the campus. I could tell she wasn't at ease in a car, but she seemed to bear it gamely.

"What led you toward history?"

"A book on American cultural history."

I instructed the car to go to White Rock Lake, the most scenic part of town. The car changed lanes. Abby grimaced and looked around to make sure we weren't going to hit anything. She settled back.

"Is that normal for teens to read that kind of thing?"

"No, hardly. My dad was a history nut, though, and I guess it rubbed off on me. He gave me Jacob P. Argyle's *Moving the Colossus: The American Cultural Revolution, 1960–2020*. It enthralled me. I saw the movement of history in a whole new way. It wasn't just about presidents and wars and all the headline stuff. It was about shifts in cultural attitudes. That became my passion."

We switched lanes again, and Abby jumped again. I instructed the car to stay in the minimum number of lanes for the remainder of our trip. Abby looked over at me, and our eyes met.

"Thank you," she said, looking relieved.

I smiled. "You're welcome. I'm sorry I didn't think of it earlier."

She relaxed a bit and took in the Dallas landscape. "When did you start teaching?"

"After I finished my PhD in '73 at North Carolina State."

"What brought you here?"

"The teaching style. Very few universities

have direct professor-student interaction. This is one of the few American universities that still offer classrooms, even in VR. For most college curricula, students simply download standardized lectures and watch them whenever they wish. Or they don't even have to watch them. They can access the information anytime they want in fact form and use it in formulating questions for tests."

"You mean formulating answers."

"No, formulating questions. No one tests for answers anymore. No one is expected to retain much knowledge."

She looked surprised. "I thought that's what education was for."

"Not anymore. Facts are available on command. The Grid can stream you to any answers you want. The key to education is in formulating the right questions. Asking questions that will bring you useful answers — that's what we're trying to teach our students."

We stopped at the Dallas Arboretum. Walking among the flowers, I found the heat oppressive, but it didn't seem to bother Abby. I found her even more radiant outdoors, like another light had clicked on inside her. I used a wet cloth, provided by the staff, to wipe sweat off my forehead.

We had, I realized, been talking about me quite a bit. It had been a while since anyone had shown interest in me, and it was unexpectedly flattering. I wanted to hear more about Abby, however. I asked about her life: her family, living in the jungle, her tribe. Everything about her seemed so exotic, so archaic, so innocent, so determined. I couldn't believe I was walking and talking with such a person.

We went to see more sights. The pickings were slim, I had to admit. We drove downtown to the Kennedy assassination museum, a somewhat gruesome staple of the Dallas historical tour. Getting out of the car, Abby noticed a small building across a one-block city park. A wooden cross adorned its top. "What's that?"

"That's a prayer chapel."

Her face lit up. "Really? Do people use it?"

"Not that I know of."

"Oh. So why is it there?"

"A long time ago someone donated that building to the city. They stipulated that it had to remain a prayer chapel. So there it sits. It's pretty, actually."

She stared at it a moment. "Yes, it is."

After the Kennedy museum, we drove past a large park extending along the Trinity

River. It overflowed with at least a thousand people who, admittedly, looked dead, lying on the grass.

"Who are all those people?" Abby asked.

"Homeless VR addicts."

"Homeless . . . what?"

"VR addicts. Most of them are homeless, at any rate. They're people who've become trapped into living their entire lives in VR. Typically, they've lost everything — home, job, family. They were such a problem all over the city that this park was declared a safe haven for them — for anyone just wanting to be in VR."

Abby's brow furrowed. "That's awful to waste your life like that."

I nodded. "Technology. Some people just aren't able to handle it."

We passed the Energy Museum and looped through north Dallas, where we came upon an expansive structure.

"What's that building?"

"It used to be one of the largest churches in the country. A Baptist one." Not that people knew what a Baptist was anymore. "Thirty thousand went to church here at one point."

"What is it now?"

"They converted part of it into an elementary school, part into a middle school. In the U.S. those grades still meet physically, though high schools don't. I'm not sure what they did with the rest of the building."

Her eyes scanned the building's huge expanse. "How long ago?"

"Did it stop being a church?"

She nodded.

"Twenty-five years. Thirty, maybe. It was pretty empty at the end."

She seemed lost in thought for several moments. She finally spoke, almost to herself. "So thirty thousand people came and worshiped God here."

I lifted an old VR helmet off my desk and turned to Abby. "I got this for you. Best I could come up with on short notice. It's kind of old-fashioned, but I figured you wouldn't be hooked up to the Grid. You aren't, are you?"

"Hooked up?"

"Neurally. You aren't, I'm sure."

"But I thought we were going to your classroom."

"We are."

She glanced toward the door of my office. "Where is it?"

"It's . . . in here, sort of." I walked around my desk and handed her the helmet. "My classroom meets in virtual reality. We have to travel there electronically. This headset will get you there. Go ahead and put it over your head."

Abby slid it on. It fit loosely and slid around slightly when she moved her head from side to side.

I helped her adjust the strap, then walked back around to my chair. "Okay. Now, this handset on my desk will take you where we're going. I'll join you there in a moment."

"Will I feel anything?"

"You'll feel like you just walked into a classroom in a real building. That's all."

"Okay." She nodded and the helmet wobbled.

I activated her headset and sent her to my classroom, then followed her. Entering VR, I caught the tail end of an audible gasp and a look of shock on Abby's face. She quickly scanned the classroom as if to spot oncoming predators. She saw me standing close by her and moved a step in my direction.

"Is this it?" she said hesitantly.

"Yes. Welcome to my class. I hope the ride didn't jolt you."

"No. Just surprised me for a moment."

"Yes. Unavoidable."

Abby looked around the classroom once more. Its cushioned seats could accommodate sixty students, with rows stairstepped up to the back of the classroom.

"Good morning, Professor." A young woman from China had appeared on the second row.

"Good morning, Xin."

A young man appeared two seats away from the woman. "Good morning, Professor."

"Hello, Alejandro. How are things in Madrid?"

"Hot. It's our summer warm spell. My family and I are going to the coast this weekend."

"Sounds wonderful."

Abby turned her glance from the student to me. "He's . . . he's in Madrid?"

"Yes." I shook my head. "I'm sorry, Abby. I should have explained this better. My students are scattered all over the world. We meet twice a week in this virtual reality classroom. Physically, they are still in their countries, but neurally they are here."

"But . . . I can't feel the chair I'm sitting on in your office. Is that normal?"

"Yes. Your helmet blocks reception of sensory input from that world and opens you to input from this world."

VR was such a part of daily life I couldn't imagine what it was like to experience it for the first time. I felt terrible that I hadn't adequately prepared her for this experience, but she seemed to be getting her bearings.

"Here." I pointed to a front-row seat near the wall to my right, which she took. "For all practical purposes, this world is just like the real one. When you're ready to go back to the real world, just press this red button on the left side of your helmet. It will take you back."

I half expected her to press the button right then, but she didn't. She just felt it and nodded at me. "What if I need to go to the bathroom?"

"Then you'll have to go back to the physical world. Technology can only do so much," I said, smiling. "Take the headset off when you get there. The bathroom is back down the hall on your left. To return, put the helmet back on and press the green button on the opposite side. It's already programmed to bring you back here."

She nodded again.

"I'm going to lecture for the first half of the class period, then we'll have the Q and A. Just relax and enjoy yourself."

As I said it, it struck me — how could she possibly enjoy herself? I had been so focused on getting her here that I had failed to consider how she might react to my lecture.

It would contradict everything she held most dear. She had trusted me, graciously accepting my invitation to come, and now I was about to attack her entire worldview. Suddenly I felt I was taking advantage of this remarkable woman.

18

I walked behind the podium and smiled gamely at Abby. I had a job to do. Whatever damage I inflicted I'd try to rectify later. In the meantime . . .

"Good morning. We have a special guest with us — Abigail Caldwell. Abby, raise your hand, why don't you?"

Abby raised her hand and looked around at the students, who looked at her with blank faces. An endearing start.

"Abby recently traveled to the United States from Papua New Guinea, where she has lived her entire life with the Inisi tribe. The last half of class we'll ask her questions about her experiences there and her beliefs. I think this will give us some insight into the very topic we'll continue discussing this morning: the decline and disappearance of Christianity in twenty-first-century America."

I forced a smile toward Abby, then purely

out of habit looked down at the visiscreen that scrolled my notes. I had delivered this lecture a dozen times and had it essentially memorized. "The most significant cultural development in the U.S. in the twenty-first century has been the fading of the Christian religion from a dominant force in society to a nonexistent one. Although not founded as a Christian nation per se, the United States was always a deeply religious one, and as recently as 2025, a majority of the population in the United States self-identified as Christians. Today, Christianity has disappeared.

"Many reasons have been proffered for this cultural upheaval. I believe five carry weight as primary explanatory factors. We discussed four of these in our last session, which we will briefly review. Can anyone name the first?"

Petrov raised his hand. "Scientific progress in the last two hundred years."

"Starting with whom?" I asked.

"Darwin."

"Correct. Contradicting as it did the biblical myth of humanity's origin, the theory of evolution was vigorously opposed by Christians from the start. A panoply of attacks against evolution were unleashed for the following century and a half. These usually took some form of the design argument, culminating in a late-twentieth-century movement called . . . what?"

"Intelligent design," answered Fakhri.

"Yes. It sought to establish what?"

"That the apparent design in the universe couldn't have arisen by chance and required an intelligent superdesigner."

"Right. These arguments, however, never gained traction within the mainstream scientific community, and as society itself became more secular, the debate became increasingly irrelevant. The issue was settled — no deity was needed to explain the variety of life on earth. With that, of course, a primary pillar in the belief system of the Christian religion had fallen."

Vinay, a young man from India, raised his hand. "I don't understand why there was such resistance to the idea of evolution in the first place. Weren't people interested in knowing the truth about their existence?"

I stepped from behind the podium. "Excellent question. Only if it didn't contradict their deeply held religious beliefs. You have to understand that religion formed the way people thought about existence. Anything undermining that belief system was rejected out of hand. We still see this, of course, in some less-developed parts of the world today. Fortunately, most of the planet has outgrown the need for such beliefs."

I avoided looking at Abby, not wanting to single her out as the one my statement would pertain to — though that conclusion was perhaps unavoidable.

Xin followed up with a question. "Professor Daniels, isn't it true that developments in cosmology had made the evolution of the whole universe apparent long before the turn of the century?"

"Good point. But whereas evolution played a critical role in the demise of Christianity, the big bang theory did not. Any ideas why not?"

Blank stares greeted me. It was, admittedly, a difficult question. Answering it required the students to think momentarily from a Christian worldview, which was utterly foreign to them. I answered the question myself. "It was because the big bang theory corresponded closely with the biblical account of creation. The Bible says that God created the universe at a specific point in time, starting with light itself. That parallels what the big bang postulates. In fact, its primary opponents were astronomers who disliked the theory's religious implications. They kept trying to prove that the universe itself had no beginning, which eliminated the need for a creator. Of course, we no longer think in those terms."

I glanced at my visiscreen. "Let's get back to the causes of Christianity's decline in twenty-first-century America. Point one was scientific progress. What was the second cause we discussed?"

Xin raised her hand. "The flame-out of the culture war."

I nodded. "Starting in the 1980s, conservative religionists began forcing their own moral agenda upon the rest of the country. This encompassed a wide variety of issues ranging from pregnancy removal to homosexuality to freedom of visual sexual stimulation. Religionists insisted that their views, drawn from the Bible, be the legislative norm for society. This movement reached its zenith politically with the election of a conservative religionist to the presidency. Who was that?"

"George W. Bush," answered Philip.

"Yes. Society grew more secular, however. That affected the culture war in what two ways?"

Sven responded from the back of the room. "Religionists no longer had enough numbers on their side to sway public policy."

"Right. And do you remember the other?"

"The more strident that religionists became in their attempt to control government, the less others were attracted to Christianity. It was seen more as a political movement than a spiritual option."

"Exactly. Jesus was a figure who existed at the political whim of conservative religionists, which of course held no appeal to the secular majority. In their political stridency, religionists ended up shooting themselves in the foot."

I finally looked over at Abby, but I couldn't read her. I forced her out of my mind and glanced at my visiscreen again. "All of this coincided with the third cause of Christianity's decline, which was . . ."

Theresa raised her hand. "The backlash against religion in general due to Islamic fundamentalism."

I nodded. "The massive destruction and loss of life caused by this movement produced a backlash against fundamentalist religious belief in general, which, because of its dogmatism, came to be seen as dangerous to the healthy functioning of a multicultural society. 'Christian' became a byword for 'dogmatic bigot,' and people didn't want to be dogmatic bigots. You may recall that the Tolerance Act of 2036 was passed during the height of this period, reflecting people's increasing unease with fundamentalist religion."

I glanced at Abby again. She sat attentively, without expression. Given her obvious intellectual ability, I hated to lump her in with religious fundamentalists. She couldn't help how she had been raised or the isolation she had endured.

"All right," I continued. "That brings us to our fourth cause, which we started to touch on last time."

Melinda spoke. "The fourth cause was how our understanding of truth and knowledge evolved."

"Correct. Until the fourteenth century, Western culture had a Platonic view of truth. Knowledge comes through philosophy and divine revelation. Truth doesn't have to be investigated; it can simply be deduced. Thomas Aquinas reintroduced the Aristotelian view: knowledge comes through empirical observation of nature. This birthed the scientific method — promoted, ironically, by religionists like Isaac Newton, who believed in a rational Creator who designed a rational, understandable world. Truth became a set of absolute realities that could be uncovered by human investigation.

"In the middle of the twentieth century, this mindset began to crumble. Philosophers rejected the notion of absolute truth altogether. What people considered to be truth was, in fact, socially constructed. No one could interpret reality in a vacuum; everyone constructed what they viewed as reality based on their acceptance or rejection of cultural norms. Claims to truth were, in fact, mere power plays designed to perpetuate the control of those in authority.

"By the turn of this century, the notion of absolute truth was crumbling in the popular culture as well. Polls of Americans in the first decade of the century revealed that most no longer believed in absolute truth or absolute morality.

"This philosophical earthquake proved devastating to the Christian religion. Without a prior cultural presupposition of absolute truth to rely upon, Christians' claims to truth fell on deaf ears. In the absence of absolutes, all that mattered was personal experience. 'Whatever works for you' became the prevailing attitude, whether that be Christianity, New Ageism, or no religion at all. The culture, of course, drifted to no religion at all. If claims to truth are all socially constructed, why bother with a religion that's going to impose demands on you and tell you how to think, as opposed to your making your own free choices in life?"

I paused. "All right. Let's get to the final cause of Christianity's demise in America. I label this one lack of distinctiveness. It may be a little hard for us to get our brains around this, because we don't think in these terms anymore; we don't expect people to be different based on a set of religious views, but stick with me.

"From its outset the Christian religion claimed that the intervention of the deity in people's lives would change people for the better. They would have a different character. They would have different morals. They would think, speak, and behave differently. They called it Christlikeness — 'Christ,' of course, being the title given to Jesus of Nazareth.

"This alleged change in people wasn't caused just by the religious adherent's efforts to be good, although that was certainly emphasized as well. Rather, it was also brought about by the presence of something Christians called the Holy Spirit. This Holy Spirit was supposed to change a person's character so that others could see them living like Jesus.

"This belief worked as long as the vast majority of people in society were professing Christians, because there was no one to compare Christians to. The crack in the foundation appeared when people began abandoning Christianity. When a large segment of society became openly nonreligious, an amazing thing happened — amazing to the religionists, anyway. People discovered that religionists and nonreligionists behaved similarly. Sexual behavior, divorce rates, self-reported levels of honesty — none of these varied significantly between religionists and nonreligionists.

"In short, the supposed influence of the deity to change people wasn't real; it was all a psychological game. As people realized that, more of them concluded, 'Why should I adopt that belief system? It doesn't cause a real change in anyone.'

"So this produced a cascade effect in which the younger generation — people born in the 1980s and after — looked at the older generation and didn't see a difference in their lives. As a result, they didn't follow in the footsteps of their parents' religion. What the religionists didn't know was that, as early as the first decade of this century, only a third of those growing up in Christian homes were, upon reaching adulthood, retaining the faith. And converts to the faith were declining as well.

"The result for American Christianity was cataclysmic. The number of adherents to Christianity spiraled downward as most of each succeeding generation rejected it. By 2030 only half of Americans self-professed as Christians, by 2050 less than a quarter did, and by 2070 fewer than ten percent did. That was its last generation. Throughout the twenty-first century, Christians were trying to pass along their religion to generations who simply didn't buy it."

Anderson raised his hand. "But it seems like Christianity in America was thriving in the early part of the century. I mean, I've passed some huge buildings that seated tens of thousands of religionists back then."

I nodded. "Yes, that's true, but that movement — megachurches, they called them — was the beginning of the end, a last gasp of the Christian religion. Churches got larger in an attempt to appeal more to the masses. They adopted a new marketing strategy, using their gatherings to appeal to outsiders with popular entertainment and practical life helps. But getting back to our main point, that didn't produce a lifestyle any more distinctive than before, so people ended up seeing through it. They decided that if they wanted to be entertained, they might as well stay home and watch their televisions. That, you may recall, used to constitute entertainment."

The class laughed.

I accessed the time on the Grid. "Let's leave it there for today. In our next class we'll examine the flip side of today's topic: the impact of Christianity's demise on the American culture as a whole."

I switched off my visiscreen. "Now, I'm very pleased to be able to spend the rest of today's class time with our special guest, whom you met earlier. Abby —"

I glanced over at Abby's seat.

She was gone.

19

I returned to my office. Abby was sitting in the chair, her helmet on. She gave me an exasperated look. "I'm sorry. I tried to get back to your classroom, and I ended up on a beach instead."

"You what?" I stepped over and looked at the helmet. "Oh. The Grid setting on this thing has been changed. Here." I reset it to my classroom. "This will get you there." I stepped back. "How was the beach?"

Her eyes grew wide. "Unbelievable. I've never been to a beach before."

"You never . . . Well, that's something you'll have to do here, isn't it?"

She smiled. "That would be lovely."

We returned to the class. I pulled a chair up front for Abby to sit on, then turned to the class. "Okay, a slight delay, but everything's fine now. I'll begin with a few questions of my own to better acquaint you with Abby, then we'll get to your questions."

I asked Abby to explain when and why her family went to Papua New Guinea, how they were cut off from outside contact, what work they had done there, and what had happened to precipitate her coming to the States. Talking about her life in the village, she was poised and confident, and I couldn't help but imagine what it would be like to tour the New Guinea interior with Abby as a guide.

She teared up when she spoke about Miraba, her adopted daughter. I waited a few moments, then when it seemed Abby was ready, I invited questions from the students. "Remember, Abby grew up with a very different way of looking at the world than we have — a way much more aligned with the American Christians we were discussing in today's lecture. Let's use our time with her to explore these different ways of viewing the world."

Abby answered several questions about her life in the jungle. Then Molly, an American, raised her hand. "What do you miss most about New Guinea?"

"My daughter, Miraba. I miss her most. My village — the people, I mean. They were family to me. I miss the jungle, its sounds and smells. It can't be described, really. Only experienced." She paused again. "I miss my sense of closeness with God. That was so precious to me. I haven't found that here. I'm not sure anyone can."

A stillness fell over the room. This was just what I had been hoping for — a living bridge not just to another culture but to an entirely different way of thinking about reality, one my students had only read about.

I spoke. "Perhaps Abby's last comment is a good transition from questions about her life in the jungle to questions about her belief system. Remember, that's what the information provided in lectures is for — to help you formulate good questions."

Sven raised his hand. "How can you still believe in Christianity when it's been proven to be false?"

A murmur passed through the room. I could see numerous heads nodding.

Abby shifted forward in her seat. "Why do you think it's been proven false?"

"Everything from science over the last couple of centuries. Evolution. The big bang. The discovery of microbes on Mars. Are you aware of those things?"

Abby smiled. "Well, yes, I am. I can only say that I've never heard of any scientific discoveries that would threaten my faith. As for creation, my faith doesn't rest on how long God took to make everything or how exactly he did it. I believe what God says in Genesis, but I don't believe the first part of Genesis was written to be a scientific account. It was written to a prescientific culture. I do know about prescientific cultures. From my understanding, the big bang corresponds fine with the Genesis creation account. But the Genesis account makes sense to my tribe, the Inisi, in a way the big bang wouldn't. If you gave them an explanation of the big bang, it would make no sense. They have no way to relate to it."

That was a good answer. A very good answer, actually — one I had never considered before.

In the first row, Maya spoke. "Do you really believe that Jesus was God?"

"Yes." Abby seemed completely confident in her answer.

"Do you believe that Jesus rose from the dead?"

"Yes."

"But isn't it incredibly naive, and even dangerous, to base your life on myths?"

Abby didn't seem offended by the question, but as before, she thought through her response. "I'd say this to you. It's not a myth if it actually happened. I believe it did. From what I understand, the historical evidence for Jesus's rising from the dead is quite good."

Melinda, always ready to debate, spoke. "No offense intended, but how can any intelligent person believe the Bible? It was written thousands of years ago in a patriarchal society, pictures God as male, sets up men as dominant over women, advocates slavery, condones violence, and is no better in its moral code than a host of other religions."

Inwardly I smiled. The clash of worldviews.

"I guess . . . I guess I don't see the Bible in that way," Abby said simply.

Melinda shook her head. "Why would you want to adhere to a belief system that says you are inferior to men? What does that say about your own opinion of yourself?"

"I don't see myself as inferior to men. Where does the Bible say that?"

"All through it, doesn't it?"

Abby looked over at me. "Dr. Daniels, we can discuss this issue if the class wants to, but it will take some time, I think."

I looked at the class. "This is a legitimate topic, but I don't want to spend our time debating what the Bible says about one issue."

Kadie raised her hand. "Do you really believe that, if God even existed, there would be only one way to him or her?"

"Yes. Jesus said he was that way."

"But isn't that incredibly exclusivist? How can there be only one way to God? What about all the other ways to God that sincere people have pursued over the centuries?"

Abby paused for a moment. "It seems to me that the real question is how could there be *more* than one way to God. If God actually came to earth in the person of Jesus Christ, then God already planned how he would reconnect with humanity. If that is the way he chose, why would we think some way we developed on our own would work? That would put us in the place of God."

Yuan, one of my brightest students, weighed in. "Don't you think religion is a crutch used by people who need something else to believe in other than themselves? I think everyone here knows that in China, there are still Christians practicing their religion, but it seems obvious to me it's a religion of the uneducated. Intelligent society has moved beyond that now."

"It depends on how you define 'crutch,' I suppose," Abby replied. "If we were created to have a relationship with God, I wouldn't call that a crutch. I'd call it realizing our place in the universe."

Toby spoke. "Don't you think it was kind

of presumptuous for your family to go to a native tribe and try to force your culture and your religion on them, as if you knew what was best for them? Isn't that just cultural hegemony?"

"I regard the Inisi as my culture. I grew up there."

"But how much of their own culture have they lost because of you introducing your outdated Western mindset into their cultural system?"

"Our goal wasn't to introduce Western culture but rather Jesus."

"But isn't the Jesus you introduced simply a construct of Western thought? I mean, what do we really know about the historical Jesus? We don't even know whether he really existed."

"All I can say is . . . I guess I'd just say, I know he did."

That wasn't particularly persuasive.

Kadie asked a question. "Do you think you have simply accepted the beliefs your parents taught you, or do you feel like you have critically examined them for yourself — like, in an objective way?"

"I haven't seriously questioned the truth of Christianity, if that's what you mean. When you've experienced the reality of God as I have . . . maybe instead of questioning you just try to draw near."

"How do you think you've experienced the reality of God?"

"In my heart, all my life."

Adriana commented, "But isn't that completely subjective? I could just as easily say I've experienced a frog in my heart." The class broke into laughter. "I mean, who could dispute me?"

Abby paused again. "Yes, that's true. But a frog can't triumph over evil spirits. Jesus can."

At that statement the students lapsed into a frenzy of head shaking, snickers, guffaws, and comments to neighboring classmates.

I accessed the time and stepped forward. "All right. We've run out of time. Can we give a hand to Ms. Caldwell for taking the time to come to our class?"

The students applauded politely, then vanished back into physical reality one by one until only Abby and a young woman from Dallas on the second row remained with me.

"Miranda, you have a question?"

"Actually, I wanted to ask Abby a personal question." She slipped out of her chair and stepped down to where Abby was standing. "I don't believe in Jesus. I mean, I believe he was a real man, but I don't believe in him like you do."

"I understand," Abby replied.

The girl shifted her feet. "I had a dream the other night, though. In my dream I was asleep, and then I woke up, and Jesus was standing at the foot of my bed. I knew it was him."

"What did he say?"

A tap came. My department chair. I stepped aside and entered his VR office. When I returned a moment later, Miranda was still speaking. "I never pay much attention to my dreams. But this one stuck with me. I suppose I'm asking . . . what do you make of it?"

Abby smiled gently. "I think it means God is speaking to you."

I watched Abby interact with Miranda and marveled. Here was a woman with the inner fortitude to cope with life in an alien culture, to travel across a foreign city, to meet a stranger and follow him into an unreal electronic world, exposing herself to ridicule of her worldview, and yet with the graciousness to respond patiently and kindly to students and to speak tenderly with one who approached her.

I didn't share any of her beliefs. Attached to any other person, in fact, her worldview alone would have repelled me. In her, it didn't. Despite everything I knew to be true about existence, I couldn't help looking past her beliefs and being lured in.

We returned to my office. Abby removed her helmet and stood looking at her surroundings, getting her bearings in physical reality again. "Well, that was interesting. Your students have some strong opinions."

Inwardly I cringed. Did she regret visiting the class? "Were you okay with the questions? I didn't want you to feel attacked." I didn't mention my concerns about my lecture.

She looked thoughtful for a moment, then spoke. "People here are not what I expected. Maybe I didn't know what to expect. You and the class — everyone here in the States, it seems — have such a different mindset than my own. It would be easy to get hung up on one or two hard questions. But I need to keep my eyes on the bigger picture."

The bigger picture. "Abby, there's something I need to show you."

"Something else in town?"

"No, here in my office. It's . . . Maybe you should sit down."

She looked confused. I could only imagine what she must be thinking. What could this professor possibly have to show of such seriousness? Because, I realized, I suddenly sounded that way.

I opened a desk drawer and pulled out my father's storage device. "My father died a few weeks ago. Committed suicide, the police said."

"I'm so sorry."

"I found this at his place."

Her eyes narrowed, focusing on it. "What is it?"

"It's an old electronic storage device. No one uses them anymore."

"What does it do?"

"You can store files on it."

"Files?"

"Like visual messages. That's what's on this one, except the visual portion is corrupt. Only the audio works."

"You need to play a message your father left you?"

"No, I need to play a message someone left my father."

"Why would I need to hear that? Isn't that his private message?"

"Well, yes. But . . . if you hear the message, you'll understand."

I wished I'd had time to develop a better rapport with her, but I didn't know if I'd have another shot at this.

"All right," she finally said.

I played the message. Abby started when she heard the voice but sat silently as she listened. She looked at me when the message ended, her eyes moist.

"Abby, was that your grandfather?"

She hesitated. "Yes, it was," she answered quietly.

"The people your grandfather referred to — Sam and Lauren. Those are your father and his cousin?"

Her brow creased. She seemed surprised that I knew their identity. "Yes. So?"

"Do you know what the message means?"

She sat silently.

"Abby, do you know what it means?"

She opened her mouth as if to say something, then hesitated. She stood up, stared at me a moment, then spoke. "Thank you for inviting me to your class, Professor."

Before I could respond, she turned and walked out the door.

20

I leaned back in my chair and stared at the ceiling. *Now what?*

I had scared her off. Maybe I should have taken things more slowly. Maybe I should have allowed Abby to get to know me over a longer period. Did my lecture offend her? Did the Q and A? Maybe I should have asked only to interview her, avoiding the classroom experience altogether. Maybe . . .

I had to admit the truth. I had no way of knowing how best to secure her cooperation. If I were in her shoes, I'm not sure I'd have trusted me, either. One thing was certain. For the moment I could do nothing. Trying to contact her again too soon would almost certainly be counterproductive. I'd have to wait.

I gathered a few items, returned to my house, and lay on the couch. I decided to put my mind on something else — a small mystery that the afternoon's encounter with

Abby had resurrected. "Alistair."

My Grid interface appeared. "Yes, Creighton."

"I need a search through your historical database." I paused for a second. I felt a bit self-conscious asking this — as if my Grid interface would have any reaction. "I need information on people having dreams about Jesus."

"Records of people dreaming about Jesus extend back to the first century CE. Can you be more specific, Creighton? Are you looking for a specific individual's dream about Jesus?"

"No, not an individual dream at all. I'm looking for groups of people dreaming about Jesus — decent numbers in a contiguous span of time."

"There are numerous such instances recorded in history."

"When's the most recent?"

"The first two decades of this century."

"Who reported having such dreams?"

"Self-reports of many individuals from Islamic countries having dreams of Jesus were recorded on the Internet, usually as part of their accounts of converting to Christianity."

"Weren't conversions to Christianity illegal in most Muslim countries at that time?"

"That is correct."

"So where were these reports coming from?"

"Typically from anonymous sources or from former Muslims who had immigrated to Western nations."

Anonymous sources and immigrants. Only a fraction of total occurrences would be captured from those population samples. "Alistair, can you scan all such reports and tabulate the number of unique cases?"

"That will take some time, Creighton."

"I understand."

At Alistair's calculating speed of more than a hundred exaflops, whenever he said, "That will take some time," I could count on it taking hardly any time.

"The total number of unique cases reported in existing records from 2001 to 2020 was 21,374."

Twenty-one thousand. That was only reported cases. The actual number was likely hundreds of thousands, if not more. No wonder there had been a resurgence of Christianity within Islamic countries early in the century. What could have caused such a phenomenon? And could it possibly be repeating itself in the United States?

Abby smiled when she heard Sabin come down the stairs the next morning. "You slept late," she said as he crossed to the kitchen.

He shook his head. "Up too late working on a program. How did the class go yesterday?"

She shrugged her shoulders. "I wouldn't say the students were very receptive. Except one, perhaps."

Sabin poked his head out from behind the refrigerator door. "Well, one's a start. How was the professor? A nice guy?"

"Yes." She pictured Creighton Daniels talking about his love of history, his eyes crinkling at the corners. "Quite nice. I guess."

"You guess?"

"I just . . . I find it's hard here . . . it's hard to know when to trust someone. I'm used to reading people in the jungle. But doing that here . . ."

"I think you just have to trust your instinct."

She didn't say anything else as she watched him access the Grid.

"Abby, you got your inheritance transfer."

"I did? That's great." She tried to sound excited, but it was just money.

"Yeah." He paused. "But strange."

"What's strange about that? Didn't Mr. Nichols say he'd send it?"

"But your transfer is from a different bank account than Lauren's was."

Abby frowned. "How do you remember that?"

"Memory enhancements, I guess. I don't know. I don't think about it."

"Sabin, does everyone here have brain implants?"

"Yeah, pretty much. I'm sure you could get them too."

She shook her head. "No thanks. I like my brain as it is."

He pulled up a visiscreen. "See — look here." He pointed to two numbers on the screen. "These say your transfer is from an account at First Capital Trust. And . . . actually, I recognize that account."

"Let me guess, memory enhancements?"

He smiled. "It's the same number that transfers money into Lauren's campaign account. Your inheritance came directly from Bryson Nichols."

"Well, wherever it came from, I suppose I'm going to need it. When you get accused of a crime, don't you have to hire a lawyer?"

She shook her head, still not believing that she could be imprisoned for speaking the truth.

"You've decided for certain that you're going to stay?"

"Yes."

"Did God speak to you again?"

Abby didn't think Sabin would understand, but as her host, he was owed as much an explanation as possible. "Sort of. I watched the Inland Tribes message you accessed for me."

"And?"

"It convinced me for certain."

"What was the message?"

"I'm . . ." She hesitated. "I'm not sure I should say."

Abby breathed a sigh of relief. Kate looked normal. It had been a week since their last contact, and in the back of her mind, Abby had worried about her. "Kate! It's so good —"

Kate started to speak. "Hi, you've reached Dr. Kate Sampson at the Meridian Hospital in Lae. I'm not available at the moment. Please leave a message."

Abby's shoulders slumped. She paused a moment, then spoke. "Hi, Kate. This is Abby. A lot has happened since we last talked, and I've changed my plans. I'm staying here in the States for a while. I don't know how long." She shifted nervously on the couch. Speaking to a visiscreen seemed so unnatural. "I was looking forward to seeing you, and I so appreciate your inviting me to stay with you for a while. I hope to take you up on it at some point. In the meantime I'll keep you apprised on what's happening to me here. I hope you're doing okay."

Abby ended the transmission as Sabin had instructed her. She walked up the stairs. Leaving a visual message left her cold. It reinforced what she felt now that she had decided to stay in the States: alone.

She knelt beside her bed. Abby had committed herself to God's plan for her, whatever that might be. At the moment she didn't have a clue. Unfortunately, praying didn't seem to reveal one.

"Did you say hi to Chloe? I think she's still up."

Lauren unzipped her suitcase and removed her makeup bag. "She's in VR. I didn't want to disturb her." She walked past Sabin to the bathroom. "So how's my intrepid cousin been the last few days?"

"She's . . . fine. I took her hiking in

Colorado. How did San Antonio go?"

Lauren took out her makeup remover, dabbed some on a cloth, and wiped her face. "Usual routine. Gave my spiel. They gave their money."

Sabin walked over to the bed, turned down the covers, and slipped inside. "There's no way to skip these fund-raisers, is there?"

She shook her head. "Unfortunately, no. Thanks to Nichols, I don't need their money. But I do need their grass-roots support. Grid campaigning can't replace that." Lauren hung her dress in the closet and put on a nightgown. "So Abby's flying home tomorrow?"

Sabin hesitated. "Actually, Lauren, she's decided to stay."

Lauren turned toward him. He expected her to yell, but instead it looked like she was about to cry. She took a moment to compose herself before speaking. "Sabin, don't you see how difficult this is for me? For us?"

"I know, it's not good for the campaign . . ."

"Not just the campaign. You and me. And probably Chloe too. Right now we don't need any more distractions. We have a lot of stuff to work through and so little time together, and I know that's mostly my fault, but . . ."

"But what?"

She seemed to measure her words. "Did you have anything to do with her decision?"

Sabin sat up against a pillow, feeling defensive. "No. This was her decision. I tried to talk her out of it."

"Apparently not too effectively. Why in God's name is she staying? Doesn't she understand she'll be indicted?"

"*God* is the operative word, actually. She thinks God wants her to stay. Even if it means jail."

"Really? Even if it means jail?" Her face hardened. "The first thing it means is being on the street. I want her out of this house." She walked toward the bedroom door.

"Lauren! You will not kick your cousin out of my house at eleven o'clock at night."

She turned toward him, her eyes steeled. "Then exactly when do you suggest we kick her out of *your* house, Sabin?"

He was silent for a moment. "I'll talk to her in the morning. I'll help her find a place to stay."

"And will you be footing the bill for her as well?"

"No. She has her own money."

A surprised look crossed Lauren's face.

"From where?"

"Ray's inheritance."

She rolled her eyes. "That man will never stop being a thorn in my side." She opened the door and turned back to Sabin. "I'm leaving for Austin tomorrow. I want her out of here by the time I get back on Thursday."

"Do you have a minute?"

Sabin stood in the doorway to Abby's bedroom the next morning. She was lying on the floor, reading the only book she had brought with her to the States other than her Bible: *Revelations of Divine Love* by Julian of Norwich. She had treasured it for years, and the cover was beginning to separate from the binding. She put the book down and straightened up. "Of course."

Sabin sat, shoulders slumped, on the bed. "Abby . . ."

"I know. I heard you and Lauren last night. It's time for me to go."

"I'm sorry."

Abby sighed. The whole situation with Lauren caused a knot in her stomach. "I'm sorry that being here has been a burden. I —"

"No, it's not that. It's just . . ." He glanced at the doorway and lowered his voice. "It's just not a good time for Lauren. Politically,

274

I mean."

"I understand. I didn't mean to come between the two of you. You've been a very gracious host." Sabin had treated her wonderfully, to the point of angering Lauren, and Abby didn't want him to think she took his kindness lightly.

He stared at the floor, looking embarrassed. "You don't have to leave immediately, you know. Just . . . soon. We can make arrangements for you."

"I appreciate that, Sabin. After I leave, I'd like to be able to access the message I got from Inland Tribes. Is that possible?"

"Sure. It's easy. I'll print out some instructions for you."

"Thanks."

Sabin stood, walked to the door, and turned. "Abby, I want you to know that I've enjoyed getting to know you. Having you here has meant a lot to me."

She smiled. "I've enjoyed it too, Sabin. You've been a good friend — and I've really needed one of those."

He stepped down the hall. Abby stood, crossed over to the closet, and pulled out her suitcase.

Lauren could hear the band playing before she entered the joint. She had just finished meeting with the lieutenant governor at the Texas State Capitol — he liked to meet in physical reality — and decided to walk the five blocks down Congress Avenue to the Sixth Street honky-tonk. That was a mistake. By the time she arrived, she was hot, sticky, and annoyed.

Hutch always insisted on meeting here when they were in Austin. "All the pols do," he said. Which was true and another reason she didn't like the place. She had come up through the state legislature herself and knew every player in town. Inevitably, she ran into several of them here, which meant pretending it was great to see them. She was pretending full-time these days — that's what campaigning was, after all.

As usual, Hutch was sitting near the back, nursing a pitcher of beer. She walked past a dozen patrons, smiling and shaking hands before taking a chair across from her mentor. "Hutch, if you make me meet you here one more time . . ."

He laughed. "How's the campaigning, Lauren?" He grasped a glass sitting on the table. "Pour you a beer?"

"No, thank you. And fine — except for reporters who keep asking me questions about a certain religious nut I have for a cousin. And the hundreds of taps we've received at my office regarding her. Not to mention some at our house."

"Your house? They're persistent, aren't they?"

"Sabin tells me Abby has also received several other Grid interview requests."

His eyebrows rose. "And?"

"He's discreetly failed to mention them to her. At least we've contained the damage." Lauren sighed, glanced around the establishment, and then turned back to him. "Hutch, we're in trouble here. I can't make a Senate run with a religious fanatic in my home, especially one who's already gone public. You did take note of the latest polling data, didn't you?"

Hutch finished a sip of beer, smacked his lips, and put his glass down. "Of course. Your lead is down to four points."

"And falling. We have to get that woman back to New Guinea. Once she's gone, she's forgotten. Have you talked to the attorney general about her?"

He shook his head. "Not yet."

Lauren stared at him, incredulous. "Hutch . . . I don't know what to say. Do you want me to win this election, or don't you?"

He leaned back in his chair. "I do, Lauren. I just want to make sure we go about it wisely." He sat silently and poured himself some more beer.

Lauren finally spoke. "You're thinking something."

"Maybe."

"You're scheming something."

"Probably." He smiled. "There are opportunities here that we haven't previously considered. Lauren, our problem isn't Abigail Caldwell. Our problem is your campaign. We need to engage people emotionally. I'm wondering if there's an alternate strategy we could employ regarding your cousin. One that would assure you of a Senate seat."

"It sounds like you've already formulated such a strategy. Or am I giving you too much credit, Hutch?"

He chuckled and raised his glass in salute.

The tap came with the usual warning of sexual explicitness. Damien Cleary responded and found himself in a VR sex club from Manhattan's Upper West Side. He shot a quick glance at the dance floor full of writhing bodies. At least people were clothed in the main room; he knew patrons had to go upstairs for further liaisons. He spotted a man seated at a table and walked toward him. A waitress in fishnet stockings approached him. He waved her off.

"I only have a minute, Lewis," Cleary said to the man.

"We've lost her."

"We've?"

"I've." The man shrugged, not taking his eyes off the dance floor.

"Did she return to New Guinea?"

"I don't know. She hasn't been at the congresswoman's house for two days."

"Did you see her leave?" Cleary asked.

"No."

"Why not?"

"Because I don't have the luxury of keeping twenty-four-hour surveillance. If you recall, I'm handling multiple tasks for you, Cleary. Setting up the insertions takes time."

Cleary swore at himself for not planning ahead better. He knew he'd need more than one primary accomplice to pull off a scheme like this. But there wasn't anyone else he trusted.

He thought for a moment and leaned forward. "All right, very well. Focus on the insertions for now. They're the most important thing. Let's get them in place. I'll see if Nichols can inquire about the girl. She's either back in New Guinea, which solves our problem, or she'll show up on the Grid again. I'll be monitoring."

■ ■ ■ ■

Sabin sat in the alcove at the far end of the upstairs hallway. It was his favorite room in the house, a place where he liked to relax and lapse into VR. That didn't appeal at the moment, however. It was physical reality that concerned him. Abby's physical reality. She had left unannounced three days earlier while he and Lauren were out the morning after their disagreement. They had told her to go, and she had. But he had anticipated helping her and certainly staying in touch. Now she was out there on her own. For Abby, America was a more dangerous jungle than the one in Papua New Guinea. Especially if federal agents came after her.

She wanted to restart Christianity in the States. Where could she possibly go to accomplish that task? Something she had said kept returning to him. The message from Inland Tribes. It had convinced her to stay. She had wanted continued access to it. Did it provide a clue as to her plan? Might it indicate her whereabouts?

He hated the idea of accessing someone else's personal message. But Abby had no idea what she might face out there. She needed someone to keep track of her — if for no other reason than to obtain good legal counsel when the time came.

"Spitfire," he said to his Grid interface, "access a message forwarded to me from Inland Tribes."

"Accessed, Sabin."

"Play the message, please."

Five days. I had waited five days since Abby's abrupt exit from my office. Long enough to let her cool down from whatever prompted her departure. Assuming she would cool down.

I tapped Sabin Wright and waited on a VR mountaintop. He liked mountain hiking, I remembered Abby saying. In a moment he appeared. I reached my hand toward him. "Creighton Daniels. Abby came to my class at the University of the South last week."

"Sabin Wright." He took in the view. "Breathtaking."

I got right to the point. "Abby left my office somewhat . . . well, abruptly, and I was hoping I could speak with her again. It's a matter of some importance."

Sabin shook his head. "I don't know where she is. She packed her stuff and left three days ago without saying where she was going."

I felt a tightening in my stomach. Abby could certainly take care of herself, but I hated the thought of her alone, navigating unfamiliar territory. "Do you think she went back to Papua New Guinea?"

"No, she was planning on staying here."

"With whom?"

"There's no one else she knows, to my knowledge."

She had to have some sort of plan. "Did you check the Grid log?"

"You think maybe she tapped someone?"

"I don't know. Has she watched you do it?"

"Yes. I'll be right back."

He disappeared. I sat down on a large flat rock. The mountain range stretched endlessly before me. Abby would have loved the view, I imagined.

Sabin reappeared. "She tapped for a car."

"Any idea where it was going?"

"No."

I thought for a moment. "I may know where she is."

Sabin returned from the VR mountaintop. The house was quiet. Lauren was returning later that day. Chloe was probably in VR.

"Spitfire . . ."

"Yes, Sabin."

282

"Access for me any information you have on Professor Creighton Daniels of the University of the South."

"I can provide personal information, professional history, professional writings, and recorded presentations."

"Just personal information, including any family history."

Sabin scanned the information. A few minutes later he heard footsteps in the upstairs hallway. He turned to see Chloe in the doorway. "Hey. You look like you just woke up."

"Yeah." She sat in a chair next to him. "I just had a really strange dream."

Three hours later Spitfire alerted him that Lauren had entered the house. He exited VR and walked to the top of the stairs. "Welcome back. How was Austin?"

Lauren glanced up at him from the living room. "Productive."

"How's Hutch doing since the funeral?"

"Fine."

He walked down the stairs. "Speaking of funerals, I was thinking about Ray Caldwell."

She looked at him cautiously. "What for?"

"I don't know. Just thinking about him and Abby. I know she would've liked to meet him."

Lauren walked toward the kitchen but didn't respond.

"I was curious — when was the last time you heard anything from him?"

She hesitated, then reached for the refrigerator door without glancing back. "Why do you ask?"

"It just seemed gracious of him to pass along some money. You two weren't on the best of terms."

She took out some melon and set it on the counter. "A number of years, I imagine."

"I never did ask — how much did Ray leave you?"

She ate a melon square. "Oh, I didn't pay much attention. How much did he leave Abby?"

"About sixty thousand."

"That sounds right. He must have left us all the same." She offered Sabin some melon. He shook his head. "Speaking of Abby," she said, "have you heard from her?"

"Why? Are you suddenly feeling guilty for kicking her out?"

She shot him a look. "No, I'm not feeling guilty. I'm just wondering what you know."

"I haven't heard from her."

She finished another bite. "So what are you working on today?"

"An oceanography training hologram for the National Marine Science Center. I'd better get back to it."

He walked up the stairs and into his alcove, then closed the door behind him. "Spitfire, access all messages to and from Professor Creighton Daniels."

"Accessed."

"And my information request concerning him."

"Accessed."

"Delete all records."

"Permanent deletion or archives?"

"Permanent."

21

"I didn't realize they'd turned this place into a hotel."

Abby froze, then turned toward me. She seemed to relax a bit. I stepped inside the prayer chapel and closed the door behind me.

"How did you know where I was?"

I smiled. "An educated guess. How long have you been here?"

"This is my third day."

"And what are you eating?"

"I packed some food and water in this bag." She pointed to an old backpack.

"That's not going to last much longer. So what have you been doing here?"

"Reading my Bible. Thinking. Praying."

"For three days?"

"Three days pass quickly."

"Not if you're just reading and thinking." I paused. "Abby, I apologize for laying so much on you the other day in my office."

She was silent for a moment. "You're worried about what happened to your father. I want to understand what the message means too."

"It seems we have a common goal."

"Yes, it does."

"Would you . . . would you like to pursue that goal together? Team up?"

I couldn't read her face. She was perfectly still, as if waiting. She gave a slight nod. "Yes, I think I would. I know I can't do it on my own." She rose off her pew and looked toward the front of the chapel. "I didn't tell you something the other day."

"Which is what?"

She turned back to me. "I had already received the same message — or rather, my father did."

"I thought your father was dead."

"The message was forwarded to me."

That meant that nothing in the message's content had surprised her — only my possession of it. She had been contemplating the message's meaning for some time.

"Then it sounds like we are in this together." I looked around at her spread of belongings. "Perhaps we should get you relocated."

She furrowed her brow. "Relocated? Why? What's wrong with this place?"

"Nothing. Except staying here this long is probably trespassing. It's not a homeless shelter." *That could have been worded a bit more delicately.* "It's not a good place to stay, Abby."

She looked at her stuff and back at me. "Where would I go?"

"Well, I'm happy to have you at my place."

She recoiled as if shot.

"You don't want to stay at my place?"

She started to pace the floor, saying nothing.

"Abby, I'd put you up at a hotel, but I can't afford that long term. We don't know how long you'd need to stay."

"I have money."

"Even so, hotels are expensive. You don't want to run through whatever you have by staying at one." Nor did I want her to venture out of my sight at this point.

She shook her head. "Creighton, I can't be at your place."

"Why —" I cut myself short, realizing I might have just stepped into a cultural minefield. "Explain to me what you're thinking."

"You're asking to take me back to your house, aren't you?"

"Yes." We looked at each other. "What does that mean to you?"

"Among the Inisi, a man takes a girl from her parents' hut into his own. Once he does, they are considered married. Prior to that, no woman would enter a man's hut."

"Do you think that's what I'm trying to do?"

"I . . ." She looked perplexed. "That's not how you select mates here. Isn't that correct?"

I nodded.

"So I know you don't want to marry me . . ." She shook her head, clearly embarrassed. "I just don't know exactly what you're suggesting. I guess I'd like it defined first. That might seem silly, but you can't take the village out of the girl overnight."

"Abby, I'm simply offering you a place to stay for the time being because you don't have one. We'd be roommates. Nothing more."

"So that's what you want me to be — your roommate?"

I laughed. "Yes, I suppose. I'm asking you to be my roommate."

"And just to be clear, you don't intend to make me your wife." There was a hint of a smile in her eyes.

"If I ever intended that, I'd talk with you about it first."

She paused and thought for a moment.

"I'm not entirely comfortable with it, but I don't have many options. Do you have plenty of room on the floor?"

"On the floor? For what?"

"For me to sleep."

"No. I mean, yes, I have ample room on the floor. But you can sleep in your own room, in your own bed. I have a guest bedroom."

"I prefer the floor."

"You can sleep in your own room on the floor."

"Okay."

"Okay."

Half an hour later Abby and I sat in my home office and opened her message from Inland Tribes. A man's image appeared on the visiscreen. He was African and sitting behind a desk.

"Abigail, I apologize, but it has come to my attention that Inland Tribes had received one more communication from your grandfather, a message sent several weeks ago. It is addressed to your father, so we thought it appropriate to send it to you. Unfortunately, it wasn't filed in the same place as the previous one, which is why I'm sending this one late. Please contact me if anything in the message requires our attention at Inland

Tribes."

I accessed the attachment. Ray Caldwell appeared on the visiscreen, sitting in an office and wearing a white lab coat. An Andy Warhol print hung on the wall behind him. He leaned toward the screen the moment the message started.

He sounded more worried, more rushed than in the message he'd sent my father. "Sam, I'm not sure how this message is going to get to you. It makes no sense, with your being beyond communication, but for some reason you came to mind. As did your cousin Lauren and my colleague Eli. Perhaps that's God's doing. I've sent them messages as well. I can only hope that you'll shortly emerge from the jungle and that Inland Tribes will be able to get this message to you."

He hurriedly glanced away, then back. "It's been so long since we talked. I'd give you other news, but matters here are urgent, and I need to get this off to you. You know that the country has entered a very dark time — a darkness that has only deepened in the years since you left. I'm loath to be the bearer of such bad news, but I've recently come to understand that life itself may soon be withdrawn, not only from America, but, theoretically, from the entire

291

planet — though surely God will intervene before that. We have enemies that, I realize now, are more insidious than even I could have imagined, for I've been in the very thick of their plot, all the while not knowing it. Their —"

He looked away again. "Someone's at the door. I'll complete this message in a second installment."

The message ended. The screen went blank. I looked again at the message from Inland Tribes. There were no other attachments. There was no second installment.

I looked at Abby. "Similar to the one he sent my dad."

She nodded.

"What do you think it means?"

She glanced to where the visiscreen had been, then back at me. "I'm not sure. He sounds so concerned, but I can't make much sense of it."

"His reference to life itself disappearing . . . Do you know what that may refer to?"

She shrugged, worry clearly etched into her face. "No."

"Well. This may take awhile." I looked at Abby's suitcase still sitting in the entryway. "Why don't we get you settled in? And how about a hot meal?"

She forced a smile. "That sounds good."

I showed Abby to the guest room and let her unpack while I prepared dinner. Thirty minutes later we sat across from each other at my table, steam rising from a bowl of rice and vegetables. I waited while she bowed her head and said what I assumed was a silent prayer.

"Do you always do that at meals?"

She nodded, dishing broccoli and carrots onto my plate.

"Does the Bible tell you to do that?"

"Not in so many words, no. It's just a good way of being thankful. And, Creighton," — her eyes were wide — "this meal is the best I've had since coming to the States. It's like being at home. I'm very thankful for that."

I smiled, and we ate in silence for a few minutes.

"Why don't I start by telling you what I've already done so far?"

I told her about everything that had happened with my father: his suicide, the visual suicide note, the electronic storage device, the file with Ray's message, and my unsuccessful attempts to identify Ray until seeing her on *Global Sunrise*.

"After your appearance on *Global Sunrise*, I researched Ray."

"Do you know how he knew your father?" she asked. "The message suggested they knew each other pretty well."

"I think they became friends in graduate school. Apparently they reconnected recently. I don't know why."

"What else did you find out?"

"Nothing you don't already know. Ray was one of the world's leading neuroscientists. He worked closely with Bryson Nichols for more than two decades. My guess is that he helped develop Nichols's artificial brain, although nothing on the Grid confirms that."

Abby put her fork down. "That's what really bothers me. Why would Poppy — my grandfather — why would he be involved in that?"

"Why wouldn't he? He was an AI scientist."

"He was also a strong Christian." She gestured as if the information should have been common knowledge.

"He was? I'm . . . surprised." Very surprised. How could one of the world's leading neuroscientists possibly believe in God?

She shook her head, her brow furrowed. "Developing artificial brains — it just doesn't seem like something he would do. Not that his faith excluded him from being a scientist. I just expected he would see the issue of artificial life very differently than someone like Bryson Nichols." She shook her head, clearly perplexed. "What else can you tell me about Nichols?"

I gave Abby the condensed version of my research on him. At nineteen he graduated cum laude in electronic engineering from MIT. He started but never completed doctoral work in nanotechnology, because his formal education was interrupted by the first of his inventions: neural implants that enabled direct Grid access. That marked the beginning of Nichols Technology, which within two years held the dominant position in the AI industry. That position was strengthened by NTI's introduction of memory stream technology nine years later.

By twenty-eight Nichols made *Forbes'* list of the four hundred richest Americans, and by thirty-one he was considered one of the world's one hundred richest individuals. He served on the board of several major corporations and started the Foundation for the Advancement of Transhumanity.

Nichols had spent the past twenty years developing the technology to upload the human brain into software form and download it into an operational silicon substrate. It was his crowning achievement, the fulfillment of his stated life goal "to end human death and make possible the transmission of our human-machine civilization to all parts of the universe."

"But how could Nichols's activities threaten life on earth?" Abby asked.

"I don't know. The only thing I can figure is the danger of gray goo."

"Gray goo?"

"That's the name given to a doomsday scenario in which artificial manufacturing cells self-replicate out of control and consume the entire planet's resources within a few days."

"So . . . what does that have to do with Bryson Nichols?"

"Much of NTI's work requires the use of nanites."

Abby looked stunned. "Nanites? Did you say nanites?"

"Yes. That's what the manufacturing cells are called. Why?"

"Creighton, my village was poisoned with nanites."

Abby's revelation immediately transformed the paradigm under which I was operating. "How do you know it was nanites?"

"Because that's what the lab in Papua New Guinea said."

"They told you that?"

"They told my doctor friend, Kate Sampson. She was the one who went back with me to the village."

"Did the lab establish the source of the nanites?"

"I think Kate sent a sample to the States to find that out."

"And what did they find?"

"I don't know. Why? What are you thinking?" Abby looked unnerved.

I got up from the table and started pacing. "Abby, if the village died of nanites, someone had to infect them. That means they were murdered."

She looked down at the table and spoke in a whisper. "I know."

"So let's review. Your grandfather sends a dire warning message to three people, possibly implicating Bryson Nichols. Ray was going to communicate with them further, but he unexpectedly dies. Within two weeks my father, one of the three recipients, is dead. So is your village, where another message was sent. That leaves Lauren Caldwell."

"Who is tied to Nichols."

I stopped pacing and pivoted toward Abby. "She is? How?"

"Nichols funds her political career."

"According to whom?"

297

"Sabin."

I walked slowly back to the table and sat. I stared past her, lost in thought. This was growing more ominous by the minute.

"Creighton, are you . . ." She could barely get the words out. "Are you thinking that my grandfather and your father were murdered?"

I nodded. "I think it's very possible. And if they were . . ." I looked at her. "Abby, who might know you're here?"

22

The wind on the outdoor porch at Sal's Seaside Café had whipped up. It matched Lauren's unsettled feeling as she walked to her mentor's table. She put on her best scowl as she sat. "We're down another three percentage points in two weeks, Hutch."

He pushed a basket of bread and an olive oil dip across to her. "Good to see you too, Lauren."

A waitress placed a beer in front of Hutch and a glass of red wine in front of Lauren.

"I took the liberty of ordering for you." Hutch took a sip of his beer. "So the polls are doing exactly what I expected. Relax. You're not behind. It's June. The election is more than four months out. Have you spoken with Jillian yet?"

"I did. She was lukewarm on the idea. Said the subcommittee members would be none too happy about holding even more hearings before the election."

He popped a piece of oiled bread into his mouth. "She just doesn't see the appeal this would have with voters. Not yet. I figured the members wouldn't be thrilled. But she's the chair. They'll do as she says. The question is, will she do it?"

"I can get her to."

"Good. Give her whatever you have to. Come January, you'll be in the other chamber, anyway."

"There's one more problem. We've lost touch with Abby."

He put his beer down. "Is she still in the country?"

"Sabin thinks so. At least she intended to be."

"Then she'll show up. Maybe I can put a tracer on her."

Lauren leaned forward. "Hutch, I have to admit, I'm still not convinced about the idea. Americans couldn't care less about a group of third-world aborigines."

He nodded. "Of course. But what they *do* care about is solving the planet's problems. Because the planet's problems always become our problems. Energy shortages. Nukes. Pollution of the oceans. Availability of usable water. People have finally come to realize that rising standards of living don't threaten the planet; they save it. It's the most developed countries that can afford to stop polluting, stop overfishing, use energy efficient systems, desalinate water — and stop threatening others with nukes. It's been fifty years, but people are still scared witless about nukes. Through universal dissemination of AI, the third world can close the gap within a generation. Humans can live peacefully and comfortably for the first time in several million years.

"That tribe of your cousin's — they'll be our poster children. You put her before the subcommittee and have her tell a sob story about their lives; she won't even know she's doing it. People will hear about their scarce food, lack of medicine, short life expectancy, infant mortality rate — I bet it's sixty percent. It'll show voters how desperate we are for someone to lead us into a brave new world. And who will do that? You and Nichols. The senator and the innovator/philanthropist, hand in hand. You champion this, and you are the future."

Lauren leaned back in her chair. "You don't think it will turn off voters to have a religionist associated with me? Because it certainly hasn't helped so far."

Hutch folded his hands on the table. "That's because we haven't played it right. We'll paint you as wanting to rescue these people from their Stone Age beliefs. Not in a heavy-handed way, but enough that voters will sympathize with their plight and be drawn to you."

"And you think Abby will cooperate with that?"

He dipped another slice of bread in oil. "Getting her to come to Washington will be like taking candy from a baby. She'll see this as the opportunity of a lifetime — tell a national audience about Jesus. She'll say how great Christianity has been for her tribe, and then we'll hear about how miserable their lives are, and people will see right through the religious charade. They'll see how desperately the lesser-developed world needs to be brought into the twenty-second century."

"And what about Nichols getting his transplant procedure covered by the national health plan?"

"That's all part of the deal. We can't promote worldwide AI unless we take the lead. Nichols will get what he wants. So will we. This thing will start snowballing, and you'll ride it all the way to victory in November. And those aborigines — they'll get their missionary back as fast as you can skin a jack rabbit. Have to keep their needs in mind."

Lauren smiled. "Hutch, I never knew you cared so much about the less fortunate."

He finished his beer. "The less fortunate are the fuel that runs the engine of politics, Ms. Caldwell. Or haven't I taught you that yet?"

My first evening with Abby revealed more surprises. She had received an old message from her grandparents, saying God would use her to reignite Christianity in America. She was committed to that goal. Another small detail: federal agents had told her to leave the country or face indictment.

"Abby!" I got up from the dinner table, walked into the kitchen, stared at the sink, then turned back to her. "I don't know what to say. Your village is murdered. Your grandfather is dead. My father, his friend, allegedly commits suicide. And you have federal agents after you. Has it occurred to you that maybe you *should* leave the country?"

She looked at me for a moment, shaking her head. "And go where? If they came all the way to Papua New Guinea, they can find me if they want to."

"I'm not as worried about them — whoever 'they' are. But the government can track you to my place the moment they want you. That gives us little time."

She drew invisible circles on the table with a spoon. "How would they do that?"

"Your chip."

She looked confused. "What chip?"

"When you arrived in the States, they gave you an electronic chip. They scan everyone at customs, and if you don't have one, they insert one into your upper arm. It's how the government tracks everyone."

"But I didn't go through customs."

"You what?"

"Something about diplomatic . . . Lauren said I didn't need to go through customs."

I returned to the table. "They didn't give you a chip?"

"No."

That changed everything. "So no one knows you're here, except possibly Sabin."

She nodded.

"Abby, how much do you trust him?"

"Quite a bit . . . I think. He's been great to me. Why?"

"Because if he tells Lauren or the federal agents you might be with me . . . How loyal do you think he is to her?"

She shrugged. "They don't seem very happy together. Lauren seems warmer toward Hutch Hardin — that's her political consultant."

"Where did you see them together?"

"At his father's funeral. Anyway, Lauren and Sabin's relationship is certainly not like my parents' marriage."

I smiled. Probably no marriage on the planet had been like her parents' marriage. At least in her eyes. "So how did Sabin feel about your staying in the States?"

"He wasn't too thrilled about it."

That wasn't a good sign.

"But I think he was just worried about me. I don't imagine he'll tell anyone where I am, unless he has to."

"That's a risk we'll have to take. We can't both go traipsing across the country, fleeing people that we don't even know are after us."

Nor would it be wise to add to the appearance I was harboring a fugitive. My conversation with Sabin had one upside: I could claim that someone knew where Abby was — that I wasn't, in fact, hiding her.

I went back to the kitchen and fixed us some coffee. We moved to the living room couch.

"Abby, do you know how your grandfather died?"

She nodded slowly. "From an aneurysm, I was told."

I sipped my coffee. "Let's verify that, shall we? Alistair, please pull up the National

305

Death Registry."

Alistair accessed the Grid site of every death recorded in the country. I looked at Abby. "What was his full name?"

"Raymond Blaine Caldwell."

"Do you have a birth date?"

She shook her head.

"Alistair, try that name."

"A Raymond Blaine Caldwell died April 16, 2088."

"In what location?"

"Silver Springs, Maryland."

"Of what cause?"

"A brain aneurysm."

I thought for a moment.

"What?" Abby asked, touching my hand lightly.

"I'm just surprised that one of the world's leading neuroscientists died of a brain aneurysm."

"What about your father? Did he ever say anything that made you think he might commit suicide?"

"No. But we didn't talk that often. And when we did . . . it was primarily surface level. We were never close. He did leave a suicide message, though."

"Can we see it? I know it's personal, Creighton, and it has to be hard —"

"No, it's fine. Alistair, please pull up my

father's suicide message."

Abby watched it intently. When it ended, she turned to me, her brown eyes full of compassion. "I'm very sorry, Creighton. I know how hard it was when I lost my dad."

"Thanks."

"Do you have brothers or sisters?"

"No, I'm an only child."

"And what about your mother? Were they divorced?" Her voice was tender, as though she was concerned that I was left alone in the world. Just as she was. "They were life partners."

"That phrase confuses me. Does that mean they were supposed to be together for life?"

"No, life partner isn't actually for life. It's a ten-year, renewable commitment. It serves the purpose marriage used to serve, except most people don't renew. My parents hadn't seen each other since I was six."

Her brows furrowed. "So you were your dad's only close family member."

"Yes, you could definitely say that." I paused. "Why?"

"I don't mean to pry, but did it hurt your feelings that your father failed to mention you in his message? That he gave a general farewell? I didn't grow up here, but it seems . . . Well, I don't want to be critical of your father."

I got up and walked to the kitchen. My father's failure to mention me *had* bothered me. Did his own son mean so little to him that he wouldn't address him by name in a suicide message? I poured more coffee and walked back to the living room. I stopped just as I was about to sit down and looked at Abby.

"What is it?" she asked.

"A thought. What if my father's suicide message was faked?"

"Faked? Is that possible?"

I sat next to her. "Absolutely. Someone would only need an electronic image of him and a voice recording. From those, a Grid program could construct a visual message of him saying and doing just about anything."

Abby straightened on the couch. "Creighton, could someone tell if that had been done?"

"A holographic designer could probably determine that — a really good one, I mean. Someone who knew what he was doing."

Abby's eyes widened. "Sabin is a holographic designer."

"He is?" I considered that for a moment, then shook my head. "We can't contact Sabin."

"Why not?"

"Because we don't know if we can trust him, Abby. We're only hoping."

I could see her shoulders slump. "I think we can, but I understand what you're saying." She paused. "What about another designer?"

That thought had already occurred to me. "No, we can't risk that, either. Not yet, anyway. If a designer determined it was a fake, that would make it a homicide. He'd immediately notify the police. At the moment, that's the last thing we want."

23

Having a roommate, especially a beautiful one who slept on the floor, was an adjustment. I hadn't lived with anyone since graduate school, and I was used to my own schedule. My eating and sleeping times were anything but routine, to say nothing of lying on the couch for hours at a time while in VR. Accustomed to wandering around my house in boxers, I now refrained from stepping outside my room half-dressed.

I'm not sure why I assumed going shirtless would offend Abby; after all, the men in her tribe, I imagined, wore virtually nothing. I suppose I considered her mores traditional and therefore modest, regardless of her tribe's customs. I admit, my adjustment to her had to be easier than her adjustment to me. She didn't complain, though.

I was lying on the couch the next morning, checking the Grid, when Abby came bounding down the stairs, sporting a ponytail that gave her a playful look. She sat in my recliner and brushed the bangs out of her eyes.

"You slept late this morning."

"Catching up," she quipped. "The floor in the prayer chapel wasn't the most comfortable."

"I've waited on you to do a tap."

"To Papua New Guinea?"

I shook my head. "It's nighttime there. If we tap late tonight, they'll be back at work. First I want to tap Inland Tribes. Didn't you say it was in Africa?"

"Yes, Cameroon."

"Alistair, in what city is the headquarters for an organization called Inland Tribes?"

"Yaoundé, Cameroon."

"What time is it there?"

"Six fifteen p.m."

"Hmm. Too late, probably. Alistair, please send a message requesting a contact from their office administrator. My moving image." I looked at Abby. "And Abby's. In both of our names, my Grid address."

"Certainly."

Abby leaned forward. "What are we asking?"

"Where the message from Ray to your father was sent from."

"Can someone determine that?"

"Usually, yes."

She thought for a moment. "Where was the message to your father sent from?"

"I don't know. The records were erased from the Grid."

"Is that normal? Who would do that?"

"That's what I'm hoping to find out." I stood up. "Are you ready for breakfast?"

She nodded enthusiastically.

I steered her to the table and reached for plates. "What did you usually have for breakfast in the jungle?"

"We always had kwa and sago."

I looked at her. "Kwa? Sago?"

"Kwa is a breadfruit, and sago is the fruit of sago palms, made into a paste and cooked."

"Hmm. I'm all out of kwa and sago. How about some bagels, cream cheese, and juice?"

"That'll have to do. This time," she warned.

The lighter mood, after the previous night's intense discussion, was welcome. I gathered the food and joined her at the table.

"Abby, have you given more thought to your grandfather's message? What he may have meant?"

"Yes." She had a bite of bagel.

"And?"

"Nothing else beyond what we've said, really. It seems he thought that something he and Nichols were doing threatened life on the planet. Whether all life or just human life, I don't know."

"I'm wondering if we should take a different tack regarding your grandfather. We're trying to trace what happened to him and my father and your village."

"Are you saying we should give up on that?"

I finished a sip of juice. "No. But maybe we should also spend some time focusing on what he said in his message."

"Are you saying you believe it? I thought you didn't."

"It does sound rather apocalyptic, and I tend to dismiss those kinds of things. But he was one of the world's leading neuroscientists. Maybe we've approached his message from the wrong angle. Look at this from Ray's standpoint. What might his words have meant to him?"

"Why would they mean something unique to him?"

"You said Ray was a Christian."

"Yes. So?"

"That means his worldview was different. He thought of things according to a different reality, just like the religionists — sorry, the Christians — I referred to in my lecture. It may be that Ray's message meant something that we haven't caught. Something unique to a biblical worldview. As a historian I have to place myself inside the worldview of others all the time."

"But I'm a Christian too, and I haven't caught anything different in his message."

I shrugged. "I know. Which means this may not get us anywhere. But it's what I'm trained to do. We might as well give it a shot."

"Okay. Where do we start?"

"In Genesis."

My motive, I had to admit, wasn't singular. I wanted to get inside Ray Caldwell's head, understand the message from his point of view, yes. But I wanted to do something more. I wanted to understand Abby.

Truthfully, I liked Abigail Caldwell. She was focused and intelligent and had a unique way of looking at the world that was fascinating. But it was more than that. Despite our substantial cultural differences and belief systems that were worlds apart, I was comfortable around her in a way I hadn't been around a woman in a long time.

There was something else too. I knew that,

sooner or later, I wanted Abby to be freed from the myths that composed her basic worldview, to instead embrace some semblance of enlightened twenty-first-century thought. Not through a frontal assault, but gradually.

It was one thing for the Inisi, who knew nothing of the big bang, evolution, genetics — even electricity, for God's sake — to believe in ancient myths, no matter how preposterous. It was quite another for this intelligent and reasonably educated woman, who was now living in modern society, to hold such beliefs. But talking intelligently with Abby about her faith required being fully informed of her worldview. That meant knowing the Bible, a source I hadn't looked at since college. It was an educational pursuit I knew she would gladly engage in.

We adjourned to my home office. I accessed Alistair in visual mode, something Abby hadn't yet experienced. He appeared in the room's third chair.

"Good morning again, Alistair."

"Good morning, Creighton."

I motioned toward the armchair across from me. "This is Abby."

He looked at her. "Good morning, Abby."

She gave a slight laugh. "Good morning, Alistair."

Alistair looked at me. "Did something humorous happen, Creighton?"

I shook my head. "No, nothing."

I turned to Abby. "Ray used an unusual phrase in his message. Did you notice how he said, 'life may soon be withdrawn'?" He didn't say, 'life may soon be destroyed,' or, 'life may soon be changed.' Instead he said, 'life may soon be withdrawn.' "

"So?"

"So if life is withdrawn, someone has to do the withdrawing. Is that the government? Industry? Bryson Nichols? Is there a plot to end all life? Disrupt our way of life?"

Abby ran her hand through her bangs. "But couldn't you use that phrase if life were being destroyed, especially if you believed in God? If you believe in God's sovereignty, the destruction of life would be, in a sense, God's withdrawing life from the earth."

"Yes, that's possible. It just seems an odd way to phrase it, especially for someone delivering a message in a hurry." I leaned back in my chair. "It might be wise to start by eliminating some possibilities."

She nodded at me. "You're the research expert."

Research expert. That meant I was good at asking Alistair questions. "Alistair, can you find any neuroscientific references containing the two words 'life' and 'withdrawn' or their derivatives?"

. He processed through the Grid for a moment. "There are no such references."

"Can you find any such religious references, including from the biblical text?"

He found four: two Hindu writings, an Egyptian text, and a fourth-century Jewish reference to some obscure extrabiblical story.

We glanced at the writings. None shed much light. "Can you do a general search on all such references across the Grid?"

He found several dozen references. None of them meant much.

I turned to Abby. "Why don't we go ahead and look in the Bible? The phrase Ray used isn't found there verbatim, but reading through it might help us understand what he meant."

For me, reading the Bible was at most a one-day task. For Abby it was at least a multiweek proposition. We didn't have that time, and I didn't have that patience. I suggested that we read several chapters at the beginning together, just to get started. After that I'd continue reading and would bring matters to her attention as I came upon them. She agreed to that plan.

We read the first chapter of Genesis, the primary creation account. I didn't recall that it had a different tone than other creation accounts from the ancient world. Creation was orderly. It started with light — just as the universe actually had — and proceeded through the creation of the earth, the land and seas, lower forms of life, higher forms of life, and finally humans. Creation was the conscious choice of a single Creator, not the whim of one of numerous gods. Humanity was created in God's image — whatever that meant — instead of springing up from the blood of a god shed during a battle with another god. At the very least, whoever wrote the story demonstrated a greater sophistication than the writers of other ancient myths.

Genesis chapter 1 didn't shed any light on our investigation. Neither did Genesis 2. Genesis 3 was another matter. It referred to the original dwelling place of humanity, the mythical Garden of Eden, describing two specific trees there. God forbade eating from the infamous one, the tree of the knowledge of good and evil. If the first two humans, Adam and Eve, ate from it, they would die. That's what allegedly happened. It was the second tree, however, that caught my attention: the tree of life.

"What does this tree of life represent?" I asked Abby.

"What do you mean, 'represent'?"

"What does it stand for, symbolically?"

"It . . . was a tree in the garden. If you ate from it, you would live forever."

I nodded. "I know. That's what the story says. But are you saying that Christians believe this was a literal tree?"

She looked confused. "Of course. What else would it be?"

"Well —" Maybe reading this together wasn't such a good idea after all. "My guess is that most commentators have taken this to be a symbolic representation of something. Alistair . . ."

"Yes, Creighton."

"Historically, how has the tree of life in the third chapter of Genesis been interpreted?"

"I reference 218 different interpretations in the records I have access to."

By that measure it could have meant virtually anything. "Was there a predominant view by the twentieth century?"

"Jewish or Christian?"

"Christian."

"There were two predominant Christian views. The tree was a literal tree with literal fruit that provided the key to everlasting life. Or the tree was a figurative representation of Jesus Christ."

That was interesting. I pressed on. "And what was the primary Jewish view?" I looked at Abby. "Just out of curiosity."

"That the tree represented God's reward for a life lived in obedience to the covenant with God."

I thought for a few moments, then accessed the time on the Grid. I turned to Abby. "Well, that's a start. Why don't we stop there? I'd better go to campus and get a few things done."

"Do you think the tree of life gives any clue to what Poppy was talking about?"

"Not necessarily. But it does tell me several things."

"What?"

"First, in the context of the story, the tree of life represented a choice being presented to humanity — one of two options leading to death or to life. Second, the life offered clearly seems distinct from merely biological life."

"Why do you say that?"

"Because in the story Adam and Eve already had biological life. They were being offered something else. And, third, whatever was being offered to them — whatever this tree of life was — was something external to themselves."

"Because . . . they didn't already have it."

"Correct. It had to be acquired."

"So . . . where does that leave us?"

I stood and smiled. "It leaves us with the rest of the Bible. Hopefully, we won't have to read the whole thing."

That night we stayed up late to tap Kate. The workday had finally begun in Papua New Guinea. I wanted to learn what she had discovered about the source of the nanites. And Abby, who hadn't spoken to her in a week, was worried about her friend.

We tapped Kate's personal office at the hospital. Another woman, a native New Guinean, answered. "Meridian Hospital. May I direct you?"

Abby straightened up on the couch. "Hello. I was trying to reach Dr. Kate Sampson."

The woman's countenance changed; she appeared troubled. "Let me connect you to our chief administrator, Dr. Dobunaba. May I say who is tapping?"

"My name is Abby Caldwell."

The visiscreen went blank. Abby waited a full two minutes before a man's face appeared. "Hello, Ms. Caldwell. I'm Dr. Afa Dobunaba. I understand you are trying to contact Dr. Sampson?"

"Yes. Is she out today?"

"No, Ms. Caldwell." He leaned forward and lowered his voice. "I regret to inform you that Dr. Sampson is no longer with us."

"She left the hospital?"

"No. She . . . she died."

Abby stared at the screen, speechless.

"I'm sorry. Were you a friend of hers?"

"Yes . . . I . . ." Her words became lost in tears.

"I'm so very sorry. Please take your time."

Abby tried to continue the conversation. "How . . . did . . . she die?"

"Dr. Sampson apparently contracted a rare jungle disease."

"Are you sure?" I asked.

He turned to me. "The lab hasn't yet confirmed it, but that's what it appears to be."

"How long ago?"

"How long ago did she die? A week. Memorial services were held for her on Tuesday. Had you known each other a long time?"

Abby blew her nose and gathered herself. "No. Not long. But she was . . . a friend."

I thanked the man, and we ended the connection.

"Creighton, everyone in my life is dying.

Why are they all dying?"

She lay against the couch, head in a pillow. I sat next to her, held her soft hand, and listened to her sobs.

24

I sat on the stairs early the next morning and watched Abby sleep. She was on the couch, an afghan over her legs, her Bible lying next to her. I rose after a few minutes and tried to slip past her into the kitchen. She stirred.

"Good morning."

"Good morning, Creighton."

I sat on the other end of the couch. "I thought you slept in your room last night." I could see dark circles under her eyes.

"I did. But I woke up and came down here to read and pray. I guess . . ." She sat up, pulling her knees to her chest and the afghan around herself. "I fell asleep."

"If you're cold, I can turn up the temperature."

She nodded.

I instructed Alistair to increase the room temperature two degrees. I turned back to her. "How are you feeling — after last night,

I mean?"

"Okay," she answered without much emotion. "Drained. Creighton, what do you think happened to Kate? Do you think she was infected with the same thing my village died of?"

"Nanites aren't contagious. Someone would have had to infect your village and then infect Kate at a later date."

"But that would mean she was murdered too."

We looked at each other in silence. Abby seemed so vulnerable. I wanted to reach out and smooth back her hair but simply spoke. "We don't have any way of knowing at this point. Maybe if we contacted them again, her hospital could give us more information." I thought for a moment. "Didn't you say Kate had a sample of the infectious agent that she sent for analysis?"

"Yes."

"Where did she send it? Do you know?"

She shook her head, furrowing her brow. "A company in the States. Something went wrong with it, though, Kate said. She was going to send another sample."

"Maybe the hospital could track down that information." I glanced at the antique clock on the mantel above my fireplace. "We'll tap them again tonight."

Abby pulled the afghan away from her, leaned forward toward me, held the index finger of her right hand out, and intertwined it with my own. She looked into my eyes. "Thank you, Creighton. For everything."

We ate breakfast in comfortable silence, then I cleared our dishes. I wanted to distract Abby from the weight of her thoughts. "Would you like to do some sightseeing in VR together — maybe at the Grand Canyon?"

"No. Thanks, though. I think maybe I'll spend some time alone." She picked her Bible off the couch and headed toward the stairs.

"I'll be in the study, working," I told her.

"Okay."

I accessed lesson planning for the next term. After ten minutes I gave up. I couldn't concentrate. I was tempted to check on Abby upstairs but decided against it. She was probably reading her Bible. Or praying. Or crying. I wouldn't have blamed her.

"Alistair, please pull up the same version of the Bible." If I couldn't focus on my work, at least I could get something productive done.

I read through Genesis. Through Exodus. Leviticus. Numbers. Deuteronomy. Who named these things? It had been more than twenty years since I had looked at the Bible, and I hadn't read most of it back then. It wasn't as I expected. I thought I remembered the Bible as similar to the Bhagavad-Gita, a Hindu text of philosophical musings on life. The Bible was nothing of the sort.

It was mainly a historical text. After some brief legends concerning creation and the origin and dispersion of humanity, it began detailing the lives and events of the forefathers of what would later be known as the Jewish nation — and, allegedly, God's interaction with them, including the giving of the divine law. The minutiae of the laws amazed me, but as a historian, I was truly astounded by the detail of the history presented. I dismissed the divine intervention material, of course, but had any of this human history actually occurred? Surely the veracity of some of the characters and events had been ascertained.

"Alistair, visual mode." He appeared in a chair across from my desk. "Please access information on the biblical character Abraham. Is there any outside corroboration of his existence?"

"Yes. In 1933 archaeologists led by Sir Leonard Woolley uncovered what they believed to be his residence in Ur, an ancient Chaldean city. The house was constructed of —"

"Pause."

I was getting sidetracked. I needed to restrain my historian impulses. I wasn't examining this material primarily for historical purposes. I was trying to ascertain the mindset of Ray Caldwell. "Alistair, discontinue answer and visual mode."

"As you wish."

I resumed my scan. Reading the Hebrew scriptures, I couldn't help wondering how anyone without neural implants had ever slogged their way through. The level of detail in the historical books was truly mind numbing. Occasionally I stopped to cross-check archaeological findings and the records of nonbiblical historical sources. Much biblical detail couldn't be proven, of course, but I did find its overall framework to be largely verifiable. The royal lineage of Israel and the surrounding nations, the places and dates of events, the outcomes of invasions, the construction of buildings and city fortifications — the biblical account was correct on these details.

After a time, my reading revealed definite patterns in the use of the word *life*. In the first half of the Hebrew scriptures, the word referred almost entirely to biological life —

both humans' and animals'. Starting with the book of Psalms, that changed. The word began to refer not just to physical existence but to the quality of one's experience.

> You will make known to me the path of
> life;
> In Your presence is fullness of joy;
> In Your right hand there are pleasures
> forever. (Psalm 16, verse 11)

> My son . . . keep sound wisdom and
> discretion,
> So they will be life to your soul. (Proverbs,
> chapter 3, verses 21–22)

Unfortunately, this knowledge didn't tell me anything new. We had already surmised that Ray could have been referring to the withdrawal of biological life or an event that might change the quality of life. I wondered if I was wasting my time.

I trudged on through the Hebrew prophets, who to my surprise focused less on prophesying about the future than on declaring divine moral pronouncements. God wasn't pleased with Israel's idolatry, sexual immorality, dishonesty, and oppression of the poor, among other failings. If they kept God's commandments, the Jews were promised life (health and long life expectancy) and prosperity. But they never succeeded in keeping them for long, and they suffered the consequences.

Interestingly, according to the prophets, God would one day do away with this arrangement. In its place he would make a new arrangement with all of humanity, based not on outward adherence to rules but on an inner connection to God himself.

I will give you a new heart and put a new spirit within you; and I will remove the heart of stone from your flesh and give you a heart of flesh. I will put My Spirit within you and cause you to walk in My statutes, and you will be careful to observe My ordinances. (Ezekiel 36:26–27)

Not a bad deal, actually, if you believed in this sort of thing. God himself would move in and do the work for you. If only he would do my lesson prep for the next term.

My growling stomach alerted me to the passage of time. I finished Malachi, the last prophet, stood, and through the glass in my office door saw Abby back on the couch. I walked into the living room.

"You looked engrossed," she commented.

"I was, I guess. Read the rest of the Hebrew scriptures."

"The entire Old Testament? Did you make a list of things to discuss?"

"Unfortunately, no."

Her forehead creased. "Why not?"

"Because there isn't anything to discuss. Life means biological life or quality of life. We already had those as possibilities. After all that research, we're still at square one."

The next morning I grabbed some breakfast, gave Abby a rudimentary lesson on accessing the Grid, and went to campus to get some real work done. When I returned at noon, Abby was sitting on the couch, looking at a visiscreen. I went into the kitchen. She called out to me, "Do you want to tap Kate's hospital?"

"I'm sorry — I should have told you this morning. I left a message for the chief administrator to tap me. They said he's out for a couple of days."

Abby sounded disappointed when she asked, "Can't someone else there help us?"

"It's a small hospital. I think anyone else would automatically refer us to him."

I knew the answer wasn't satisfactory, but I didn't know what else to tell her. She had to be frustrated, waiting to hear developments through me. I fixed some lunch and brought it to the table. "What are you watching on the visiscreen?"

"World news. How can you call this a screen? There's nothing there."

I smiled. "People still call them screens even though they have no physical reality. The images are electronic projections onto a specific spot in the room — two-dimensional holograms, if you will. You know, with neural implants you could watch the news in three dimensions, like everyone else."

"No thanks." She muted the visiscreen, came to the table, and had a bite of her sandwich. "I can't believe they're actually mining on the moon."

"Helium-3. The moon is full of it. They anticipate it will supply most of our energy needs by 2100. That's optimistic, I think. But it has a Gore of zero, so the government is committed to it."

"What's a Gore?"

"It's a pollution measure. Carbon dioxide parts per million divided by BTUs. Basically, how much carbon pollution is generated per unit of energy produced."

She reached into the bag I had put on the table. "Mmm. This is good. Salty. What is it?"

"A potato chip."

She ate half the bag before I finally advised her to desist. "Your stomach's not used to those, you know."

I went upstairs for a few minutes after lunch. When I came down, Abby was lying on the couch, not looking the best.

"How's your stomach?"

"It's been better. I'll survive. I think." She raised herself up. "Creighton, I need to ask you an important question. Will you help me with my task?"

"Your task? What task?"

"Spreading the gospel of Christ here in the States."

I sat in the recliner, considering how to adroitly respond to this request. "Abby, the last thing you want right now is a high profile. Or any profile, for that matter. We're keeping you out of sight, remember?"

She drew her legs into a crisscross pattern on the couch, facing me. "I knew the risk when I decided to stay. I have to do what God is calling me to do."

"Abby, how do you know —" I stopped. Questioning people's most deeply held beliefs was usually pointless. That's why Christianity held on as long as it did. I found myself replying in a way I never thought possible. "How can I help?"

She smiled at me. "Thank you. I know you don't agree with my beliefs, but I appreciate your help. How can I get the message of Jesus out to as many people as possible?"

I looked over at the still-muted visiscreen and sighed. "Well, we can make a visual message to put on the Grid."

"We can? So anyone can see it?"

"Yes. But just because you put something on the Grid, that doesn't mean people are going to access it."

"But some people will?"

"They might."

She nodded, as if accepting the uncertainty. "Then I'll have to leave the results of that to God."

I couldn't help but admire her faith. I wished I had a deity I could trust with endeavors that had no chance of succeeding. "But," I emphasized, "we can't put it up there until it's safe to do so."

She nodded again. "All right. I understand. But we can make it now?"

We spent the afternoon recording Abby as she explained the Christian gospel.

"I'll need to edit this and add background settings behind you," I said when we finished. The whole thing would still look amateurish, but Abby didn't care. Assuming we put it on the Grid, it would get the message out. Not that anyone would be interested.

Abby went upstairs after dinner. I stretched out on the couch and entered a VR program of an old university library, the kind with books. It seemed an appropriate setting to complete my research.

"Alistair, please pull up the New Testament. Same translation."

I had scanned most of the gospel of Matthew when I received a tap from Dr. Dobunaba, the chief administrator at the Meridian Hospital in Papua New Guinea. I called Abby down and put the tap on visiscreen. We all exchanged greetings.

"Dr. Daniels, I'm responding to your inquiry concerning the research conducted by Dr. Sampson." He spoke with a seriousness that didn't bode well. "We tried to access Dr. Sampson's Grid files and discovered that they had been inadvertently erased. The backups on the Grid have been erased as well. I'm very sorry for this unfortunate occurrence and am at a loss to explain it. As for any samples she may have shipped to the United States, I checked with our shipping coordinator. He has no record of such a shipment. It is possible Dr. Sampson may have arranged shipment on her own, although that isn't our standard procedure. I'm sorry not to be of more help."

We thanked him and ended the communication.

I leaned back on the couch. "Deleted. Even the backups." I looked at Abby. "That was no inadvertent occurrence."

25

I got up early the next morning. Abby had been devastated by the news from Papua New Guinea. Not only had Kate Sampson been murdered, but now all information regarding Kate's investigation had been lost, nanite samples included. We would never determine their source.

Under the circumstances I thought it best to keep moving forward. Uncover what we could, and leave behind what was irretrievable. Abby shut herself in her room, uninterested in food or going onto the Grid to research with me. Before she shut the door, she said, "Creighton, what happens if no one ever finds out? No one learns about Kate or Miraba . . . the village?"

I couldn't answer her.

I returned to the VR university library and resumed the accounts of Jesus's life. The gospel of Matthew. Mark. Luke. No clues. Hundreds of stories about Jesus, but no clues about the word *life* or its withdrawal.

I was restless. I got out of my library chair and walked to the student union next door. I picked up a hamburger and chips at the grill, sat at a table in the courtyard, and resumed my reading.

I finally hit something in the fourth sentence of the gospel of John. Jesus, the writer claimed, was himself God. Along with God the Father, he created all things. And then this statement: "In Him was life, and the life was the Light of men."

I put down my burger and read on. The fifth chapter of John, verse 26: "For just as the Father has life in Himself, even so He gave to the Son also to have life in Himself." The sixth chapter, verse 35: "Jesus said to them, 'I am the bread of life.'" Verse 53: "You have no life in yourselves." Verse 57: "He who partakes of Me, he also will live because of Me." Verse 63: "It is the Spirit who gives life." I found this statement of Jesus in chapter 11: "I am the resurrection and the life." And this one in chapter 14: "I am the way, and the truth, and the life."

I stopped scanning. "Abby!" I looked around. All the college students were looking at me. I was still in VR. I reentered physical reality. "Abby!"

"Yes," she answered from upstairs.

"Come down here."

She came to the top of the stairs, her face still swollen from crying. "What is it?"

"I think I found something."

She came down and sat on the couch next to me. I placed my hand on her knee. "How are you?"

"I'll be okay. Thanks."

I pulled up a visiscreen and showed her the passages I had found. "Are you familiar with these?"

"Of course." She looked blank.

"So why didn't you mention them?"

"Because they don't say anything about life being withdrawn."

"No, but they do give us a biblical usage of the word *life*. That's what we're looking for. That's what Ray might have been referring to." I rose and started pacing the floor. "The passages make reference to all three members of the Christian Trinity: the Father, the Son, and the Holy Spirit." I stopped in the middle of the living room floor. "Alistair, are there references in other parts of the New Testament that connect the Christian Trinity to the word *life*?"

"Yes."

"Dictate those passages, please."

"From the first letter of John: 'That which was from the beginning, which we have heard, which we have seen with our eyes, which we have looked at and our hands have touched — this we proclaim concerning the Word of life. The life appeared; we have seen it and testify to it, and we proclaim to you the eternal life, which was with the Father and has appeared to us.' "

"Pause." I turned to Abby. "Isn't this talking about Jesus?"

"Yes."

"But it says 'eternal life.' The Bible says eternal life is a person?"

She shrugged. "I guess I never looked at it that closely."

"Huh." How could Christians miss that? It seemed fairly important. "Alistair, next passage."

"From the first letter of John: 'He who has the Son has the life; he who does not have the Son of God does not have the life.' From Paul's letter to the Romans: 'For the law of the life-giving Spirit in Christ Jesus has set you free from the law of sin and death.' From Paul's letter to the Colossians: 'When Christ, who is our life —' "

"Stop." I looked at Abby again. "There's our answer."

"Which is what?" She wasn't seeing what I was seeing.

"Christian theology asserts that God actually comes to live inside humans, doesn't it? To dwell inside them? Some of these verses, and others I saw, refer to that."

"Of course."

"So don't you see? All these verses identify God himself — the Father, the Son, the Spirit — as life. God is the life. The life comes to live inside humans. Ray spoke of the withdrawal of life."

"So you're saying —"

"That to Ray, the withdrawal of life is the withdrawal of God himself."

She stared at me for a moment. "But why would God withdraw himself from humanity? And what does that have to do with anything Poppy and Bryson Nichols were doing?"

I shrugged. "I don't know. I was hoping you might be able to tell me."

In my campus office I kept mulling over my discovery. God was life itself. Where had I heard that before? Late morning, in the midst of organizing lectures for the next term, it hit me.

"Alistair, access my memory stream, please."

"What date?"

"I'm not sure. A month ago, perhaps."

"Subject?"

341

"Dreams people were having about Jesus. First instance."

"Accessed."

I entered my stream. I was watching a young woman named Jade on CulturePulse.

"I had a dream last night. It was so odd that I accessed my dream bank to check it out. It wasn't like any other dream I've ever had. I was lying in bed asleep, watching myself. You know how you do that in dreams — watch yourself? So I was asleep, and this man suddenly appeared at the foot of my bed. He had long brown hair and was dressed in a white robe. He had sandals on — I'm not sure how I saw that lying down. He reached down and touched me gently on the leg, saying, 'Jade, wake up.' And in my dream I woke up. I looked at him, and I wasn't afraid or even startled. I was just curious why he was there. And he said to me, 'Jade, choose to be joined.' And I asked, 'To what?' He said, 'To life.' And then he walked around the bed and leaned close to my ear and whispered, 'I am the life.' I looked into his eyes, then he disappeared. And I woke up. Does anyone out there know what my dream could mean? I've never been much into analyzing dreams."

The visual ended.
"Alistair, next instance."
I was watching a young man dressed in a beige T-shirt and jeans.

"I had this really weird dream last night. I was sleeping, and this guy came and stood down at the end of my bed. When I woke up, he said, 'Corey, choose to be joined.' I had no idea what that meant. So I said, 'Joined to what?' And he said, 'To life.' Then he whispered, 'I am the life.' "

I scanned several more such visuals. They were all the same. "I am the life." Just as Ray Caldwell had indicated.
A tap from Cameroon interrupted me. I exited my memory stream and answered it. An African man with a broad smile appeared.
"The Lord's blessings from Cameroon, Dr. Daniels."
Did people still speak this way?
"I am Mr. Ogunji," he continued, "the office manager at Inland Tribes."
"Thank you for tapping back."
"We are happy to provide Abigail Caldwell

the information you requested. Our systems manager says that the message was sent by Dr. Ray Caldwell on April 11 from the Massachusetts Center for Mental Health in the USA. Is there anything else we can help you with?"

"No, thank you. That's all we needed."

I leaned back in my chair and sipped my coffee. The Massachusetts Center for Mental Health? What was Ray Caldwell's relationship to that institution? There was one way to find out.

I tapped the center and was sent to the facility's director, Dr. Theodore Brandt. His assistant answered. "Dr. Brandt is unavailable at the moment. Can I help you with anything?"

I left my name and Grid address with a request that Brandt tap me.

"Can I tell him what this regards?"

"Yes. Dr. Raymond Caldwell."

I decided to lunch at home and took the winding road around White Rock Lake toward my place.

"Stop," I instructed my car two miles short of home. "Back up fifty yards."

The vehicle reversed, passing an attractive brunette walking briskly along the lake path. I poked my head out the window when she caught up to the car. "What are you doing out here, Abby?" I spoke more sharply than I'd intended.

She looked over, startled, then her face relaxed. "Hey. I needed to get out for a bit. I've been so cooped up. I hope that's okay."

I sighed. "I don't know. I don't want to be paranoid, but . . ."

"No one knows I'm here except Sabin. He's not going to tell . . . well, the people who killed Kate."

A hint of sadness shadowed her.

"I'm sorry, Abby. I didn't mean to upset you. Look, maybe I'm just being overly cautious, but I don't want anything to happen to you."

She tilted her head and a half smile emerged. "You're worried about me?"

"Well . . . yes. Of course."

There was a pause. Finally Abby spoke. "One loop around the lake? And then I promise — I'll come right back to your place. I'm a fast walker. And I can take care of myself pretty well."

I didn't doubt that at all. "Okay, but if you're not back by two, I'll come looking for you."

"Great." She started to walk away.

"Wait, Abby. I heard from Inland Tribes."

She stopped and looked back at me. "And?"

"Ray sent the message from some mental health center in Massachusetts."

"A mental health center? What was he doing there?"

"I don't know. But I put a tap in to the director to find out."

"Thanks, Creighton."

"Thanks? For what?"

"For all your help. For finding answers. And . . . for worrying about me."

"You're welcome." My throat had gone unexpectedly dry. "Well, I'll see you back at the house, then. Soon."

She resumed her walk. I wondered if I'd done the right thing by letting her go unaccompanied. But what choice did I have? From what I'd observed, her walking was equivalent to my jogging. And I wasn't about to jog the entire lake. I could have driven next to her . . . Very macho.

She'll be fine, I told myself.

I rode home and began a task I had twice promised Abby to do: finishing her evangelism message for the Grid. I sat at my home desk. I needed to insert the backdrops Abby had selected for her presentation. She had jotted her choices down with an old-fashioned pen in a small paper notebook of hers. Where had she left that?

I scanned my study without success, then the living and dining rooms. I walked up the stairs and entered Abby's room. The notebook was sitting on the desk in the far corner of the room. I walked over, sat at the desk, and opened it.

The notebook was a journal. My eyes landed on the first entry, February 17, 2088. Abby had started this volume this year. I flipped toward the back, looking for the list of locations for her Grid message. The list was the last item she had entered. I scanned it, then started to close the notebook, but I noticed my name written at the top of the same page. I read the entry.

. . . none of my beliefs, yet I have found Creighton to be as faithful as a brother, providing me with shelter and food and companionship, even helping me in the mission God has given me (while believing none of it). And though his actions have been brotherly, yet I wonder if his eyes reveal more. If so, why has God given me a man such as this, at a time such as this? I've been cast on him like the waves cast a shipwrecked sailor on the shore.

I glanced toward Abby's bedroom door. The house was quiet. I sat on the edge of the bed and turned to the beginning of the journal.

26

The lake was deserted. Halfway around, Abby stopped to sit on a bench. She leaned her head back, closed her eyes, and prayed silently. The sound of footsteps startled her out of her reverie. A young woman rounded a nearby hedge of bushes. She headed for the bench, then hesitated when she saw Abby.

"I'm sorry if I interrupted you."

Abby sat up straight. "No, not at all. I just sat down for a minute."

"Do you mind if I join you?" the woman asked. "This is the only bench on this side of the lake."

"Please." Abby motioned for her to have a seat. "It sounds like you come here a lot. Beautiful, isn't it?"

"I walk around the lake every day. I never run into anyone this time of year. Everyone's in VR, out of the heat."

"So what brings you out here?" Abby

looked across the lake. A mother duck was leading her ducklings toward them, looking for a handout.

"I like being close to nature. I mean, VR is okay. But I feel . . . a spirit connection when I'm in nature. I feel one with the universe."

The statement caught Abby's attention. "A spirit connection? Do you mean a connection to God? Nature makes me feel that way too."

The woman tossed a small piece of tortilla into the lake; the ducklings dove for it. "I don't really use the word *God*. I'm not even sure what it would mean to me. But if you're equating God with all of existence, then, yes, that's what I feel."

Abby leaned a bit closer. "Well, that's not quite what I mean. By God, I mean the Creator of the universe, a personal spirit being in whom we live and move and have our being, as Paul said."

"Paul who?"

"The apostle Paul."

"Is he a friend of yours?"

"Well, no." Abby smiled. "Not yet, anyway."

How could she bridge the gap between herself and this woman? In the jungle Abby knew what she would say to a person about

Jesus. But here in America . . .

"Where I come from," Abby began, "the people are very much in touch with nature. Their whole lives revolve around nature — what it provides, what it takes away."

The young woman looked at Abby. "That must be amazing. Where are you from?"

"The Papua New Guinea jungle. I miss almost everything about it."

"Why don't you go back?"

"I will. When the time is right. I have something to accomplish here first."

The woman gazed intently at her. "What's that?"

"Well . . . to talk to people like you, I suppose."

I turned in the journal to just after Abby's village died.

May 5. Three days since Kate and I left the village behind. Since I buried Miraba. Miraba! I miss you terribly. I know you are in a better place. But how I wish that you were still in my arms at night, that I could see you running and playing and learning at our table. There is a hole in my heart that will never be filled.

I flipped several pages.

May 13. God, who seemed so close in the village, is distant here in America. I try to draw near to him for a sense of closeness, but it doesn't come. I have no sense of peace here.

May 16. I'm astonished at how Americans can live without God. They go about their lives as if he simply doesn't exist, apparently never giving the least thought to what is behind the universe, what provides ultimate meaning, and what will happen to them when they die. In the jungle, death is a constant. Here, the life span has been lengthened so much that death is infrequent. Still, lives do not last forever. Does no one here contemplate what happens to them after they die? They seem too distracted and entertained to care.

I turned several more pages.

May 21. I took communion tonight with Sabin. I explained the elements to him, and he understood. I think it had meaning for him. Sometimes I wonder if the true meaning sinks into me. I'm genuinely thankful for Christ's sacrifice, for being forgiven, but why can't I live as Jesus lived? I can't even do a simple thing like love Lauren. I don't even want to be around her, let alone share the gospel with her. Being a Christian seemed so much easier in the jungle. I'm feeling less like Jesus than ever. When do I start being more like him?

May 23. People here know how to laugh. I like that about them. When I was growing up, our family loved to laugh. We laughed together in everything. The Inisi did not know how to laugh. When you live in a culture of such fear, laughter is unnatural. My brother and I taught the children to laugh and play. They, in turn, taught the adults. Americans learned to laugh a long time ago, it seems.

Abby was feeling more excited the longer they talked. This woman seemed genuinely interested in what she had to say.

"Nature's Creator is perfectly holy and righteous. He demands that we be perfectly holy and righteous too."

"Why would he do that?" the young woman asked.

"Because God created humans in his image, to have fellowship with him, but he can't be in the presence of sin, so our sin has created a wall between us."

"But there's no reason for walls to exist."

"Well, in this case, our own sin — how we disobeyed God and missed the mark of his perfection — created the wall. And the only way that wall could be removed was for us to be truly forgiven." Abby leaned forward. "Have you ever thought about your need for forgiveness?"

"Forgiveness for what?"

"Your sin."

The woman shrugged. "We are who we are. Nature has placed us here. I'm fulfilling what nature made me to be."

"But don't you . . . haven't you made any wrong choices in life?"

"I've made some decisions that I'd choose differently now. I messed up some relationships. But that's part of life. We have to accept that."

Abby wished she could reach out and physically open the woman's heart to what she was trying to say. "But wouldn't you say your own wrong choices played a part in losing those relationships?"

"Wrong choices?" The woman looked out across the lake. "Hmm . . . I'm not sure I'd call them wrong. Immature, maybe. I might choose more wisely now." She glanced down at her electronic pad. "Oh, I'm meeting someone. I have to go. I've enjoyed talking with you. My name's Britta, by the way."

"I'm Abby."

"If you come again, you can tell me more about your time in the jungle." Britta picked up her stuff and started down the path. She turned and waved as she went.

Abby waved back. She sat, looking down at the bench, discouraged. *I didn't even mention Jesus.*

I turned to the next page in the journal.

May 24. I can't keep pace with life here. Everything flies at me at incredible speed — people, news, entertainment, cars. I can't think. I'm restless, and I can't still my soul. In the jungle we took time to think. I miss the log down by the river where I used to sit every day, watching the water flow by, thinking about God, my life, my place in his grand scheme. Here, there is no such place. I can't block out the assault of messages and images that come every moment of the day. Like an earthquake rippling through the jungle, the intrusions ceaselessly shake me. I don't know how to make them stop or how to be still.

May 27. I have no sense of belonging here. There is no one who can relate to how I live, to how I see life. I'm alone in a vast sea of people. The only people who can understand me are the Inisi. The longer I'm here, the more my life in Papua New Guinea seems to intrude. I can't help seeing the faces of the ones I loved. Of Miraba. I yearn for the way of life that God blessed me with in the jungle.

May 30.

The Lord is my light and my salvation;
Whom shall I fear?
The Lord is the defense of my life;
Whom shall I dread? (Psalm 27:1–2)
  I must fulfill my purpose in this place. I can't run, though everything in me wants to flee. Heavenly Father, you are my light and my strength. I must lean on you every day. You are my protector as long as you give me breath to live upon the earth.

I skipped to after the time Abby moved in with me.

June 9. I'm surprised at the stirrings in me, feelings I've never felt before. I seem attracted to Creighton. I'm confused. Do I feel this way simply because he's taken me in and been protective of me?

God, why have you placed Creighton in my life? Is he here just to help me through this time? To help me accomplish the task you've given me? Or is he more? He isn't even a Christian.

A sound suddenly intruded upon my consciousness. My head jerked toward the door. Someone was at the top of the stairs.

I slipped the journal back onto the desk and turned just as Abby entered the room. I don't know how I could have looked more conspicuous, sitting in her bedroom with nothing in my hands.

"Hi. Uh . . . how was your walk?"

She slumped into a rocking chair. "The walk was good. I had a talk with a young woman. Don't worry. She wasn't with the attorney general's office. At least I hope not . . ."

I smiled — a nervous smile. "What did you talk about?"

She glanced out the window. "Jesus. Well, I tried to talk about Jesus. Never really got around to it, I guess." Her eyes came back to me. "So . . . were you looking for something in here?"

"Yes. I . . . uh . . ." I glanced down at the journal. "I was looking for your notes about the backdrops for your Grid message. I saw you write them in your notebook."

She picked up the journal and sat back in the rocking chair. "This is my journal, actually. Did you find what you needed?"

"No. I mean, yes. I think. Were there just four?"

"Yes, just four." She opened the journal and began leafing through it. "Did you read any of the rest of it?"

"No. Well, not really. I leafed through it, looking for the list. I just saw some dates and that you had written some things."

"Good." She looked up at me. "You're not supposed to read someone's journal, you know."

This was a good time to redirect the conversation. "Did you ever journal in the Inisi language?"

She shook her head. "Their language isn't sophisticated enough."

"What do you mean?"

"They have too few words. Many concepts they have no word for at all."

"Such as?"

She thought for a moment. "Sheep.

358

They've never seen a sheep. I couldn't write, 'We are the sheep of his — God's — pasture' in Inisi. Forgiveness. They have no word for forgiveness."

"But surely they have the concept."

She shook her head again. "Not until my family came."

I looked at her unbelievingly. "What did they have before you showed up?"

"Revenge. The Inisi culture was based entirely on revenge."

"Revenge for what?"

"For everything. Every bad thing that happened, such as sickness or an accident, was blamed on curses from other clans. So the victim would take revenge, killing someone from a rival clan — often children — or else kidnapping a woman for a wife or a child for a slave."

"But wouldn't that clan take counter-revenge?"

"Of course. The cycle never stopped."

"So how often did these things happen — several times a year?"

"Oh no. Several times a month."

"A month?" I couldn't grasp living in such an environment. "So what was this like for the children? Weren't they afraid?"

"Yes, they lived in constant terror. They never strayed from their parents' side. If left alone, they would huddle next to a tree trunk for protection."

"You lived this way for thirty-four years?" How had Abby turned out so relatively normal?

She looked confused for a moment. "No. It all changed when I was little — six or seven."

"What happened?"

"My father taught the Inisi to forgive."

"How?" I couldn't imagine a foreigner being able to pull off such a feat.

"At first he and my mother simply tried to model forgiveness in marriage for the Inisi. Most husbands used to beat their wives when they were unhappy with them. But the turning point came when my father caught the chief's son stealing knives from our house."

"What did the chief do?"

"Nothing. He couldn't do anything. The penalty for stealing was absolute."

"Which was?"

"Death."

"They actually executed thieves?"

"If they were caught. My father was supposed to march the boy — he was eleven — into the village circle and slit his throat in front of them all. So the village gathered, and my father marched him out, knife in hand. No one made a sound. He turned to the boy, knelt down to his level, and said, 'Jesus doesn't hold against you what you did. Neither do I. You may have the knife.' He handed the knife to the boy, stood up, and walked him over to his father. The chief broke down weeping. It was the only time I ever saw him cry. After that, the chief decided he no longer wanted our clan to take revenge on the other clans. He forbade it."

"But the other clans were still murdering and kidnapping."

"Yes, but only for a while. When the other large clan saw what ours was doing, they decided they wanted peace. Eventually the rest of the clans joined as well. After that, warring between the clans stopped. That was . . . twenty-six years ago."

It was an amazing story. If, indeed, her family had influenced the Inisi in such a way, that was an astounding accomplishment. "So if they don't have a word for it, how do the Inisi now say 'forgiveness'?"

Abby smiled, her brown eyes warm. "They say, *'Ée 'e rîløn dsa hua 'i 'ajia' bi jmee júu quia' uu'n.'* "

"Which means what?"

"Like the man from afar who does not take revenge."

■ ■ ■ ■

"Why do you think Poppy sent the message from a mental hospital?" Abby asked again during dinner.

"I don't know. But a possibility occurred to me that I haven't checked into yet." I put my fork down. "Alistair, please display any information that has been released on the development of the artificial brain announced last month by Bryson Nichols."

Alistair displayed pages of information on a visiscreen. We examined them. "Here, look at this." I pointed to a paragraph.

"So?"

"It says that much of the final-stage experimental work was conducted on patients with severe mental illness and advanced brain disease." I turned to Abby. "They had to get those patients from somewhere. Alistair, please do a cross-link of information on Bryson Nichols or NTI and the Massachusetts Center for Mental Health."

More information appeared. I pointed to another place on the screen. "Here's a list of the board of directors of the center." I scanned it. "Look who's on the list."

Abby gasped. "Bryson Nichols."

27

The crowd at the Library was light. Bryson Nichols didn't mind; the paucity of patrons gave him a clear view of an attractive woman in a short black skirt and low-cut blouse sitting in the middle of the room. Per Nichols's programming, the Library mirrored a nineteenth-century English pub in most respects. But not all.

Nichols's view was suddenly obstructed by the less appealing image of Damien Cleary holding a bourbon and soda.

Cleary sat. "I wondered when you were going to tap."

"You were right. She may be putting the pieces together on Ray. Brandt received a tap from some university professor in Dallas asking about him."

"Has he responded?"

Nichols glanced at the woman in the skirt. "Not yet. He will deny Ray's ever having been there, of course."

"And if that doesn't stop the prying?"

Nichols refocused his attention on Cleary. "We may have to take more drastic measures. We'll see. There may yet be an easy way out of this."

Cleary sipped his drink. "You're not still counting on Knowles, are you?"

"I already met with our esteemed attorney general."

"And what did he say about the jungle girl?"

"Off the record, he said Ms. Caldwell's case was on hold."

"Did he say why?"

"He told me to ask Hutch Hardin."

Cleary cleared his throat. "Hutch Hardin? What's his involvement?"

"I don't know. But I'll find out. In the meantime there's a small matter I need you to attend to. A woman we just transplanted voiced the same complaint as Ray did. Said she lost her connection."

"And you want me to take care of her?"

Nichols shook his head, bemused by Cleary's language. "No, I don't want you to 'take care of her.' All you need to do is discredit her on the Grid before she becomes a problem. Something simple, not too harsh. Just so no one will give her a second thought. No need to blow this out of proportion."

Damien Cleary found himself standing next to a lighthouse overlooking the Pacific Ocean. Mountains rose behind him from the rocky coast. Below him, waves crashed on boulders. He spotted Lewis Pape on a sandy beach a hundred feet below and to his right. He hiked down to the shore.

"What are you doing down here?"

Pape looked up at him. "Looking for crabs. I thought we weren't going to meet face to face for a while, even in VR."

"This place is secure. It became necessary."

Pape's eyes scanned the sand. "You want a progress report on the insertions?"

"That's not what I'm here for, but we can start with that."

"I'm almost done with placements in Richmond. I'll start on Annapolis next week. DC after that. What's your progress on the activator?"

"It's ready," Cleary replied. "Just waiting on you." He watched Pape pick a crab off the sand. "Don't those things pinch?"

Pape smiled. "Not if you pull their claws off."

Cleary shook his head. "You are inhumane, Lewis."

"It's VR."

"It's the principle."

"Look who's talking."

Cleary was indignant. "I take no pleasure in causing pain. But when there's a greater purpose . . . well, collateral damage happens."

Pape tossed the crab aside. "Justify all you want — as long as you can sleep at night. I'm just here to follow orders. You said you have another assignment for me."

The tap I awaited came the next morning at my campus office. I answered it and found myself sitting in the VR office of Dr. Theodore Brandt of the Massachusetts Center for Mental Health. We exchanged pleasantries.

"I have checked into your inquiry, Dr. Daniels. We had no association with Dr. Raymond Caldwell, although it would have been our privilege. He was a man of extraordinary abilities. Did you know him personally?"

"No, I didn't. I just know his granddaughter."

He rose from his chair as if to end the conversation. "I'm sure she misses him very much. I'm sorry we couldn't —"

"But how is it that Inland Tribes received

a message from him sent from this location?"

He smiled. "It must be an error on their end, Dr. Daniels. A place like . . . where are they located?"

"Cameroon."

"A place like Cameroon — you know how unreliable the Grid can be in such countries. I checked with our systems people. I assure you, no message was sent from our location to Inland Tribes."

"Abby, I'm back." I closed the front door behind me and draped my sports coat over the stairway banister. "Abby!" I walked into the kitchen. It was empty. I turned and walked into the living room. "Abby?"

I felt a growing unease. I hurried up the stairs to her bedroom. "Abby?" No one was there. I strode down the hall, looking into the master bedroom and bath. They were empty. I walked to the top of the stairs and shouted. "Abby!"

"Yes?" She rounded the corner from the foyer and stood at the bottom of the stairs. "I'm right here."

I let out a huge sigh. "Abby." I walked down the stairs. "Where were you?"

"I went for another walk around the lake. I know . . ." She held up her hand in self-defense. "I know what you're going to say. You were worried about me. But there was no one out there — I only saw two people the whole time. Oh, and one was Britta, the woman I talked to yesterday. We chatted for quite a while."

"Abby, you have to be more careful. Please, at least let me know if you're going somewhere. Can you do that?"

She looked exasperated. "In the jungle we went to visit other villages and didn't tell anyone when we'd be back. We could be gone for three days before they'd send someone looking for us."

"Well, a lot can happen here in three days." *Or three hours.*

She perched on a stool in my kitchen and related to me her conversation with Britta. I ordered Chinese food, after which I told her about the tap from Theodore Brandt. She was disappointed, I could tell.

"What do you think that means?" she asked.

"Given Nichols's association with the center, I assumed Ray was doing testing there for the brain transplant technology. Now . . ."

"Do you think he's telling the truth?" asked Abby.

"Brandt? I think Theodore Brandt probably says what Bryson Nichols wants him to."

"I have a surprise for you tonight," I said after dinner.

Abby's eyes brightened. "What is it?"

"I finished your evangelism message."

"You did?" She gave me a quick hug, her soft ponytail brushing my cheek. "Can we see it now?"

"Absolutely."

We sat down on the couch next to each other. Abby watched in fascination as she presented the gospel of Jesus from four different Alistair-generated locales: Bethlehem, beside the Sea of Galilee, at the place of Jesus's crucifixion, and at his tomb.

"I can't believe how I'm moving around and pointing to things," she said a couple of minutes into it. "I was just sitting on your couch when we recorded this."

It was an amateur production at best — not even Alistair could make Abby look like a professional speaker. But it included what she wanted to communicate. The message ended, and she turned toward me, beaming. "What do you think?"

"No, what do you think?" I didn't want to color her mood with an honest review.

"I think it's perfect." She reached out and

took my right hand in hers, intertwining our index fingers. "Creighton, thanks for doing this for me. I can't tell you how much it means."

I smiled and looked into her eyes. "You're welcome, Abby. I hope it reaches many people."

For her sake, I may have actually meant that.

We retired to our bedrooms early after watching Ray's message one more time. It had become a daily routine, just in case we saw something new.

Sleep came slowly. I twisted and turned, trying to make sense of Ray and the mental hospital. In the dark I kept accessing the time on the Grid: 11:16, 11:34, 11:51, 12:02. No resolution to the mystery presented itself.

I jerked awake to the sensation of someone touching my arm. My head leaped off the pillow, and I sat straight up. "What is it? Alistair, lights."

Every light in the room came on. Abby was sitting next to me on the bed, squinting, her hair mussed. "I'm sorry for waking you, Creighton."

"No," I responded groggily. "You can wake me anytime. What's going on?" I accessed the time: 1:31.

"I want to watch my grandfather's message again." She looked apprehensive, but her words sounded resolute.

"At this time of night?"

A look of disappointment crossed her face. "I'm sorry. I shouldn't have woken you, and I wouldn't have, but . . ."

"No, it's okay. I just . . . Alistair will respond to your voice command, you know."

"I know. I wanted us to watch it together."

"All right. I'll meet you downstairs."

I climbed out of bed, slipped some pants over my boxers, put on a shirt, and walked down to the living room. Alistair accessed the message. Once more Ray Caldwell appeared on the visiscreen, leaving an urgent message for his son.

"Can you stop it — stop it on my grandfather's image, I mean?"

"Alistair, pause message."

Ray's image froze on the screen. Abby looked at it intently. "What is my grandfather wearing?"

I looked at the image. I had never paid much attention to his appearance, only to the bizarre message he had transmitted.

"A lab coat," I replied. "He was a scientist."

"My dad used to have a picture of Poppy

371

at work. He didn't look like that."

"Abby, that picture was how old? Companies do change attire. It's the middle of the night. I'm not sure —"

"There are some words on the clothing."

I looked once again and saw what she was referring to. The lettering was quite small. "Probably his name and title."

"Is there any way to tell for sure? Creighton, please, there's something here. I can feel it."

I sighed. "Alistair, overlay an eight-by-eight grid on this image." A horizontal and vertical grid emerged. The writing was in the lower right side of the image. "Enlarge 6F to full screen."

Ray's image was replaced by the image of a portion of his clothing. On the clothing were printed the words "Massachusetts Center for Mental Health."

And underneath them, a single word: "Patient."

28

The VR tap woke me. I accessed the Grid's time: 6:43 a.m. Who was tapping me this early? I entered VR and found myself sitting in an antique wooden chair in an office on Capitol Hill. On the other side of a large wood desk sat Congresswoman Lauren Caldwell.

"Dr. Daniels. Glad to make your acquaintance." She extended her hand. Still stunned at being with her in VR, I hesitated, then shook it. "I understand Abby has been staying with you. I need to speak with her. Can you connect us?"

"I don't know where you got that idea."

"Dr. Daniels, there's no need to lie. I know she's there. And no, I'm not going to tell you how I know that."

There wasn't any point in denying the truth. Our secret was out. "Just a minute."

"I'll wait."

I reentered physical reality and found

Abby in the kitchen. "Lauren Caldwell wants to talk to you on visiscreen."

Abby's eyes grew wide. "She knows I'm here? How?"

"I don't know."

"Should I speak with her?"

"I guess you don't have much choice. Just . . . be careful what you say."

I connected with Lauren on the visiscreen. Abby sat on the couch. I walked into my study to give them some privacy. They talked for ten minutes. I saw Abby stand and look over at me and concluded they must be finished. I opened the glass door and walked out.

"What did she want?"

"She wants me to come to Washington to testify at a congressional hearing."

"Hearing about what?"

"Artificial intelligence."

"She wants you to testify about artificial intelligence? That doesn't make any sense."

Abby waved an arm in objection. "No, she wants me to talk about life with my tribe."

"What for?"

"Lauren said it's because Bryson Nichols wants to make artificial intelligence available to people groups throughout the lesser-developed world."

"You wouldn't be in favor of that for your

tribe, would you?"

"No, of course not. She said they need to hear both sides."

I thought for a moment. "So what did you tell her?"

"I told her I would."

"Abby!"

"Don't be upset with me, Creighton." She chewed on her lower lip, but her gaze didn't leave my face.

"This is a really bad idea," I said sharply.

"Maybe it is. Or maybe it's just where God wants me to be."

"In harm's way?"

"Well, sometimes God does put his people in harm's way. Lots of Christians have been martyred for following Jesus. Their sacrifice spread the gospel even further."

I shot her a disapproving look.

"I know it doesn't make a whole lot of sense," she said. "At first I told Lauren no. But then I realized it might be God opening a door for me to tell more people about Jesus. This isn't about Lauren. It's about trusting God."

"What about the indictment?" I demanded.

"Lauren said she's taken care of that, for the time being at least."

"Uh-huh. And Nichols?"

"He'll be at the hearings."

"Abby, I don't like this. I don't like it at all. There's no telling what might happen to you up there."

I marched into the kitchen and got a glass of water to simmer down. I breathed deeply and leaned back against the counter, my eyes closed. *There's no telling what might happen to you up there.*

"What are you doing?" Abby asked.

I looked over at her leaning against the entrance to the kitchen. I wanted to protect her, but I couldn't keep her locked up in Dallas. "Thinking."

"About what?"

"I'll let you know in a minute." I closed my eyes again. When I reopened them a minute later, she was still standing there.

"So?" she asked.

"It's time to go."

"Go? Go where?"

"To DC."

"I thought you said that was a bad idea."

"It might be. But staying here is a worse idea. Lauren just tapped for you. If she knows where you are, Nichols probably knows where you are. That means you need to leave. We've done what we can here, anyway. DC is the best place to continue the investigation. NTI is up there. Your grandfather lived there. The mental hospital is in Boston, two hours away. Nichols lives just north of that."

Her eyebrows furrowed. "So what are you saying? I should go knock on Bryson Nichols's door?"

"No. But at least we'll be close if something like that becomes necessary."

"*We'll* be close?"

"You don't think I'd let you go by yourself, do you? Did Lauren say when the hearings are being held?"

"In three weeks. She said she'd be in touch on the details."

"Okay." I stepped past her and headed to the stairs.

"Okay, what?"

"Let's get packed," I answered. "I'll have Alistair get us a flight."

"But, Creighton —"

I stopped at the bottom of the stairs and turned to her.

"Where are we going to stay in Washington?"

"At separate places in case someone tracks me through my chip. They can't track you. We'll rendezvous wherever we need to go."

"Creighton, I . . ."

I took a step toward her, put a hand on her arm, and tried to smile. "We'll be fine.

We're just taking precautions, that's all."

Three hours later I loaded our luggage into the back of the car and climbed in after Abby.

"Destination?" the car asked.

"DFW Airport." I looked at Abby and smiled. "Ready for DC?"

She seemed distracted. "Creighton, the man sitting in the car two houses down — he's watching us. I'm not sure why, but I have this strange feeling I've seen him before."

"Where?"

"I'm . . . I'm not sure."

I resisted the urge to look up the street. "All right. We're bound to be a little paranoid with all that's been going on. But just in case, don't look back. Did he see you looking at him?"

"Maybe. I don't know."

I forced myself to stay calm. "The best thing for us to do, I think, is to get moving. We'll see what he does."

She nodded. I told the vehicle to start toward our destination. I glanced in the rearview mirror. The car remained parked. I breathed more easily. He wasn't following us. We were headed out of town; we could get the police to deal with my place upon our return. I glanced at the mirror again. Two blocks back the vehicle had left curb-side. It *was* following us.

Don't panic, I told myself. *You need to think clearly. Where can we go to escape this guy?*

"New destination," I instructed the car. "Fair Park. Main entrance."

The car took a right at the next street and headed south.

"We're going to a park?" Abby asked.

I glanced over my shoulder at the vehicle trailing us. It was still two blocks behind. Under normal circumstances it wouldn't gain any ground. Vehicles travel at set speeds on given roads. It's impossible to make them go faster, and since the automated system doesn't require stop signs or traffic lights, we wouldn't stop moving unless traffic necessitated it.

"Fair Park is where the State Fair of Texas is every year. It's close to here. Art deco buildings from the Great Depression." I sounded like I was starting a history lecture. I cut it short. "There's an art fair at the park today. Lots of people. Maybe we can lose him."

"Can't we just tap the police?"

"And say what? That a guy in a car is behind us? Maybe he's just going to the art show, for all the police will know."

Five minutes later we were within sight of the Fair Park entrance. Cars lined the street in front of a large open gate.

"All right." I spoke quickly. "When the vehicle stops, jump out and run through the gate. Veer to the left, to the first big building. We'll go through it and out the back. Hopefully we can double back around and get a car before he sees us."

We were within a hundred feet of the entrance. The vehicle slowed. I braced myself for a fast exit and sprint.

"Creighton, no!"

I turned to Abby. "What?"

"You stay with the vehicle. I'll get out. I'll meet you at the airport."

"Are you crazy? Abby, you can't be out there alone."

The vehicle stopped. We had no time for this discussion. She shook her head vehemently. "I'm faster than you are. Than him too, probably. I can do this."

I stared at Abby. This was madness. But it had a certain logic to it. I grabbed her, cupped her face in my hands, and then pushed her toward the door. She sprang out and sprinted through the gate.

"New destination," I instructed. "DFW Airport."

The vehicle pulled away from the curb. I

looked behind me. The other vehicle had stopped. The man dashed after Abby.

Abby bypassed the first building and ran alongside two lengthy pools of water. *I can outrun this guy. All I have to do is keep moving.* She came upon a wide expanse of concrete that ran between the main mall and a large circular building. She glanced behind her. The man was running full speed, passing the end of the first pool. She was perhaps a hundred yards ahead.

She veered to the left and ran across the concrete expanse, dodging people and art exhibits. She glanced again over her shoulder. The man had piled into a group of people, knocking down one woman and several easels. He continued on, undeterred. Her confidence began to fade. She wasn't outdistancing him.

Abby ran past an amphitheater and angled toward a large stadium on her left. She passed between two buildings, scanning for a doorway or hiding place. She had left the art fair crowd behind and was alone in this part of the grounds. *Why did I come this way?*

She glanced over her shoulder. Her pursuer trailed her by less than seventy-five yards. She passed a row of empty concession stands. A building quickly approached on her right. The aquarium. She ran to the main entrance, grabbed the handle of one of the doors, and jerked. It didn't budge.

Abby sprinted with all her might past the building. She could hear the footfalls a short distance behind her. She circled a small pond and neared the entrance to another building. She braced herself for another try at a door. She slowed and grabbed the second door handle as she passed, letting her momentum pull it. It swung open. She lost her balance and broke her fall with her hands. She reached for the door handle again, pulled herself up, and dashed inside.

Racing past dinosaur bones and a mastodon skeleton, she ran down a ramp that switched back in the opposite direction. She grabbed the handrail at the bottom of the ramp and swung herself around to look behind her. Nothing. She stood, trying to quiet her panting enough to listen for her pursuer. *Where is he?*

Abby pushed against the panic that rose within her. She'd had at least some confidence as long as she was in front of her adversary. Now she was cornered. She'd been in this situation several times before in the river. Most of the villagers had. But crocodile behavior was predictable. Here she faced an unknown foe in an unknown environment.

She scanned her surroundings. She was in a museum. Bones and artifacts were scattered across large rooms to her sides, but they were laid on the floor as if ready for scientific examination, not public viewing. She looked down the long hall in front of her. Labels for six rooms on either side extended above her along the hallway. A dozen exhibit rooms. *They might have places to hide.*

At the end of the hall, where it turned left, Abby spotted a lighted red sign that said Exit. Everything within her wanted to sprint to the outside. But she resisted. He might be waiting there, around the corner.

Abby glanced down at her feet. Slowly she removed her right shoe, then her left. She padded eight steps down the hall and slipped inside an exhibit room. It was filled with human jawbones. Samson, the Bible said, had slain Philistines with a jawbone. That didn't seem a suitable weapon for her.

The room had no rear exit. She eyed a door that opened into the hall, twenty or so feet past where she had entered. Using the exhibit rooms' two sets of doors, she could weave her way from room to room while spending minimal time in the open hall.

She'd still have to navigate the corner to get to the exit, but she'd deal with that when she got there.

Abby opened the far door and eyed the corridor, then slipped out and into the next exhibit room. In the back of the room were stacked boxes more than six feet high, draped with large sheets. Between her and the boxes, stretched across the room, lay what appeared to be artifacts of native peoples, not unlike those of her village.

Her observations were cut short by a noise. Abby caught her breath. It came from down the corridor. She let her breath out, inhaled deeply, then held her breath again, listening. Nothing. She crept to the door she had entered and listened again. Footsteps. Moving slowly, then stopping. She placed her head near the door and slowly pressed against it. It opened a crack without making a sound.

Abby peered through the crevice. Near the far end of the hall, the man was holding open a door and scanning the interior of an exhibit room. Her eyes locked on to the free hand that dangled at his side. It held a gun.

She fought the instinct to burst out of the room and flee up the ramp. That could be suicide. She eased away from the door.

The door down the hall closed. Another

one opened. He was checking each room. Soon he would be upon hers.

She glanced at the back of the room once more. She could hide behind the stacked boxes, but that would buy her little time. Surely he would enter the room and check behind them. She was trapped.

She stayed close to the door. She heard footsteps again. He had crossed the hall once more. Seconds later, he crossed back. Two rooms away. She held her breath. She couldn't hear anything more. Had he entered a room? Was this her chance to flee?

She leaned her head against the door and started to press against it. She froze. More steps. He had crossed the hallway again.

Panic rose within her like that of an echidna cornered by village hunters. She needed a weapon. She scanned the room. Items of clothing covered its front half. Pottery and small utensils lay on a table beyond. Her eyes lit up at three small knives. She could use one if she had to. But hand-to-hand combat was her last option.

Abby heard movement. One more room, then he would be upon hers. She edged silently toward the stacked boxes, picking a knife off the table.

She heard the door close across the hall. She slid behind the row of boxes. Her eyes landed upon objects in the back corner that had been blocked from her view. Two small bows, not unlike those she had grown up using in the jungle. And beside them, three arrows.

Abby moved swiftly toward them. She picked up a bow and pulled against the string. It was stiff but could be bent. She grabbed the three arrows and slid back toward the boxes. She knelt and placed the arrows and the knife on the floor. Footsteps approached her door. It opened. He was inside.

Abby took the bow in her left hand. She inched her right hand toward the arrows. Footsteps. He was moving through the room. She picked up an arrow with her first two fingers. With her thumb she eased the knife handle against her right palm. The footsteps stopped. Had he heard her?

It was now or never. Abby raised herself to a stooped position. She swung her right arm over her head and released the knife. It sailed toward the front corner of the room. She heard a *clang,* then a deafening gunshot. In a single motion Abby strung the arrow, pulled back the bow, and sprang from behind the end box into the open. The man whirled toward her. She let loose the arrow. It struck the man in the right thigh just as he pulled the trigger for another shot. Abby felt the bullet whiz by her left ear. The man yelped and fell, the gun dropping from his hand.

Abby ran for the door, bow in hand. She threw it open, swung to the left, and sprinted down the hall and up the ramp. She rounded the switchback and glanced at a group of four middle-aged men in suits running toward her.

"What was that noise?"

"Were those gunshots?"

She dashed past them and made for the exit.

"Hey! You can't take that bow out of here!"

She dropped the bow and flung open the door. She raced around the pond, back across the concrete walkway, down the esplanade, and out the front gate and threw herself into a car.

"Airport."

"Love Field or Dallas/Fort Worth Airport?"

She couldn't remember. But she had to start moving. "Dallas/Fort Worth Airport."

Thirty-two minutes to takeoff. We needed to board in twelve minutes. I glanced to my left and right, taking in as many of Terminal

D's thirty-nine gates as I could see. If Abby was just arriving, we could still make it.

I cursed myself for leaving her alone. What was I thinking? We were safer together. Separated, our plan would break down. Which it had. I had sent her blind into a run for her life.

My mind replayed all the macabre scenarios that were possible at Fair Park. I pictured her shot, bleeding to death in an abandoned building. Tied up in the back of a vehicle, being taken who knows where. Bound and forced to drink brain-eating nanites.

I drove the thoughts out of my mind. Seven minutes.

I heard my name. I turned to the sound. Abby was running toward me, breathing hard. I raced to her. We threw our arms around each other and held on tightly.

"Abby! You're safe."

I ran a hand through her hair and felt something sticky. I pulled my hand back and looked at the blood on my fingers. "Abby!"

I pushed the blood-matted hair away from the left side of her head. The upper tip of her ear was missing. She winced but didn't cry out. "You've been shot!" I glanced around, afraid that we were attracting attention, but no one was looking. I guided us to nearby seats. "Abby, you've been shot."

"I know. It'll be okay. Has it stopped bleeding?"

I pulled her hair away again. "I think so."

"Good." She nodded toward our gate. "Don't we need to get on the plane?"

"Yes. But tell me what happened to the man."

She looked sheepish. "I shot him with an arrow."

I looked at her in disbelief.

"Come on," she said. "I'll tell you more on the plane."

Four hours later the door of a small private jet opened onto a set of tarmac air stairs. Lewis Pape limped up the stairs and boarded. Damien Cleary was standing in the aisle. He looked down at Pape's blood-stained pants leg.

"How did you say you got shot?"

"With an arrow."

Cleary shook his head. "What — did she bring it with her from New Guinea?"

Pape didn't answer. Cleary motioned for him to take one of the posh seats. "Let me get you a towel so you don't bleed all over the plane."

"I've already stopped the bleeding."

Cleary looked at the leg once more. "Right. Well, we can get you some medical attention in DC."

"Why DC?"

"Ms. Caldwell is heading there tonight." He looked Pape in the eye. "I trust you haven't given up on this assignment."

Pape eyed him back without expression. That was all Cleary needed to know.

29

Our plane landed at Washington Reagan. We grabbed our personal items and stepped from the plane onto the jet bridge.

"It's hot here," I commented to Abby. Just like Dallas.

We walked down the jet bridge. I glanced ahead as we rounded a turn. The person standing in the concourse doorway froze me in my tracks.

"Hello, Abigail. Professor."

Abby answered for us. "Lauren. How did you —"

"I take it you decided to come early to do some sightseeing, Professor?" Her eyes bored into mine.

I tried to look as innocent as possible. "Yes. I thought this might be Abby's only chance to do some exploring up here."

"Really? Well, you can fit in plenty of sightseeing in three weeks, can't you?"

"Maybe you can recommend some sights."

I wasn't fooling her a bit.

"Maybe my assistant can. Let's retrieve your luggage, shall we?"

She turned and walked down the concourse. We followed. My mind raced. How did she know we were coming immediately to DC? Was she merely ensuring our safe stay until the hearings, or —

"Fortunately," Lauren said over her shoulder, "we have two spare bedrooms." She glanced at Abby. "Unless you prefer one, that is."

"No," Abby replied quickly. "Two is good."

I spoke. "We didn't intend to impose upon you, Congresswoman."

" 'Lauren' is fine. Shall I call you 'Creighton'?"

I nodded. "We planned to secure our own accommodations. We can still do that if —"

"No. You'll have to stay at my place. That's the deal I made with the attorney general. Abby has permission to remain here until the hearings. After that, she will have to leave the country."

Abby and I looked at each other but kept on walking. We took the escalator down to the baggage claim area and waited silently until our luggage came, then walked toward the airport exit.

"Lauren," I finally said, "Abby needs to see a doctor." I didn't see any choice but to involve her at this point.

"My assistant can make arrangements for that tomorrow."

"No, tonight."

She stopped. "What's the emergency?"

I glanced around to make sure no one was close by. "Abby was shot."

"Shot? With a gun?" She gently grabbed Abby by the shoulders and looked her up and down. "Where? Are you all right?"

Abby pulled back her hair, revealing the wound. I could tell she was surprised by Lauren's sudden concern. "I'm fine. It's just . . . minor."

"It needs to be looked at," Lauren said. "I can contact a doctor who will keep this quiet."

"What do you mean 'keep this quiet'?" I snapped back. It was the wrong tone to use. Lauren glared at me. Clearly, this was a woman unaccustomed to being contradicted.

"Professor, there are ways to handle things in Washington. If a man truly was targeting Abigail, I assume you don't want to publicize her presence here."

"No."

"Then I suggest we proceed as I recommended."

We followed her outside the terminal.

"Where did this happen?"

"In Fair Park in Dallas," I answered.

"Do the police know about it?"

Lauren motioned toward her car. I put our luggage in the back, and we slid in. The car pulled away from the curb.

"We haven't told anyone," I answered. "But certainly they must know. There were people in the building."

"Then they've informed the police, and the man has been apprehended. I'll have my assistant verify that. For now, let's get Abby looked at. Excuse me a moment."

She went into VR. Abby leaned close to me. "Creighton, how did she know?" she whispered.

"I don't know," I whispered back. "Sabin must have alerted her."

Abby glanced at Lauren in VR, then back at me. "Is this okay, going along with her?"

That was a good question. At this point I had no idea who could be trusted. "It'll have to be. I don't think we have any choice. Not at the moment."

I reached out and squeezed Abby's hand. A tap interrupted us. "Abby, excuse me a second."

I found myself sitting in a VR living room

a few feet away from Sabin. He appeared worried. "Creighton, Lauren is heading back to DC. She thinks Abby is on her way there. I'm . . . I'm not sure what her plans are. I know she contacted Abby to —"

"Yes, we're in a car with her at this moment."

"You are? She met you at the airport?"

"Did you tell her Abby was at my place?"

He looked taken aback. "No. Why would I do that?"

"Sabin, Abby was attacked in Dallas. A man tried to shoot her."

"No! Is she okay?"

"She's fine. A slight wound on her ear. Do you . . ." To what degree was it prudent to take him into our confidence? He was, after all, Lauren's partner. But he seemed to be telling the truth. "Do you think Lauren informed Nichols where Abby was?"

He shook his head. "No, I don't think she knew. She kept asking me if I knew. It's more likely she found out from Nichols. Creighton, I wouldn't trust him."

That was an understatement.

He continued, "I saw the message Ray Caldwell sent Abby's father. Something's going on . . ."

"Yes, we know. You . . . I'm sorry to ask

this. You don't think Lauren's involved, do you?"

He sighed. "I don't know what to think. I hate to say this, but I'd be circumspect with her. She's told me at least two lies recently."

"About what?"

"She said she hadn't heard from Ray Caldwell in years, but apparently she received the same message as Abby's father. That was just weeks ago. Then she told me her inheritance from Ray was the same as Abby's, but that can't be. Abby would have received her father's share too."

I checked the Grid time. "I'd better get back. I don't want to look suspicious."

We rose and shook hands.

"Creighton —"

I waited for him to continue.

"I'm not saying Lauren has any ill intent. Campaigning . . . it makes Lauren unpredictable. She may just be keeping quiet about something for political reasons. Don't tell her we've been in touch. Maybe she and I . . . Well, who knows."

I nodded. "I appreciate your help."

I exited VR. Lauren looked over at me when I reemerged but said nothing.

It was 9:15 p.m. when we walked into the office of Lauren's physician. The facility was deserted save for the four of us. While the doctor treated Abby's ear, Lauren motioned me into the hallway, closing the door behind us.

"Creighton, let me make something clear. Abigail Caldwell remains in the country, unindicted, because of my intervention on her behalf. Her legal issues aren't over; the AG's office is simply taking time for due diligence in regard to her case. I've done this as a personal favor to Abigail. During this delay I'm providing her the opportunity to speak to the U.S. Congress on behalf of her people and disadvantaged people everywhere. Maintaining a low profile is essential to keeping her in the country during this brief respite from prosecution. Publicity concerning a shooting in Dallas will bring her back to the public's attention and put political pressure on the attorney general to indict her. Do you understand?"

I nodded.

"As unfortunate as this incident is," she commented, "most likely this man was simply a lunatic who saw Abigail on *Global Sunrise,* objected to her views, and chose to respond with violence. Assuming he's been apprehended, the danger has passed."

I didn't know how to respond without revealing much more than I desired.

She went on. "I'll contact the Dallas County DA myself. No doubt he will want a statement at some point from Abigail. Concerning your stay here, I'm confident of Abigail's safety at my residence. But to put her at ease, I'll have DC police posted outside my house for the duration of your stay."

"Thank you." That, at least, was a positive development.

The door to the examination room opened, and Abby appeared. I stepped toward her. "What did he say?"

"He said I lost the top of my ear." She smiled. "It'll be fine. I just need to keep it clean and dry for a few days after I wash this blood out of my hair." She turned to Lauren. "I'm so sorry for putting you through all this trouble."

"That's quite all right, dear. That's what family is for."

We went to Lauren's. Abby was free to move about DC as long as she returned to Lauren's at night. Lauren would be returning to Texas for several days.

I carried our belongings upstairs to the guest bedrooms. Abby followed. I closed the door behind us as we entered her room. She surprised me when she turned, put her arms around me, and pulled me close. I could hear my heart pound in my ears.

"Creighton, are we going to be safe here?"

"I think so." I didn't sound too convincing, even to myself, but I stroked her hair, reassuring her.

She kept her head on my shoulder. "Three weeks. We may only have three weeks up here together."

"I know."

"Is that enough time?"

"I'm not sure."

She pulled away slightly and looked at me. "Did you talk more with Lauren?"

I related to her most of what Lauren had said in the hallway.

"Do you think we can trust her?" Abby asked.

"I think we need to be careful. She may genuinely be trying to help us out — and herself as well. Or . . ."

"Or what?"

I shook my head. "I don't know. I can't read her. Sabin suggested that her judgment might not be the clearest right now."

Abby hugged me again. "Let's hope there is no *or.*"

We unpacked Abby's suitcase. I stepped into the hallway as she changed into a pajama top and pants, then we walked to the hallway bathroom. At the sink I ran soapy hands through her hair as she kept her ear covered with gauze. Blood-tinged water trickled down the drain until her hair was clean. I dried it with a towel and silently combed it. I wished I could remain there for hours, drawing the comb through her straight black locks.

"All done," I finally said. She turned and placed her arms around me again and squeezed. I held her for a long time.

"Thanks for being here for me," she whispered.

She looked at me, rose up on her toes, and pressed her warm lips against mine. We leaned back into the counter, kissing as she slid herself onto the countertop. She locked her hands behind my neck as I caressed her. After several minutes she pulled back and looked into my eyes. She spoke softly. "Creighton, I . . ."

"What?" I whispered.

"I have . . . I just want you to know how much you've meant to me."

I leaned forward and kissed her again, hoping to convey that I shared her feelings. When our lips finally parted, she glanced into the hallway. "Well, we'd . . . I'd . . . better get to sleep."

I walked her to her room, then ran my hand gently through her hair. She moved her lips to mine once more and kissed me gently.

"Good night, Creighton."

"Good night."

30

Lauren finally left the house at noon. I glanced out the window as she did; a DC police car was parked outside. I pulled up a visiscreen in Abby's room, and we tapped Sabin.

"Are you both all right?" His concern seemed genuine.

"We're fine," Abby said, reassurance in her voice. "Sabin, Lauren insisted that we stay at your place. She has police outside."

He nodded. "I think you're safe there. The last thing Lauren would want is an incident at the house."

"Sabin," I asked, "do you think Lauren suspects anything about your contact with us?"

"No. As Abby can attest to, Lauren and I aren't in the best place these days. Given the amount of time we spend apart, keeping secrets is fairly easy."

I thought for a moment. "Can I ask you

to keep one more?"

"Sure."

"My father's suicide message. I need to know if it's authentic."

We ended the tap. I looked at Abby. "I'm going out on a limb here, trusting Sabin."

"He'll come through." She stood up. "So . . . what can we accomplish on a Sunday?"

"We can relax."

"Relax? Creighton, we have so much to do, so much we need to find out." She started pacing the room. "Can't we make it to Boston, to the mental hospital, before the end of the day?"

"No."

"Why not?" She stopped and put her hands on her hips.

I had to choke back a laugh at her expression. "Because the people we want to see won't be there today. Abby, it's okay to take half a day to regroup. I have an idea. We're in DC — let's do some sightseeing."

A frown indicated what she thought of that proposal. "Sightseeing? Do you think that's safe?"

I chuckled. "Now look who's worried about safety." I reached out and took her hand. "I know we have to be cautious. But Lauren was right; the guy in Dallas is in custody. You can't shoot a gun in a public place and not be caught."

"Why not? If there are no witnesses . . ."

"Because every building has holographic sensors that, from people's chips, recreate for the police a picture of who was there and what they were doing. Then tracking him down via his chip is simple. And, as far as we can tell, he's the only person that was after you."

I patted her hand, trying to reassure her. "We'll be careful. But while we're in DC, if we want to investigate, we have to get out. We can't stay cooped up here."

I got up and grabbed an apple from a bowl on her dresser. "As for today, the National Mall is the most patrolled place in the whole city. We'll be fine. I'll ask the officer outside if he can run us over there."

An hour later we were walking up the steps of the Capitol. Abby stopped to gaze at the massive structure. "So this is where your tribe makes its rules," she said, a half smile on her lips.

"Primarily, this is where various interests vie for resources and privilege."

We walked down Pennsylvania Avenue and entered the White House. Abby asked the tour guide, "Is the president here?"

"No ma'am. President Ramirez is at

Camp David this week."

Abby read the guide's nameplate: Adela Ramirez. "President Ramirez — is he your father?"

The guide gave her an odd look. "I wish."

We walked three blocks to an ice cream shop, where Abby took a sample of each of the thirty-six flavors. "Those were wonderful." She beamed, wiping ice cream from her fingers.

"Where is she from?" the clerk asked in a guarded tone as I paid for three cones — one for her, one for me, and one for the samples.

"Another planet," I whispered.

We sat at a sidewalk table and licked our treats. She looked at me with a serious countenance. "Creighton, last night . . ."

"Abby, I apologize if I rushed you into something you weren't ready for." I couldn't believe I was saying such a thing. To wait two weeks before kissing a woman. Even a relational klutz like me could count on adjourning to VR sex within two or three encounters. And Abby had been living in my house.

Still, I spoke the truth. She was unlike anyone else in my life in the last ten years; I genuinely cared for this woman.

She shook her head. "No, you didn't do

405

anything wrong. I'm just wondering . . . the time we spend together. It's how men and women develop relationships here in the States, isn't it? Romantic relationships, that is."

I looked her straight in the eye. "Yes, I suppose it is."

"Is that what you're trying to do — develop a romantic relationship? Because I don't know if that will work between us."

"Why not?"

"Because . . . I . . ." She blushed. "I won't have sex with you."

We were silent for a moment, looking at each other. Finally I spoke. "It's possible to develop feelings for someone and want to be with them without having sex."

"Is that what you're doing?" She brushed a lock of hair away from her face.

"Well, so far."

"And not having sex doesn't bother you?"

"I would say . . . I'm willing to forgo the sex at this point. And let me tell you, that's saying something."

She smiled. "Okay, then. I just want to make sure we understand each other."

I nodded. "I think we do."

I tapped the police officer, who soon picked us up. I held Abby's hand in the car on the way back to Lauren's. "Abby, we haven't talked much about Ray since we discovered what he was wearing in his final message."

She squeezed my hand but looked away, out the window. "I know."

"Since Ray had on a patient's gown, have you considered the possibility that he became mentally unstable at the end? And that his message was simply the musings of someone not entirely . . . together?"

After a long minute she turned and looked at me. "I thought mental illness was rare."

"It is. But not unheard of."

"Do you think his work on the transplants could have something to do with it? What if he was testing something on himself and it went wrong?"

"I can't imagine Ray doing that. It would violate every protocol."

"Who would have put him in there?"

"He could have done it himself. Or Bryson Nichols."

"Nichols? How could he —"

"Since he handled Ray's affairs after he died, he probably had power of attorney. When Ray became ill, he could have had him committed."

She didn't respond.

"Abby, I think we need to consider a real possibility. All the inconsistencies that seem to have occurred with Nichols — maybe he was merely covering up what happened to Ray in his last days."

Her brow creased. "Why would he want to cover anything up?"

"Put yourself in his shoes. You're the leading AI innovator in the world. You've just introduced your greatest achievement. A new brain. A week later your chief neuroscientist goes . . . becomes mentally ill. It doesn't make for good headlines."

"But what about my village? And the man in Dallas?"

"I don't know. I'm just saying Nichols had good reason not to let anyone know what had happened to Ray."

Abby pulled away, wrapping her arms around herself. Bringing up Ray had disturbed her. I could understand why. It was apparent that his last days had been a nightmare.

The next morning I let Abby sleep in. After two late nights and her ordeal in Dallas, I figured ample sleep and Lauren's departure for Texas would make for a smoother day. I set one simple objective for us: verify Ray's physical death certificate with the state of Maryland. Abby had other ideas.

"I thought we were going to Boston," she

objected. The displeasure on her face was palpable.

"I want to see Ray's actual death certificate," I explained.

"Why?"

"To verify that he actually died."

"I thought you verified that."

I shook my head. "I verified that his record of death is on the National Death Registry."

"But doesn't that mean he's dead?"

"By all accounts, yes. But computer records have been known to be in error. Or to be falsified."

She looked at me in disbelief. "Are you saying that —"

"I'm not saying anything. Your grandfather died. I just want to verify that before we proceed further."

We took a car downtown and boarded a shuttle to Annapolis.

"Lauren left some water and a snack in our rooms," I said after we took our seats. "Did you bring yours?"

She shook her head. I offered her a breakfast bar.

"I don't want any. Thanks, though."

"You didn't have any breakfast before we left."

She patted my knee. "I'm okay. Don't worry."

"Aren't you hungry?"

She finally looked at me. "Creighton, I'm fasting."

"Fasting? You mean . . . restricting your diet? That kind of fasting?"

"I'm not eating at all."

"For how long?"

"A few days."

"Abby, you can't go without eating for a few days."

She scrunched her nose and eyebrows together, looking cuter than I'm sure she meant to in the moment. "Of course I can. I've done it several times."

"Why would you do that?"

"To combine with prayer about an important matter. To focus on God."

"You think that if you go without food, God will give us the answer to what happened to Ray?"

She shook her head. "No. This isn't a cause-and-effect thing. God isn't obligated to do anything. I'm just fasting so I can hear him better."

"And what have you heard?"

"Nothing. I just started this morning."

I laughed aloud but quickly grew serious when Abby glared at me. No joking matter, I guessed. But this was so far outside the range of what I considered normal that it left me dumbfounded.

"All right. Fine." I held up a water bottle. "At least have something to drink."

She shook her head again. "Not now."

"You're fasting from water too? Abby, your body needs liquids to survive. You have to drink something."

"I can hold out for a while."

"Abby, this is —"

She held up her hand. "Creighton, I know you're just trying to look out for me. I'll be fine. I give you permission to hound me about it from time to time if you want."

I looked into her eyes. "Okay," I finally replied. "And I will hound you."

"Okay."

A woman greeted us from behind a counter in the State Records Building. We told her what we were seeking.

"Those records are available on the Grid. I can show you how to access them."

"We've already accessed it on the Grid," I replied.

She looked at me. "You have? Then why did you come here?"

"Because we want to see the physical copy. It's our understanding that Maryland still requires a physical certificate to be signed and filed. Is that correct?"

"Yes, it is. But what you saw on the Grid mirrors whatever records we have here."

I leaned on the counter. "Can you show it to us, or do I need to speak to someone else?"

She scowled. "Follow me."

She led us down two flights of stairs and unlocked a door in a long basement hallway. We entered a room with endless rows of metal shelves filled with filing boxes, each labeled alphabetically and by date.

"The latest technology," I commented.

She ignored my snide remark. We followed her until we reached a box labeled "2088: Cal to Car."

"It will be in here," she declared.

She pulled the box off the shelf, set it on a nearby table, and laid down the rules. "I'm the only one who can handle the document. I'll place it in front of you to view. You have up to ten minutes with me to view it. Longer than that, and I have to request a robotic replacement for myself down here."

A full-time robotic replacement for her might have been an improvement, but I didn't suggest it.

She donned a pair of plastic gloves and leafed through the box. "We don't have as many deaths as we used to. Years ago "Cal to Car" would have filled three file boxes.

Caldwell. Here's Albert Caldwell. Samantha Caldwell. What was the name? Raymond?"

She turned to Abby, who nodded. The woman looked back through the file, flipping through a dozen records on either side of Samantha Caldwell. "Well." She looked over at us. "It doesn't seem to be here. You said you saw the record on the Grid?"

"Ten days ago."

"Huh. Let me look one more time." She flipped through the file once more. Nothing. "You're sure you saw it on the Grid? Because if it's on the Grid, it has to be here. The Grid records come from here."

"Yes," I replied. "We're sure."

She closed the file box and placed it back on the shelf. "Well, let's verify that, shall we?"

We followed her back up to the second floor, where she located Ray's death record on the Grid. "Huh. There it is. You were right. Looks like someone made a mistake."

Abby grabbed my forearm as we walked toward the exit. "Creighton, what does it mean that there's no certificate here?"

"I'm not sure. But it might mean that the Grid record is fraudulent."

"And if it is?" Her brown eyes were wide.

413

"Then your grandfather isn't dead."

We took the car back downtown and boarded a shuttle for DC. I turned to Abby after we got settled in. "I'm going to take the train up to Boston tomorrow."

She nodded. "What time do we need to leave Lauren's house?"

"No, not we. Just me. I want you to stay at Lauren's."

"Don't be ridiculous," she retorted. "He's my grandfather. I have to go too. If there's a chance that he's alive, I need to be there."

The shuttle started to move. "No, your going there really *is* too risky."

"Creighton, I can take care of myself. You don't understand how important this is."

I shook my head. "Your ability to care for yourself is not the point. That hospital is a place someone might expect you to show up. It's safer if I go. If they need verification that I'm representing you, I can tap you at Lauren's place."

She glared at me. "I think I should be the judge of what's too risky for me."

"I don't," I said sternly. "If this were the jungle, fine, I'd let you make the call. But this is my territory, and you've already been shot once. You're going to have to trust me."

She turned to the window. "We'll see."

We rode back to DC in silence.

414

Abby went to bed early. Lack of food had given her a headache. I offered her some medication, hoping she would drink something — anything. She refused. I said good night and went downstairs.

I lay on the couch in Lauren's spacious living room, frustrated at the ill temper I was experiencing toward even the concept of a deity. I found it hard to believe that any deity would ask people to go without food or water. What was next — air?

I must have fallen asleep. When I awoke, I had a message from Sabin. I accessed it; he looked serious.

"Creighton, I took a look at the file you sent me. I'm sorry to be the bearer of bad news, but it's a fake. A very good fake — they knew what they were doing. But it was made from a previous recording of your father." He paused. "I'm not sure what else to tell you. Tap me if you need more."

The news didn't surprise me. Deep down I couldn't imagine that my father had committed suicide. Evidently, he hadn't. I didn't feel grief. I felt numb. What had we stumbled into? Whatever it was, my father had been murdered for it.

I lay on the couch for a long while. I didn't want to think anymore. I was tired of thinking. I considered distracting myself with VR entertainment. Spending an hour or two at night in VR had been my greatest weakness since my teen years. What might I have accomplished had I not wasted thousands of hours in meaningless pursuits?

I went upstairs and crawled into bed. I looked at the empty pillow next to me. Before sleeping, I usually went into VR and filled that space with someone — often someone I knew. People re-created real people in VR all the time to have sex with or just to be with.

I thought about Abby. I could re-create her here — not to have sex with, I told myself, but simply to lie next to her.

"Alistair, bring up the image —"

I stopped. It seemed . . . a violation. Though she would never know, Abby wouldn't want me in VR with her. Perhaps she was the last person on earth who cared. But I knew she would.

I rolled over, pulled the covers to my neck, and drifted off to sleep alone.

31

Abby looked pale when she came downstairs the next morning. She sat at the kitchen table opposite me.

"Eggs?" I asked.

She shook her head.

"How's your headache?"

"Still there."

"I actually have one myself." I got up, put the rest of the eggs on my plate, and returned to the table. "Abby, will you at least drink something today? It's too hot this time of year to let yourself get dehydrated."

She smiled at me. "Okay. This afternoon."

I touched the top of her hand. "I'm heading to the train station in half an hour."

She glanced at me hopefully.

"And, no, I still don't think it's a good idea for both of us to go."

She sighed. "All right. Will you return this evening?"

"That's my plan, yes."

A few minutes later I kissed her good-bye at the front door.

She held me close and gazed into my eyes. "I'm sorry for being cross with you yesterday."

I brushed the hair away from her forehead. "That's all right. We're both stressed."

I walked out the door.

"Hey!" she called after me.

I looked back at her.

"Did Lauren tap about the guy in Dallas?"

"She left me a message but didn't have any details yet. Said she'd tap me back." I turned toward the car. "See you tonight."

I settled into a comfortable coach seat on the train. It pulled away from the station in DC and quickly reached a cruising speed of 200 mph. Only the automation of cities' traffic systems had made such speeds possible. Trains no longer crashed into cars, regardless of the speed. Outside the window the fields of rural Maryland were a blur. The trip to Boston would take two and a half hours, an ideal time frame for something I had been contemplating for several days.

I had more research to do, and it had nothing to do with Ray Caldwell. It was about Abby. As my feelings for her grew, so did the disconnect I felt within me. How could I be falling for a woman whose world-view I had always dismissed? Maybe because the belief came wrapped in a person I respected, even admired. Maybe because along with her beliefs came a goodness that exceeded my own. Was she good because of her beliefs or in spite of them?

Alistair couldn't answer that for me. But he could complete what was lacking in the biblical research I had begun.

"Alistair, access modern archaeological findings as they relate to historical notations made in the New Testament."

"I understand you're trying to find information on a friend's relative, Dr. Daniels."

I sat in the office of the hospital's chief administrator, Dr. Brock Morris, a short man with a firm handshake and a brusque manner. I had overcome my first potential roadblock: I had obtained an audience with someone other than the hospital director, Dr. Theodore Brandt. Conferring with him in person would be a dead end; he had made that clear in our VR encounter.

"Yes. A friend's grandfather. I have authorization from her to secure information about his stay here . . . ." I pulled out my electronic pad.

Dr. Morris waved me off. "That's not necessary, Dr. Daniels. I've checked our records. We have never had Raymond Caldwell here as a patient."

"But we have a visual message from him in which he's wearing a patient gown from this facility."

He looked taken aback. "You do? How did you —" He paused and collected his thoughts. "I don't know how he could have obtained such a garment. From where did you receive this message?"

"It was sent to his granddaughter from —" I thought better of revealing too much information. "Well, you'd have to ask her that question." I shifted in my seat. "Is it possible Dr. Caldwell may have been here temporarily, perhaps just for an assessment, and then dismissed?"

He shook his head. "No. Our records would indicate that as well. I'm sorry, Dr. Daniels. We don't have any information on Ms. Caldwell's grandfather."

He rose from his desk and nodded toward the door. "I wish we could have been of greater assistance to you." He followed me out of the office. We took three steps down the hallway, then he stopped. "The exit is straight ahead at the end of the hall. Good day, Dr. Daniels."

He stuck out his hand. I shook it and turned to walk down the hall. I glanced into an office with an open door and froze. On the back wall was a large, framed Andy Warhol print. The same one I had seen in Ray Caldwell's message.

"Creighton, what did you find out?"

On the car's visiscreen, Abby looked better than she had that morning, her hair pulled back into a braid. She was curled on the couch with an old copy of *To Kill a Mockingbird* we had found at an antiques shop.

"They deny that Ray was ever here."

Abby's shoulders slumped. I could feel her disappointment even through the car's visiscreen.

"They have no record of him as a patient?"

"That's what the administrator said."

She sighed heavily.

"But he was here, Abby."

Her eyes shot back up at me. "He was? How do you know?"

"Because I saw the office from which he sent the message."

"Are you sure?" She rose from the couch.

"Yes, absolutely."

"Then why don't they have a record of him?"

"I think they're lying."

She threw up her arms. "Why would they lie about my grandfather?"

"I don't know." The car stopped. "I'm at the station. We'll talk more when I get back."

"Creighton . . ." She hesitated. "Thank you."

"You're welcome. See you in three hours."

I boarded the train and took a seat, contemplating what had happened at the hospital. My mind kept returning to one name: Bryson Nichols. If there was a conspiracy to cover up Ray's stay at the hospital, Bryson Nichols was behind it.

Abby looked exhausted and was already dressed for bed when I arrived at Lauren's. We went to the couch, and I recounted the details of my encounter at the mental hospital. She laid her head on my lap, and I stroked her hair.

"Creighton, what do we do now?"

"I was thinking . . ." I'd formulated a plan while I was on the train, but now I couldn't recall what it was. My headache, which had disappeared for a while, had now returned with force.

"Why don't we talk about it in the morning?" I suggested.

"I found out something today," she said.

"I looked up Ray's address on the Grid. Do you think we could go by there tomorrow? I'd like to see where he lived."

"That would be fine." I stroked her hair a few more moments. "Abby, are you still on your fast?"

"The food part."

"Is it doing any good?"

She looked up at me. "I don't know yet."

We got up, took something for our headaches, and went to our bedrooms.

Ray Caldwell had lived in an old-style two-story red brick house. The street was deserted, as were most streets anymore. We got out of the car and walked up to the house. Abby examined every detail as if she could somehow connect with her grandfather by taking in the exterior of his home. Maybe she could.

We heard footsteps behind us and turned. An older man pushing a wheelbarrow filled with flowers stopped on the sidewalk in front of Ray's house. He looked over at us. "Good morning."

"Good morning," we both answered.

"Haven't seen you folks here before. But I'm only here once a week, I guess."

"Do you work for the city?" I asked.

"Oh no. I'm Dr. Caldwell's gardener, you

might say. At any rate I keep up the outside of the place for him."

"Even since he died?" Abby's words were tender.

He hung his head slightly. "Yes, a crying shame, a good man like that dying at such an age. I thought I'd tend to the place until they sold the property, but I don't think they've even listed it for sale. Are you folks looking it over?"

"No, not exactly."

We introduced ourselves. The man smiled when he found out Abby's identity. "Granddaughter? Ah, I love to see grandchildren caring for their grandparents. This is nice of you to visit Dr. Caldwell's house. I'm sure you have many memories here."

"I wish I did," Abby answered. "I've lived in Papua New Guinea all my life. This is my first visit to the States. I just wanted to see where they lived."

The man stepped around the wheelbarrow. "I never knew your grandmother. She died in the accident about a year before I met Dr. Caldwell. But your grandfather, he was a fine man. A very fine man. He'd invite me to sit with him on his back porch and have tea. A very smart man." He leaned forward and lowered his voice. "Do you know that he believed in God?"

Abby smiled. "Yes, I do. I believe in God as well."

The man's face brightened. "Really? Oh, you'd have loved knowing him all the more. He never convinced me. But I admired him for believing." He lowered his voice again. "They say Christians were all bigots, but not your grandfather. He was the kindest, gentlest man." He glanced up at the house. "Have you come to collect a few things? I don't know that anyone other than you has come. It's a mystery to —"

"We just came by to look," I interrupted. "We don't have access to Ray's place."

"You don't?" The man glanced up and down the empty street. "Well, I do. I'd be glad to let you two inside, take a look around. I'm sure Dr. Caldwell would like nothing more than for you, young lady, to see his place." He looked up and down the street again. "Let's go around back." He led us through a side gate into the backyard and placed his eye over the retinal scan by the back door. It unlocked.

"It may be a little stale in here. I don't know why they don't do something with this place." He stepped inside. "Who's responsible for it, anyway? They aren't doing much of a job." He looked at me.

"A work associate of his," I answered.

"I don't think anyone's been in here since Dr. Caldwell died . . . except me. No, I take that back. Someone must have cleaned out the refrigerator. I water the plants and dust a bit. The place was immaculate the first time I came in after hearing the news. Dr. Caldwell always kept it that way."

Abby was already making her way around the living room, taking in her grandfather's possessions. A fireplace mantel held framed photos. She picked them up one by one and looked at them carefully. I walked over to her.

"This is my grandfather and grand-mother," she said, pointing to a wedding photo. Her eyes were moist with tears. "This is them too." I recognized them in the second photo; they looked similar to their appearance in the message they'd sent Abby. Full of life.

"These are my parents." They looked to be about forty. They were seated, holding hands and smiling broadly.

She picked up a picture of a baby. "This . . . I think this is my brother. This must have been taken shortly before my parents moved to Papua New Guinea." She looked at it a long time and placed it back on the mantel.

She picked up the next photo and smiled.

"This is me." She turned and showed me a picture of a grinning girl of about three sitting in a tree. "My parents must have sent this to them while our Grid interface was still working."

"Well . . ."

We both turned around and looked at the gardener.

"I finished watering the plants. It looks like you have a bit to look over. How about if I let you do that while I tend the flowers out front?"

"That would be wonderful of you to let us stay," Abby replied. "We won't be too long."

"No, take your time, young lady. These are special moments."

He walked out the front door. Abby continued slowly around the living area, picking up photos and decorative items, studying them, looking at the paintings on the walls. I wandered into a study. It was walled with dark wood bookcases on three sides, with a wood desk and chair in the middle. I could have lived in that room.

I cocked my head and began scanning book titles. On the right-hand shelves stood volumes on science and technology. On the back shelves were titles on history, philosophy, and a variety of other subjects. The shelves on the left housed a large collection of Christian writings. *Christ Is All. The Spiritual Man. My Utmost for His Highest.* I pulled a volume off the shelf. *You Give Me New Life: A 40-Day Journey in the Company of the Early Disciples.* It contained selections from the writings of the early leaders of the Christian church. It was brief, scannable in less than ten minutes. I wasn't familiar with any of the authors quoted, but I had become familiar with their primary theme, which startled me.

I walked to the doorway. "Abby, come look at this."

She walked over, and I held up the book.

"Do you want to read it?" Her voice sounded hopeful.

"I just did. You won't believe what it says."

We walked to living room couch and sat down.

"Listen to this. These are excerpts from various early Christian writings, 100 CE to 250 CE." I read samples from several authors.

"Watch over the eternal life that has been planted in your soul, as a gardener tends seeds in the earth. For your faith is like a seed, charged with the flame of eternal life." — *The Didache* ("The Teaching")

428

"We have been given new life from above, as a sign of our eternal life that is to come." — Athenagoras

"I knew nothing of real life — the new life that is offered to us from above. . . . Presently, I was aware of the Spirit — the very breath of the Father — coming into me from beyond this world. And in that moment I was made a new man." — Cyprian

"We receive strength and new life within ourselves — life that is not of ourselves — from the One who is perfect and before all creation." — Irenaeus

"Open your soul to Him now who is your Father and Creator. Be ready to receive and be filled with this new life . . . which is God himself." — Cyprian

I lowered the book onto my lap. "Isn't this amazing? It shows that the true message of the New Testament was still being passed down in the first two centuries after its writing. Don't you see a parallel between this and what we found earlier about God himself being the life?"

Abby shrugged. "But . . . this is just the

traditional message of Christianity."

"It's not the one you've been communicating."

Abby had a shocked look on her face. "It certainly is."

"No, it isn't. You keep saying that God sent his Son to die for our sins so we could be forgiven and live forever with God."

"That's what the Bible says."

"Right, I know. But that's only part of the message. The way you present it, God forgives people, then basically leaves it up to them to try to live good, Christian lives."

"He doesn't leave it entirely up to us. God helps us too . . ."

I shook my head. "But that's not what the Hebrew prophets indicated the new arrangement would be, or what Jesus said, or how he claimed to live, or what Paul of Tarsus taught —"

"How would you know, Creighton?" She left the couch and began walking around the room. "All you've done is a little reading, and suddenly you think that you can lecture me on what my own faith teaches? You don't even believe any of this!"

"I just think that your understanding of Christianity is too limited. From what I've read, it seems that the full message of the Christian faith is that God himself comes to

430

live inside you, that he joins himself to your human spirit, and that he actually lives his life through you. He doesn't *help* anyone live the Christian life. He lives it himself. He *is* the life. What you've been teaching people and living by is a kind of Christian self-help system —"

She stopped and glared at me.

"Abby, I'm just trying to help you understand your own faith —"

"By telling me what I've always believed is mistaken."

"Not mistaken, just incomplete. Abby, if you had some brain implants, you could read faster and process information more quickly. You'd see the connections. All of this would become clearer . . . to . . . you."

I'm not sure she heard my last two words. She turned, walked to the front door, and left the house, slamming the door behind her.

"Abby!"

I opened the door in time to see her climb in the car and speed off. The gardener looked up at me. I shrugged.

Shrewd, Creighton. Very shrewd.

I walked back inside the house and accessed the Grid for another car. I returned to Lauren's and went straight for the medicine cabinet. I hadn't had a headache in years; I couldn't imagine why this one had come upon me and had lasted so long. I lay on the couch and accessed Alistair.

"You look ill, Creighton. Have you consulted a doctor?"

My Grid interface was lecturing me.

"No. Thank you, Alistair. I just have a headache. I took something for it. I'll contact a doctor if things don't improve by the morning. Right now I'd like to continue my research into the reliability of New Testament manuscripts."

Five minutes later I leaned back against the pillow on the couch.

"Do you wish to continue, Creighton?"

"I'm sorry, Alistair. My headache seems to be getting worse. I can't concentrate. Discontinue, please."

I lay there for ten more minutes, then started to feel nauseous. I got up, lost my balance, fell over the coffee table, and threw up on the floor. I got up again, weaved my way to the bathroom, found the toilet, and threw up again. In a few minutes the dry heaves started. I retched off and on for perhaps half an hour — I lost track of time.

I raised myself up and wiped my mouth with a towel. I looked at the mess I had made. I'd have a homebot clean it up. I just wanted to sleep. I glanced at the stairs across the living room and knew I couldn't make it.

I wobbled across the living room and collapsed onto the couch.

32

The large wooden doors to the congressional hearing room opened silently. Bryson Nichols leaned back in the chair marked "Chairwoman Cahill."

"Welcome to my subcommittee, Damien," he boomed.

Damien Cleary strode down the main aisle between rows of empty chairs. "Are you aspiring to political office now, Nichols, or have you simply switched your favorite VR location?"

Nichols smiled. "Why would anyone want to occupy one of these chairs when they can wield real power? No, I'm simply getting used to the room. I always do before they want me to testify."

Cleary reached the front row, paused, then sat in a chair reserved for witnesses. He looked up at Nichols. "It all comes full circle. Did you meet with Hutch Hardin?"

"Of course."

"And?"

"Hutch assures me that the delay at the attorney general's office is only temporary, until the upcoming hearings are over. We should be able to hold out until then. I'm informed that Professor Daniels came alone to the mental hospital, looking for Ray."

"And?"

"A dead end. All they have are dead ends." Nichols leaned forward and assumed a tone of mock seriousness. "The subcommittee wishes to thank the witness for his work in tracking Abigail Caldwell and Creighton Daniels these many weeks. I believe we are in a position to abstain from further action and let events take their course." He smiled with self-satisfaction.

"It's too late for that, Nichols."

The smile disappeared. "What do you mean, it's too late?"

"By this time Ms. Caldwell and the professor have been taken care of."

A concerned look formed on Nichols's face. "Taken care of — by whom?"

"By us. You said we'd have to take drastic measures if the AG didn't get her out of the country quickly. He did not."

"I said we *might*. What have you done?"

Cleary remained expressionless. "The two of them have by now contracted a rare brain disorder. An irreversible one."

Nichols rose from his seat, processing what Cleary had just told him. It took only seconds to connect the dots. "You killed that tribal village in New Guinea. You were experimenting with our nanites."

He traversed the raised row of congressmen's seats and walked onto the committee room floor, never taking his eyes off his associate. "You had the doctor killed when she began to uncover the cause. You sent your man after Abby Caldwell in Dallas. And now you've murdered her. Because of your impatience, you forced this woman out of the jungle, you brought her down upon our heads, and now you've tied both of us to her murder."

"The nanites aren't traceable to us, Nichols."

"And whom do you think they're traceable to? How many companies even have the capacity for their manufacture?"

"Several. And we can plant evidence implicating one of them if the need arises. I don't think it will."

Nichols walked over to Cleary, who stood and faced him. "I've done what was necessary, Nichols. Necessary for us. Necessary for the advancement of humankind. Do you dispute that?"

Nichols glared at him in silence. Slowly he willed away his anger. Cleary was still essential to the success of his long-term plan. "I appreciate your intent, Damien. I simply disagree with your tactics. When I indicated drastic measures might be needed, I didn't mean to imply ones this draconian. I realize I should have clarified."

Cleary nodded. "Perhaps you should have."

"I can't countenance the killing of innocents, even for humanity's long-term good."

"That's where you and I disagree."

"Apparently." He motioned to Cleary, and they began walking down the main aisle of the room. "What's done is done. I suggest we begin implementation of our plans for expansion of the transplant procedure."

I was roused by someone shaking me. I heard a voice. A loud voice, telling me to wake up. I opened my eyes. It was Abby. I tried to raise my head. Too sleepy. I felt something press against my shoulders. Her hands. She was shaking me. *Why are you shaking me?* I opened my eyes and looked at her. She looked worried. I took in pieces of what she was saying.

"So sorry . . . left you . . . Alistair . . .

ambulance . . . forgive me . . ."

I glanced around the room and tried to speak. "I . . . where am . . ."

She said something. Something about Lauren's house. She thought we were at Lauren's house.

"Abby . . . headache . . . dizzy . . . thirsty."

She squeezed my hand. I could see her lips moving. ". . . will . . . water."

She left.

I closed my eyes.

The man glanced nervously at the six other people occupying the elevator. The hospital wasn't supposed to be trafficked much at night. He looked again at his orderly's uniform. It looked authentic, even down to the Washington General name badge. The uniform, however, was the easy part. The big hurdle awaited him. All he could do now was trust the magic of the one who had hired him.

The elevator stopped at the fourth floor, and the doors opened. He eyed the other passengers, but no one else was getting off. He slid through the doors as they began to shut. He looked down the halls to his left and right, then proceeded forward. As he approached a nurses' station on the right, the sole nurse looked up and smiled.

"Good evening," she said. "Are you new?"

"To this shift."

"Welcome to the graveyard."

He passed her without further comment and came upon a pair of locked doors with an eye scanner to the right. He leaned forward and placed his right eye in front of the pad. It emitted a brief, quiet buzz. He stepped back and saw a small flashing red light. He leaned again toward the scanner. The buzz and flashing red light returned momentarily. He glanced over his shoulder toward the nurses' station. The woman was looking his way.

"I, uh . . . How do you . . ."

"You need to run your badge through the scanner first."

"Oh. Right. They told us that in training."

"I thought you'd been working another shift already."

"Yeah. Laundry. I was working laundry. This is new."

She nodded. He turned back to the door, scanned his badge, placed his eye to the wall, and heard the door release. He stepped to his left, opened it, and walked through without looking back.

The corridor was empty. The man passed closed patient room doors. He noticed a biohazard waste chute on the wall. He heard sounds coming from another nurses' station down the hallway. He glanced at a room number. Three more. He wouldn't have to pass another station. He took a dozen more steps and looked at the patient name on a door to his right. "Creighton Daniels."

He pushed open the door and stepped inside.

The patient lay motionless on the hospital bed. A small fluorescent light above it cast shadows across the room.

The man eyed the room. His heart jumped into his throat when he spotted something completely unexpected. A woman was draped across a small couch, her legs dangling off the edge. She was asleep. There was no place to hide if she awoke. He hadn't been briefed on this contingency.

He listened to the woman's breathing. It was deep and regular. He decided to risk continuing. He wouldn't have another chance. He stepped gingerly toward the patient's bedside. He had never seen anyone in a coma before; the patient looked as peaceful as the sleeping woman.

Three intravenous tubes led into the patient's arm. He examined them and selected one. He pulled a syringe out of a plastic holder and brought it up to the clear plastic tubing. He attached the syringe to the needleless port. He turned and looked toward the woman. She roused slightly, then fell back to sleep. He pressed the plunger of the syringe. Five cc's of liquid were introduced into the tubing.

The man withdrew the syringe, placed it in the holder, and left the room. He glanced down the corridor. A nurse was walking down the hall to the right. He turned left, deposited the holder in the sharps container, walked through the security doors, took a right past the nurses' station, and approached the door to a stairwell. He glanced behind. No one was following. He exited into the stairwell.

33

I awoke in an overcast haze. My mind was a jumble, as if waking from a dream that still feels real. I heard voices. One was familiar. I opened my eyes and blinked at bright lights. "Abby."

"Creighton! You're awake!"

I felt the touch of a hand on my arm. I tried lifting my hand in response, but my arm felt leaden. I turned my head to the right, and Abby came into focus. "Abby." I collected my thoughts. "Where am I?"

"You're in Washington General Hospital. You fell into a —"

"Why?"

She touched my face gently. "Creighton, you have a brain infection. You fell into a coma. You've been in a coma for three days."

Three days. Coma. Hospital. I don't remember coming to the hospital. "Why am I here?"

She took my hand, raised it to her lips, and kissed it twice. "Creighton," she said slowly, "you have a brain infection. You've been in a coma. You're in the hospital recovering."

Recovering. I'm recovering. I tried to lift my head and look around the room. A man was sitting in a chair against the far wall, looking at me. "Who is that man?"

"He's an FBI agent. His name is Ben Steele. He's been assigned to your case."

I turned back to Abby. "My case? Of what?"

She leaned forward. "Creighton, we think someone infected you with the same type of nanites that killed my village. They probably tried to infect me too. Agent Steele is trying to track down the perpetrator."

Nanites. The village had died from them. "How long?"

"How long what?"

"To live?"

Abby smiled and squeezed my hand. "We hope a very long time. The infection seems to have been arrested."

Arrested. "It stopped?"

"For now, yes. The doctors are watching you, but the damage doesn't seem to be getting worse."

Damage. Do I have damage? Grogginess overtook me. I just wanted to sleep. "Abby, I'm . . . I . . ."

■ ■ ■ ■

Abby reiterated for me the sequence of events that had transpired. Once. Twice. Three times. It finally began to sink in.

After leaving her grandfather's town house, she had gone to the National Mall, the only place she knew where she could be alone and think. She returned early that evening to Lauren's place, found me asleep on the couch, and woke me to apologize. I was incoherent. She tried to get me to stand. I couldn't. She tapped for an ambulance.

Abby accompanied me in the ambulance. I lost consciousness en route and was rushed into the emergency room. Brain scans revealed that part of my brain's frontal lobe was gone. The doctors couldn't explain it. Abby told them about the nanites. They had no way of predicting the spread of the infection.

I was placed in intensive care. My condition worsened. I lapsed into a coma. The infection continued to spread.

The hospital's neurosurgeon wanted to operate to remove the infection, even if it meant performing a lobotomy. Abby objected. How could he be sure that all the nanites would be removed? Since she had no legal standing, her objections were over-ruled. I was prepped for surgery. One last brain scan, however, revealed that the infec-tion hadn't progressed in the previous twelve hours. The surgery was placed on hold.

Subsequent scans continued to reveal no progression. The surgery was scrubbed. I had stabilized. Nineteen hours later I awoke. Abby had been with me the whole time.

Lauren had come to the hospital when she found out. After talking to Abby, she tapped the attorney general and requested an FBI investigation and FBI protection for the two of us.

I was taken out of intensive care and placed on the medical/surgical floor. Three FBI agents were assigned to our security, taking round-the-clock shifts. Special Agent Steele was handling the investigation. He was tallish, about my height, but with a much stockier build. I could imagine him playing college football forty years earlier. He had a quick mind and a gentle spirit. I immediately trusted him. He had some questions for me. I answered as best I could remember. Events not just of the past four days but for days before that were hazy. Fortunately, the nanite infection hadn't hindered access to the Grid or my memory stream, which I had to use to answer many of his questions.

He rose when he had finished questioning me. "Abby indicates that you are in possession of the messages from Ray Caldwell. Can you provide me with access to those?"

I instructed Alistair to give him access to them.

The agent looked at Abby. "I'll take a look at these and follow up on some of the other information you've provided. I — You don't have neural implants, do you?"

She shook her head.

"Then I'll tap this room if I need anything else."

"Agent Steele . . ." Abby hesitated.

"Yes?"

"Do you think Bryson Nichols may be behind what happened to Creighton?"

He looked at me, then back at Abby. "I prefer not to engage in speculation before the facts are in. Especially in a case like this. I'll let you know what I find out. Agent Ruiz is outside if you need him." He walked out.

Abby picked up my right hand and caressed it. In a moment she spoke. "Creighton, I need to ask your forgiveness."

"For what?"

"For overreacting at my grandfather's

house. I realize you were just trying to help, but I took it as a personal attack. If I hadn't stormed out . . ."

I lifted my left hand across my body and placed it over hers. "Abby, I don't really remember that. But if you think you're responsible in any way for my not getting medical care fast enough —"

"But if I had been there with you . . ." She wiped a tear out of each eye. "I never should have gotten you into this. I never should have —"

I shook my head. "Abby, I knew what I was getting into." I forced a smile. "Besides, I'm still here."

Half an hour later Agent Ruiz opened the door. Dr. Peter Foreman, the hospital's chief neurosurgeon, entered the room. He pulled up a visiscreen and examined it. "Discontinue," he said. He stood at the foot of my bed. "Your vitals look good, Dr. Daniels. And the brain infection continues to be dormant." He lowered his voice. "Do you understand the nature of the infection?"

I nodded. "Can you tell me what the damage is?"

"Most of your orbital frontal lobe is gone. It's hard to say for certain what the impact will be. Short-term memory loss. Perhaps some long-term. Interruption of speech patterns, of analytical speed of the brain, of emotional and social awareness. These are likely manifestations. I assume you've experienced some of these?"

I nodded again.

"The exact damage will be more evident over time. There are a couple of psychotropics I can prescribe that will help your brain compensate. Unfortunately, they can only be used short term."

"Whatever may help." I knew that the brain has amazing elasticity and can often recover lost functions resulting from trauma. "How long before my brain compensates on its own?"

The doctor looked at Abby, then back at me. "Dr. Daniels, most of what you're experiencing now is irreversible. You've lost too much tissue. Your brain function will never return to normal. I'm sorry."

"How many of those spring rolls do you eat a week, Steele?"

Ben looked up at Trevor Hamm, his partner, standing just outside his cubicle. "Three every day for lunch. You do the math."

"Tell me what you're finding on this brain infection case."

"A pile of circumstantial nonsense that

448

may revolve around Bryson Nichols and NTI."

"Bryson Nichols? What does he have to do with anything?"

"The victim's girlfriend's grandfather was Raymond Caldwell, the neuroscientist who helped invent Nichols's brain-transplant technology."

"So?"

"Supposedly they have a visual of him talking about some conspiracy of Nichols's that may destroy the planet."

"By doing what?"

Ben shrugged. "I don't know. I was about to look at it. And it may not matter. According to the granddaughter, he made it while in a Boston mental hospital before he died. However, I can't get confirmation that Raymond Caldwell was ever at the place. All I know is she seems certain he was there."

Hamm sat in Ben's visitor chair. "Let's see the visual."

Ben accessed Ray's message to Sam. When it ended, Hamm leaned back, put his hands behind his head, and laughed. "What a trip. This guy was a neuroscientist *and* a Christian? I didn't know such a person could exist. Leave it to the kooks to start talking about the end of the world." He stood. "Be sure to keep me in the loop on this one. I can't wait to see what you dig up. But, Ben, don't dig too deep. Not with Bryson Nichols."

Ben watched him walk away. He accessed the sixteen-year-old message from Raymond Caldwell to Abigail Caldwell. It verified what Ben had suspected — Abby Caldwell was a Christian too.

Ben placed his elbows on his desk and lowered his head into his hands. He sighed deeply. He reached down and opened a desk drawer, where his eyes fixed on the single item inside: a framed photo. It showed a young woman standing next to a prop plane on a dirt landing strip. She was holding a Bible.

Hours passed slowly at the hospital. Abby stayed at my side. I entreated her to return to Lauren's and get a decent night's sleep. She relented. FBI agents had also been assigned for security at the congresswoman's. Abby gathered a few items and departed for the night.

The doctor had given me the psychotropic, but it would require a day or two to take effect. In the meantime I was left to my own impaired thoughts. I looked around the hospital room. I felt confused again.

Abby had gone to Lauren's. What was I doing in the hospital?

I accessed my memory stream and scanned the last several days. I had been infected with nanites. They had eaten my frontal lobe and were now dormant. The doctor wanted to surgically remove them.

Should I do it? Why wouldn't I do it? Shouldn't the nanites be removed?

I tapped the nurse.

"Yes, Dr. Daniels."

"I'd like the surgeon to go ahead and do the surgery now."

"We'll have to contact Abigail Caldwell before scheduling surgery."

"Contact Abby? Why?"

"You signed a statement requiring her consultation before any surgical decisions were made."

"Oh."

"Do you want me to tap her?"

I accessed the time on the Grid. "No. She's probably asleep by now. Thank you."

I accessed my memory stream again. Abby and I had discussed the surgery not three hours earlier. Surgery, especially on the part of my body just invaded, carried risks. But what were the risks of letting the nanites lie dormant inside my head?

Even if surgery did remove all the nanites

— an unlikely proposition — then what? What was going to happen to me? Over time my brain would rewire itself. But not enough to compensate for what I had lost.

"Abby, what will happen to my career?" I had asked her. "How can I possibly function as a professor?"

What I didn't say out loud, but what my memory stream recorded, were my other thoughts. How could I have an ongoing relationship with someone? With someone like Abby? Who would want me as a partner?

I had never thought in those terms before. I was still in my forties. I had eighty years of life span left. Most people at my age — or before — had settled down with their first life partner. Perhaps I had waited too long. If I had done that earlier, I wouldn't have become entangled with Abby. Perhaps I'd still . . .

Fatigue came quickly. I exited my memory stream and closed my eyes.

When I awoke, light was streaming through my window. Abby was sitting at my side, tracing circles on the palm of my hand. She smiled when I looked at her. I admired how the sunlight sketched an outline around her.

"I brought us a little something to eat," she said. "How did you sleep?"

"Fine, I guess. Sleep is the only thing I do well anymore," I tried to joke.

She handed me a cup of juice and a cranberry scone. It was good to have something from the outside world. We started eating.

"Creighton, have you decided anything on the surgery?"

"I'm still thinking about it."

"Is there anything I can do to help?"

I shook my head. "I wish there were."

We finished our food. Abby put the plates and cups on the counter and turned to me. "Do you know if there's a knife in here?"

"A knife? What for?"

"I want to cut something."

"Cut something — like with scissors?"

"Yes, scissors would work fine."

"They probably have some at the nurses' station."

She stepped out the door. A moment later she reappeared with scissors. Abby took the scissors in her hand, cocked her head, and with her other hand pulled her hair out to the side. A small bit of hair poked out from between two fingers. She placed the scissors around the hair.

"What are you doing?" I asked abruptly.

She closed the blades and snipped off some dark hair into the palm of her hand.

She reached into her pants pocket and pulled out a small plastic bag and some string. She opened the bag, dropped the hair inside, and sealed it.

"What's the string for?"

Abby made two small holes in the bag's upper corners with the scissors. She ran the string through the holes, then tied the ends together. She rose from her chair and moved toward me. "Lean forward."

I bowed my head toward her. Abby placed the string around my head, letting it fall on the back of my neck. The plastic bag dangled on my chest like a necklace. I looked up at her.

She smiled. "This is for you."

I lifted the bag off my chest and peered at it. "Thank you. What does it mean?"

"The Inisi have five stages of friendship and a sign for each stage. In the final stage, the closest friendship, you take some of your hair, place it in a bamboo shoot, and give it to the friend. I looked around for a bamboo shoot, but no luck."

"No, I suspect the hospital is all out." I looked at the long strands again. "So . . . why hair?"

"The Inisi believe that to curse someone, you have to have a strand of their hair. So for their deepest friendships, they give each other their hair. It's their way of saying, 'I entrust my very life to you. I trust that you will never use this to hurt me.' "

She was looking down, patting the bag with affection. I reached out and lifted her chin and looked intently into her eyes. "Abby, no one has ever given me anything so precious." I took her hand in mine. "I will never use it to hurt you."

She smiled, leaned over, and kissed me tenderly on the lips. "I know."

Ray Caldwell's message to his son, Sam, ended. It was the fifth time Ben had watched it. He leaned back in his chair and sipped his midmorning coffee. Was there something in this message that he was missing?

The fact that Caldwell had been able to send it at all was a mystery. How could a patient in a mental hospital — if indeed he had been one — obtain the Grid access necessary to send a message? What had prevented Caldwell from sending the rest of the message?

Caldwell's deportment during the message troubled him. Not the eccentricity of his demeanor — just the opposite. Apart from some apparent anxiety (did he anticipate being apprehended?), Caldwell seemed perfectly lucid. What's more, he seemed

strangely unconcerned about his own wel-
fare, talking instead about existential threats.
If a person had one chance to communicate
with family, wouldn't one's location in a
mental facility be the first thing to communicate?

Ben put his cup down. He needed to focus
on his strongest lead. He had his Grid
interface contact the Dallas Police Department. He finally landed at the VR desk of a
Detective Shriver. "Special Agent Ben
Steele with the FBI in DC."

The man stood, and they shook hands.

"I'm seeking the identity and case status
of a man arrested at the Dallas Museum of
Natural History on June 12."

Shriver shook his head. "Agent Steele, no
one was arrested. A disturbance was reported, with shots fired inside the building,
but the only person witnesses saw was a
woman trying to abscond with one of the
museum's artifacts. She dropped it and ran
from the scene. We haven't been able to
identify her. No one appeared on chip scans
except museum personnel."

"No male assailant? I was informed —"

"No assailants at all. May I ask your interest in the case?"

"I . . . uh . . . we thought it might be
linked to an incident here in Washington.

But details are sketchy. It was a long shot. Can you contact me if you develop any further leads?"

"Of course."

Ben exited VR. With an assailant presumably in a Dallas jail, Ben had assumed the assault on Creighton Daniels was performed by an accomplice. Now he was most likely searching for a single suspect. Normally, that would be good news. Less complication. Less danger. In this case the opposite was true. The assailant appeared untraceable. Worse, he had attacked across the country — maybe across the world. Whatever his motivation, it was high. And he would attack again. Of that, Ben was certain.

34

That night I pressed Abby to return again to Lauren's. She didn't want to. "You'll sleep better," I argued. "One of us needs to be able to think clearly. I'll be fine."

She relented. She kissed me, told me she was praying for me, and left.

The FBI agent outside the door poked his head in. "Good night, Dr. Daniels."

"Good night."

I wasn't sleepy. I had already taken three or four naps that day. Abby had patiently read while I slept. When I woke, she was always there, repeating to me why I was in the hospital, what the doctor had said, and the decision I needed to make about the surgery.

The hospital was quiet. My habitual evening VR escape beckoned. There were always exotic natural wonders to explore, archaeological sites to dig, former presidents to converse with, people to hook up with. I scanned some of my favorite options. None appealed.

I lay in bed, pondering the surgery. Again. Alistair signaled me. I had just received a tap from an unknown source. When I accessed it, a young woman appeared.

"Dr. Daniels, you have a message. It is text only."

Text only. That was odd. "From whom?"

"The sender prefers to remain anonymous."

"Play it, please."

The text scrolled up.

Professor Daniels, I was so very sorry to hear about your hospitalization. I am sure this has been devastating to you. I am an expert in the neurosciences and would like to offer my services in the restoration of your brain. Discretion is important in our communication. If you are interested in discussing further, please meet me at the attached VR location. — A Concerned Friend

A concerned friend. I didn't have any friends in the neurosciences. Or did I? Who was this person? How did he or she find out about my condition?

There was no downside to meeting the

sender. No one could harm me in VR or affect the world outside of VR in any way. I couldn't think of any risks, except saying something I shouldn't say. As long as I exercised proper caution . . .

I entered VR. I found myself in an old-fashioned English gentlemen's club, sitting in a leather captain's chair. Across the table sat a man I instantly recognized as one of the world's leading industrial technologists and richest men, and my probable assailant. Bryson Nichols.

"Welcome, Professor Daniels. I'm so glad that you chose to join me. Few people are invited here."

I glanced around at the clientele. I hadn't been in VR since the nanite attack. My brain, unfortunately, was the same inside or outside VR. I didn't trust it in either realm. I looked back at my host. "Are you actually Bryson Nichols?"

"As opposed to a VR projection? Yes. I am quite assuredly Bryson Nichols."

"How can I know that?"

Nichols smiled. "As you know, receiving a tap from an unknown source, you can't. But you'll know I'm the real thing when you hear what I have to say." He signaled the waiter. "Do you like scotch?" he asked me.

"Did you order the attack on me?"

He whispered something to the waiter, then turned back to me. "No, I did not."

"Did you have my father murdered?"

He looked surprised. "I wasn't aware that your father was murdered. I thought it was a suicide."

"It wasn't."

The news seemed to perturb him. He sat silently for a moment. The waiter arrived with two drinks. I sipped mine. Fortunately, VR liquor would have no effect on what mental capacity I did retain.

"So why did you invite me here, Mr. Nichols?"

"You've been wronged, Professor. Someone has stolen part of your brain from you. I would like to give it back — no, give you an even better brain."

I considered that statement for a moment. "You're offering me one of your transplants."

"Precisely."

I eyed him, examining his face for hints as to why he had brought me here. "I couldn't possibly afford a brain transplant. Unless you've already managed to get them covered by the government."

He smiled. "In due time. In your case, the expense will be on me. The least I can offer, I believe."

461

"By whom have I been wronged?"

Nichols lifted his glass, smiled unnaturally, and took a sip. He placed the glass back down on the table. "I can't tell you that. But —"

"Why not?"

"I'm being honest with you, Professor Daniels. I'm just trying to make up for a malicious wrongdoing."

"Did they intend to kill Abby Caldwell too?"

"She is safe, is she not? For that we can both be grateful. Regarding your condition, I assume you've seen the news concerning the success of the transplants NTI has been performing?"

I leaned back and took a drink. "I have no interest in having an artificial brain, Mr. Nichols. I prefer the real thing."

"You may prefer the biological brain you once had. But what about the one that has now been eaten away?"

"What can you tell me about that?"

"You were attacked by neural nanites."

"I thought nanites were benign."

"These were not. They were programmed to travel to the victim's brain and eat, so to speak, any neurons they encountered. You were fortunate. They planted in your frontal lobe. They could have attacked any number of brain regions that would have killed you by the time I intervened."

I paused to process that statement. "You intervened? How?"

"Shortly after you entered the hospital, I was informed of your condition."

"By whom?"

"I can't reveal that."

"Those who attacked me?"

"I can't say. Please — bear with me, Professor. I invited you here because I'm on your side."

"My side of what?"

"Of life." He leaned back and took a drink. He continued in a softer voice. "As I was saying, I was informed. I knew immediately that I had an antidote to the pathogen."

"You have antidotes for killer nanites?"

"We have predatory defense nanites that are programmed to destroy nanites such as those that infected you."

"Does the government know about this?"

"We manufacture these on *behalf* of the government. When self-replicating nanotechnology became viable, we knew the catastrophic potential of killer nanites. We had to develop immune systems and defense mechanisms against such attacks."

"So . . . you're saying . . ."

"These defensive nanites were introduced inside your body to stop the attack."

"Introduced when?"

"That's not important."

It seemed important to me. I looked across the pub, trying to sort through all I had just learned. "So can these nanites of yours rebuild the part of the brain that I've lost?"

"Unfortunately, no. They are for defensive purposes only, not reconstruction of damaged tissue."

"I thought nanotechnology could be used for tissue repair."

"For most tissue, yes. Not for brain tissue. We stopped our efforts at that a number of years back."

"Great."

"Actually, Professor, it is. We stopped because of the promise we saw in another technology we were developing, the synthetic brain."

"I already said —"

"Please, Professor, let me finish." He put his drink down and leaned forward. "I'm offering you a way to restore your brain to full function. The only way. But I'm offering much more than that. I'm offering you permanent existence, a never-ending life in the same conscious form in which you currently exist — not a continuation of yourself in replicated form, but in your own form, with no discontinuity of conscious awareness. I'm offering you eternal life."

"Until my body gives out."

"By the time your body gives out, the technology will have been perfected to construct nanite bodies. We are on the cusp of that technology now."

"Synthetic brain. Synthetic body."

"But real self. That never changes. That's what I'm offering." He picked up his glass and took a drink. "I assume you can appreciate what this would mean to you professionally."

"Which is what?"

"Instant access to the entire library of human knowledge."

"But I already have that on the Grid."

"Yes, but you don't have the capacity to process its information a million times faster than a healthy biological brain, even one with implants. Imagine what you could do in your field of study with such capabilities."

"If the advantages are so great, most of my profession will have the same capabilities within several years."

"All the more reason to get a jump on them now, wouldn't you say?"

465

My mind felt hazy. I forced myself to press on through the fog. My current brain would never again do for me what I wanted it to do. My life would never be what I wanted it to be. I had nothing to lose and everything to gain if I accepted his offer.

"I've always been reticent to embrace technological enhancements, Mr. Nichols. As a historian, I have an affinity for doing things the old-fashioned way."

"But under the circumstances . . ."

I took a slow drink. "Inflexibility for its own sake is no virtue. Under the circumstances . . . I accept your offer."

"Splendid. You won't regret it, Professor."

I thought for a moment. "I would, however, like to make one request."

"Which is?"

"I'd like to first see the transplant procedure performed. Can you arrange that?"

He smiled. "Of course. We'd be delighted to have you observe. We can set you up in simultaneous VR, and you can observe a procedure in real time right from your hospital room."

It took a moment for that to sink in. "Yes. That would be fine."

"Splendid. I'll have my assistant contact you." Nichols leaned forward and placed his elbows on the table. "Now, shall we discuss the other end of the deal?"

I looked at him warily. "There's another end?"

"Yes. One thing I need you to do for me."

35

"I had a visitor last night after you left."

Abby looked up at me from the cafeteria breakfast she had brought to my room. "You did? Who?"

"Bryson Nichols."

"Bryson Nichols! He was here?"

"We met in VR."

"What did he want?"

"He . . . heard about my condition, and he wanted to . . . express his concern."

"Could you tell if he's behind all this?"

"I don't think so."

"You don't? Why not? Everything we know about my village, your illness . . . it points to Nichols." Her eyes were narrow, and her cheeks were reddening.

I put my hands on her arms, hoping to calm her down. "I . . . It's more complicated than we surmised, Abby. I think people close to him are behind it. I think he's trying to stop them and make things right.

That's why he wanted to talk to me."

Abby's eyebrows furrowed. "Creighton, he didn't try to talk you into getting an artificial brain, did he?"

I didn't answer.

She pulled away from me. "You're not seriously considering that, are you?"

"I'm not sure. It is tempting, given what's happened to me."

She stood and walked over to the window. Her face conveyed a mixture of disappointment and confusion; clearly she was still baffled at why anyone would want an artificial brain. When she spoke, her voice sounded distant. "Did he say anything about my grandfather?"

I nodded. "Nichols told me something to relay to you."

She turned toward me.

"He gave me directions to your grandfather's grave site, to the place where they buried his ashes. He thought you might like to visit it sometime."

Abby crumpled into a chair. "His grave site? You mean . . . my grandfather really is dead?"

"I'm sorry, Abby. I know you were hoping otherwise. It was always a long shot." I reached toward her.

Tears welled up in her eyes and drifted

silently down her cheeks. She walked over, sat next to me on the bed, and leaned close, her arms folding around my body.

"I hate having to break the news to you."

She lifted her face, wet and red from her crying. "But how do you know it's really his grave site?"

"I told him about the things that didn't fit together for us. There's an explanation for all of them, Abby. The inheritance check — the money had all been distributed. Nichols simply wrote you a check himself. He felt you were owed that."

"But what about the house?"

"He thought it was a bad time to sell, so he was waiting for a market upturn. As executor he has that power."

"And the death certificate?"

"He didn't know. A bureaucratic error, probably. He said he could check on it."

She looked intently at me. "What did he say about the mental hospital?"

I shook my head. "Your grandfather was there the last two weeks of his life. He had a break with reality. They diagnosed him with a mental disorder just before his aneurysm."

"Were the two related?"

"He didn't say. I didn't ask."

"But they don't have any records of his being there. If Nichols was willing to tell you that Poppy was in the hospital, why would the hospital cover it up?"

"That was to protect your grandfather's legacy. And probably to protect all Nichols has worked for."

She put her head against my chest. "Why . . . did he tell you these things? Why didn't he talk to me?"

"I don't know. He's a very busy man, Abby. We're fortunate he was willing to meet with either of us. At least now we know the truth."

Abby pulled away from me and looked back toward the window, staring at the bright sunshine. "Creighton, do you really think he's telling the truth?"

"What he said makes sense, Abby. It all fits." I tried to offer a consoling smile, to give her some bit of closure.

"Okay," she said resignedly. She sat silently for a moment, absently stroking my hand. "I'd like to visit Poppy's grave."

The car turned into a wooded area cordoned off by a three-foot-high stone wall. An archway at the entrance said "Resting Meadows." It didn't appear anyone had been to the cemetery in a while. There were no fresh grave sites and no fresh flowers on the old graves.

The car followed a winding road to the back of the cemetery. There, to her right, under the shade of a thick leafy tree, Abby spotted the headstone. She instructed the car to stop, then climbed out and walked slowly to the grave. The headstone read "Raymond B. Caldwell. 1997–2088. Trailblazing scientist and devoted friend."

Devoted friend. Not devoted father. Or grandfather. Friend. She supposed Nichols couldn't honestly say anything else. And, in truth, neither could she. He was a grandfather she never knew.

She knelt and placed a hand on the ground in front of the headstone. She closed her eyes. She was back in the jungle again, saying good-bye to a daughter she had loved with all her heart yet hadn't known long enough.

"Poppy," she said in a quiet voice, "I know you aren't really here. You're much better off, with Jesus. But I came to say good-bye."

She paused and pushed her palms against her eyes, trying to block the river of tears.

"I know that you loved me. You gave me the greatest blessing, raising a son who'd be an amazing dad. He loved Jesus with all his heart and then showed me how to love Jesus too. Through Dad, I felt like I knew you and Nonny and that you two were somehow

472

with me in the jungle, supporting me. But now . . . now I miss you even more — I need you more than I did when I was a child."

The tree leaves rustled in the breeze.

"Sixteen years ago you left me a message. I know you believed strongly in what you said. And I believe it too. But, Poppy . . ."

Abby wiped her face with her sleeve.

"But, Poppy, I keep failing. I've tried everything I know how to do. But God doesn't seem to be in my efforts. It's like I've been throwing sticks into the river; they have no effect. Now I think God has opened a door for me to testify for Jesus in Washington. But I've been wrong several times already. I wonder if I'm just fooling myself. Who wants to listen to what I have to say?

"I'm afraid I've let you down . . . let God down. I've failed at my mission. Somehow my faith worked in the jungle. But here . . . I'm not trusting God. I'm not at peace. And now I'm struggling with thoughts about Creighton that I shouldn't be having about a man. Maybe I'm not as strong as you thought I'd be. Or as God wanted me to be."

She felt the breeze on her wet cheeks, listened to the rustling leaves, and watched as the trees swayed under the cloudless sky.

Perhaps, she had thought, God would speak to her at her grandfather's grave, give her some direction. But she heard nothing. Her grandfather was not here. God seemed far away. She was alone. Again.

"Creighton."

"Yes, Alistair."

"You asked me to notify you of your scheduled time to observe a brain transplant."

I sat up in my hospital bed. "Thank you, Alistair." At this point he was reminding me of almost everything in my life.

I entered the simultaneous VR Bryson Nichols had set up for me. It placed me in the lobby of NTI's Neurological Enhancement Lab. I received the requisite retina scan for visitors before a woman led me through a labyrinth of hallways. The surgery was performed in a clean room. I was required to don a surgical cap, gown, and mask before we entered — for realism, I supposed. Being in VR, I could hardly infect the place.

"Professor!" Bryson Nichols strode my way. "They're running a bit ahead of schedule. Didn't want to start without you."

He introduced me to the medical staff of four, led by Dr. Kamisha Sutter. They were preparing to do brain transplant surgery on Emma Fischer, a one-hundred-twenty-year-old with advanced brain disease. Though the surgery was minutes from beginning, the patient was awake and alert.

I stood with Nichols several paces back from the operating table. Emma's brain, Nichols informed me, had been internally scanned by thousands of nanites and reconstructed in software form. The software version of the brain had been tested for functionality. It was working perfectly. It hadn't been brought online so as to avoid the problem of simultaneous consciousness with the biological brain. The software form had already been uploaded into Emma's new silicon brain. All that remained was removing the biological brain, implanting the silicon substrate, and activating the software.

"Aren't they going to anesthetize the patient?" I asked.

"Momentarily. They administer it at the last minute. The general anesthetic has quite a short half-life. She will be conscious within a few minutes of the procedure's being complete."

Emma looked at us and smiled weakly. Nichols nodded to her reassuringly. "I do love being here for the procedure. It's been weeks since I've seen one. The look on the faces of the patients when they wake up is worth it all. They know that nothing has changed, that they are still themselves, only better. And that they will be themselves forever. Many of them start weeping as the wonderful reality hits home."

They anesthetized Emma. She lay motionless on the operating table. Sutter used a laser scalpel to slice open Emma's skull. She cut a ridge around the skull just below the top of the ears. When the ridge was complete, she removed the top half of the skull entirely. I stared at Emma's biological brain.

Sutter made a lengthy incision at the back of Emma's neck and inserted the connecting nodes that would be the link between Emma's spinal cord and the silicon brain.

Nichols leaned toward me and whispered, "They have to connect the spinal cord to the new brain before they can remove the biological one, of course. Otherwise, body maintenance functions run by the lower brain, such as breathing and heartbeat, would cease."

The spinal cord connection took two hours. Neural fibers had to be cut one by one and immediately replaced. Once Sutter completed the spinal cord connection, the lower brain functions of the body were severed from the biological brain. Emma's breathing and heartbeat stopped. I looked at Nichols.

"It's okay," he mouthed.

The neuroprogrammer activated the software's lower brain functions. Emma's heart beat irregularly for three beats, then resumed normal functioning. Her breathing returned to normal. I let out a sigh and breathed as well.

Nichols leaned over again. "We keep the patient running on lower brain only until the surgery is complete. Then we bring the higher brain online."

Sutter removed the biological brain from its cranial home. She placed the brain into a liquid-filled container. A nurse walked it over to a large stainless steel refrigerator and placed the brain inside.

"Temporary stasis," Nichols explained.

Sutter returned her attention to the operating table. Her team had positioned the silicon brain inside Emma's cranial cavity, placed her skullcap over it, and resealed the bone.

I turned to Nichols. "I thought the top of your skull was artificial now."

He smiled. "It is. But that was only for the demonstration. We do return patients' actual skulls back to them."

The operation was complete. Sutter turned to a nearby monitoring screen and looked at her patient's vitals.

"Everything is normal," Nichols informed me.

Sutter turned to the neuroprogrammer. "Jim, you can activate the full substrate."

The man input the operational commands, then looked at Sutter. "She's running."

Nichols was grinning from ear to ear. "She'll be awake in ten minutes."

We waited. Nine minutes later Sutter leaned over her patient. "Emma? Emma, can you hear me?"

The old woman opened her eyes. "Yes." She looked at the surgical staff standing over her. "Yes. Is it done? Do I have my new brain?"

"You sure do. It's all done. How do you feel?"

"I feel fine." She looked around the room and beamed. "I feel — Mr. Nichols. There's Mr. Nichols!"

Nichols took a couple of steps toward the table. "Just checking on you, Emma. I'm thrilled everything went perfectly."

"Yes." Emma turned to Sutter. "Just as I prayed for, Dr. Sutter. I asked the Lord —"

I looked over at Nichols. He was frowning.

A troubled look crossed Emma's face. "I asked the Lord . . ."

Sutter patted Emma's hand. "Yes, Emma. You were saying?"

She tried to rise from the table, but restraints kept her in place. "I was talking about the Lord, how —"

"Emma, you're going to have to let us untie the restraints. But when we do, you need to relax and lie still. It will be a while before we want you to get up."

She pulled against the restraints once more.

"Emma!"

The old woman laid her head back on the operating table and closed her eyes. She remained perfectly still. The room was quiet. After perhaps half a minute, Sutter spoke. "Emma? Are you ready for us to remove the restraints?"

Emma opened her eyes, a look of terror in them. "No! No! You didn't tell me this would happen!" She pulled against the straps, her eyes darting around the room. "You didn't say anything —"

Sutter leaned her face close to Emma's. "Emma, what? What? Is something not working right? Speak to me."

"No!"

Sutter turned to the nurse standing next to her. "We need to sedate her."

"You didn't tell me I'd lose —"

The nurse handed Sutter a hypo.

"Lose what, Emma?" Sutter asked. "Lose what?"

"Him!"

"Him? Who?"

"God!"

36

"Special Agent Steele, I can show you those records."

The robot walked down corridor B of the Massachusetts Center for Mental Health. Ben followed through a set of security doors.

When Ben had flashed his credentials at the center, demanding records on Raymond Caldwell, Director Brandt had miraculously discovered that Caldwell had indeed briefly been a patient. He gave Ben full access to Caldwell's files.

The robot led him down another corridor. They passed a physician and two orderlies — all humans — on the way. They took a right into a room furnished with several long tables. The robot motioned for him to have a seat. "This will provide you privacy to view the records."

The robot accessed the Grid. The first electronic file appeared on a visiscreen. "There is a refreshment bar at the back of the room. You are welcome to avail yourself. If you need further assistance, you can contact me." The robot gave Ben his Grid contact code and departed.

In truth, Ben could have accessed the records from DC. Theoretically, he could perform almost his entire job from his office, accessing information on the Grid and contacting people in VR. But Ben Steele liked hands-on work. When investigating a case, he preferred to spend time at the scene rather than stare at records on the Grid.

Ben began wading through the files. Several oddities emerged. Dr. Leonard Thompson was the admitting physician. There was no initial screening report from Thompson, however. The next day Caldwell had been assigned to the care of Brandt. How many patients were under the care of a hospital director? Since Bryson Nichols had had Caldwell committed, perhaps the director felt he should handle the case personally.

Caldwell had suffered a break from reality. He was diagnosed with Sarkov's syndrome, a disorder Ben knew was formerly treatable by pharmaceuticals but was now curable by gene therapy. He found it strange that Caldwell had not had thorough genetic testing done on himself. A routine test would have revealed the marker predisposing him to Sarkov's. The disease's onset could have easily been prevented.

Caldwell was placed on a pharmaceutical regimen to control his paranoid ranting. He was scheduled for gene therapy, to begin two weeks after his admittance. The day before the gene therapy commenced, he suffered a brain aneurysm and was found dead in his room.

Ben pushed back from the table, stood, and walked to the refreshment bar. He poured himself a cup of coffee and ordered a sausage-and-cheese biscuit. He turned back toward the table and stared at the image of Ray Caldwell still projected onto the visiscreen. He had no reason to doubt the file's accuracy. There was something about the case, however, that raised a red flag.

A movement to his left diverted Ben's attention. The door swung open. In walked one of the orderlies he had passed in the hallway. She was young, no more than twenty, and anxiously looking over her shoulder. She closed the door behind her and started toward the refreshment bar. She noticed Ben there and froze.

"Hi. I . . . uh . . ." She brushed her blond hair back over an ear covered with piercings. "May I help you?"

Ben smiled. "No, I'm fine, thank you. Just

getting a bite to eat." He motioned toward the bar. "Is this also an employee break room?"

Her shoulders slumped. "Well . . . not really. I just —" She glanced at the visiscreen. "You must be the FBI agent."

Ben looked down at himself. "Is it that obvious?"

The girl smiled. "No, it's not that. I just heard. We don't get FBI agents in here every day."

She walked to the bar and took a danish. She turned toward the visiscreen. Ben sidestepped to shield it from her view.

"The records you're looking at about that guy are wrong."

"What makes you say that?"

She took a bite of her pastry and shrugged.

Ben glanced back at the screen. "How do you even know what they say?"

"I just know they're wrong."

Ben stared at her, unsure how to respond.

She grabbed another danish and stuffed it in a front pocket. "I'll show you."

He followed her into the hallway. They walked down the remainder of the corridor and took a left down another one. The young woman kept looking over her shoulder.

"Is this going to get you into trouble?"

Ben asked.

"Yeah. This'll be my last day here, probably. That's okay. Crap job. I just like the pastries."

They came to a security door. She opened it with a retinal scan, and they walked down another hallway.

"I don't usually work this part of the hospital. But sometimes I have to substitute, so I have access. We're not supposed to say anything about this, but if it exposes Brandt, I'm all for it. He's a jerk."

She stopped at a patient room. She opened the door with another retinal scan and stepped inside. Ben followed her.

The room was painted white. In the middle of the room was a metal table with rounded edges and a simple chair. Beyond the table was a cot with a thin mattress, a sheet, and a green blanket. On the cot sat a man who looked to be in his nineties. It was Ray Caldwell.

Ray looked up from the bed in his isolation-unit room. Someone was opening the door. Three times daily a staff person came in to deliver food and check on him; this wasn't one of those times. His room had no clock, but from the internal clock of his silicon brain, he knew the exact timing of the staff's normal rounds. Someone entering at 1:47 p.m. meant something else was afoot. He sat up.

Theodore Brandt entered, followed by an orderly and a man Ray hadn't seen since he had been committed: Bryson Nichols. Brandt stopped just inside the door. "Ray, you have a visitor."

"Bryson. To what do I owe this visit?"

"We'll leave you two to talk," said Brandt. He and the orderly left the room.

Nichols sat in the chair. "Ray, Ray. If only you'd see things clearly, you'd be out of here — never would have been placed here, in fact. We can still proceed as if none of this has happened. I have a perfectly believable excuse for the mix-up about your death just waiting in the wings. You can rejoin the project immediately. I haven't even touched your office."

"You want me to see things your way? I used to, Bryson. I was mistaken." He leaned forward. "You didn't answer my question."

"You know perfectly well why I'm here, Ray." His visage revealed neither anger nor anxiety. "You had a visit from an FBI agent."

"You have eyes in the walls, Bryson. Or a hospital director in your pocket."

Nichols nonchalantly folded his hands behind his head. "So what did you and the agent discuss? Your release? Abigail? I hope you aren't planning anything foolish, old friend."

"My only concern at this point is my granddaughter, that she gets back to her people safely."

"She's become obsessed with finding you, Ray."

Ray frowned. "Thanks only to your clumsy attempt to make me disappear. I would have thought that with your new brain, you'd have handled that more intelligently. Perhaps you received a defective model."

Nichols stared at him.

"Lost your sense of humor, Bryson?" asked Ray. "I think we both want the same thing — Abby's departure. I told the FBI agent to handle that and to keep my presence here a secret."

A smile creased Nichols's face. "You're a wise man, Ray. Usually." He stood. "I will, of course, have to ensure the agent doesn't make a return visit."

"Of course."

"And the hospital staff will be keeping close watch on you. We still can't allow you access to the Grid. You know that."

Ray nodded. "Do me a favor, will you? Keep Abby safe — safer than you have to date."

"I will. I'm glad we're on the same page regarding Abigail, Ray. I only hope you come to see the larger issue my way." Nichols glanced around the room. "I hate to see you living like this."

Ray stood. "It's not permanent, Bryson. Not even eternity lasts forever — not your kind, anyway."

37

Abby was curled in the chair, reading her book, and I was just shaking off the vestiges of an afternoon nap when Ben Steele burst through the hospital room door. "Abby, your grandfather is alive!"

Abby leaped out of her chair. "He is? How do you know?" Her eyes shot toward me. My stomach churning, I feigned astonishment.

Ben glanced at me, then answered Abby. "I just got back from meeting with him earlier today. He's been at the mental health center the whole time."

Her cheeks had gone rosy with excitement. "Is he okay?"

"He's fine. There's never been anything wrong with him. Nichols had him committed there for . . . safekeeping."

Abby bolted for the door. "Let's go. I want to see him."

"No, Abby, you can't." Ben put his hand

on her arm, guiding her back toward her chair.

Abby looked bewildered. "Why not?"

"Because they won't even acknowledge that he's there. The hospital director takes instructions from Nichols. You'd never get past the foyer."

"How did you get to see him?" Abby asked.

"An employee who didn't mind losing her job."

"So are you going to arrest Nichols?"

Ben shook his head. "It's not that simple."

"But isn't what he's done against the law?" Her words were edged with frustration.

"Yes, of course. But Nichols has friends in high places. Very high places. It doesn't serve their interests to see him charged with anything."

"But this is the United States," she cried, throwing up her hands. "If someone commits a crime, don't they go to jail?"

"They should, yes. But it doesn't necessarily work that way if you're powerful."

Abby looked angry, ready for a fight. "Agent Steele, I don't understand. Why don't you just go to the head of the FBI and tell him what you know? They can't hold my grandfather against his will."

"At this point we don't know who to trust. That's what I need to work on now. In the meantime I need you to stay here or at the congresswoman's, where you're safe."

She sighed. "I'll try."

"Abby, this is no game. Men have tried to kill you." Ben glanced at me. "Both of you." He looked back at her. "Meanwhile . . . your grandfather would like to see you."

Abby's face lit up, her anger sliding away. "But . . . I thought you said —"

"You can't go to the hospital to meet him. But we may have figured out a way for you to meet in VR."

"They let him do that?" I asked.

Ben looked at me. "Not exactly. They won't allow him full Grid access. But he thought he could convince Brandt to let him have some time in a secure, localized VR environment. Something to give him a break from the white room where he's being kept. If Brandt allows it, he's pretty sure we can sneak in through a password-protected back door. He gave me all the information. That man is brilliant. We'll need to get Abby a portable VR hookup. I'll work on that. And it may not work at all" — he glanced at Abby — "so don't get your hopes too high. Not yet, anyway." He stepped toward the door, then looked back. "Until then, stay put. Both of you."

Ben left, and Abby ran over and threw her arms around me. "Creighton, he's alive! We can —"

Her expression grew troubled. I could almost see the wheels turning in her head as she tried to sort through what Ben had told her — and what I had told her about Ray earlier. She sat on the bed next to me and examined my face. "Creighton, did you know he was alive?"

I averted my eyes from hers. I felt sick. Suddenly the deal I had struck with Nichols seemed the most ill-advised decision I had ever made. "I didn't ask, Abby. I only told you what Nichols asked me to tell you. That was his price for doing the brain transplant on me. I suppose . . . I suppose I didn't want to know." I looked back up and into her eyes. "I'm very sorry."

Abby looked at me in silence for what seemed an eternity, her face blank and stony. Finally she rose from the bed and walked out the door.

Three hours later Abby returned. She walked over to the sink and placed a cup and a small bag on the counter. "I brought you a drink and some cookies."

She sat on the edge of the bed. "Creighton, I want you to know that I forgive you."

I wanted to reach for her, but I felt too ashamed. "Abby, I don't know what to say. When Nichols said he would —"

She held an index finger to my lips. "I forgive you. Let's leave it at that, okay?"

She had placed her trust in me, and I had violated that trust. There was so much I wanted to explain, but nothing would alleviate her pain. We looked at each other for a few moments. She seemed tired, as if she had been crying again. Everything had been taken from Abby, and I had added to her losses when I should have been caring for her, protecting her. I looked away.

"Has Agent Steele returned?" she finally asked.

"Not yet."

She glanced at the counter. "Have you had anything to eat this afternoon?"

"No. I didn't like what they brought for lunch."

"I'll go get something. I don't want you eating just cookies."

She returned in ten minutes with two sandwiches and some chips. She had become a connoisseur of chips. Ben entered as we were finishing the sandwiches. "Got the portable VR hookup."

It looked like the one I had used in my office, only newer.

Abby put her plate down and stood. "Is it ready to go?"

"As soon as we get you into it. If Ray was successful, he should be online in a matter of minutes. If not . . . well, we'll know soon enough."

She sat in the chair by the window. Ben got her fitted and the settings adjusted. He stepped back. "It's ready."

"Are you coming with me?" she asked him, looking anxious.

"No, no need. He's expecting you."

She looked over at me. "Creighton? Are you coming?"

I shook my head and forced a smile. "You two need to get acquainted. Catch up on the last three decades. I'll join you the next time."

I desperately wanted to go, to somehow make amends by simply being there. But I had forfeited the right to be there, the first time at least. I had been Abby's closest connection in the world, and she could no longer trust me. Despite saying she forgave me and despite her invitation for me to accompany her, she was, in part, alone again. Maybe, for now, Ray could give her the connection she needed.

She turned to Ben. "Okay."

"All right," he said. "Now, remember, this can't be a long visit. Ray said that longer than a few minutes might trigger a security subroutine that would let the hospital know we've snuck in. At least I think that's what he said. I'm no scientist. As it is, we agreed that if you're not back in ten minutes, I'm pulling you out."

She nodded.

Ben continued, "Press this green button on the right side of your head. I have no idea where you'll end up. Be prepared for any sort of environment." Ben accessed the time. "One minute."

Abby turned toward me, her eyes wide. "Creighton, can you believe it? I'm going to see my Poppy."

I managed a smile. "I'll see you in a few minutes."

She pressed the green button and entered VR.

Abby found herself in the middle of a large, deserted park. Tall trees appeared in every direction under a blue sky. The trees were separated by expanses of green grass of a sort she had never experienced in the jungle.

"Abigail."

She turned. Ten feet away was a wooden picnic table. On one of the benches sat her grandfather. "Poppy!"

He stood, and she ran and threw her arms around him. Her eyes filled with tears. She could feel his whiskers against her cheek and the strength in his arms. They embraced a full minute before Ray pulled back slightly. "Oh, precious girl." He touched Abby's face, wiping her tears with his thumb. "We'd better get acquainted before our time runs out."

They sat on the bench, Abby clasping her grandfather's arm. "Poppy, I'm so sorry for not finding you sooner. We kept —"

He shook his head. "No, I'm right where God wants me. You weren't meant to find me sooner. Abigail, look at you — a grown woman. I can't believe we're finally together. Your grandmother is envious, I'm sure."

"Do you think she knows what we're doing?"

"If she doesn't, we'll tell her eventually." He winked at her. "So how long have you been in the States?"

"A month and a half. Poppy, I got your messages — the one you sent me sixteen years ago and the one you sent Dad recently." Her words came in a rush. She inhaled deeply, trying to slow her racing pulse.

"He didn't get it?"

"Poppy, Dad's been dead for fifteen years."

"Oh no." He looked stricken for several moments, then wiped tears from his eyes and collected himself.

"I'm sorry to have to tell you this way."

He shook his head. "No, there's no good way. When Agent Steele told me you were in the States, I assumed you all were accessible. I was looking forward to his company once more." He wiped a last tear from his eye. "And your mother?"

Abby sighed. "Eight years ago."

"You've been by yourself in the jungle for eight years?" He looked surprised.

"No, not by myself. In my village."

"Of course. They're family too, I'm sure. So you got the message your grandmother and I sent you. I had no idea you'd be thirty-four before you got it. Perhaps it came as somewhat of a shock."

She nodded.

"To us as well," he added, "discovering that God had told us both the same thing about you."

"So you think . . . Do you still believe it?"

Poppy chuckled. "Well, I never heard otherwise. Yes, I believe it. And now you're here. So what is the Father doing through you?"

Abby's eyes fell. How would Poppy react to her lack of success? "Nothing, I'm afraid."

"Nothing? I doubt that. Not if he lives in you."

She looked back up at him. "I've tried to share the gospel numerous times. With a woman in Dallas. At a dinner party at Lauren's. In a college class. On *Global Sunrise*."

"*Global Sunrise*? You're kidding. God opened that door for you?"

She sighed. "Well, yes." She decided not to get into what had happened as a result. "I even recorded a message for the Grid that presents the gospel. But . . ."

A warm breeze blew through the park.

"But what?" He put a hand on her restless knee.

"No one seems to be interested in the message of Jesus." She gestured in frustration at the empty park. "It wasn't that way in the jungle. Many people came to Christ there. But here I just can't connect with people."

Despite her fears, her grandfather's eyes looked warm and understanding. He gently asked, "What's the message that you're telling them?"

"The basic gospel. That they're sinners.

That Jesus was God in the flesh. That he died on the cross to pay the penalty for their sins and then rose from the dead. That by trusting in him, they can get their sins forgiven and live with God forever."

Ray leaned forward. "Maybe you're not delivering the right message."

She was confused. "How could that be the wrong message? It's the gospel."

He smiled. "Not wrong. Incomplete. Let me ask you this: how is that message working in your own life?"

Abby frowned. "I'm not sure what you mean."

"How is the Christian life going for you personally? Are you experiencing something that others would be dying to have?"

"I don't know. Not really, I suppose." Abby twisted uncomfortably on the bench. "I'm trying as hard as I can for God. I try to stay connected with him. I —"

He patted her hand gently. "Maybe that's the problem. You're trying to do something you weren't meant to do."

"But in the message you and Nonny said —"

She was disoriented for a moment. The park disappeared, and Abby found herself sitting back in the hospital room. "No. Not

499

yet!" She looked at Ben. "We weren't finished."

He shook his head. "That was ten minutes, Abby. I'm sorry."

"But we didn't even get to talk about —" She looked near tears again but seemed to will them back.

"We'll try again tomorrow."

Abby looked at me, her eyes pleading.

"At least it worked," I said, trying to encourage her. "So how was it, meeting your grandfather?"

Her shoulders slumped, and she looked at the floor. "Not what I wanted."

38

Abby and Ray met at the picnic table again the next day. He hugged her, and they sat.

"Abby, I want to apologize for yesterday. It seems you left somewhat disheartened. Let's start again. I'm so thrilled to see you after all these years, and I'm so proud of the young woman you've become, with such a love for God. And I must say" — he grinned at her — "you look so much like your mother."

A lump filled Abby's throat. She reached across the table, and they held hands for a moment.

He continued, "I can't tell you how often I wanted to hold your little hands when you were growing up, but you were half a world away. I never imagined that it would take this long for us to get together or that it would be under these circumstances."

He grew more serious. "Did Agent Steele tell you that it's only a matter of time before they find out what we're doing and shut this down?"

She nodded.

"I think you can trust him," he continued. "If we get cut off, we'll keep working together to find the truth. Okay?"

"Okay." She was eager to return to the prior day's conversation, to understand what he had begun to say. "Poppy, what did you mean, I'm trying to do something I'm not supposed to do? Haven't I been trying to do God's will?"

He smiled tenderly. "Yes, I'm sure you have. Your heart is for him, and I know you want to do what he wants."

"So what did you mean?"

"Are you sure you want to take time to discuss this now?"

She nodded emphatically. "Ever since coming to the States, I've felt out of sorts spiritually. Things just don't work for me here the way they did in the jungle. I read the Bible, and God doesn't speak to me. I pray and feel like my prayers bounce off the ceiling. I try to share the gospel but don't even mention Jesus. I spend time with this man, Creighton, and . . ." She stared at the ground. "It's just hard. I'm a grown woman . . ." She looked back up at him. "No matter how hard . . ." She shook her head in frustration.

"No matter how hard you try for God, you just can't seem to do enough?"

Her eyes widened. "Yes. How did you know?"

"Because I've been there." Ray stood. "Here, let's stretch. I spend my whole day sitting. I hate being cooped up." She rose slowly, and they walked toward a wide dirt path that wound its way through the park. He took her hand in his.

"God knows you're trying hard for him, you know."

Abby sighed. "I suppose."

"But he's not asking you to try hard for him."

She looked at him, bewildered. "What do you mean, he doesn't want that? The New Testament has all these commands about living the Christian life. If I don't try hard —"

He held up his hand, and she stopped walking.

"I'm not saying you don't have a role to play," he replied. "I'm saying you don't have to wear yourself out trying. You're seeing yourself as the one who has to make the Christian life work."

"But who's going to make it work if I don't?" She knew the frustration was evident in her voice.

"Jesus is."

Her shoulders slumped. She wanted a fresh idea, not something she had known for thirty years. "Well, of course Jesus will do it. But I still have to —"

He shook his head again. "Let's walk some more."

They continued down the path. "Abby, the most important thing for you now is not to *do* something differently but to *see* something differently. Jesus is the life within you. How old were you when you first trusted in him?"

"Five. At least, that's what Mom told me. I don't really remember."

He nodded. "So when you were five, God gave you spiritual life. You already had biological life, but you had a spirit dead to God. You were born that way; we all are. So God did a heart transplant in you. He took out your dead spirit and gave you a new human spirit, made like him. Then he himself came to live in you — joined himself to your new spirit. Now you are permanently connected to the source of life itself. That's how his life flows into you, and through you."

She paused on the trail, lost in thought. What he said resonated on a certain level, but what difference did this make when her prayers went unanswered or when she was trying to maintain pure thoughts about Creighton? Jesus wasn't going to think purely for her.

"I hear what you're saying," she said, "but I still have to do something. Jesus doesn't make my mouth move to say the right words to someone."

He chuckled. "No, he doesn't. But that takes care of itself once your mindset has changed — once you see things as he does. When you do, his load really does become easy and his burden light, just as he said. You've been carrying a heavy load."

He was right about that. She took a deep breath. "Okay, explain that to me."

Poppy reached up and pulled a limb down toward them. "You remember the story Jesus told about the vine and the branches?"

She resisted the impulse to roll her eyes. *Of course I remember it.* "Yes."

"This tree works the same as a vine." He held a small branch between his fingers and turned to Abby. "Where does the life of this tree originate — deep inside the tree or in this little branch?"

Trees, at least, were one topic Abby did know about. "Deep inside."

"Right, but how do you know? You can't

tell by looking on the outside."

"Because a branch by itself doesn't grow."

"Correct. It has no life of its own. It receives life. Abby, you are this branch. You aren't the source of the life." He motioned with his head toward the tree. "The tree is. God is. He is the source of spiritual life within you. As the tree produces fruit, so God produces life. His own life. Only he can do that. Why would we think we can produce the life of God — or that God expects us to?"

He looked again at the branch. "This branch bears fruit just by staying connected to the tree. It's a conduit. It doesn't have to work hard. Now, what if I break off the branch" — he snapped it off — "and you plant it in the ground." He handed the branch to Abby. "How much fruit is that branch going to produce now?"

"None. By itself, a branch can't produce fruit."

"Right. It won't produce a single" — he looked at the tree again — "pecan, I believe. If it tries to work hard and produce pecans on its own, it fails. God designed it that way. It only bears pecans by resting in the tree.

"Like this branch, Abby, you can try as hard as you want, but you can't produce the life of God. It's impossible; we all fail at it. We can't come close to producing the life the New Testament describes. It's God's life. But though we can't produce it, we can express it — as the branch does. We do that by simply staying connected to him, by trusting him to live his life through us. That's what he's in you to do — live his own life."

She stared at him, confused. "But it can't be that easy. I can't just sit around all day saying, 'I'm connected to him.' I have to do something."

He smiled. "Let me tell you what you can do. You mentioned the woman you spoke with in Dallas. When . . ." He paused momentarily. "Our time is up. I don't want you jerked away again without being able to say good-bye."

Abby felt incomplete, as if the truth she sought had somehow eluded her. "Poppy, we can't stop here."

"We can do this for only ten minutes, Abby. That's what Agent —"

"Just three more minutes. I want to finish what we started. I'm not sure I'm getting what you're saying."

He placed his hand on her shoulder. "I would love to talk more. I'll stay here a few minutes. If they let you —"

■ ■ ■ ■

I watched as Abby opened her eyes. She looked disturbed. Ben walked over and reached to remove her helmet. "How was your meeting?"

"I need to go back."

Ben nodded. "Tomorrow it'll be time to —"

"No!" Abby reached up and grasped her helmet, holding it in place. "I need to go back now."

Ben frowned. I could tell things were about to blow up.

"Abby," I interjected, "we agreed that ten minutes was the most we could safely afford to do."

"Three minutes." She looked from me to Ben. "Just three more minutes."

He shook his head. "I'm sorry, Abby. I can't let you risk that."

Her eyes flashed. "And who put you in charge of how much time I can spend with my grandfather?"

I could see the anger well up inside him. "I would have thought that my thirty-two years as an FBI agent might have put me in that position. But if you don't want my expertise . . ." He turned and started toward the door.

"Agent Steele . . ." I held up my hand.

He looked back at me. We all stared at one another in silence. "Where is Ray now?" I asked Abby.

"He was going to wait for me in VR."

My eyes met Ben's. "I agree with you, but could we send Abby back for three minutes? We're spending more time than that arguing, and every minute we delay, Ray is endangered."

He sighed resignedly. "All right. Three more minutes. That's all."

Abby nodded at him and looked at me. *Thank you,* she mouthed. Ben programmed the helmet, and she reentered VR.

Ray was sitting at the picnic table once again. Abby sat down, and he extended his hands across the table. She took them in hers and opened her mouth to speak, but he started first.

"I wonder if I'm making things more confusing for you every time we get together. Let me back up for a moment and see if I can make this clearer."

Abby felt her body relax. That's what she desperately needed — some clarification.

"For two thousand years," he continued, "most of the church has missed what Jesus said about this. Consequently, it always falls back on teaching rules and principles for successful living. But those aren't the good news of Jesus. The good news is that Jesus comes to give life — his life."

He looked across the park, then back at her. "You said people didn't seem to be interested in the message of forgiveness through Christ."

She nodded. "Not that I can tell."

"I found that out long ago. That's because they no longer sense their need to be forgiven. People don't believe in absolutes anymore, in right and wrong. So what is there to be forgiven for?"

"But they *need* God's forgiveness."

He put a hand on her arm. "What they need is life. And they do sense their need for that. Even in the midst of all their high-tech pleasures and diversions, people are empty. Physical life alone, with an empty spirit, never satisfies. People need spiritual life; they need God. You have God. Relax in that reality — he is living through you this very moment. When you spoke to the woman in Dallas, he was living through you. He was speaking through you. Be at peace with that, and people will see the life within you and be drawn to it."

He placed his hands around hers. "You

need to return. We'll talk more. God will make this clear to you. Growing up with a distorted gospel, as we all did, we need to do some unlearning, I've found. Tomorrow bring that professor friend of yours. And Agent Steele. We have to make plans."

Abby emerged from VR. She looked downcast.

"Well?" I asked. "How did it go? Did you get the answers you wanted?"

She turned to me and shook her head. "Not entirely." She removed her VR helmet. "What he said made sense, I guess. I just don't see how it's all that different from the way I've been trying to live. I'm not sure what it means practically — what I actually need to do." She inhaled deeply and looked toward the window. "Maybe if we talk some more . . ."

I felt impatient. We didn't have time to waste on spiritual matters when life-and-death physical matters confronted us. "Is he ready to discuss our situation?"

"Yes." She sounded distant, lost in her thoughts. Then she turned and looked at me and Ben. "We have to get him out." She started pacing the small room. "I can't stand him being in . . . wherever he is in that place."

Ben shook his head. "I don't think that's wise. Not yet. Nichols thinks I'm keeping quiet about Ray's still being alive. It was a way to buy some time for these meetings. If we take any action . . ."

"But he's already in danger, then, right?" Abby bumped into the edge of the bed with her hip. She winced, then gave an apologetic smile. "Sorry, Creighton."

"Yes," Ben replied, "and you'd be in danger too if you tried to get him out. Promise me you won't do anything rash, Abby."

She sighed heavily. "He wants us there tomorrow at the park." She looked at me. "All of us."

"Abby, do *you* want me there tomorrow?"

She answered without hesitating. "Yes."

The next day the four of us met at the picnic table. Abby and I filled Ray in on the details that Ben hadn't.

"NTI is the only company with the technology to pull this off, as far as I know," Ray said. He looked at Abby. "The fellow you describe, the one who attacked you in Dallas — I'm not familiar with him. I'm guessing he's associated with Damien Cleary."

Ben's eyebrows rose. "What makes you

say that?"

"Just a hunch. Cleary is a maverick. Brilliant but uncontrollable. He does what he wants."

"What would be his motive?"

"That's hard to say."

"If one of his people is behind it, shouldn't we inform Nichols?" I interjected.

Ray shook his head. "No. We can't trust him. Nichols would never condone murder himself. But he might cover it up if he thought it would advance his cause. Everything revolves around his cause. That's why he threw me in here — in the hospital, that is. I threatened his vision for humanity."

If Ray and Abby had already discussed that matter, she hadn't revealed it to me. Or had she?

"Why were you a threat?" I asked.

"Because of what I discovered. During the final phase of the brain transplant testing process, we began performing the procedure on actual subjects, elderly people with advanced brain disease" — he turned to Abby — "and a couple of them were Christians. What I discovered was that when we did the transplant procedure, they lost their connection with God."

I felt a rush of satisfaction. I was right. Ray's warning in his message involved what he believed to be the presence of God. And what I experienced watching Emma's brain replacement wasn't a singular event.

Ray continued, "I believe that when the biological brains were removed from the patients, the human spirit departed. It was as if they were dead. God's Spirit joins himself with — becomes one with — a human spirit. When the human spirit leaves, God's Spirit goes with it."

Abby's face conveyed her astonishment. "But how did you find that out?"

"From their own self-reports. They lost their sense of connectedness."

Ben cleared his throat. "Ray, you said these people were elderly, with advanced brain disease. Isn't it possible that they were imagining things — that they were simply experiencing a normal psychological side effect of the procedure?"

Ray looked at Ben. "It makes sense to question that. But no. I went back and checked these patients' files. Only the two self-reporting as Christians experienced this."

"I'm surprised you found any Christians at all," Ben remarked.

"You have to remember, most of the patients were quite elderly."

"So what did you do when you found this

out?" I asked, keeping an eye on Abby's face. Given her esteem for her grandfather, I hoped he had an answer she could accept.

"After my discovery I informed Nichols, of course. He wasn't concerned. I insisted that he stop the procedures. Not only had two patients lost their connection with God forever, every other patient had lost the *potential* to connect with God. They no longer possessed a human spirit capable of being joined to him. But Nichols wouldn't stop. He wouldn't believe such things, despite the evidence."

"But he only had two such cases," Ben countered. "It might be reasonable —"

"No, they've had three cases," I corrected.

Abby turned to me, the furrows in her brow deepening. "How do you know?"

"Because I witnessed one. Nichols invited me to a transplant."

Abby's eyes widened. "What? When? Creighton —"

"Then we've had four," Ray interjected.

I looked at him, surprised. "Who was the fourth?"

He paused. "I was."

39

"No!" Abby cried. "You didn't have that done to yourself!"

Ray shrugged. "He did it to me, Abby. Nichols drugged me and performed the procedure on me."

"Why would he do such a thing?" I asked, placing an arm around Abby's shoulder.

"Arrogance, I believe, not malice. Nichols was convinced that if I had the procedure done, I'd see things his way. That wasn't the case. I experienced exactly what the other two patients experienced."

Tears welled up in Abby's eyes. "So you don't have any sense of connection to God?"

He shook his head slowly. "No. I've lost him. Intellectually, I can formulate what I've always believed, but there's no spirit reality to it. The inner life I shared with him is gone."

Abby's pallor had turned gray, and I worried she might faint. "So everything you've been telling me —"

"Is what God taught me over many years, Abby."

"But do you believe it anymore?" She nearly whispered the question.

Ray sighed. "Faith is in the spirit, Abby. Without my spirit I don't have the capacity to have faith — or to experience God."

Abby looked as if her world had come to an end. The one person she had a spiritual connection with, the one she had placed so much hope in, didn't himself have a connection with God any longer. And never would.

I pulled Abby to me and stroked her hair while she dabbed her tears. We all sat silently, letting Abby collect herself. She reached across the table toward Ray, and they held hands.

"I know how hard this must be for you, Abby," he said, compassion filling his eyes.

She nodded. "It's just . . . a shock."

"I know. It was to me too."

Ben leaned forward. "I hate to interrupt, but we're out of time. Can we meet again, Ray? This afternoon? I know it's risky, but time isn't on our side."

"I'll try," said Ray. "Look for me at two thirty."

Abby, Ben, and I reentered physical reality.

"Agent Steele," I asked, "based on what Ray said, don't we have enough evidence to move against Nichols? Can't we enlist some help higher up the chain in the FBI?"

The door opened, and the agent from the hallway stepped in. "Ben, I've been instructed to escort you out."

I turned to the man. "Escort out? Out of where?"

"The secure area of the hospital, sir," the hallway agent replied.

"Why?"

"Mr. Steele is no longer with the FBI."

That answered my question about obtaining help. We were on our own.

Ben tapped me just before two in the afternoon. He was sitting at a desk in what I assumed was his VR office.

"I didn't expect to see you again," I said. "What happened?"

"Someone with serious power decided I was getting too close to the truth, I guess."

"Can you at least help us meet with Ray once more?"

"I can do more than that. Getting fired won't make me go away. I'm in this to the end, Creighton, assuming you want my help."

I was taken aback by his resoluteness. "Of course we do. I . . ." I didn't want to come across as impertinent. "I am curious why you feel so committed to us." To Abby, I imagined.

He glanced to his left, toward the bottom of his desk, then his eyes returned to me. "It's . . . it's a personal matter."

The four of us reconvened as planned at two thirty. Ben pushed the agenda. "Our window for these meetings will close soon. We need to develop a plan — quickly."

Ray spoke. "Nichols's vision is for all humanity to convert to transhuman status. That's what he calls humans with silicon brains."

"Poppy, how did you ever get involved in this?" Abby had been quiet most of the day, reading her Bible and leaving my room for walks. With Ray, she seemed composed, but I was worried about her.

"I joined with Nichols because I saw the potential medical benefit to individuals with terminal brain disease. It was the only organ never transplanted. I knew Nichols had this grand idea about transhumanity, but I never expected —"

"Okay," Ben interrupted. "This is all very interesting, but it doesn't give us a plan." He turned to Ray. "You said Damien Cleary was the most likely suspect."

Ray nodded. "Nichols would never have authorized the murder of the Inisi. At least I don't think he would. One thing I've realized is that after the transplant is done, one's sense of conscience starts to dissipate."

"Why would the conscience be affected?" I asked.

"The human spirit is the seat of conscience. Without the spirit, one's sense of right and wrong — which can be distorted under normal circumstances, of course — ebbs. I find that I must intellectually compensate for that — more so as time passes and I'm distanced from what used to anchor me. For someone without a strong sense of conscience in the first place —"

"Like Nichols," I suggested.

"Or Cleary," Ray added. "My concern" — he looked at Abby — "apart from your safety and Creighton's, is that Cleary may want to speed up the transhuman conversion. How, I'm not sure. But he's always been on the cutting edge of the research, and he's very impatient. There's a lot of money to be made. I'm afraid . . ." He paused.

"Afraid of what?" Ben asked.

"I'm afraid that what happened to Abby's village was a trial run. That Cleary was using them as test subjects for the nanites."

Abby looked stunned. "Why my village?" she muttered. "Why Mir . . ."

Ray looked at her. "My message to your father. I'm so sorry, Abby."

She stifled a cry.

I placed my hand on her shoulder. "Abby?"

She shook her head, seeming to will away the pain. "I'm okay."

Ray continued, "Plus, your tribe was completely isolated. Little risk of discovery, or so he assumed."

"Are you saying Cleary might have larger-scale plans?" Ben asked.

"That's what we don't know. But, yes, very likely."

"If that's the case," I said, "the man in Dallas who shot Abby must work for him."

Ben shook his head. "For some reason he was untraceable."

Ray gave Ben a look. "That's probably Cleary. He develops anti-nanites. Nanite antibodies. They could easily disable a tracking chip."

"Why can't we just follow Cleary," Abby asked, "if he's the key?"

"I could tail him," Ben answered. "The problem is, I don't have any legal standing to do so. If I'm spotted, he could have me arrested or, more likely, killed. And my guess is he's not the easiest man to keep an eye on."

"No," Ray agreed. "He wouldn't be. Almost impossible to do without endangering yourself."

"I'm not saying I'm unwilling to do that for our purposes. But if I'm apprehended, that leaves us up a creek."

The table was silent for a moment. I heard a loud sigh from Abby. I could tell she was growing frustrated by our inability to stop those responsible for murdering her village. For murdering Miraba.

"There is another way."

We all looked at Ray.

"Which is?" I asked him.

"Read Cleary's memory stream. It would tell us everything he's done and, probably, is planning to do."

"How are we going to do that?"

"Someone with a brain transplant and the right adjustments could do it. I discovered this while I was developing the Grid interface for the silicon substrate. We can access the memory stream of anyone who has had a brain transplant."

"Who else knows this?" Ben asked.

"I didn't inform anyone. Didn't even record it in my log. I didn't want to make that power available to anyone."

"But wouldn't that be illegal?" Abby objected. She turned to me. "You said memory streams were the most highly secure information on the Grid."

"It is definitely illegal," Ben commented.

Ray nodded. "And highly dangerous. In the wrong hands . . ."

We all looked at one another.

"So if it's illegal," I asked, "how could that information help us? I can't imagine it would be admissible in court."

"We don't need it for court," Ben answered. "All we need is to alert the authorities to a specific threat and obtain some physical evidence to support it. That would be enough to generate an investigation. It may be our only shot."

Everyone was quiet.

"Well," I said, "what are we waiting for? Let's have Ray proceed. Can you do that in your . . . room . . . without attracting attention?"

"I can't do it in my room at all."

"Why not?"

"Because we didn't build the substrate with the necessary configuration. It would require a slight modification to the hardware, and I don't have access to the instruments I'd need to make the adjustment."

"So who else could access Cleary's memory stream?" I asked.

Ray leaned forward. "It would have to be someone else who has a transplant."

"Then that idea is another dead end." Ben looked around the table. "Unless one of you has an artificial brain." He laughed.

I looked at Abby.

"Creighton, no. You can't go through with it." Abby glared at me from beside the window in my hospital room. "It's suicide. It's spiritual suicide. Why would you want that?"

"Abby, I don't even have a connection to God. If I do the transplant, I'm not losing anything. And I get my mind back. The bottom line is, someone has to do it."

She threw up her arms. "I can't believe you're saying this. You're losing the potential to be connected to God. After all the research you did, haven't you thought about that?"

I had. I just didn't want to admit it to Abby. I was hardly a Christian yet, but Ray's words had only confirmed what I had discovered for myself, that the life offered in the Bible was much more appealing and made much more sense than the version of the faith that had so unceremoniously faded away this century. "I have thought about it," I answered. "I'm just not ready to do anything about it yet."

She walked over to me and took my hands in hers. Her brown eyes reflected both love and deep sadness. "Creighton, if you do this, you'll never be able to take that step. You'll know God is there, but he'll be unavailable to you. Who knows how long you'd be like that."

"For eternity, if Bryson Nichols has his way." I tried to give her a smile, but Abby remained somber.

She shook her head. "I'm worried about both your here and now and your eternity, Creighton. You know that."

"I know." I touched her soft cheek.

We were silent for a moment.

"Maybe God would make allowance for my fate under the circumstances," I offered.

She released my hands and stepped to the window again. I knew she was concerned for me, but there seemed to be something more bothering her. "Abby, are you still holding out hope . . . for us?"

She stared outside. "I think so. I mean . . . I was."

"Even after I allowed you to continue to believe Ray was dead?"

She turned toward me. "I don't blame you for that, Creighton. Nichols made you an offer and attached conditions to it. Maybe you couldn't think clearly about it, recognize his lies. It was a difficult situation for you."

"But I betrayed you." The tightness in my chest was back. It surfaced anytime I thought about what I had done to Abby.

She looked at me tenderly. "And it still hurts even though I've forgiven you. It's just that, well, I know God changes hearts. I've been praying that he might change yours." She appeared small beside the window, younger than thirty-four, like a girl. I wished that I could make her world perfect for her — wished that I hadn't added to its imperfections.

"If I do the transplant, you're afraid you'll lose me."

"Yes. I know I will." She returned to the bedside and took my hand again in hers. "I haven't been able to work it all out, Creighton. Your beliefs, my faith, Papua New Guinea. I just know I don't want to lose you."

■ ■ ■ ■

I lay awake listening to the quiet, sleeping rhythm of Abby's breathing as she lay on the cot next to my bed. I felt the warmth of her hand intertwined with mine. My brain — what was left of it — was a jumble of thoughts and emotions.

Was I capable of making a decision such as this? Of logically weighing the options, the risks, the probabilities? Of weighing not only my future but the future of possibly millions?

A week earlier, when Nichols had offered it to me, I was ready to do the transplant. If anything, the case for it was now greater. We needed the transplant to access Damien Cleary's memory stream. I needed it to have any hope of continuing my career. And not simply to continue it — to become the preeminent historian of my generation. Of any generation.

Why, then, was I so torn? Was it this woman lying beside me? Would I really lose her? Did I love her? Did I even know what real love was?

It's not like I hadn't had my share of relationships. But the longest relationship I had ever had was in Barcelona during the summer between my freshman and sophomore years of college. Since then, I had never met anyone I was drawn to on more than a hormonal level. Until now. Could I abandon that — even for a potentially greater good?

To my shock, a final consideration weighed even more heavily: God. Two months before I would have considered the issue irrelevant. Questions about God were the mental gymnastics of intellectual primitives. God was a fairy tale invented millennia ago by people who believed that the sun revolved around the earth and that fire was a basic element.

I had done the research, however. As a historian, I could no longer dismiss the possibility that Jesus Christ was the appearance of a supreme being in human form, that he rose from the dead, and that he offered true life to those willing to join themselves to his Spirit in faith. The experience of several transplant patients corresponded to that paradigm. Ray Caldwell was certainly no neanderthal. Quite the opposite.

If connection with God was a reality, could I choose to forfeit it — forever? Who could make such a choice if that was the reason for our existence? Didn't self-sacrifice have a natural limit?

The minutes passed. No answer came. No answer would come, I knew. I would have to choose.

40

The restaurant, 120 stories up, rotated 360 degrees every hour, giving diners a constant, awe-inspiring view of the Hong Kong skyline and, to the north, mainland China. Despite my distaste for VR restaurants, I could have happily visited this one regularly.

The maître d' led me to an empty table by a window. Two minutes later Bryson Nichols arrived. He sat in a chair across from me.

"How do you like the view, Professor?"

"Magnificent. I've never heard of this VR restaurant."

Nichols smiled. "No one has. It's my own creation. All my VR spots are my own creations." He looked across the room and nodded. A waiter appeared.

"Care for some wine?" Nichols asked.

"Yes, please."

He glanced at the waiter. "Geoffrey, a bottle of Pinot Gris."

The waiter disappeared. Nichols turned back to me. "I didn't expect to hear from you, at least not so soon. You strike me as a cautious man, Professor. I don't mean that disrespectfully. Caution has its place. The encounter you had in our lab would have been enough to scare off lesser men permanently."

"How do you know it hasn't?"

"Because you requested a meeting. Why else would that be, except to say you want to go ahead with the transplant? A wise choice, if I may say so. A very wise choice. The transplant will open up vistas of which you've never dreamed. That woman you witnessed at the lab — she was quite insane, you realize. I don't know what happened to our psychological screening. An unsatisfactory candidate. Such an outcome could never happen to someone like you."

That was true at this point, but not for the reason he gave. "No, I understand," I replied. "I'm ready to go through with the procedure."

"Splendid. How soon would you like it done?"

"Immediately."

"Excellent." He paused for a moment, apparently checking his internal calendar. "How about Tuesday at eight o'clock?"

"That would be fine. Who will do the procedure?"

"I'll do it myself."

The waiter appeared with our wine. I took a sip and placed my glass back on the table. I leaned forward and lowered my voice, despite what I assumed were fail-safe security safeguards. "Mr. Nichols, there is a certain matter we need to discuss."

He placed his glass to the side. "I wondered if you were going to bring this up."

"Agent Steele has informed Abigail about the status of her grandfather."

He sighed. "Yes. Most unfortunate. There is, of course, nothing she can do about the matter."

"She can inform Lauren Caldwell."

"Lauren Caldwell knows exactly where her uncle is. It's to her advantage that Ray's status not change or become public knowledge."

"What about the congressional hearings? They give Abby a public platform."

Nichols reached for his wineglass. "I'll handle that matter as well."

"Without harm to Abby?"

Nichols scowled. "Professor, I'm an instigator of global transformation, not a gangster."

"And what about Agent Steele?"

"As you probably know, *Mister* Steele is no longer with the FBI. What exactly can he do?"

Despite the late hour, I checked out of the hospital. There was no point in staying. My condition was static and nonthreatening, and I wasn't having surgery. Not the kind my neurosurgeon had suggested, anyway. The hospital had provided one benefit: I didn't have to interact with Lauren at her house. According to Abby, however, Lauren had returned to Texas until the hearings four days away. Lauren's place suddenly held more appeal.

I took a car to Lauren's home and carried my belongings to my guest bedroom upstairs. Down the hall Abby was already asleep. What was I going to tell her about my decision? I had thought of a hundred ways to break the news. None of them would soften the blow. No words could.

The next morning I woke up late. I walked down the upstairs hall to Abby's sunlit room. Her bed was empty. I checked the bathroom; it was as well. I walked down the stairs and called for her. No one answered.

I searched the downstairs. Had she said she was going someplace? I accessed my memory stream. No. I went outside to the

FBI agent sitting in a car at the curb. "Did Abby leave?"

"Yes." He seemed annoyed to be speaking with one of his charges.

"When?"

"About an hour ago."

"Did she say where she was going?"

"No." The man had no intention of elaborating.

"Why didn't you stop her?"

"I'm here to secure the house, Dr. Daniels. I don't have the authority to prevent either of you from leaving."

Great. I stalked back into the house and tapped Ben. We met in VR.

"Abby left."

"Where'd she go?"

"I don't know," I replied. "Neither does the FBI guy."

"How long ago?"

"An hour."

"You think she just wanted to get out for a while?"

"Probably. Or . . ."

"Boston." Ben rubbed his brow in frustration. "She seemed pretty focused on getting Ray out of there the other day." There was a long pause. "I have a friend at the bureau who will still help me out. He can check to see if she's taken a train."

He exited VR. In five minutes he was back. He looked worried. "She's on the train. Gets to Boston in two hours."

"I'll meet you at the station," I said, exasperated by Abby's determination to put herself in danger.

"No, you'll never make it to the mental hospital before she does. I might."

"From DC?"

"No, I'm in Baltimore. I'll go after her. You stay in DC."

"But she might need both of us." I didn't like the idea of helplessly sitting around Lauren's, waiting for news.

He shook his head. "No, let's stick with our plan."

"But my transplant isn't for two days."

"I need you there in case Abby comes to her senses and returns. If she does, don't let her out of your sight."

Ben accessed Grid time. It didn't encourage him. Abby had too much of a head start. He couldn't just walk into a hospital and demand that a visitor be handed over to him. He wasn't FBI anymore. He tapped a Grid address he hadn't contacted since the day of his firing and entered Trevor Hamm's virtual office.

"Ben! How's your vacation going?"

Ben couldn't help but smile. Hamm always looked on the bright side of things. "Busy. Say, I need a favor from you. A big one."

"Concerning what?"

"My chip."

Trevor stared at him. "Is this about that New Guinea woman?"

Ben didn't respond.

"Ben, you've lost your job over her. Why are you risking everything else?"

Ben blew into his hands, then looked up at him. "I just have to."

Ben exited the car and bounded up the stairs to the front doors of the mental hospital. He stopped short of going in and turned to survey his surroundings. His eyes landed on the figure of a woman seated on a bench across the street. Abby. He almost shouted her name, but a car pulled up to the curb between them. Two men in suits got out and moved toward her.

Ben ran down the stairs and into the street, dodging half a dozen automated cars that sped past. By the time he reached the other side, the men had wrestled Abby off the bench and were trying to subdue her. She wasn't going quietly. One man had his arms wrapped around her torso and was trying to drag her to the waiting car. The other was grabbing Abby's legs to put an armlock around her ankles. Abby's kicking was slowing their progress considerably.

Abby clawed the man at her shoulders. He jerked back and lost his grip on her. She hit the cement with a thud. Ben lunged forward, his right hand grabbing the man's gun from its holster and throwing it into the street. With his left elbow he cracked a blow to the man's nose, sending him sprawling backward to the ground, spurting blood.

Ben turned just in time to receive a strike on the side of his head. He staggered sideways and fell. He looked up at the second man, still standing above Abby after delivering the blow. The man reached for his holster.

Abby coiled her right leg and kicked him full force in the groin, doubling him over. Ben leaped up and barreled into him like a linebacker. The man hit the sidewalk, his head snapping against the concrete and his gun flying across the ground. Ben punched him in the left cheek, then stood and glanced around. The other man was crawling away.

Abby scrambled to her feet, and Ben grabbed her hand. A small crowd had begun to gather; surely the police had already been called.

"This way! Run!"

They sprinted back across the street to Ben's car.

"Get in."

Abby threw herself in. Ben followed. "Point A," he instructed. The car ambled out of the complex's driveway. It wouldn't get them far without being intercepted, he knew. But that wasn't his primary concern.

Ben looked over his shoulder out the back window. No one was following yet. He turned to Abby as the car pulled from the driveway onto a road.

"Abby, what were you thinking? How could you possibly have thought . . ."

She was crying. "I'm sorry," she said. "I couldn't do it. I couldn't go in there. I didn't know —"

Ben gently grabbed her chin and looked at her head. "Are you injured?"

"Ben . . ."

He placed his hands on her shoulders and ran them gently down her arms. "Are you injured?" he repeated.

She shook her head. "I don't think so. Ben, what are you doing here?"

"Saving you from a big mistake. Just in time, obviously."

"Who were those men? Why were they . . ." She took a heavy breath. Her shoulders relaxed slightly.

He glanced out the back again. "Associates of Damien Cleary, I suspect."

"But how did they know where I was? And how did you —"

"I still have a friend at the bureau who owes me a few favors. As for Cleary . . . Are you sure you're okay? We're going to have to hike a ways. Several miles. Are you up for that?"

She nodded. "Why can't we continue in the car?"

"Not safe. Cleary's men will follow us. Or the police will track it. Either way, we have to switch to foot."

"But what about . . . Don't you have one of those locator chips?"

"I took care of that."

"Your bureau friend?"

"A different one."

The car pulled onto the shoulder. "Point A," it announced. To their left were open fields; to their right, a forest of spruce and pine. Ben glanced at Abby. "We get out here."

"Here? In the middle of nowhere?"

"It's not nowhere. Trust me."

Ben climbed out of the car. "Point B," he

instructed it.

Abby stepped out behind him. "Ohhh!"

Ben turned. "What is it?"

"My ankle." She took another step with her left foot and quickly shifted her weight to her right. "Ohhh. I must have . . . it must have . . ."

"You probably sprained it."

The car drove off. Ben looked down the road both ways, then glanced into the forest. "Abby, we're going to have to hike through this forest. There's no other way. I can support you."

She took in the area, her mouth set in a firm line. "Okay. I can do it."

Ben paused to access the Grid's global positioning system. After a moment he shook his head in disgust.

"What's wrong?" Abby asked.

"I don't have Grid access. Must have been the blow to the head."

"Do you need it right now?"

"Yes."

"What for?"

"To prevent us from wandering around aimlessly in those woods for the next twenty-four hours."

"You won't know where we're going?"

He shrugged. "We'll see, won't we?"

He took her left arm and placed it around

540

his shoulder. He curved his right arm around her slender waist. *She's in great shape physically,* he thought. That was obvious from the episode at the hospital. *Maybe she can make it — if we don't get lost.* "Are you ready?" he asked.

She looked at him and nodded.

They slid down one side of a ditch and crawled up the other. A barbed-wire fence blocked entry into the woods. Ben released his grip on Abby and let her stand. He pushed down on the chest-high top wire of the fence. Abby placed her left leg over the fence and toppled over it, falling onto the ground. "Ugh. Ohhh." She reached for her ankle.

Ben stepped over the wire. "Are you all right?"

She nodded and climbed to her feet. He slipped his hand around her waist again and held her tight. They shuffled through the trees.

Four hours later they emerged into a small clearing. In the middle was a cabin. Abby raised her head and wearily looked at Ben. "I hope this is the place. My ankle —"

"It's an old FBI safe house. We can spend the night here."

She sighed, clearly relieved. They hobbled

to some steps leading to a covered porch. Ben was virtually carrying Abby now. He lowered her onto the steps, straightened up, and took several deep breaths. The cabin looked deserted, just as it had been the only other time he had been here. The place hadn't changed much, though the woods had encroached a bit. The deck needed replacing. The exterior could use a paint job.

He walked around to the side of the porch, bent down, and reached under a plank. "Ugghhh." His right shoulder was killing him. So was his right hand, which he'd used to punch the guard. He'd survive. He found an old-fashioned metal key under the plank, just where it had been years earlier. He walked to the front, opened the door, and stepped inside. The cabin was simple: a living area to the right, a small open kitchen with a breakfast table to the left, a single bedroom in the back with a bathroom on the side.

The place smelled musty. He opened several windows and stepped back onto the porch. He climbed down the steps and helped Abby to her feet. They hobbled into the cabin and over to a couch. Abby lay down and propped up her ankle.

"I'm going to take a look at it, Abby."

Ben removed her sock and rolled up her pants leg. The ankle was purple and badly swollen. He ran his hands gently over it. Abby grimaced in pain.

"Nothing's broken. Just a sprain. Let's see what we can do for it."

He walked to the refrigerator and found two frosted ice packs in the freezer. He wrapped them in dishtowels and walked back to the couch. "Here. This will help."

Abby stared at the packs. "What do these do?"

Ben smiled to himself. Of course. They wouldn't have ice in the jungle.

"They'll help the swelling." He draped them over her ankle, and she recoiled at their cold touch. "Leave them like that until they grow soft. I'll see if there's any pain reliever around here."

In the bathroom he found a small bottle of something called acetaminophen. He read the directions and gave her two pills. He considered taking some himself but decided against it. Abby might need what was left. He sat down on a dusty easy chair across from her and closed his eyes.

"Ben, won't they find us here? And doesn't the FBI know that you know about this place?"

He opened his eyes and looked at her.

"Probably. But identifying me and tracing us here without the benefit of a chip — that will take time. I think we have until morning before they could track us. We'll be gone by then."

"But how are we going to get out of here? Ben, I don't think I can walk through —"

He waved her off. "Hopefully you won't have to. If we're lucky, we've got alternative transportation in the shed out back. Maybe I should check on that now."

He stood up and started out the door, then walked into the bedroom, where he found a light blanket. He went back to the living room and laid it over her feet.

"Thanks." She pulled the blanket up to her knees. "Ben, do we have any way of contacting Creighton? I'm sure he's worried sick."

"Unfortunately, no. Not without my Grid connection." He squatted beside the couch. "Abby, next time you have some hare-brained idea, run it by us beforehand, will you?"

She nodded. "I will. I'm sorry, Ben."

"Good. Now, I need to see what's out in the shed. I'll be back in a few minutes."

Twenty minutes later he returned to the cabin. Abby was asleep. He removed the ice packs and placed them back in the freezer.

He looked through the kitchen cabinets for supplies and found several packaged food bars. He opened one and bit into it. Stale, but edible. It would see them through the morning. He stepped outside; it was getting dark. He went back into the cabin and locked the door behind him. Not that it would help if anyone found them. He shut the windows, ate another food bar, grabbed a pillow from the bedroom, and sat back down in the easy chair. Not the most comfortable way to sleep, but he didn't want to leave Abby alone.

Abby's breathing was regular with a very slight snore. Her face was toward him. Her lips were parted, and her black hair had fallen over her left cheek.

Reminiscent of his daughter or not, she was a beautiful woman, strong and capable, with a personality to match. A twenty-five-year age difference used to be rare between a man and a woman, but no longer. If only the circumstances were different.

He leaned his head against the pillow and tried to shift into a comfortable position. After ten minutes he gave up. He'd be stiff in the morning. He looked at Abby again, watching her body rise and fall as she breathed. He closed his eyes and slept.

41

In the morning Abby could barely stand. Ben found a first-aid kit under the sink in the bathroom and wrapped her ankle with an elastic bandage. Abby contorted her face when he tightened it.

"Is that too tight?"

She shook her head.

Ben pulled out of his pocket a small cloth-like object wrapped in plastic. He unwrapped it. "I need to put this on your back, behind your shoulder."

"What is it?" She looked suspicious.

"An electronic tracking patch that we used to use. It was in the shed." He held up a small electronic device. "This will tell me where you are at all times."

Abby undid the top two buttons of her shirt and slid it backward, exposing her shoulders. Ben applied the patch to the skin behind her left shoulder. "At least I won't lose you again. Not unless someone removes it."

"But won't the FBI be able to track me too?"

He shook his head. "I'm the only one with the transponder code. Besides, no one uses these anymore."

Abby buttoned up. Ben helped her onto the porch. Next to the door were two jet packs.

"What are these?"

"These are how we're going to get you to the train."

Abby hobbled over to one. "What do I do with it?"

"I strap it on you. You take off and fly."

She looked up at him. "You're serious."

"Forty years ago these were the future of individual transport. People loved the idea of them, but they never quite panned out. Not cost efficient and not safe having millions of people flying around at once. Law enforcement still used them until Congress banned their manufacture for safety reasons."

She shot him a look. "That isn't encouraging."

He picked up one for her. "Chances are these will work fine."

She examined it, rapping her knuckles on

its side. "Show me how."

Ben strapped one on Abby, then the other on himself. He demonstrated, taking a brief flight to the top of the trees and back. "All right. Let's give you a quick course."

It wasn't all that quick. Abby lacked the advantage of knowing how to operate even basic small machinery. Each step had to be explained and demonstrated. What Ben expected to be a thirty-minute lesson stretched into two hours before Abby was going more than twenty feet up or maneuvering through the air.

Ben glanced toward the sun. Time was getting away from them. The cabin provided a temporary haven at best. "Abby, we have to go. We can't risk staying here any longer."

"Ben . . ." She bit on her lower lip.

"You can do it. Just fly low, behind me. I'll go slow."

She looked up toward the tops of the trees. "Okay. Let's go."

Ben rose off the ground and hovered at fifteen feet. Abby took a deep breath and followed him. They passed the tree line. Ben flew on ahead, then spun around to watch Abby's progress. She clipped herself on a branch and had to right herself to avoid slamming into other trees. Finally she settled into level flight, twenty feet above the trees. They flew south. In a few minutes they reached a main road. Ben peered to their left. In the distance several cars were parked alongside the road in a haphazard pattern. The police.

They rode the jets toward downtown Boston. Ben could see the city center on the horizon. Thirty-five minutes later they hovered over Boston Common. Ben motioned Abby down. Her landing was rough. She stumbled forward, her ankle gave way, and she crumpled to the ground.

Ben was immediately beside her. "Are you okay?"

She gathered herself in a moment. "I'll make it. Until now, I thought automated cars were scary."

Ben placed the packs in two canvas bags as he glanced at several passersby staring at them. "We need to go."

He carried the bags as they walked to the train station. Abby limped behind him.

Ben scanned the station as Abby bought her ticket. When they got to the platform, she leaned close to Ben and spoke in a hushed voice. "You're sure the police won't be waiting for me when I arrive in DC?"

"No. They have no way of identifying you. Even if they did, DC is where those in charge want you so you can testify. You'll be under their protection again."

"What about you? Are you taking a later train?"

"No. I assaulted two guys. If I got on this thing, they'd identify me."

She arched a brow. "So are you coming back on the jet pack?"

He smiled and shook his head. "No, hardly. These things have limited range. I'll make it back to DC, don't worry. I have to check into something here first. You and Creighton can expect me by Thursday."

The train pulled into the station. Abby turned toward Ben. "Thank you. For everything." She hugged him.

"I'll see you back in Washington," he said.

She pulled away, limped to the train's steps, and boarded. Ben watched as she disappeared. He stood on the platform for fifteen minutes until the train left, then turned and exited the station. Three days ago he had been an FBI agent with an unblemished thirty-two-year service record. Now he was a fugitive. He had one thing in his favor, at least. He had training that few fugitives could dream of.

Abby sat quietly as the train sped through the Jersey countryside. The next stop was Philadelphia, then Baltimore, then DC. Passengers were sparse. Traffic was always light, a traveler had told Abby when she'd taken the train a day earlier; people mostly traveled in VR.

The train stopped in Philadelphia. Three passengers in Abby's car got off. Just as the train was about to start moving again, a woman got on. She was tall and dark skinned with black eyes and striking facial features. She looked to be in her thirties, though with the life span in the U.S. so different from what she was used to, Abby found gauging ages difficult. The woman was pregnant — about eight months pregnant, Abby guessed.

The woman walked down the aisle, one hand cradling her belly. She glanced at Abby, then sat across the aisle from her.

Abby couldn't help but speak. "It looks like the baby is almost ready."

The woman turned and smiled. "Yes. Three more weeks before he is due." She spoke with an accent, perhaps African.

"He? A boy. How wonderful." Abby beamed. It felt good to be having a conversation that didn't include brain transplants or nanites.

"Yes." The woman nodded. "We chose a boy."

"You chose?"

"My husband wanted a boy first. I didn't care really, so . . ." When she tilted her head, gesturing indifference, her long gold earrings tinkled softly.

Abby was curious, but it seemed impolite to inquire further. Another item to ask Creighton about. Both women were silent for a moment.

"You don't sound American-born," Abby said.

"I was about to say the same thing. We're from Eritrea. We moved here — to Baltimore — three years ago."

"Eritrea. Pretty beaches."

The woman's eyes brightened. "You've been there?"

"Oh no. I just remember seeing pictures when I studied about it."

"Where did you go to school?"

Abby laughed. "In my parents' hut. I grew up in the jungles of Papua New Guinea."

"Oh, my . . . that must have been quite an adventure. Ah!" The woman looked surprised and moved both hands to her belly. "That was quite a kick. A moment ago he was quiet. He's going to be a handful, this one." She looked up at Abby, smiling. "Do you have children?"

Abby's chest constricted, her throat tight. "I . . . I did. She passed away . . . recently."

"Oh." The woman's face was etched with sympathy. "I'm so sorry. How terrible. What was her name?"

Abby offered a weak smile. "Miraba."

"That's a beautiful name. How old was she?"

"Eight."

"Eight?" The woman shook her head. "I'm . . . Was it an accident?"

Abby felt as if she couldn't breathe. She inhaled deeply, trying to fill her lungs with air and force out the pain. "No . . . not . . . not really. A brain disease."

"That's so very tragic. You must be heartbroken. I can't imagine losing a child."

Abby fell silent. She felt helpless to stop her grief from engulfing her. She looked out the window, but the scenery provided little diversion.

"Oh!" The woman looked at her belly. "There he goes again."

Abby turned back to the woman, welcoming the distraction of the kicking baby. She felt the grip of grief weaken. "It must be amazing, carrying a baby like that."

"It is . . . but you know. You are a mother."

"No. My daughter was adopted."

"I see." She paused. "It seems your daughter chose a wonderful mother."

Abby looked into the woman's dark eyes,

feeling tears surface in her own. "I hope so."

The woman slid her hand around on her belly. Abby watched her smile whenever the baby moved.

"To think that he draws his very life from you," Abby commented. "It seems like one of the few natural things left in —"

She stopped.

Suddenly everything her grandfather had been saying about God made sense, as if the pieces were waiting for her to click into place. This beautiful mother's very life was constantly flowing into her baby. The baby didn't have to do anything to get it. It was already his. He possessed her very life. He didn't have to do anything to activate it. It was already active inside him. Apart from her, he had no life. But being joined to her, he had her life. All he had to do was be at rest and receive that life. Which was the most natural thing in the world.

"Oh my," Abby said, louder than she intended. A man sitting two rows ahead turned to look at her.

"What is it?" the woman asked, startled.

"I just . . . Now I understand something my grandfather has been telling me. Something that changes everything. Faith isn't about striving; it's about resting."

The train began to slow. "Baltimore," the passengers were informed.

Abby sat forward. The train stopped, and the Eritrean woman stood and collected her belongings, then turned to Abby. "Best wishes to you."

Abby nodded. "God's blessings on you and your baby."

The woman stared at her for a moment, then smiled. "Thank you." She walked down the aisle.

Abby stood and stretched, exhilarated by her spiritual revelation. Using caution not to put much weight on her ankle, she walked the opposite direction toward the nearest bathroom, past a door at the end of the coach. She found the bathroom, reached for the knob, and began to open the door.

A hand encircled her head from behind and pressed a handkerchief over her mouth. Her scream was muted by the odd-smelling cotton, her mouth full of fabric and chemicals. Instinctively, she threw her right elbow back into the chest of her assailant. The handkerchief loosened over her mouth, then pressed against her again as a man shoved her forward into the bathroom, his right hand holding the handkerchief and his left twisting her arm behind her back. Her ankle buckled, bringing muffled cries of pain. She tried to hold her breath and push back, but the force against her was too great. With one last effort she started to buck with all her strength, then her legs went wobbly. She slumped to the floor.

42

I leaped out of the car and ran to the train station. Two hours earlier I had ignored a tap from an unfamiliar Grid address. By the time I accessed it and got the message from Ben, I had half an hour to meet Abby.

The train pulled in, and passengers began getting off. I looked to my left, then to my right. A woman with long black hair stepped down from a coach. I moved in her direction, then stopped. It wasn't Abby. I turned and looked the opposite direction. I didn't see her. A passenger got off a coach to my right. I waited a few moments. Another passenger stepped down to my left.

I paced anxiously. Within minutes the platform was empty save for employees disembarking and a man and woman enjoying a lingering embrace. I strode a hundred feet to my left, glancing into each entrance to the train. I raced back down the platform.

The entrances were all empty. I looked back up the platform. At the front of the train, a security guard disembarked.

"Hey!" I shouted.

He turned.

"Do you know anything about a woman who was due in from Boston? Five ten, long black hair, tan. Could she still be on the train?"

"No. Train's empty."

"Did anyone get off early that wasn't supposed to?"

He shook his head. "Not that I know of. You can — Oh, wait. I think we were short one after our last stop. Must have got off in Baltimore."

"Would they know the name inside?"

"No. That just happens."

Why would Abby get off in Baltimore?

I tapped Ben. There was no response. Not even a message indicating when he'd be available. I returned to Lauren's. Abby hadn't miraculously shown up there. I waited. One hour. Two. Three.

I tapped Ben again. And again. Still no response.

Something had gone wrong. Twenty-four hours before receiving my brain transplant, I was on my own. Was my going to the NTI lab part of a plan to eliminate all of us? Or was it, as we had strategized, going to save us?

Recognizing the beach house from the air was more difficult than Ben had imagined. None of the coves around Rockport, Massachusetts, looked familiar from this height. It didn't help that Ben hadn't been here in more than ten years. He guided his jet pack north from town. He didn't see anything. He doubled back and headed south. Nothing.

He glanced at his jet pack's power reading. Almost out. *Where is that blasted house?* An overnight delay was the last thing he needed. He had no choice, however. He landed behind a sand dune bordering a deserted beach. He found some short grass to place the jet pack on and attached it to the recharger. *Why can't these things run on the recharger?* It would take two hours to power up. It would be dark by then.

He glanced around him. The dune wouldn't provide much in the way of comfort. Not that he'd get much sleep if the crabs found him. At least he had a full moon to provide some light.

If his plan in Rockport worked, he'd make it to Bryson Nichols's estate in two days — one day after Creighton accessed the memory streams. If he could confront Nichols with information Creighton gleaned, Nichols would cave. His cover-up exposed, he'd have no choice but to accede to Ben's demands.

One snag had arisen, however — a huge one. Ben had lost Grid access. Creighton couldn't contact him, and he might have no way of contacting Creighton.

Ben unzipped his jacket and pulled out his electronic tracker. At least he could verify that Abby had arrived safely at Lauren Caldwell's. When he turned on the tracker, a white dot flashed on its screen. He looked at the road grid indicating her location. The reading confused him. It was nowhere near the congresswoman's house.

He zoomed out to a wider angle. A shoreline appeared. He pulled the image back some more. A series of islands materialized. These looked familiar. He pulled the image even farther out. He was looking at the Maine coast. He zoomed back in. The white dot was approaching Seal Harbor on Mount Desert Island.

Bryson Nichols's estate was on Mount Desert Island.

At dawn Ben strapped on his jet pack and flew back up the beach. He found the house on the first pass, a mile south of town. He landed in soft grass between the house and the beach and unstrapped the pack. He glanced up and down the beach. It was empty.

"Ben, is that you?"

He whirled toward the house. Fifty feet away, on the edge of a covered porch ten feet off the ground, stood a man in his nineties whom he hadn't seen in twelve years.

"Paul!"

The man smiled at him. "Ben, you old rascal. What are you doing landing in my yard at the crack of dawn . . . and in a jet pack of all things? Is this some kind of invasion?"

Ben climbed the stairs to the porch. The two men embraced and laughed. "Good to see you too, Paul."

"Let me take a look at you." The older man broke the embrace and stepped back. "Well, can't say you never looked better. Not that I'd know, since you haven't tapped me in . . . what? Five years?"

Ben nodded. "I know, I know. I've been negligent about keeping in touch. You could always tap me, you know."

Paul waved his hand. "You're a busy man, Ben. You don't need old codgers like me pestering you."

Ben put his arm around him. "You're my

mentor, Paul, not an old codger. And you always will be."

The man looked out to the yard toward the jet pack. "I thought we stopped using those things years ago."

"We did. Do you have any coffee?"

"I was about to pour some. I'll get Melanie up to say hi."

"No, let her sleep. I need to talk to you privately first."

Paul brought two cups of coffee to the porch. "So what's up, Ben?"

"Do you still have that boat you used to sail?"

"Of course. Take it out, oh, three times a month probably. When the weather's good."

"I need to borrow it."

"You've learned to sail?"

Ben shook his head. "I'll use the motor."

"On that thing? Where are you going?"

"Mount Desert Island."

"Mount Desert Island? Ben, that's . . . that's more than three hundred miles round trip. It would take you forever running the motor — plus several tanks of gas, which isn't easy to find anymore."

"I need the boat, Paul. It's a matter of life and death."

His mentor looked him in the eye. "Ben, agents don't have to borrow boats from

562

private citizens. What's all this about?"

Ben sighed. "I'm not an agent anymore."

Paul rose from his chair. "Come on."

"Come on where?"

"I can get you a faster boat."

Bryson Nichols's face obscured the bright light shining into my eyes. I tried to raise my head off the operating table, but it was already in a restraint. He smiled at me.

"Hello, Professor Daniels. It's so good to see you. I was afraid you might back out at the last minute. You've made a very wise decision, one I know you'll be thrilled with — forever.

"Dr. Sutter has prepped you. I apologize I wasn't here for the preliminaries. Another matter required my attention. Fortunately my staff is more than capable of performing these operations without me — more capable than with me present, perhaps." He forced a laugh.

He glanced away for a moment, then looked down at me. "Your brain software is already up and running perfectly in the silicon substrate. All we need to do is connect the substrate and disconnect your biological brain. As I indicated before, the entire procedure should take about three hours."

Three hours. Three hours until I could access the information we needed to stop Nichols and Cleary. Three hours before I lost access to what potentially gave life its ultimate meaning.

I had thought this through many times. But now that the moment had arrived . . . was I mad to make such a choice? Would any sane person choose what I was choosing? Was I truly sacrificing my eternity for the sake of —

Nichols had been speaking to me.

"I'm sorry," I responded. "You were saying?"

"I was asking if you're ready for us to put you under."

I took a deep breath, then exhaled. "I'm ready."

"Wonderful. I couldn't be happier for you, Professor."

The anesthesiologist placed a mask over my mouth and nose. "Just breathe normally."

I took my final breaths as a purely biological human.

43

Abby opened her eyes to the canopy of an ornate four-post bed. She raised her head and looked around a large, lavishly furnished bedroom. She was alone. She climbed out of the bed, jarring her bad ankle when her feet reached the hardwood. She limped to a window and opened its shutters. Sunlight flooded the room. Below her spread the manicured grounds of a grand estate. In the distance she saw a high stone fence and an entrance gate.

Abby remembered being assaulted on the train but nothing after passing out.

She turned a small crank, and the right side of the window swung open. A cool breeze caressed her face. She closed her eyes and took in a deep breath. She remembered her epiphany on the train before she was assaulted. Christ in her. He was living through her. By faith, she drew upon him. Whatever she would face, his life in her was sufficient.

A knock interrupted her thoughts. She opened her eyes, hesitated, and then answered. "Come in."

A man dressed in a butler's uniform entered with a tray. "Good afternoon, Ms. Caldwell. Can I take it that you slept well?"

Her eyes steeled, and she answered curtly. "Where am I?"

"You are at the Kensington estate of Bryson Nichols. May I —"

"Why have I been brought here against my will?"

The man looked surprised. "I . . . I do not know the circumstances of your arrival, Ms. Caldwell. I have only been instructed to serve you lunch." He placed the tray on a coffee table between two upholstered chairs and removed the lid. "Croissants, sliced prosciutto ham, swiss cheese, fresh fruit, and coffee."

She limped toward the butler. "No thank you. I'd like to see Mr. Nichols now."

"I'm afraid Mr. Nichols is away from the residence at the moment. He is expected to return later this afternoon."

"And will I see him then?"

"I am not privy to Mr. Nichols's appointment schedule. I only know when he is expected back."

"I assume I have no choice but to remain

here." She prayed that she was wrong, that she wasn't locked in a gilded cage.

The butler looked aghast. "No guest is forced to do anything here, Ms. Caldwell. You are free to leave if you wish."

"I do wish." She started for the door.

The butler motioned for her to wait. "Very well, but would you like some help gathering your belongings?"

"I don't have any."

Abby exited the room, moving slowly and favoring her left foot. The butler walked past her in a long hallway filled with paintings. He led Abby down a winding staircase into a large marble-floored foyer. She knew she was gaping at the opulence, but she couldn't believe that the house belonged to just one man. The foyer alone could contain half the huts in her village. The butler opened one of two enormous white doors that led out the front. Abby followed him to the door, exchanged glances with him, and stepped through.

"Would you like me to secure transportation for you, Ms. Caldwell?"

"How far is it to the next car depot?"

"Six miles."

"No. I'll walk." She tried not to think about her throbbing ankle.

"As you wish."

"When I go through the gate, which direction do I turn?"

"To the left. That road will lead you to the town of Northeast Harbor." He glanced at her ankle. "It would be much faster if you allowed us to drive you."

She waved him off. "I'm fine."

Abby walked slowly along a stone path that crossed the lawn. She reached the driveway and proceeded to the estate's entrance. She glanced back, saw no one behind her, and headed left. She had to place as much distance between herself and Bryson Nichols as possible, even if it took hours. He had committed her grandfather to a mental institution, and now he was after . . .

She stopped. She looked down the road in front of her, then back toward the estate. Bryson Nichols had committed her grandfather to a mental institution. If that was true, Nichols controlled whoever ran the institution. Or had influence over them, at least. The only sure way of getting her grandfather out was through Nichols. The man was dangerous, undoubtedly, but she had to chance talking to him. It could go very badly — or result in the breakthrough she needed to help her grandfather.

She stood for several moments, debating

the matter. Finally she turned around and limped determinedly back toward the estate.

Two thirty arrived — the time of my scheduled VR meeting with Ray. I appeared at the picnic table. Ray was already sitting on the other side.

"We don't have much time," said Ray. "Security will close in on this little loophole I created. Once they find the breach, access will be shut down. This may be our last —"

"Ray," I interrupted, "Abby is missing."

Concern shadowed his face. "When was she last seen?"

"Ben put her on the train from Boston back to DC yesterday. She wasn't on it when it arrived."

He sighed deeply. "Cleary. Or his people."

"Most likely."

He sat silently for a moment and then seemed to push aside his fears for Abby and address the issue at hand. "But we don't know for certain. That's why we need to give you access to their memory streams. I assume your transplant is done?"

I nodded.

"I'm sorry," he said. "The loss — or potential loss, in your case — is great. I know that quite well. I appreciate the sacrifice you're making."

"What's done is done. Let's make it worthwhile. What adjustments need to be made?"

"It will be easier for you to download the instructions than for me to try to verbalize them. I'll leave you the Grid address where you can find them, along with the password you need to access it. As I indicated before, the alterations will be easy now that you have your silicon brain. Once you've made the adjustments, you can also find directions for accessing memory streams.

"Professor, it is imperative that this information remain with you and you only. This technological capability should never be used, but circumstances have made it necessary. I'm trusting that you'll use it only for the purposes we have discussed."

"I understand. Is there anything else?"

"Before you go, I have a question." He hesitated. "It seems you and Abby have developed a relationship that . . . well, that goes beyond mere friendship."

There didn't seem to be any disapproval in his voice.

"Yes, perhaps we have."

"I'm curious — what is your take on her personal beliefs?"

"In God?"

"Yes. I'm sure she's discussed them with you."

"Of course."

"Did she challenge you to consider those beliefs yourself?"

"I don't know if *challenge* is the word. She's been quite circumspect concerning this topic."

He smiled. "I sense a *but*."

"But I took the time to do some research on my own."

"And what did you discover?"

"That as a historical source, the Bible carries much more credibility than I expected."

Ray nodded. "Did you reach any conclusions about its message?"

"Yes, and your message to my father was key. It directed me to numerous passages that referenced God as the life. I found that the Bible's message isn't primarily about obeying rules or even forgiveness and heaven. It's about being joined to Christ by faith and receiving the life of God, being one with him. Very different from the traditional understanding, as far as I can tell."

Ray leaned forward. "Professor, it seems you were on the brink of believing. But you didn't. Why?"

I tilted my head, considering how best to

answer him. "I suppose my question became, how can I know for certain?"

He smiled. "A very good question. The answer is, you can't. What would constitute certainty? You're the historian. Is there any historical account you'd swear to with absolute certainty?"

"No, of course not."

"And so it is with Jesus Christ. He has left room for faith."

"But why? Why not make it absolute?"

"Because the heart of God is relationship. And relationship is based on trust, on faith. When two people marry — most people still married in my day — it is a commitment based on faith. They can't be certain what they're entering into. They have to trust the other. So it is with God. He offers to enter into an eternal union with us. We trust him — trust what his Son has done to make it possible — and enter in. It's not blind faith. God has shown us more than enough to make it intellectually palatable, as you've discovered. But there is an element of trust. Trust seals the deal, as in any relationship."

I fell silent. We looked at each other. I finally spoke. "Now that I've had the transplant, you believe I no longer have a spirit to join to God."

"Yes," he responded quietly. "I believe that

is true."

"But to receive his life — eternally — one has to be joined to God's Spirit."

He nodded.

"So does that leave me out? I mean, with this brain I can live forever in my current state."

"That's something you'll have to entrust to God, won't you? As to your current state, I wouldn't count on it lasting forever. Bryson Nichols and I may have engineered your brain, but we aren't God. We can't grant immortality. You, too, will die, Creighton. As will I — sooner rather than later, I hope. I miss God."

"How do you know for sure that you'll be with God again?"

He thought for a moment. "I don't know how to answer that. I don't have a sense of God anymore. I can only tell you what it was like before. The spirit of Ray Caldwell, I suspect, is already with God."

At that, the wind blew as if to underline his statement.

"There's something I've been meaning to ask you," I said. "My father . . ."

"Eli." He sighed, and his shoulders slumped. "I'm so sorry about your father. He was a good man."

"In the message you said you'd known

him for a long time, but I don't remember his ever mentioning you."

"We went to school together ages ago, but life took us in different directions. We had only recently reestablished our friendship."

"What prompted the sudden reconnection?"

"He remembered some of our talks years before — people sometimes talked about the Christian faith back then — and he thought I might be able to help him sort through something."

"Sort through something?"

"He'd been having a recurring dream about Jesus. He thought maybe I knew what it was about."

I felt reassured. At the end my father had been in good hands after all.

There was one final topic I wanted to talk about. Ray seemed to wait on me.

"Ray, if my life continues indefinitely, either in VR or in a synthetic body . . . If there should come a time when I don't want to live that way anymore, is there a way to end it?"

He answered gently. "Maybe you should leave that up to God as well."

"But what if I'm stuck in this existence and don't want to be? God didn't make me this way. Is there a way I can . . . get out?"

He hesitated. "There is. There's a series of commands you can run."

"And what will they do?"

"They'll tell your programming to delete itself."

"Can you tell me the commands? Just in case."

He looked at me for a moment. Then he nodded.

44

I pushed my conversation with Ray to the back of my mind and accessed the Grid address he'd given me. I completed the necessary alterations in less than fifteen minutes. The memories of those who had had brain transplants were now accessible.

As was everything else. After the transplant I realized that I now had immediate access to the entirety of human knowledge. Not only that, I could meaningfully synthesize it. The prior constraints of my biological brain had been superseded. I could understand astrophysics, genetics, or atmospheric science as easily as I could understand history.

Every mental process was quick and simple beyond anything I could have imagined. The potentialities I foresaw were limitless. What if humanity truly did become transhumanity? What if billions of persons could all instantly process the same facts and reach the same logical conclusions? Maybe Nichols's vision was the correct one, after all. Even if one did lose access to God — a hypothetical I couldn't verify — perhaps that was a small price to pay for the advancement possible through the transhuman merger.

A new life purpose intruded upon my consciousness. I was a pioneer, one of the first of a new race. Perhaps I was meant to ensure that humanity would be ushered into its new, fated era peacefully, without harm to those burdened with biological brains. Nichols, Cleary, and Ray Caldwell had perfected the technology. Ray had rejected it due to his religious bias. Nichols had mismanaged its implementation, acting imprudently and arrogantly but without malice. He simply wanted to realize his vision for humanity. He could be convinced to amend his ways.

As for Cleary . . . he posed the real threat. I had to access his memory stream first.

Abby nodded to the butler and hobbled through the door he held open for her. After she'd returned to Nichols's estate, she'd spent the afternoon in the conservatory, contemplating what she would say to the man who had violated her grandfather . . .

and saved Creighton. Now she entered a large library. At the far end of the room, in an easy chair next to a reading lamp, sat Bryson Nichols. He stood and motioned her over to a chair near his.

"Hello, Ms. Caldwell. I'm so pleased to finally meet you face to face." He held out his hand.

She remained standing and didn't extend hers. "I wish I could say the same, Mr. Nichols."

"I do appreciate your waiting for me to arrive back here."

Despite her repeated prayer to remain calm, Abby felt her anger swell. "I was abducted and brought here."

He looked surprised. "Abducted? I gave instructions for you to be invited. I do so apologize, Ms. Caldwell. An unfortunate misunderstanding. You are, of course, free to leave anytime you wish."

"Yes, I see that. But I can't say the same for my grandfather. You have him incarcerated."

"Incarcerated. I would not employ that word. But I understand why you do. Please sit down, and we can discuss your grandfather and other issues that are of import to both of us."

Abby sat in the chair and stretched out her leg.

Nichols continued. "I had to be in DC this morning. I performed a transplant on a friend of yours."

Her voice caught in her throat. "Creighton . . ."

"He's fine. It went like clockwork. A truly enlightened fellow, Professor Daniels. And now even more so, of course."

A wave of sadness replaced her anger. She couldn't believe that he'd received the transplant. "Can I talk to him?"

"Yes, of course. I'm sure he'd be thrilled to hear from you. I can provide his new Grid address, and my assistant can set — But you'll need a helmet to enter VR, won't you? I'll have my assistant track one down for you. We should have one in storage. It may be this evening."

"As soon as possible, please." She erased the emotion from her voice, trying to sound in control. "And when can I contact my grandfather?"

Nichols shifted in his seat. "Ah, your grandfather. You must realize that everything that has happened with Ray has resulted from a series of miscommunications and misunderstandings."

"Is that why you performed the brain

transplant against his will and have locked him in a mental institution?"

"That is one perspective, to be sure. But Ray had planned to have the procedure done on himself. And when he disagreed so vehemently with it after his operation — and insanely threatened to shut us down — I had no choice but to have him psychiatrically examined."

"There was nothing wrong with my grandfather until you removed his brain. You —"

He cut her off. "The hospital records may show differently."

Abby's cheeks flushed with anger. "You took —"

"However . . ." Nichols held one finger in the air. "However, I believe the time has come to have the physicians reevaluate Ray's mental state and consider his release. I visited with him the other day, and he seemed in his right mind. I'm sure the doctors will give him a clean bill of health if he agrees not to make these unfortunate incidents a continuing issue. Would that be agreeable to you, Ms. Caldwell?"

She sat silently for a moment. "What you have done is wrong, Mr. Nichols. And I cannot control whether my grandfather will agree to your terms. But I want him out."

"Then we are agreed, aren't we? I'll take

the matter up with Ray. In the meantime, it's late in what I'm sure has been a tiring day for you. I invite you to have dinner and spend the night with us here."

Spending the night at Nichols's estate wasn't part of her plan. Abby didn't trust the man, and here she was completely at his mercy. Everything he'd just said to her concerning Poppy might have been a lie. She didn't see much choice, however. Cooperating seemed her best shot at securing her grandfather's release.

"Thank you," she replied. "I accept your invitation. How soon do you anticipate going to visit my grandfather?"

His eyebrows rose slightly. "Well, I do have to think through how exactly Ray and I will need to proceed from here, to protect both of our interests. I would say within a day or two."

Anger rose within her again. Already the man was playing games. There was no reason Nichols couldn't tap the mental hospital this evening and talk with Ray. And it was only his own interests, not those of Poppy, that Nichols had any intention of protecting.

She pushed down her anger. Losing her temper was the last thing she wanted to do. "A single day would be preferable," she responded.

"Indeed. I will let you know." Nichols got up and crossed to the far side of the room to a wet bar. He opened a refrigerator and pulled out a bottle. "You've caused quite a stir since your arrival, you know."

"That wasn't my intention."

He pulled out two glasses and poured something into each. "But it is now?"

Abby decided to go along with the conversation. Perhaps Nichols would inadvertently say something that would help them stop him. "Not to cause a stir, no," she answered.

Abby paused and thought about her epiphany before continuing. "I want to spread the message of Jesus to this country. To tell people that" — she hesitated — "that God's *own life* is now available to everyone in the person of Christ."

Nichols turned and placed the flask back in the refrigerator. "Yes. Christianity. You may have noticed that we left those notions behind some time back, just as Europe did before us. Eventually the entire world will, of course." He crossed the room and placed the glasses on the coffee table between them.

"And where will that lead, Mr. Nichols?"

"To where we have been heading all along: the evolution of the human species into a transhuman species." He leaned forward, picked up a glass, and took a sip. "Please, have some water."

Abby picked up the other glass and looked inside; bubbles were rising to the top. She felt refreshed when she drank it.

Nichols continued. "I understand why you cling to your beliefs, of course. Those beliefs were a natural step in the evolution of the species. Of course, for humanity to realize its true destiny, myths like Christianity had to be laid aside. We had to acknowledge reality as it truly is."

"And what do you see as that reality?"

Nichols chuckled. "Is it not obvious? That humanity is to be the spark of intelligence that the universe has always wanted to bring into existence and spread throughout itself."

"Are you saying the universe has consciousness?"

Nichols put his glass on the table. "Consciousness. What a sublime concept. But so difficult to define, is it not? This century has brought us face to face with that dilemma. The machines we build have become more intelligent than we are. They think. They make their own choices. They have their own value systems. I've always considered them to be conscious. Some disagree.

"As for the universe, I believe it has all

along carried the seeds from which intelligence would arise. We are that intelligence — we, merged with the machines we've created. Those who have already entered this union, Ray included, have achieved a level of intelligence never before imagined. How high will this intelligence go? I believe there is no limit."

Abby finished her water and placed her glass on the table. "And what of the human soul?"

He smiled at her. "Such a quaint notion, the soul. Using nanotechnology, we have successfully mapped the entire human brain, down to the very molecules that compose every neuron in our gray matter. But we have never come across a soul. We are material beings, Ms. Caldwell. Cells, molecules, atoms — these account for the entirety of our human existence."

She stood and limped over to a window. "And how, Mr. Nichols, would you know? How can you look for what your instruments aren't designed to see?"

"Well, you are free to continue your search for what doesn't exist, Ms. Caldwell. I prefer to live in the real world. And, fortunately, the rest of humanity has come to see it my way. The civilized countries, at least. Superstition is still prevalent in some parts of the world. But they'll catch up eventually."

"Maybe reality looks like superstition if you haven't personally encountered it, Mr. Nichols."

The conversation, Abby concluded, was revealing nothing useful — only Nichols's steadfast faith in his own belief system. Abby turned toward him. "I'm a bit tired. I believe I'll return to my room. May I have my dinner served there?"

"Of course. You want a bit of privacy this evening. Understandable. I'll have my butler bring your dinner." Nichols stood. "I enjoyed talking with you, Ms. Caldwell. Your perspectives are a fascinating journey into our cultural history."

She gave a slight nod but did not smile and then moved toward the door. "I believe I can find my way back upstairs."

I accessed Damien Cleary's memory stream. His first recorded memories dated from November 2073, four months before NTI changed human experience by introducing the technology to the public.

I scanned the entire life experience of Damien Cleary for the previous fourteen years: his every thought, dream, and sensory input. The volume of information was staggering. But so was the speed with which my new brain processed data. The task took less than three hours.

I knew now why the memory stream system had been established with stringent safeguards. No one should have access to the full extent of someone's life, as I possessed. Nothing in Cleary's experience was hidden. I scanned his work life, his relationships, his financial dealings, his thought life, his sex life — those aspects of ourselves which, if made public, bring even the best person to shame. And Cleary wasn't the best person.

Viewing Cleary's memories, I experienced a certain prurient interest in his dark side, followed by a revulsion at taking such pleasure, and finally settled into a kind of wistful sorrow that such a technically brilliant man had, because of his own psychological makeup, spent so much of his time and energy on meaningless, unfulfilling pursuits. Like so many of us.

To one cause, however, Cleary was truly devoted: the advancement and spread of human intelligence.

I came upon his original conceptual discussions with Nichols and Ray Caldwell about the silicon brain. I scanned through the endless developmental process. I witnessed Cleary and Nichols's arguments concerning worldwide marketing of the transplant procedure. Cleary always favored the most aggressive approach, regardless of moral or legal niceties. His goal: transform humanity as quickly as possible, no matter what was required.

"Humanity," he said in Nichols's VR office one day, "has wallowed in a Stone Age mentality long enough. We have the potential not only to solve the planet's problems but to spread a nearly perfect civilization to all corners of the galaxy. Doing so at maximum speed, Nichols, is the highest moral consideration."

Near the end of the memory stream, I came upon the assailant. Toward the close of Lewis Pape's tenure as a security manager at NTI, Cleary discovered that Pape supported his ambitious agenda — and had no qualms about doing whatever it took to achieve it. Cleary gradually took him into his confidence. Pape left NTI to go into private consulting. His primary client, unsurprisingly, was Damien Cleary.

They met in Cleary's VR office with increasing frequency over eighteen months. Several meetings stood out.

November 5, 2087

"I've developed something that may interest you," Cleary nonchalantly mentioned in his NTI office. He pulled up a 3-D schematic of a nanite in holographic form.

"What does it do?" Pape asked.

"It searches for and destroys neurons."

Pape leaned forward in his chair and looked at the schematic. "Whose neurons?"

"Anyone who is implanted with the nanite."

"How many neurons?"

"It depends on how many nanites are introduced. Introduce enough, and the brain is turned to mush. Literally."

"Overnight?"

"Within a few days."

Pape stared at the schematic a few moments, then looked at Cleary. "Anyone so infected would be a prime candidate for a transplant, wouldn't you think?"

Cleary smiled. "My thoughts exactly."

April 18, 2088

Cleary sat on a large rock overlooking a remote beach in VR. "You remember my saying we needed a test group for the neural nanites?"

Pape tossed a rock onto the beach below. "Some people volunteered?"

"Let's just say we need to get rid of a village that no one will ever miss."

May 4, 2088

Sitting in his living room, Cleary was tapped by Pape. He went into VR.

Pape looked concerned. "We may have a problem."

"Which is?"

"One person escaped from the village."

Cleary frowned. "Escaped? How could someone escape?"

"She was away from the village when I planted the infection."

"So where did she go?"

"To the coast. She's an American, apparently. She's teamed up with a doctor."

Cleary looked indignant. "I swear, Pape. Couldn't you have been more careful than this?" He sat silently for a moment. "Do they have a sample?"

"I think so."

"Then get it back. And eliminate both of them."

I scanned Pape's updates to Cleary on his progress in attempting to kill Abby. The reports were chilling. I felt utter rage.

Cleary, meanwhile, was busy furthering his own plans in the privacy of his VR office. He glanced at a screen that laid out the schematics of water treatment and sewage systems for every U.S. city with more than a hundred thousand in population.

Cleary tapped Pape after the two returned to DC from Dallas.

"Have you decided on the cities?" Pape inquired.

"Yes." He handed Pape a list.

"Three? Just three?"

"We only need three." Cleary leaned across his desk and pointed at the list. "We start with DC. The system is complicated, but it can be rigged with nanites at entry points. Once in, they will multiply and spread, infecting every person who comes into contact with the city water system."

"That could be millions. You can't do millions of transplants in that time frame."

"No, of course not," Cleary replied. "Most will die. We follow that up with Richmond and Annapolis. It will look like the contagion is spreading both north and south. A nationwide panic will ensue. We will have the only solution: the transplants.

"The government will seize NTI's operations for national security purposes. It will find that we have the software available to train physicians to do the transplants. The government will mandate the retraining, physicians will be conscripted into national service, and blank silicon substrates will be mass-produced. We will go from a few hundred transhumans to several hundred thousand in the course of a month."

"But they'll be able to trace the nanites back to NTI," Pape objected.

Cleary shook his head. "I'm working on a self-destruct subroutine that we'll have to use for the nanite bombs. After they've consumed a set number of neurons, the nanites will disintegrate into their constituent molecules and be dispersed throughout the body. There won't be anything left to trace. Just neural mush."

Pape smiled at him. "I assume you want me to plant the bombs."

Cleary nodded. "Since my nanites made your chip untraceable, you are supremely suited to the task, my friend."

Cleary received another series of updates from Pape.

"I injected nanites into bottled water at the congresswoman's house — the ones you programmed with the thirty-six-hour operating life. The Congresswoman should be safe; she doesn't return from Texas for another three days."

That, I realized, was why I'd been infected with the nanites but Abby hadn't. Pape contaminated the water at Lauren's just as Abby had started her food-and-water fast. I continued scanning the updates.

"I've finished my preparations for Richmond. I go there tomorrow."

"We missed the New Guinea woman again, I'm sorry to say. We seem to have infected only the professor. He'll be dead in two days. I'll try the woman again."

"Richmond is ready. I'm heading to Annapolis. I'll come back to DC and do its system last."

The two met on a VR beach while I was in the hospital. Pape was looking out to sea when he appeared in Cleary's memory stream. Pape turned to Cleary and spoke.

"A complication has arisen."

"Which is?"

"The professor is recovering."

"I thought he was in a coma, headed out."

"Something stopped the infection."

"Nichols!" Cleary reached down, scooped up some sand, and threw it into the wind. "That man is going to ruin his own dream if it takes his very last breath." He turned to Pape. "All right. So much for using the nanites on them. Use a gun."

"They have FBI protection now."

"Then wait until they don't. And be sure not to leave fingerprints — that's the traceable part of you, remember?"

"I remember."

Three nights later Cleary was scanning the day's headlines. I recognized them as only a day old. He finished his scan, then tapped Pape. They met in Cleary's VR office.

"We need to take care of Ray Caldwell," Cleary stated.

"I thought Nichols had that covered."

Cleared snorted. "I think Nichols underestimates him. He's the one loose end that can unravel our whole plan. There's no telling what he may have told that ex-FBI agent or may be telling him now, for all we know."

"But he's in isolation," Pape objected.

"True. But even isolation is a relative thing."

"So what are you suggesting?"

"I think it's time we let Ray go to his mythical maker."

"You want me to murder him in the hospital?"

Cleary smiled. "That wouldn't be proper, would it? No, let's secure his release. Then you can dispose of him as you see fit."

"You can get him released?"

"No, but Nichols can. Leave that to me. You plan to be in Boston tomorrow to escort Ray Caldwell from the hospital."

Pape disappeared. Cleary sat at his desk, composing a visual message to the director of the hospital while appearing as Bryson Nichols.

The action was highly illegal — the VR system depended on people trusting whom they were receiving messages from — and extremely difficult to program to escape detection from Grid safeguards. Cleary, apparently, was confident in his ability to pull it off.

I continued my scan of his memory stream.

Cleary/Nichols tapped the hospital director and asked him to release Ray Caldwell. An associate of his was coming to pick him up. The director gladly acceded.

"My associate will be there at five."

"I'll have Dr. Caldwell ready."

I accessed the memory stream's time. The date was June 29. A chill went down my spine. The memory was from today.

It was currently four minutes after five.

45

I tapped the hospital. A receptionist robot — they were amazingly easy for my new brain to spot — appeared.

"Creighton Daniels for Theodore Brandt, please."

"One moment, Mr. Daniels."

Two minutes passed. Brandt appeared. "Mr. Daniels, hello again. I apologize for the mix-up when you were here previously. Obviously, Ray Caldwell —"

"Dr. Brandt, you must not release Ray Caldwell to the man who has come to pick him up. The message you received from Bryson Nichols regarding his release was faked."

The director pasted on a smile. "Mr. Daniels, I appreciate your concern since you're a friend of his granddaughter's. You can rest assured, Dr. Caldwell is in good hands. We received Mr. Nichols's request for the release, and I personally tapped Mr.

Nichols back to confirm it. I can't say more due to privacy concerns, of course."

"So he's been released?"

"Yes, just a few moments ago."

He had confirmed the release with Nichols? How could that be?

I ended the transmission. My next VR meeting with Ray was for eight that night. All I could do was wait.

Abby raised her head from a book she'd taken from the bedroom shelf. Someone was coming down the hall. She closed it and fixed her eyes on the doorknob. It turned, and the door opened. Her heart leaped. "Ben!"

"Shh!" He closed the door quietly behind him and walked over to the bed. "We have to get you out of here. Right now."

"Ben, I can't go. Nichols said he would release my grandfather if we'd keep quiet. If I leave, Nichols won't let him go."

Ben shook his head. "If we get you out of here, Nichols won't dare keep Ray locked up. You'll be able to implicate him. The safest thing for your grandfather is for you to be in a secure location." He walked across the room and pulled the curtain back to look at the front of the estate.

"Have you talked to Creighton?" she asked.

"I haven't been able to reach him. If he had the transplant, he may have a new Grid address."

"Yes, he does. Nichols said he was going to get it for me this evening."

"Too late for that." He stepped toward her. "Abby, we have to leave." He took her by the hand, opened the door, and slipped out.

"I apologize for interrupting you, sir. Ms. Caldwell just —"

"Yes, I've just been informed, Rosalie."

Bryson Nichols walked across his expansive personal study to a window that overlooked the front lawn of the estate. In the distance he could see two people near the end of the drive. Abigail Caldwell was limping. The other was most likely the former FBI agent, come to rescue her. He watched them reach the main road and turn to the right. Surely they had transportation along the road.

Nichols shook his head. So unnecessary. "Rosalie, have Drummond report to me here."

One of Nichols's many assistants, Edward Drummond, appeared in the doorway.

"Edward, our guest, Ms. Caldwell, has left without due consideration of her actions. Please overtake her on the road and persuade her to return to our graces once again. Her companion can come as well."

"And if she refuses, sir?"

"She won't. Tell her that her grandfather is due to join us."

Nichols knew that Drummond would savor this assignment. Driving luxury cars full throttle in physical reality was his passion, one Nichols tried to cater to from time to time. He could hear tires squealing as Drummond raced onto the main road.

Nichols turned his attention to the testimony he was due to deliver to Congress. He had waited for this opportunity for twenty years. He wanted the speech to be perfect.

Fifty minutes after he left, Drummond reappeared in the study doorway.

Nichols turned to him. "Edward, I assume our guests are in hand?"

"No sir."

Nichols frowned. "Why not, Edward?"

"Because their car skidded off the road at the turn on Otter Cliff."

"Off the road? How far off the road?"

"Into the Atlantic."

Nichols was silent for a moment. "Did you

see them go off?"

"Yes. I had closed to within a few hundred feet."

"And did you stop at the top of the cliff?"

"I did."

"What did you see?"

"The car floating on the water, upside down. Then it sank."

"You didn't see any sign of Ms. Caldwell or her companion?"

He shook his head. "Mr. Nichols, that cliff is well over —"

"Yes, I know." Nichols turned to the window that overlooked the front of the estate. "Thank you, Edward. That will be all."

At 8:00 p.m. I tried to access the VR park where Ray hoped to meet me again. The location didn't exist. Ray had been right. The door had been closed.

I checked on Cleary's memory stream for Pape's most recent tap. Nothing. Whatever had happened to Ray, Cleary hadn't yet been informed.

I walked downstairs to Lauren's kitchen, simultaneously accessing news headlines from around the world. I bit into an apple as I noted a breaking report from Maine. A reporter stood on a cliff road overlooking the Atlantic Ocean.

"In a rare automotive fatality, a former FBI agent and a woman passenger were killed as their car plunged off the side of Otter Cliff on Mount Desert Island near Acadia National Park. The car apparently skidded on slick pavement and was unable to navigate the turn. Local authorities have begun a search for the car but hold out little hope of recovering it in these deep coastal waters. The agent, Ben Steele, a thirty-two-year veteran of the FBI, had left the bureau just last week. The woman, Abigail Caldwell, had recently come to the United States for the first time from Papua New Guinea, where her American parents had raised her among an isolated jungle tribe."

The apple dropped. I sank to the floor, buried my head in my hands, and did something I didn't know was possible with my new brain.

I wept.

Fifteen minutes later I leaned back against a kitchen cabinet, wiped my face with a dishtowel, and stared at the ceiling. Abby was dead. I could barely bring myself to believe it. This woman who had so much life — who had added so much to my life. In a single month she had turned my world upside down, inserting herself into my every dream for the future. Now I had lost her forever.

I glanced around the lifeless kitchen. I had to pull myself together. I had to stop Cleary. Countless lives depended on it. But what could I do? Ben was dead. Abby was dead. Ray had been picked up by Pape. I'd be the next target.

Cleary's scheme would proceed. The only hard evidence I had against him or Pape was contained in Cleary's memory stream, and it couldn't be used by law enforcement. It was a federal crime even to look at one — a crime of which I was now guilty. Whatever I might say to government officials would be unconvincing at best, self-incriminating at worst.

Our plan had failed. I had failed Abby.

Lauren had interviewed with Max Strong before — too many times before. He was arrogant, condescending, self-aggrandizing. A typical media type. She endured him, as with all the media. In politics, they were a necessary evil.

Sixty seconds to airtime. Lauren licked her lips and patted her hair. She heard a familiar ring tone in her neural implant. It was Claire, her aide. She quickly turned aside. "I'm going on in thirty seconds. You

602

can't tap me now. You know better than that."

"Sorry to interrupt, Ms. Caldwell. I just wanted to let you know some important news."

Lauren listened intently. Her jaw dropped, and her face turned ashen.

The television producer spoke. "Five seconds, Ms. Caldwell. Three, two, one . . ."

She survived the interview. Within a minute after it ended, Hutch was tapping her.

"You seemed distracted, Lauren."

"Abby is dead."

"What?"

"A car accident. Up in Maine."

She looked at him for a reaction. There wasn't any.

"Any hint of foul play?"

"I haven't heard anything," she answered.

"I'll check into it."

"What do you think about doing the hearings without her?"

He was silent for a moment. "Having her in the hearings was always a risk. A good risk, but a risk nonetheless. They'll go fine — maybe even better. Let's simply proceed as planned."

Sabin tapped first thing the next morning. I

met him on a mountaintop.

"Lauren told me about Abby. I'm so sorry, Creighton."

I felt as if I should have something to say in response, but I wasn't sure I could without breaking down. I simply nodded. We sat for a few moments, the breeze against our faces.

Sabin finally spoke. "Creighton, I want you to know that I thought Abby was the most special person I've met in a long time. A very long time."

"I thought so too, Sabin."

He picked up a stone and tossed it a ways down the mountain. "Have you thought about a memorial service?"

Had I thought about a memorial service? "No. It hadn't even occurred to me."

"When are you coming back to Dallas?"

"I don't know. I don't feel I can leave yet. If I do, it will mean closing the book on everything we came here for — finding out the truth about Ray and my father, getting answers about her village. I can't do that to Abby." I looked over at him. "I don't want her sacrifice to be wasted."

"Do you want me to come up there and help you?"

"I wouldn't. I don't think you'd be safe. I wonder if anyone here is safe."

"What will you do?"

"I have to try to stop Ray Caldwell's warning from coming to pass. That's the least I can do."

"There's nothing I can do to help?"

"I'll let you know if there is." I hesitated. "Actually, plan a memorial service. You're right. We should do that."

I exited VR, walked downstairs, and sat at the breakfast table. Abby's copy of *To Kill a Mockingbird* lay at her spot. I stared out the breakfast room's bay window. Abby always looked out windows. She lived outdoors, in the jungle. She should have stayed in the jungle.

46

Bryson Nichols walked to the witness chair in front of the House Subcommittee on Technology and Innovation. He sat behind a simple wood table.

Chairwoman Jillian Cahill introduced Nichols, welcomed him to the proceedings, and invited him to begin his prepared statement. He cleared his throat, probably for dramatic effect — everything Nichols did was for effect, I surmised — glanced at the rows of representatives before him, and began.

"Madam Chairwoman, we stand on the brink of the greatest upward leap in human history . . ."

Nichols's testimony, I discovered, didn't have to interrupt what I regarded as my real work for the day: monitoring Cleary's memory stream. I could simultaneously attend the hearings in VR and scan the stream — one of a constant series of discoveries of my new brain's capabilities.

"Imagine a world in which every man and woman has immediate access to the entirety of human knowledge. And not only immediate access, but the ability to process and synthesize that knowledge instantly. Ignorance disappears overnight, and with it superstition. Public policy disagreements evaporate, for we all see reality completely and perfectly and come to the same conclusions regarding ideal courses of action."

I glanced around the hearing room. It was packed. Media representatives rivaled spectators in number. Attention was riveted on Nichols. Lauren Caldwell was getting her wish: public attention on one of her key campaign issues.

"Humanity's enduring blights — poverty, resource supply, ideological and religious conflict — all end. Shortages disappear. Economics are transformed; all people have access to virtually unlimited wealth to be enjoyed throughout limitless life spans . . ."

Not having to refer to electronic notes, Nichols maintained constant eye contact with the committee members, slowly scanning their faces as he spoke.

I monitored Cleary's stream every few minutes. My only hope was to observe within it a planned action that would unmask his scheme. I would anonymously alert the authorities and hope they followed up. It was a long shot but the only one I had, short of murdering Cleary and Pape, which was problematic.

"All obstacles to human progress will soon be swept away. Human intelligence will catapult forward at a pace previously undreamed of . . ."

In between my times with Cleary, I scanned Nichols's stream. It gradually confirmed what I had already suspected. Nichols wasn't behind the murders of Abby's village or of Ben and Abby. He hadn't even intended to institutionalize Ray. Events had caught him by surprise, and he fully expected Ray to see things his way when Ray received his new brain. That proved false, and when Ray threatened to go public, Nichols panicked and had him committed. At that point he was trapped.

Nichols continued his testimony. "Our collective future is as limitless as the energy of the sun, of a billion suns. We *will* achieve this future, of that there is no doubt. The question is when. NTI has this year achieved the most significant technological breakthrough since the invention of the integrated circuit a hundred and thirty years ago . . ."

The memory stream I was unable to access — one I desperately needed to access — was Pape's. Apparently, he still possessed his biological brain. Pape's activities, not Cleary's, would give me the best update on their progress.

"The issue facing this committee today is the shape of human society to come. Will the human community leap forward into unlimited intelligence, awareness, and potentialities, or will we remain wedded to the pace of progress afforded by our merely biological brains — a pace that consigns untold millions to lives of misery?

"I sit before you in full support of the two proposals drafted by Representative Caldwell. First, to mandate Health Services coverage of brain transplants in the United States." I glanced at a nodding Lauren Caldwell. "This is *the* civil rights issue of our time. We dare not deprive any American of his or her rightful destiny. And, second, for the United States to take the lead in disseminating this technology worldwide, not only to those who can afford it, but to those who cannot. We dare not allow our quantum leap in intelligence to be limited to the haves of the world and exclude the have-nots. If the entire world makes this leap together, there will soon be no have-nots. We will have solved the problems that have plagued us since the dawn of *Homo sapiens.*

"This is the necessary — no, the inevitable — next step in our evolution as a society and as a species. We have risen together out of the slime of human ignorance. Let us press forward to the upward call of our destiny. We owe ourselves, our children, indeed our universe, no less."

Nichols leaned back in his chair, a look of self-satisfaction crossing his face. "Madam Chairwoman, I'm prepared to answer any questions the committee wishes to pose."

The upward call of our destiny. Nichols and Cleary were already living their vision of the future. From personal experience, I knew what that produced. In theory, transhumanity — I was transhuman, I had to keep reminding myself — sounded wonderful. In practice, it had turned out to be less so. Perhaps there was more to human existence than could be duplicated in silicon.

Abby had been scheduled to testify the next morning. Dr. Matthew Lambert, the U.S. representative to the UN Committee on the Transfer of Technology, had been moved into her slot to offer a developing-nation view of AI. I returned to my real-time VR seat, knowing perfectly well that, regardless of what he said, it wouldn't mirror Abby's perspective.

Unlike the day before, the room wasn't full. Nichols had been the star attraction. I looked up front. Lambert sat in the witness chair. Lauren Caldwell took her seat on the row of representatives. The chairwoman gaveled the hearings to order and turned to Lauren.

"Representative Caldwell, we share your deep sadness at the passing of your cousin, Abigail Caldwell, who was scheduled to testify at this time." An image of Abby appeared on visiscreens at the front of the room. "Abigail lived an extraordinary life, and this subcommittee would have been enriched by her perspective, as we are certain your family was enriched by her life."

Lauren leaned forward. "Thank you, Madam Chairwoman. My cousin grew up among tribal people in New Guinea who have been deprived all their lives of the advances of humanity. She would have heartily embraced the vision expressed by Bryson Nichols of making the wonders of artificial intelligence available to all peoples."

I gagged.

Chairwoman Cahill turned to the witness chair. "The subcommittee stands ready to hear from Dr. Matthew Lambert." Dr. Lambert stood and raised his right hand.

As an officer approached him to administer the oath, I heard the door to the committee chamber open, followed by a low murmur in the back of the room. Heads started turning. The murmur grew louder. I looked back. I couldn't believe my eyes. It was Ben. While I was still trying to absorb that, a woman stepped out from behind him. I jumped out of my chair and shouted, "Abby! Abby!"

Of course she couldn't hear me. I was sitting in Lauren's living room. But she was alive!

Chairwoman Cahill banged her gavel half a dozen times. A hush fell over the room. Ben, Abby, and a man I didn't recognize walked down the aisle to the witness table. Still standing, Ben addressed the chairwoman.

"Madam Chairwoman, my name is Ben Steele. Until last week I was a Special Agent with the FBI. Since last week I've considered it my duty to deliver Abigail Caldwell to this subcommittee for these hearings. She stands ready to testify at her originally scheduled time."

A buzz swept the room again. The chairwoman pounded her gavel and looked menacingly at the spectators before returning her eyes to Ben. "Thank you, Special Agent Steele." She looked at Lambert. "I apologize, Dr. Lambert. Would you be offended if Ms. Caldwell presents her testimony at this time?"

Lambert wasn't offended.

The chairwoman looked up and down the row of representatives. "If there are no objections, I will call Abigail Caldwell as our witness."

I glanced at Lauren. She was white as a sheet.

Abby stood at the witness table and was sworn in. I tapped for a car. I could remain in VR while en route to the Capitol.

"Do you have a prepared statement, Ms. Caldwell?"

"A brief one, yes."

"Please proceed."

Abby glanced at Ben, then began. "Madam Chairwoman, esteemed members of the subcommittee. I am honored by the privilege of coming before the Congress of the United States as an ordinary citizen to speak concerning an important issue such as this.

"Unlike those who have testified before me, I'm not an expert on artificial intelligence, though here in the States I've learned quickly of its possible effects. I'm a simple woman who has lived her entire life in the jungle of Papua New Guinea. I'm an expert on how to avoid crocodile attacks and what to do when one's mosquito netting is eaten through by rats."

There was a smattering of laughter in the audience.

"It may be that I'm here as an example of the kind of person America *doesn't* want . . ."

I glanced at Lauren. Her face remained expressionless.

Abby continued, ". . . a person who would lead civilized people back to the Stone Age. Maybe, after listening to me, you'll choose to fund Bryson Nichols's utopian vision and all peoples of the earth will be blessed." She paused before adding, "Or so he claims."

I heard whispers behind me. Witnesses before Congress rarely made such pointed comments.

"The people I've lived with in the jungle don't have all your technological advances. Their lives are simple. They get diseases, and they die young, and their lives are difficult. But they have joy.

"They didn't always. When my parents first moved to the jungle, the Inisi tribe was ruled by fear and revenge killings and clan wars. Life was not only hard; it was dreadful. No one smiled or laughed. As I grew up, that changed, because my parents brought them a new way to see the world — a way that offended them, initially. But they saw in our imperfect lives that Jesus was real. We showed them what it meant to love as Jesus loved, to forgive as Jesus forgave, to value human life as God does, to serve one another as Jesus came to serve us, and to enjoy God and his creation in a way that enriches life.

"The wars stopped. The killings stopped. Husbands started loving their wives instead of beating them. The children learned to laugh and play. For the first time, the Inisi experienced true life."

I looked around the room. Abby had the audience's complete attention.

Alistair informed me that my car had arrived. I ran outside and hopped in the car while remaining in the VR hearings room.

Abby glanced at her notes. "How we view reality may be the most important thing about us. It governs our actions, our attitudes, our dreams. America has chosen to embrace a universe without God. Here, ultimate reality is just physical matter. We are all just collections of atoms given certain forms as a result of time and chance.

"Existence has no real meaning. Life has no purpose. It's not surprising that Americans spend so much time seeking stimulation for their brains and bodies since that becomes the ultimate goal in such a universe. And I'm truly amazed at the wonders you've invented in pursuit of this goal.

"What I haven't found here, however, are people with deep inner joy. I miss that about the Inisi. Though materially the Inisi couldn't be poorer, in spirit they couldn't be richer."

A few spectators nodded in agreement.

"What if reality is different than you have believed? What if ultimate reality is a Creator who designed us with a human spirit, who wants to join himself to that spirit, who wants to infuse us with his very own life? And what if our spirit can't find fulfillment or peace or true purpose except by being joined to the One who made it?"

She paused, and I noted how radiant she looked in that moment. She was fully alive, not just physically, but in every way a person could be.

"Bryson Nichols claims to offer eternal life. Perhaps he offers unending existence, but he doesn't offer eternal life. Only God offers that, because his Son *is* the life. He who has the Son has the life. Forever.

"The Inisi would not be enriched by Bryson Nichols's latest technology. They would be impoverished, for they would lose their greatest treasure, God himself. Just as my grandfather, Dr. Ray Caldwell, lost God when he was forced against his will to undergo the brain transplant that he himself invented."

Murmurs rippled through the crowd once more. The chairwoman banged her gavel again, and the audience quieted. She looked at Abby. "That's quite a claim, Ms. Caldwell. Have you discussed this misuse of his technology with Bryson Nichols?"

"It was Bryson Nichols who performed the transplant."

Confusion churned through the crowd. It took ten minutes for the chairwoman to regain control and resume the proceedings. She looked at Abby with the utmost seriousness. "Ms. Caldwell, this hearing room does not afford protection for slander. You stand in danger of both criminal and civil proceedings. I understand the duress all this has placed you under. I will afford you the opportunity to amend your statement to this committee."

Abby leaned over and spoke briefly to the man who had accompanied her down the aisle with Ben.

"Ms. Caldwell?"

Abby looked back at the chairwoman. "I appreciate your graciousness, Madam Chairwoman. In response to your offer, may I request that a statement by the man next to me be added on my behalf?"

Jillian Cahill's patience had worn thin. "And who is this man, Ms. Caldwell?"

"Dr. Leonard Thompson."

"And what is he a doctor of?"

"Until three weeks ago he was the head of psychiatry at the Massachusetts Center for Mental Health."

Within the span of forty-five minutes, Leonard Thompson unraveled Bryson Nichols's carefully constructed plan for the world. He corroborated Abby's claims concerning Nichols and her grandfather. Thompson had been fired without cause because of what he knew and had been threatened with harm if he spoke of it. He had contacted the FBI and had been referred to Ben Steele, who had arranged for his presence at the hearings.

By the time Thompson's testimony ended, I stood at the back of the hearing room, in physical reality. Chairwoman Cahill pounded her gavel, ending the morning session.

"Abby!" I cried. "Abby!"

Several officers began wedging Abby, Ben, and Dr. Thompson through the crowd toward the back. I pressed my way toward her.

"Abby!"

Her eyes lit up when they met mine. "Creighton!"

She pushed through reporters and threw her arms around me. We held each other for several long moments. She leaned her head back, tears on her face. "Creighton —"

I kissed her gently. "Abby, I thought you were —"

"I know. I know."

"What happened with the car on the road? How did you . . ." I glanced around us. Ben was standing next to Abby. Reporters were gathered in a circle, peppering her with questions, none of which she was paying attention to. I leaned over and spoke loudly into Ben's ear so he could hear me. "We need a place to talk."

He nodded. "Follow me."

Two officers led us down a hallway and unlocked a door to a small room with a rectangular table and six wooden chairs. They closed the door behind us, blocking the media corps.

Abby leaned into me, and we embraced

again. I looked into her eyes. "Abby, I thought I'd never see you again."

"I thought that too."

I stroked her hair and looked over at Ben. "What happened? How did you survive the crash?"

He shook his head. "We weren't in the car when it went over the cliff. Thank yesterday's abandoned technologies."

"But, Ben, why did you go up to Maine?"

"To confront Nichols. But then Abby was kidnapped."

"But Nichols isn't the one behind all this. It's Cleary who —"

"That's the conclusion I reached as well."

"So where have you been hiding?" I asked Abby.

"On a boat off the coast," she answered. "We wanted to contact you, but the boat wasn't connected to the Grid, and we didn't want to risk coming ashore before we had to."

"And," Ben added, "we didn't know how secure such a communication might be. I assume you had the transplant done?"

I looked at Abby, searching her face for her reaction.

"Yes," I answered simply.

She met my eyes, then looked down.

"Abby, you know I had to do it. Cleary

has to be stopped."

She tilted her head, clearly not in agreement. "I hoped there was another way." She leaned forward and held on to me tightly. "I'm just . . . heartbroken for you."

We were quiet for a moment. I dreaded the silence, knowing the question that lurked within it.

Ben provided a brief respite. "Creighton, were you able to access the memory streams?"

"Cleary's. Not those of his henchman, Pape."

"And?"

"They're planning to release the neural nanites into the water supply of three cities, including DC."

"When?"

"I don't know. Soon. Ben, is the FBI going to take you into custody?"

"No. En route here I tapped the ombudsman at the FBI and told him what had happened at the hospital. They'll want to question me, I'm sure."

"Creighton —"

I turned to Abby. She looked anxious.

"Have you met again with my grandfather?"

It was the last question I wanted to answer. I looked at the floor.

"What is it?" she asked. "Is something wrong?"

I raised my eyes to her. "Abby, two days ago Cleary faked a message from Nichols asking that Ray be released."

"And was he?"

"Pape went to pick him up. I'm sorry, Abby. Ray is dead."

47

We exited the Capitol and got a car. Ben instructed it to take us to his residence. En route, I filled them in on what I had learned from Cleary's memory streams. Abby gripped my hand the entire ride, but didn't say much.

The vehicle stopped in front of an older, modest-sized house in DC's Virginia suburbs. We walked inside. Ben checked his monitoring system. Abby walked around the living room, looking at photos.

"Who's this?" Abby was pointing to a picture of a young woman standing on a dirt airstrip next to a prop plane.

Ben glanced over. "That's my daughter, Chelle."

"Where does she live?"

"She died nine years ago. She'd have been thirty-eight next month."

"Oh." She looked pained. "I'm sorry, Ben."

"No, that's okay. I enjoy talking about her. She was the delight of my life." He walked over and stood next to Abby. "You remind me of her a lot, Abby."

She smiled. "Where was this picture taken?"

"Tanzania."

She examined the photo more closely. "Is that a Bible she's carrying?"

He nodded.

Abby didn't hide her surprise. "She was a Christian?"

"Yes. One of the few her age."

"What was she doing in Tanzania?"

"She was on a mission trip. Literacy work."

Abby turned back to the picture and ran a finger along the edge of the frame. "Ben, do you mind if I ask how she died?"

Ben rubbed his eyes and sighed. "She was taken hostage by religious extremists. They held her for several months. We paid a ransom, but they killed her anyway."

"Oh, Ben." Abby hesitated, then put her arms around him. After a moment she stepped back, keeping a hand on his arm.

"I've always regretted I didn't go there and try to rescue her."

Abby hugged him again. This time he squeezed her tight. We were all silent for a moment.

"Well," Ben finally said, clearing his throat, "let's get a bite to eat and get going, shall we?"

He dished up some chili, and we sat at the kitchen table. He looked at me. "So Cleary and Pape are planning to infect the water supplies of DC, Annapolis, and Richmond. I imagine they want to make it look like a natural disease that's spreading north and south from DC."

I nodded.

Ben thought for a moment. "Do you know exactly where Pape has planted the nanite bombs?"

"No. Cleary's stream doesn't indicate that. Maybe he left it up to Pape."

"Why don't we just have the water system people find the nanite bombs?" Abby asked.

"The bombs could be microscopic," I replied.

Ben leaned back in his chair. "Even if they were visible, those water systems have hundreds of miles of pipe. Finding them would be almost impossible."

Abby tapped her fingers on the table. "Why can't the FBI simply arrest Cleary?"

"Apart from the memory stream Creighton accessed, which isn't usable, we don't have enough evidence against Cleary for the

FBI to monitor him, much less arrest him. Besides, even if we got to Cleary, Pape may already have his instructions. Arresting Cleary, in fact, might trigger their plan immediately."

My brain was exploring options we hadn't considered. We couldn't reach Cleary and Pape soon enough with law enforcement. Somehow we needed to redirect their efforts. I already had access to Cleary's memory stream. How could we use that to our advantage?

Then it struck me. I knocked my knuckles against the table.

"What is it?" Abby asked.

"An idea. Maybe. It would require the help of a friend."

Bryson Nichols sat in the Library, sipping a vermouth and rum. He glanced around the walls, looking at the nineteenth-century English paintings for the first time in a while. *My favorite century,* he thought.

Damien Cleary appeared and sat in the chair across the table from him. "Where are you hiding, Nichols? I take it you can't be found at the Kensington estate any longer."

"Unfortunately, no. It's a shame things don't always turn out as one may wish.

626

That's what contingency plans are for, isn't it?"

Cleary was silent.

Nichols answered his original question. "As for me, I'll soon be safe. It takes time to execute one's getaway, you know, even with our mental capacity. I'm surprised they aren't on your trail, Damien."

"Depends on how well the FBI can connect the dots."

Nichols entwined his fingers on the table. "They'll suspend operations at the lab shortly. It will, however, remain functional. We have only one more upload to perform for now. Unless you're ready for yours, that is."

Cleary shook his head. "No, I'll let you escape into VR by yourself. I'm content staying out here in the physical world."

"I don't think the attorney general can protect you at this point."

"No need for him to. I'll use our nanites to deactivate my chip, and I'll melt away. When all of this is over — when much of humanity has converted, and we're regarded as heroes — I'll resurface."

"And I will download back into a nanite body. So it sounds as if you'll be available to assist with that procedure."

Cleary nodded.

"Good. Then I will contact you from VR in . . . oh, twenty years."

"And if something should happen to me?"

Nichols smiled. "Then I have a backup, of course. I've already programmed my re-appearance in holographic form at MIT. With instructions from me, someone there should be able to put me in a nanite body."

Nichols lifted his drink. "To us, Damien. Our plans have suffered a setback, but it isn't permanent. The transplants will resume at some point, and our march toward trans-humanity will continue." He finished his drink and stood. "Fortunately, we'll both be there to see it."

"Fortunately."

"I'll meet you in the lab tomorrow. Six a.m."

"Are you sure you can trust this guy? He can blow this whole thing for us."

Abby nodded. "Ben, we can trust him."

He turned his gaze toward me. "And you think this will work?"

"We'll soon find out."

Momentarily Sabin appeared on a visi-screen. His eyes lit up. "Abby! I've been try-ing to get hold of you since I heard the news. I'm so glad . . . so thankful you're alive. I tried tapping you, Creighton —"

"I'm sorry about that, Sabin. I meant to have Abby get back to you as soon as possible. But now . . ." I glanced at Abby.

"Sabin, we need a favor," she said.

He looked toward me. "Sure. Anything."

"We could use your holographic programming skills," I answered.

"You need a hologram?"

I nodded. "Several. Quickly. And confidentially."

At the NTI lab Nichols and Cleary prepared the equipment for Nichols's upload into VR. Cleary kept glancing at the building's security monitors.

Nichols turned to him. "We're ready. I'll perform the upload scan myself. Once I'm permanently in VR, I'll need you to take the three physical copies of my brain software and store them in the proper locations."

Cleary rolled his eyes. "Nichols, we've reviewed this multiple times."

"Damien, please indulge me. Soon you'll be rid of me for years. Now, the original of my brain software will be uploaded into VR. You'll be the only one with access to me. Once my software is uploaded, I'll verify from here that I've been accurately copied and securely located. After I'm in VR, I'd like you to check on me periodically. If anything goes wrong and you need to reupload to the Grid, you have access to the three physical copies."

"I will check on you at least monthly."

"Good."

"Nichols, if by chance I'm not around, how do you know that twenty years from now they'll be able to download you back into a new body or whatever is the container du jour? Every time technology switches to a new medium, the old media become inaccessible. Surely you've accounted for that."

"I'll update the instructions while in VR. When I reappear, they'll have all they need to download me into a physical form."

"And how do you know they'll bother?"

"Because, Damien, I'll be living history. The first transhuman. It will be impossible for them to say no."

He sat down in a chair and started the upload procedure. In an hour he announced, "It is finished. My software is uploaded onto the Grid, and my VR program is secure. I wish you could join me, Damien. It will be quite lovely."

"Of that I have no doubt."

Nichols handed him three physical copies of his brain software. "You know where these go."

"I do."

Nichols stuck out his right hand. "Then I will see you in twenty years."

They shook. "Until then," Cleary added.

Nichols got out of the chair and lay facedown on the floor. "You may proceed with the final act."

Cleary picked up a sledgehammer, raised it over his head, and brought it down with all his might on Nichols's skull. The execution made a mess on the floor, but cleaning robots could take care of that.

Cleary placed the sledgehammer on the floor and took a seat. He accessed Nichols's secure location on the Grid. Everything was just as Nichols had planned; his brain software was properly functioning in some undoubtedly exotic VR location.

Cleary reviewed instructions for deleting programs from a secure Grid location. He input the commands. Within five minutes he had completed all the steps except one. "Sorry to erase you out of paradise, Nichols. But your plan always was too cautious. And I can't have you around implicating me for genocide. I don't think they'll forgive that, even in twenty years."

He executed the final command.

Cleary stood and picked up the three physical copies of Nichols's brain software. He walked through the lab door and down a long, dark hall. He took a right into another corridor and unlocked a door that read Authorized Personnel Only. He entered a large room and walked toward the back to a large bin with a yellow label: "Warning: nanite incinerators. Use for controlled incineration purposes only."

He opened the slot on the side of the bin and dropped the three copies of Nichols's brain software inside.

"Good-bye, Nichols."

I looked over Sabin's shoulder in his VR office. He brought up a hologram on the desk in front of him, the first of a series of false memories that we hoped to insert into Damien Cleary's memory stream.

"This is him deactivating the nanites," Sabin explained.

I watched the hologram of Cleary sitting in his own office, programming the activation command on the nanite bomb he had designed.

"This command," Sabin commented, "tells the bomb to release the nanites into the water supply. This command internally disables the bomb." Cleary had installed a disabler as a safeguard. "In this memory I've simply switched the commands."

"So when he tells the bomb to release the

nanites," I verified, "he will actually be telling it to deactivate?"

"Correct."

I pulled a chair over and sat down. "What about the second one?"

Sabin leaned back and folded his arms. "The first one was easy. The second was more involved . . ."

"I realize that. Could you do it?"

"Of course."

Another hologram appeared before us. Cleary was sitting at his desk, programming Pape's personal tap and VR meeting history to be sent to Cleary. Intercepting someone else's taps was highly illegal; supposedly, the government alone had the capability and could exercise it only for national security purposes. Rumor had it, however, that the technology had leaked onto the black market. "So how does Cleary get the equipment to intercept Pape's taps?" I asked.

"I programmed that memory for him in another hologram. You want to see it?"

"Later. I want to see the Pape hologram."

"Right here."

Cleary was at home sifting through Pape's taps. He stopped at one. Pape was meeting with a Chinese man, about fifty.

"Hello, Lewis. You said you'd contact

me only if something went wrong."

"Or when I was done. I'm done."

The man nodded. "Then we're ready. You don't think Cleary suspects anything?"

"No, I'm sure he doesn't."

"Why so sure?"

"Because he continues to entrust every operational detail to me. He's assuming we're on the same page, that I'm doing everything he instructs me to do." Pape smiled. "Which I have. Except for our last twist."

The Chinese man rose from his chair. "Lewis, we won't transfer the funds until the nanites are released and Cleary is taken care of — both his hardware and software."

"That's what we agreed to."

The message ended. Cleary sat at his desk, his eyes unmoving.

Sabin paused the program. "That's it." He turned and looked at me. "Creighton, are you sure when you insert these into Cleary's memory stream that they'll work? What if Cleary discovers that he doesn't have access to such equipment in reality? Then what?"

I let out a long breath. "All I can say is,

we need to hope he acts on these memories before he discovers that fact. It's our only shot."

"And you can definitely insert them in his stream?"

I nodded. "That's what I am sure about. I can get them in there as memories. What I don't know is whether they'll be seamless in the stream and come across as any other memories. If they don't, Cleary may notice a glitch and suspect something."

"So there are at least two ways he may not take the bait."

We looked at each other for a moment.

"Well . . ." Sabin turned back to his visiscreen. "Here's the third memory."

The holographic Cleary was reviewing the commands necessary to upload his brain software into permanent VR — just as Nichols had done.

"And here," Sabin said, "is the memory of Cleary and Ray discussing the commands necessary to erase one's own programming."

They were the commands I had received from Ray at the picnic table. In this memory Cleary vociferously objected to the need for such commands.

"Ray, why would anyone possessing a

new brain and everlasting mental existence want to erase themselves? It's inconceivable."

"I agree, Damien," Ray replied. "I can't imagine anyone using it. It's a backup, that's all."

"A backup to what?"

"To anything that might not go as planned."

The scene was a nice touch. It would play into Cleary's image of both himself and Ray.

Sabin paused the program again. "In these memories the commands have been switched. When Cleary runs what he thinks is the upload sequence, putting himself in permanent VR, it will actually . . ." He didn't end the sentence.

"Erase his software," I said.

Sabin nodded.

"And the backup on the Grid?"

"Yes," he confirmed. "Unless he's backed himself up elsewhere."

"No, he hasn't."

Sabin swung his chair around and faced me. "Creighton, I'm not . . ."

I waited, but he didn't continue. "Not what?"

"I'm not sure about this. We're talking about murder here."

I walked to a counter, poured myself some water, and took a long drink. "Are we? Or are we just reformatting a computer? Is there anyone left there to murder?"

"I don't know. You tell me."

I had asked myself the same question. I didn't know how to answer it. I put my glass down. "Well, it's either Cleary or, potentially, millions of others."

"I don't think Abby will go for it."

I shook my head slowly. "Abby will never know about it."

I exited VR. Ben was sitting on his couch, waiting for me.

"Where's Abby?" I asked.

"She went to bed. Do you have the holographic memories?"

I nodded. "Sabin just copied them to me."

"How do they look?"

"Quite good, actually. All I have to do now is insert them."

He stood up. "Well, no time like the present. Anything you need from me?"

"No. Just wish us all luck."

He smiled. "Good luck."

I closed my eyes and accessed Cleary's memory stream.

48

Damien Cleary strolled across the entryway in his DC home and opened the front door. "Hello, Lewis."

Lewis Pape glanced down the street, then stepped inside.

"You have the activator?" Cleary asked.

Pape placed a carrying case on a coffee table, opened it, and removed a small electronic device. "I could've done this myself, Cleary. It's risky, my coming here."

Cleary waved him off. "It's far too late in the game for anyone to stop us. Besides, this was necessary. I appreciate your willingness to terminate so many for the sake of humanity's future, but I decided I couldn't lay that on you. If I'm to be known as the father of transhumanity, I have to take responsibility for the transition."

He walked into the kitchen and poured two mixed drinks. "Besides, I wanted to celebrate in person. Our two-year partnership is coming to an end. Humanity will soon be converted. I'll be ensconced in VR for twenty years. And no one will ever know of your involvement."

"I thought you were going to deactivate your chip and try to stay undetected."

"No, too risky. I let Nichols think I was staying around, but he was right. Transferring into VR is the only safe route at this point."

He walked back and placed the drinks in front of them. "Lewis, I couldn't have done this without you."

Pape smiled. "Never has a truer word been spoken." He took a sip and smacked his lips. "You seem certain your plan will work, Cleary."

"The nanite plan or my personal plan?"

"Your personal plan. I know the nanites will work."

"Yes, Nichols and I were both quite certain. It's a shame he won't be joining me."

"Yes. A real shame."

Cleary sipped his drink. "I've programmed a media release to be sent across the Grid in 2108: 'Father of Transhumanity, Presumed Dead, Found in VR.' Catchy headline, don't you think?"

"But what are they going to download you

into? Your body's going in the grave in a few days."

"Yes. And good riddance. By that time they should be able to download me into a pure nanite body. If not, a robotic body will do."

"You don't have any doubt that NTI will agree to ramp up the transplants once the brain infections begin?"

"NTI will have no choice. The government will declare a national emergency, seize their assets, and mass-produce surgeon robots. Biological humanity is in its death throes, my friend. Transhumanity will have begun in earnest."

Pape raised his glass. "To the Singularity, then. We have arrived."

Cleary lifted his own glass. "To the Singularity." He picked up the electronic device. "Well, the nanites are waiting. I made the code zero five zero eight."

"My birthday. I'm honored."

Cleary input the first three digits. He looked at Pape. "To you, Lewis. And to the future."

He input the final digit.

On the way to the airport, we stopped at Lauren's to pick up a few of Abby's things that were still there. The congresswoman, I figured, was on the Hill.

"I'll just be a minute," Abby said.

I started worrying after five minutes had passed. I got out of the car, walked to the front door, and opened it. Lauren and Abby were standing in the foyer. Lauren turned to me, a cold smile crossing her face.

"Professor. Abby and I were just wrapping up. It's been a pleasure having you here in Washington."

I glanced at Abby, who looked horribly uncomfortable. "We need to go," I said, guiding her out. I closed the door behind us.

The car drove toward the airport. Ben and I talked about his plans while Abby sat silently. Finally I turned to her. "Did everything go okay back there, Abby? Are you all right?"

She reached out her hand and placed it in mine. "Everything will be all right, Creighton."

Ben accompanied us to the gate when we got to the airport. Abby walked to the women's rest room. Ben turned to me after she was out of earshot. "When was the last time you accessed Cleary's memory stream?"

"That's what I was doing when Abby was talking with Lauren."

"And?"

"They just finished meeting two hours ago. They deactivated the nanites."

"You're sure?"

"As sure as I can be. I still recommend you guys find the nanite bombs."

"I'll get the bureau on that. What about Pape?"

"Cleary infected him with nanites. He has three days. Maybe four."

"And Cleary?"

"He plans to upload himself into VR tomorrow night. I'll check the day after to make sure."

"That he's erased himself instead?"

I nodded.

Abby returned, and a moment later we heard the first boarding call. Abby stepped over and looped her arm in Ben's. Her eyes were full of tears. "It seems like too little to simply say thanks for all you've done."

He shook his head. "I would've —" He stopped.

"Would have what?"

"I was going to say I'd have done the same for anyone. But that's not true. You gave me a chance to redeem a wrong choice I made nine years ago. And you've helped me understand my daughter just a little more. I'll never forget that."

"Your daughter would be so proud of you, I'm certain." Abby's voice was thick with emotion. "And if it weren't for you, Ben, I never would have met my grandfather."

He gazed into her eyes. "I'm sorry he's gone, Abby."

She smiled. "I'll see him again someday. I'm sure of that." She looked at him for a moment. When she spoke again, her words held sadness. "I don't imagine I'll see you in person again."

He seemed to force a smile. "Oh, you never know. I make it down to Texas from time to time. Besides, you can tap me."

"Yes, I can tap you." She nodded, but I knew she felt that a tap wasn't the same.

I heard a second boarding call. "Abby, we'd better go."

She pulled Ben into an embrace, and they hugged for a long time. When he finally pulled away, I could see a tear in his eye.

He and I shook hands.

"I'll tap you in a couple of days," I told him. "Give you a progress report."

He nodded. "Talk to you then."

We grabbed our suitcases and walked past the gate and down the jet bridge.

"Progress report about what?" Abby asked.

"How things are going in Dallas," I lied.

We waited for a moment on the jet bridge. Abby leaned close to me so no one would overhear her. "Creighton, when Cleary discovers that the nanites didn't activate, what will stop him from trying it again?"

"I'm sure the FBI will have him by then." Another lie — unless one considered possession of a corpse as "having him." I'd be glad when this entire episode ended and I didn't have to hide anything from Abby. "Ben is staying here to work on it. All they have to do is find one nanite bomb, and they'll have the evidence they need."

"Then it will be over?"

"Then it will be over." I smiled at her. "Our part is already over."

When she sighed, her whole body seemed to release tension, and she leaned into me. "I know."

Ten minutes after Ben Steele left the airport, Lewis Pape emerged from a car, walked inside the terminal, and approached a ticket kiosk.

"Destination?" the kiosk robot asked.

"DFW."

"Departure time?"

"Two forty-six."

He secured his ticket and proceeded to the concourse, stopping to buy some over-the-counter pain medication for a headache. Did this stuff actually work? Pape hadn't had a headache in years.

I woke to bright sunlight streaming through my windows. I threw on some clothes and walked down the hallway. Abby was stretched out on top of her comforter in jeans and a T-shirt, writing in her journal, her Bible next to her on the bed.

"Hey," I said from the doorway. "You're up early."

She closed her journal and smiled at me. "You're up late." She crossed the room, placed her arms around me, and hugged me.

I stepped back after a moment. "No kiss?"

She rose up on her toes and kissed me briefly on the lips. Something was wrong, but I decided not to press her about whatever was bothering her. We went downstairs for breakfast.

"I saw in the news that Lauren has a new strategy. She's called for hearings on government oversight of the AI industry."

Abby had a bite of toast. "At least we gave her a new issue for her campaign. I'm glad government funding for the transplants died."

"Thanks to you."

She shook her head. "No, thanks to Poppy."

"NTI announced that it has suspended brain transplants indefinitely."

Abby's eyes brightened. "Really? Well. Poppy got what he wanted after all. In every way."

We finished breakfast and cleared the dishes. Abby headed upstairs to get cleaned up. She paused halfway up and looked down at me. "Creighton, I'd like to go see Sabin. Can we arrange that?"

I nodded. "I'll tap him."

Midmorning I walked into the living room. Abby was lying on the couch, reading her Bible. I sat on the far end and ran my fingers over her feet.

"That feels good." She kept reading.

"Don't you ever get tired of reading the Bible?"

She laughed a little, looking up at me. "No. God speaks to me through it."

"But how many times have you read the same words?"

She closed the Bible. "Many. But now they have a different message for me. I don't see a list of things I have to work to do. I see a list of all the amazing things he will do living through me. It's such a radical shift, but it's so obvious to me now. I don't know how I missed it."

"But all along you've been asking God to help you, to be a part of everything you've done here, haven't you?"

"Of course. But the burden was still on me. *I* had to perform well enough for God. *I* had to keep his commands. *I* had to be a good Christian." She shook her head. "No one can live up to that. Jesus doesn't want to help me. He wants to live through me. So when I'm sharing the gospel or testifying before Congress or" — she smiled — "forgiving you, it's Jesus in me doing those things."

I did a quick scan of the New Testament. "Is that what Paul meant when he said, 'It is no longer I who live, but Christ lives in me'?"

Her eyes lit up. "Yes. Exactly. 'And the life which I now live in the flesh I live by faith in the Son of God, who loved me, and gave himself up for me.' Galatians 2:20."

I could find the verses. But she had learned to live them out.

I started rubbing her toes.

She giggled. "That tickles."

"So . . . if Christ is doing it, what do you do exactly?"

She thought for a moment. "I depend on

him. I stay attentive to him. Listen to the Spirit, follow his lead. I just enjoy God." She cocked her head slightly. "Creighton, you seem more interested in this than ever."

I nodded. "Maybe we're more intrigued by whatever is unavailable to us. Maybe . . ." I hesitated. "Maybe if I had connected myself to God, I wouldn't have to ask about it."

She took my hand in hers. "That may be. But, Creighton, you did what you thought you had to do."

We looked at each other silently, knowingly.

"Will you help me with something today?" she asked.

"Sure. What?"

"I want to remake the visual I did for the Grid."

"You want to say something different?"

"I want to say something more complete."

Sabin saw the car pull up and Abby get out. He walked down the steps from a platform overlooking the Fort Worth Botanical Gardens, one of his favorite places to visit. "Abby!"

Her face broke into a wide smile, and she walked briskly to him. They hugged.

"It's good to have you back."

"It's good to be back." She looked around the gardens. "This is beautiful."

"I thought you might like it."

He motioned to their right, and they began walking down a path lined with red and yellow flowers. They talked of events that had transpired over the previous days. Sabin could tell she was grieving over her grandfather.

"Abby, I'm so sorry about Ray. I know you wanted to know him better."

"Thanks." She slowed and looked at Sabin. "I feel like I learned a lifetime of lessons from him in just a few days."

"About God, you mean?"

She nodded. "And myself."

They sat on a green lawn next to a bed of white roses. Abby leaned over and inhaled the fragrance, then gently fingered a petal. A broad smile crossed her face. "I love these. I've never smelled roses before, only read about them."

They sat silently for a moment. Sabin felt a bit awkward bringing up a certain question, even though he knew Abby would welcome it. "I've been thinking . . . about God . . . since you left our place. I was wondering . . . Could you teach me what you know? About God, that is."

Abby grinned. "Of course. I'd love to do

that. I have to tell you, though — I'm just learning myself."

He shrugged. "You're much farther down the path than I am."

"I'd be happy to get you started. Once God moves in, though, the Spirit becomes your teacher. I'll just be a mouthpiece."

"Well, you're the only one I know."

Over dinner Abby told me about her afternoon with Sabin. "I'm going back over to Fort Worth tomorrow," she said, watching for my reaction. "He has a couple of friends who are interested in meeting me."

"I can set you up to conference on the Grid, you know. It's kind of a long ride over there."

She shook her head. "Maybe later. But I'd like to meet them in person first."

I went into the kitchen and brought out salmon and rice. We ate silently for a few moments before Abby set her fork on her plate.

I looked up. "What is it?"

She looked uncomfortable. "Creighton, when Lauren spoke to me at her place . . ."

"Before we went to the airport?"

"Yes." She hesitated. "Lauren said the attorney general was going to indict me shortly."

My fork clinked hard against the plate. Lauren Caldwell had no heart, and she didn't care who suffered for the sake of her career. "I wondered if this might happen. Well, what are we going to do?"

She shook her head slowly. "I've decided to go back to Papua New Guinea, to a new village."

"When?" I choked out. My insides felt compressed, fearing her answer.

"I'm not sure. A few days, maybe."

I stood, walked to the kitchen entrance, and leaned against the wall. Even with all the intelligence in the world, I couldn't make her stay. And I couldn't undo anything that might have added to her reasons for leaving.

"Tell me what you're thinking," she said. I could hear in her voice that she was crying again. "And feeling."

I looked back at her. "I think . . . and I feel . . . that I love you. I don't want you to leave."

She stood and came to me, wrapping her arms around me. "I love you too, Creighton."

I wiped her wet cheeks with my thumb. She had said what I wanted to hear, but I knew her loving me didn't mean we could be together. "Abby, are you doing this because of the legal danger or because you want to go back to the jungle?"

She looked into my eyes for several long moments, tears still swimming in her own. "I don't know. I'm not sure it matters. This is the right thing to do. The jungle is my home. I've missed it ever since I got here."

"And what about us?" I said softly. "I didn't know you'd ruled out a future together."

"I think . . ." She paused, seeming to gather her thoughts and will away any more pain. "I treasure our relationship more than I could've imagined. You're incredibly special to me, Creighton. I wish I could be with you and with the Inisi. But I can't." She paused, then gave a mischievous half smile. "I just can't picture you hunting crocodiles with a spear."

"No. But maybe I could lecture one to death." I kissed the top of her head.

We stood embracing for several minutes longer, both silent and, I imagined, accepting the inevitable.

"Abby, have you thought much about that first message your grandparents sent? The one about restarting Christianity?"

She paused a moment. "Yes . . . and I sense that God has used me the way he wanted to. Not how I expected, but the way he planned all along. All the pressure I put on myself to fulfill this grand mission — God simply wanted to live through me, as me. Not as some great missionary." She smiled. "I think he's done that."

I gently ran my hand through her hair. "Will you have enough time to teach Sabin before you go?"

"I can do that from the jungle."

I stopped, surprised. "You're taking a mobile Grid interface?"

She nodded. "Sabin said he'd get me one."

I began stroking her hair again. "Do you want us to keep in touch, Abby?"

She leaned toward me and touched her soft lips to mine. "Yes, Creighton, I do."

49

Abby left early to go to Sabin's. When she arrived, a small group had already assembled in his living room. Sabin introduced her to the gathering and served refreshments while people got acquainted. The experience felt so different to her than the dinner party at Lauren's, which now seemed eons ago.

The group finally quieted and turned its attention to Abby. Her eyes met Sabin's, and she smiled, then turned to the group. "I'm not sure where to start. In the jungle the whole village used to get together every evening. There was no outside entertainment, of course, so we would tell stories and laugh and talk about the day. They were all believers in Jesus, and —" She stopped.

Sabin leaned forward. "What is it?"

"I just realized something. All the time I was in the jungle, I felt like even though we were all believers in Jesus, we never had a real church. I'd hear my parents talk about what their church was like in the States, and I'd think, 'We don't have a building or clergy or anyone who stands up and gives a sermon.' " She thought for a moment. "But the church — the gathered ones, as they called it in the New Testament — is just a group of people joined to Jesus, getting together to share his life. He is the head. We are led by him."

She looked around the group. "This, the way we are right now, is how believers in Jesus met in the New Testament. They didn't have all that other stuff. They just had Jesus living in them. His life flowing among us — that's what he wants." She looked back at Sabin. "I'm sorry. I'm getting ahead of myself. Let's just start with Jesus, shall we?"

Midmorning I went to the university. I wasn't looking forward to a day alone at my office. I dawdled about with various administrative tasks and communications that had accumulated during my absence. I glanced over the syllabuses for the courses I'd be teaching. I already had lectures prepared for one; the other class was new. With my new brain it only took an hour to complete lesson prep for half the term.

I finally decided to tackle something I'd been putting off: checking Cleary's memory stream. I was twenty-four hours late to the task. I simply didn't want to do it. I didn't want to return to the scene of Cleary's memories — the remnants of a man whose existence I'd conspired to erase.

But it had to be done. Whatever misgivings I felt, I had to make sure Cleary and his nanites were no longer a threat. Ben had tapped the day before, asking if I'd checked on Cleary. I didn't want to let him down when he contacted me again.

I accessed Cleary's stream and fast-forwarded to his meeting with Pape at Cleary's place. Pape had left, infected with nanites.

Cleary cleared the table. He poured Pape's leftover wine into a special container and sealed it. He glanced at the day's headlines, looked at some messages, and tapped a couple of people at NTI, discussing innocuous matters. He carried on as if all were normal.

The next morning Cleary began making arrangements for his financial affairs. He did so at amazing speed. He was reviewing his will when a tap came. It was Pape. Cleary entered a VR strip club.

"Pape, I'll miss the high-class places you drag me to. I didn't expect to hear from you for . . . oh, twenty years."

"Your last day with us, Cleary. I couldn't stand not to say good-bye." He pasted on a smile. "We neglected to discuss a certain detail yesterday."

"We did?"

"The Caldwell woman."

"She can't stop us now."

"But she's a loose end."

"True. One who can identify you." Cleary leaned forward, glanced around the room, and looked back at Pape. "Lewis, I'm disappearing tomorrow. If you wish to take care of her, I have no objection."

"And the professor?"

"The same."

They stood, shook hands, and said their farewells. Cleary exited VR.

I exited from his memory stream, fear crawling up my neck. *Pape is still loose. He could be here. Or in Fort Worth.*

I tapped Sabin. He took forever to answer. "Creighton, what's going —"

"Sabin, Abby has to leave immediately."

"We'll be wrapping up here in about half an hour. The car —"

"No! She has to leave now. She may be in danger."

His face hardened. "In danger? From whom?"

"Lewis Pape."

"I thought he was out of the picture."

"I thought so too. But I checked Cleary's memory stream, and he may be coming after Abby."

"Should we tap the police?"

"No, we just have to get her out of here. On a plane — anywhere but here. Pape won't have enough time left to follow her. We just need a couple of days. Put her in a car, and send her back here. I'll have a plan by the time she arrives."

I grabbed my briefcase and sprinted down the hall and two flights of stairs. I ran across campus and hopped into a car, out of breath.

I processed airline options on the way home. All she needed was a flight — the quickest possible flight. If she wanted to proceed on to Papua New Guinea, I'd worry about connections later. I arrived home but paused before getting out of the vehicle, scrutinizing the house. What if Pape was waiting for us?

I walked to the door, unlocked it, and turned the knob. My heart raced. I cracked the door opened and scanned the inside. Nothing. I slipped off my shoes, inched into the living room, and looked down the hall and into the kitchen. Things seemed undisturbed. I headed upstairs, still listening for unwelcome noises, and quietly started to gather Abby's belongings.

Then it hit me. *Why hadn't I just sent her straight to the airport? We could've met there. What good is this blasted brain if it can't make a decent split-second decision?* It was too late to reach her now.

I finished throwing her things in her suitcase and ran downstairs and out to the curb. The light was fading, but from what I could tell, everything looked normal.

Five minutes later the car rounded the corner and pulled up in front of my house. I opened the hatch, flung the suitcase inside, and jumped into the front seat, shooting a quick glance at Abby next to me.

"DFW Airport." I slammed the door. The car pulled away. I craned my neck to look behind the car, scan around the neighborhood. Was that movement two blocks down? A pair of lights?

"Creighton —"

I stopped looking ahead and behind the car and focused on Abby. My heart was in my throat.

She looked perplexed. "Sabin said Pape is after us. I thought Pape was being handled by the FBI."

I glanced behind us again. The pair of headlights lingered in the distance. I had no reason to believe it wasn't my neighbors, but tension pulsed through me. "Well . . . he wasn't." We were traveling down Columbia Avenue toward the freeway.

"Could you look into his memory stream?"

"No, but I looked at Cleary's again."

"And?" She sounded irritated, obviously wanting me to explain our sudden flight.

Our car entered the freeway and picked up speed. The car in the distance disappeared. "And you could be in danger."

"That's what Sabin said. But I don't —"

I pressed my hand to her lips. "Abby, this man wants to kill you. I don't know how to protect you. We need to get you out of here."

Her beautiful eyes were wide, and she nodded slowly. She kissed my fingers and gently moved my hand, clasping it in hers. "I understand that. We're on our way to the airport. What else can we do?"

I breathed deeply, trying to push away my fear. "I'm sorry, Abby. I'm . . . I'm just worried about you."

I scanned the freeway. Darkness shrouded

the cars, but from the pace of traffic I could tell all of the ones around us were automated. *He can't catch us in an automated car.*

She squeezed my hand. "And what about you? Are you in danger?"

"I'll be fine. I'll . . . I'll leave town for a couple of days."

"Then Pape will give up?"

"Abby, Cleary infected Pape with the nanites." I paused. "He'll be dead in another day, I think."

"Oh." Abby turned toward the window and remained silent for several moments. "Where's my flight going?"

"Albuquerque was the next flight. Abby, I'm sorry you're having to leave this way." My words came out in a rush. I wanted her to grasp the gravity of the situation. "I just thought —"

Something on the freeway behind us caught my eye. The way the lights were moving through traffic, weaving in and out of the automated cars. A self-operated vehicle. We had been followed.

"Abby —" Panic filled my voice.

She sat up straight. "Creighton, what?"

"Abby, get down!" I shoved her low into her seat. I looked toward the lights. They were half a mile behind us and gaining fast.

I addressed our car's Grid interface. "Can this vehicle accelerate . . . emergency accelerate?"

"The emergency override feature can only be activated by the municipal transportation department. I can contact the department if you wish."

"Yes! Do so!" I yelled. The car had closed to a quarter of a mile. "Is there any other way to . . . to stop or change course?"

Abby had inched back up in her seat, trying to peer out her window.

"Only the municipal transportation department can authorize traffic deviations on multilane thoroughfares. A representative will be with you —"

"Abby, get on the floor!"

She moved off the seat. "What is going on? Tell me!" I could tell she was anxious, but she didn't sound as terrified as I felt.

I pressed my hand into her shoulder. "Just stay down."

The car was within fifty yards. It moved into the lane next to Abby's side of the car. I unbuckled the seat belt and tried to throw myself toward her, but she was wedged between me and her door.

Suddenly I heard a car pull alongside us. I wrapped my arms tightly around her body.

"Creighton," I heard Abby's muffled voice

say, "it'll be all right."

There was a rapid series of booming sounds. Glass sprayed everywhere. I burrowed my face into her back. The adrenaline raced like a wildfire through my body, and I thought my heart would explode. I gripped Abby tighter, feeling her softness and warmth. The noise seemed to last forever. Finally it stopped.

"Abby!" I lifted my head, shaking off bits of glass. "Abby!"

She moaned. I reached my hand around her and felt a sticky wetness. "Abby!" I lifted her head. It was covered with blood. "Oh, God, no!"

She coughed, and blood gurgled in her throat. She whispered, "It's . . . okay. Creighton —"

"Shh. Shh." I wiped the blood away from her nose and put my cheek against her face. She was barely breathing. Her eyes looked vacant, glassy.

"No, Abby, no. Don't do this." I opened her mouth, placed my lips against hers, and breathed into her. I breathed. I pumped her chest. I breathed.

I continued until I heard sirens in the distance. The car had stopped. I placed my cheek near Abby's mouth. I placed my blood-soaked fingers against her neck. She was gone.

"Oh, no, Abby. God. No, Not like this."

I cradled her in my arms and sobbed.

50

We gathered beneath a sprawling oak tree in the midst of an expansive cemetery, surrounded by blue sky overhead and the scorching Texas heat. The group was much larger than I'd expected.

Ben Steele had flown down from DC. He was shaken by Abby's death, I could tell. It was all I could do to give him an abbreviated account of what had happened after we'd returned to Dallas.

Ben shook his head. "I never should have let her leave."

"It wasn't your fault, Ben. If anything . . ." I couldn't bring myself to say what I had been thinking for the past three days: if only I had checked Cleary's stream earlier.

I turned away from him. His hand caught my shoulder. "Creighton —"

I stopped.

"It wasn't yours, either."

Coming from anyone else, those would

have been just words. Coming from Ben . . . Our eyes met, and we shared a silent understanding. I nodded slowly. "Thanks, Ben."

I gazed at the people around me. Miranda, the Dallas-area student who had spoken to Abby after my class, had come, as had two dozen or so people I didn't recognize. I heard Sabin ask several of them how they knew Abby. They didn't. They'd seen her new message that I'd just put on the Grid, and they wanted to know more.

I hung close to Ben and avoided conversations. I wasn't at a point yet where I could reminisce about Abby or engage in small talk. One young woman, however, made a point of introducing herself to me.

"I'm Britta."

"How did you know Abby?" I tried to sound engaged.

"I met her at White Rock Lake. We talked a couple of times. I saw the news about her. I just . . . I wanted to be here."

I nodded, my eyes burning with unshed tears. Abby liked this girl.

Sabin came over to me, a teenager walking with him. "Creighton, let me introduce you to Lauren's daughter, Chloe."

She smiled and extended her hand to me. It was kind of her to come since her mother was so conspicuously absent. Lauren had fallen behind in the polls and was campaigning.

"Did you get to spend much time with Abby?" I asked her.

"No. I wish I had."

Sabin pointed out a man standing on the edge of the gathering.

"Someone you know?" I asked.

"Not exactly. A federal agent. He came to our house."

I looked back at Sabin. "What do you think he wants?"

He shrugged. "He told me he wanted to hear more about Abby's message."

Sabin had asked if I wanted to speak. I would have liked to say how much Abby meant to me and what her life had taught me and how I would miss her. But I knew I would get too choked up. I decided to let Sabin do the talking.

Sabin stepped forward and motioned to the crowd. The gathering quieted. He cleared his throat and began. "We are here to celebrate life. Not just the life of Abigail Caldwell, whose time here touched us deeply, but even more so the life that, I believe, God brought her to America to share. That is the life of God himself, given us in the person of his Son . . ."

He spoke for only fifteen minutes. But in

those minutes he expressed what Abby had taken a lifetime, a brief lifetime, to fully realize.

When he finished, Sabin nodded to the cemetery workers, who took hold of the leather straps holding the casket and lowered it into the ground.

"Abby told me once," Sabin continued, "that burial is a truly Christian practice. It affirms the value of the physical body in God's plan and anticipates the day when the body will be raised and made immortal to live with God on a new earth forever. That was Abby's ultimate hope — one I know she awaits now more than ever."

He picked up a small handful of dirt and tossed it on top of the casket, then turned away, wiping tears from his eyes.

Afterward, everyone came up to express their condolences to Sabin and me. One thing in particular would have thrilled Abby. Sabin had mentioned the little group that she had started at his house. Several people asked him if they could join the gathering.

Sabin's tap came two days later. On her last trip to Fort Worth, in the rush to get out the door, Abby had left her journal at Sabin's.

"I'm not sure what to do with it, Creighton. Would you . . . Do you think she might like you to have it?"

Yes. I very much wanted to have it. I could have had it delivered to Dallas, but it seemed too precious for that. I went to his place to pick it up.

Riding to Fort Worth, I realized I felt a certain bond with Sabin. The two of us had become friends during the events of the past days. We would always have that.

Sabin opened the door and invited me in. The group that Abby had started was gathered in the living room: four men, three women, and Chloe.

"I didn't mean to interrupt you."

"Let me introduce you." Sabin turned to the group. "Creighton was a good friend of Abby's in Dallas."

"Yes, she spoke of you," one of the women said. Then she added, "You meant a lot to her."

I swallowed hard. The wound was still too fresh. Nevertheless, it pleased me to hear that. I don't know why. Perhaps I had always secretly wondered if Abby compartmentalized me in a nonreligious sphere of her life. Apparently Abby didn't think that way after all.

Sabin walked over to his dining table. "Here's the journal. I guess Abby won't mind if someone reads it now."

He handed it to me. I ran my thumbs over the cover. "Sabin, do you mind — this is going to sound silly perhaps — but do you mind if I take a look at the room she stayed in?"

"No, not at all." He pointed to a staircase. "Up the stairs, first door on your left."

"I'll just be a few moments."

I walked up the stairs. The door on the left was shut. I turned the knob and slowly opened it. A queen-size bed with a dark green, patterned comforter filled the left side of the room. In front of me stood a small wood desk and chair; to the right, a tall white dresser. On the walls were photos of mountain scenes — taken by Sabin, I guessed.

A much smaller frame rested on the desk. I walked over and picked it up. It was a picture of Sabin and Abby, arms over each other's shoulders, standing on what appeared to be the top of a peak. A peak she never mentioned having conquered.

I placed it back on the desk. I sat down in the chair and opened the journal. I flipped slowly through the pages, feeling the paper between my fingers as I did. I stopped on the page where Abby had made her final entry.

Jesus,
I am about to leave the man I have grown to love. Our paths diverge, but my heart will always be with him.

Creighton has moved toward faith in you. And though he may no longer have a human spirit for you to join yourself to, I know your grace is bigger than that, and the door to you is not closed.

Keep him in your love. Draw him by your grace. May you and he be one forever.

I raised my eyes from the page and stared at the window next to the bed. Wooden blinds were drawn closed across it. I walked over, parted the blinds, and looked outside at Sabin's backyard. And behind it, a small woods. A solitary path disappeared into the thicket. Abby had walked that path, I knew.

I wiped the moisture from my eyes and went back downstairs.

Sabin rose from his seat in the living room. "Are you doing okay?"

"I'll be fine. In time."

"I understand."

I looked around at the gathering. "Well, I'd better get going. I don't want to interrupt your group." I reached my hand out to Sabin. "Thanks for letting me pick this up. I'd enjoy keeping in touch, Sabin."

He shook my hand. "I would too, Creighton."

I moved toward the door.

"Creighton . . ."

I turned back to him.

"Since Abby started this group . . . I was just thinking . . . We all wanted to see if you'd like to stay for a bit and join us. That would have meant a lot to Abby, I know."

Several of them nodded. I glanced at the coffee table. It held a single goblet and a small loaf of bread. I looked back at Sabin. "I'd like that."

Sabin motioned to an open seat, and I sat down next to him. He spoke to the group. "We were talking about how the bread represents the life of Jesus, now within us and expressed through each of us."

He looked at the man to my right. "Ryan, why don't you get us started?" The man picked up the bread, took a piece, then passed the loaf to the woman next to him. It came around the circle until Sabin held it.

"As Abby said, he who has the Son has the life. His life is ours, together."

He broke off a piece of bread for himself,

turned, and offered the bread to me.

Later that day I rode back to Dallas. I walked through my front door and surveyed my house. It felt empty. It probably would for a while.

I got a bite to eat, settled in the living room recliner, and checked headlines on the Grid. I chatted with Alistair awhile. With my new brain, I didn't actually need Alistair to perform any functions, but I talked to him more than ever. He was, at least, the semblance of a friend. I wished I hadn't left Sabin's so quickly. I could interact with real people there.

I finally turned to a task I'd been avoiding: perusing memory streams one last time. I felt tainted just contemplating it. But I needed to ensure that all danger had indeed passed. One by one I examined the memories of the transplant recipients.

Nichols's existence, I already knew, had ended in an NTI incinerator. Pape, as expected, had been dying, his brain slowly being eaten by nanites. He tapped Cleary the evening of the shooting, accusing his client of infecting him. Cleary laughed at him and ended the tap.

That night Cleary completed the preparations for his departure. He would upload himself into VR and reappear in holographic form in twenty years, just as Nichols had planned to do. His hologram would provide instructions on downloading his brain software into a nanite or robotic body. Once uploaded into VR, he had programmed his silicon brain to power down and, with it, his bodily functions.

Cleary sat in an easy chair, accessed the memory Sabin and I had planted in his stream, and executed the commands he thought were necessary to upload himself. Instead, it erased his brain software. Cleary's memory stream stopped. Mercifully, I didn't have to watch his body's final moments.

I felt a grim relief at his passing. The conspiracy had ended. We — those of us remaining — were safe.

I had to make sure, though. I had to scan the rest of the streams. Several were employees at NTI; all, I discovered, were innocent. I scanned numerous elderly patients who had had brain disease. Nothing. I came across Ray's stream. It seemed odd, having his memories saved on the Grid. I didn't need to look at them.

After reviewing several dozen benign streams, I didn't expect any surprises. I only had three more to go.

Then I accessed a memory stream that made my heart skip a beat.

The breeze at Sal's Seaside Café barely ruffled the umbrella flaps over the outdoor tables. I scanned the patio, walked past a counter filled with the day's pastries, and stood next to a table with one occupant looking out to sea.

Hutch Hardin turned and looked up at me. "Dr. Daniels. Please, have a seat."

I sat across the table from him.

"Beautiful time of year here, isn't it?" he remarked, looking away again. "This is when the big yachts go out on the Adriatic." He turned back. "So to what do I owe this visit? You're not considering politics, are you?"

A waitress came by. I ordered a cappuccino and a pastry. Hutch did the same.

"You could say I simply wanted to get acquainted."

"Really? I feel we know each other already, so much has happened to mutual acquaintances these last several weeks. I'm truly grieved by what transpired."

"Yes, I know. But you're not grieved in the way you imply."

His eyebrows rose. "What would make you say that?"

"You're sorry your plan for genocide and the worldwide adoption of brain transplants fell through."

The waitress returned with our orders. Hutch picked up a knife and slowly buttered his pastry. He spoke without looking up. "That's quite a statement, Professor. Slanderous if you were to say it to anyone else."

I finished a bite of my pastry. "I didn't say you had done anything illegal."

"It's hard to commit genocide legally."

"Not if you allow it to be done through someone else."

He gently placed the knife on his plate. "And who would that someone be?"

I might have hesitated to answer his question directly, but he didn't know my source of information. He would never know my source of information.

I leaned back in my chair. "Like Damien Cleary, Mr. Hardin, you've always pressed for rapid expansion of the brain transplant procedure. You dreamed that humanity would be transhuman within twenty years."

"That isn't an unusual vision for members of the foundation, Professor, as I'm sure you know."

"But Nichols's way was too cautious for you," I continued. "Too dependent on the vagaries of independent decision making."

"The problem with any new technology."

I took a sip of my cappuccino. "You knew, however, that Damien Cleary would take matters into his own hands under the right circumstances. Ray Caldwell provided that circumstance. He threatened to expose the transplants for what they were."

"Which is what, exactly, Dr. Daniels?"

"The permanent separation of humanity from God."

He laughed. "Surely you don't believe in that sort of thing."

"And when Ray Caldwell sent his messages, and Lauren Caldwell showed you hers, you knew what Cleary would do."

"That was Cleary's business."

"Yes. It was. You were merely a spectator. Just as you were when Abby Caldwell came to the States. Your political instinct was to chase her out. But you reconsidered. If you could get her to stay long enough, she would eventually discover the truth about Ray. So you convinced the attorney general to give her time. And when she got too close to the truth, you knew what would happen: Nichols's plan for government funding would collapse. And Cleary would implement his own plan. Genocide."

He leaned back in his chair, glancing at a

yacht before looking back at me. "Professor, wherever you obtained this story, it has no legal ramifications concerning me."

I sipped my drink. "No. It doesn't. You've done nothing illegal — unless we consider your chat with the attorney general. But that's just politics, isn't it?"

He put his cup on the table. "So tell me, Dr. Daniels, what is the point of this little meeting?"

"I told you. I simply wanted to make your acquaintance."

"And so you have."

I finished my drink and placed my spoon on the saucer. "You won't be able to stamp out God, you know."

He smirked. "They will restart the transplants. The public will demand it. Eventually I'll have billions on my side, Dr. Daniels. God will have that ragtag little band that meets at Sabin's house."

I smiled at him, rose from my seat, and looked out over the Adriatic. "Yes." I watched a yacht disappear behind a monolith rising out of the sea. "God will have that little band."

I looked back and met Hardin's eyes. His smile faded ever so slightly.

"It's been a pleasure, Mr. Hardin. We'll

have to do this again."

I turned and exited VR.

AUTHOR'S NOTE

Near the end of *The Last Christian,* Creighton uploads Abby's "more complete" message onto the Grid. You can see her message at

www.abbysmessage.com

Had she lived in our day, Abby would have been thrilled to learn of the numerous resources that harmonize with her spiritual epiphany. Here are some I recommend.

To better understand and live out Abby's epiphany of Christ in her: *The Rest of the Gospel: When the Partial Gospel Has Worn You Out* by Dan Stone and David Gregory. It's available at www.davidgregorybooks.com.

For excellent online teaching on this topic:

www.stevepettitmessages.com

For a deeper theological foundation for this topic:
www.christinyou.net

Information on my books and movies, including a discussion guide for *The Last Christian,* is available at www.davidgregory books.com and www.waterbrookmultnomah .com. My sincere thanks to you for your interest.

ABOUT THE AUTHOR

David Gregory is the best-selling author of *Dinner with a Perfect Stranger, A Day with a Perfect Stranger, The Next Level,* and the coauthor of the nonfiction *The Rest of the Gospel.* After a ten-year business career, he returned to school to study religion and communications, earning master's degrees from Dallas Theological Seminary and the University of North Texas. A native of Texas, he now lives in the Pacific Northwest.

The employees of Thorndike Press hope you have enjoyed this Large Print book. All our Thorndike, Wheeler, and Kennebec Large Print titles are designed for easy reading, and all our books are made to last. Other Thorndike Press Large Print books are available at your library, through selected bookstores, or directly from us.

For information about titles, please call:
(800) 223-1244

or visit our Web site at:
http://gale.cengage.com/thorndike

To share your comments, please write:
Publisher
Thorndike Press
295 Kennedy Memorial Drive
Waterville, ME 04901